ULTIMATE RESORT

David Scott Ewers

Pelekinesis

Library of Congress Control Number: 2017955945

Copyright © 2017 David Scott Ewers

This work is licensed under the Creative Commons Attribution-NonCommercial-NoDerivatives 4.0 International License. To view a copy of this license, visit http://creativecommons.org/licenses/by-nc-nd/4.0/.

Book Design by Mark Givens
Cover Art by D. Broth

First Pelekinesis Printing 2017

For information:

Pelekinesis, 112 Harvard Ave #65, Claremont, CA 91711 USA

www.pelekinesis.com

To Paco and Mara

Ultimate Resort

David Scott Ewers

1

"Call me Al."

"Okay."

"We will start when you're ready."

"Okay... okay." Shit.

"Try to relax."

"Okay." Avery Krizan turns from the resort's oversized window and the cluster of tripods dotting the valley road below. From there (where he was just yesterday, looking up here) the resort resembles an open drawer overflowing with adobe architecture. Terraces, footbridges, balconies and stair steps spill down the pink sandstone cliff in an elegant mess. According to the brochures in the rack by the registration counter, "The dance of light and shadow created by Kasbah Kandisha's tasteful tumble draws a steady flow of photographers, who gather at both ends of most high-season days." From the valley floor it's a 90-minute mule ride up to the resort and its abundance of faux finishes, ersatz oil lamps and trompes l'oeil, all artfully placed to enhance those distant effects. The brochures head off the dissonance by contextualizing it as "A Successful Merger of Present and Past with an Eye to the Future." Now here he is, inescapably. He shifts in his seat and nods at the interviewer. They're in a meeting room just off the resort's main atrium. His breathing is shallow. He woke up this morning with pelvic tendons plucking, and had to chase his toast with water to get it past his throat. He dabs his palms on his pant legs and tries to envision the eye of a merger.

The resort is quiet and relaxed. Employees outnumber guests by about two to one, he guesses, although the ratio could be more lopsided than that. A sinus-scouring scent of industrial disinfectant mingles with more genteel aromas of rosewater and tea. The combination is not doing his sour stomach any favors. He feels the sun on his back and wonders what Aisha's up to right now, out there. She's probably hiking around in some cool canyon, or standing on some cliff. He'd much rather be out there with her than sitting here doing this interview. Something about it feels funny, and he's been nervous since he agreed to do it.

He faces a camera, and behind it the varnished cobblestone intersection he recognizes from the brochure as the resort's "exclusive retail experience." It's a typical day-napping piece of luxury mall as far as he can tell, and more mandatory than exclusive, since it's located between the resort's main entrance and registration counter. The camera is mounted to the right of and behind the interviewer. It is to be operated by remote. Avery's best guess, judging by position, lens length and convexity, has the camera capturing maybe a crescent of the table in front of him, a bit of the traditional rug beneath his feet, probably all of the couch he presently occupies, and a lot of the large windows behind him. The couch he's sitting on is a clownish assemblage of paint-splattered triangles, presumably intended to clash playfully with the rest of the resort's conventional, generically locally-inspired decor. It isn't the most comfortable thing for sitting on, that's for sure.

Speaking of eyes, it occurs to him that as this tableau was arranged by the time he got here, and the interviewer is positioned several feet away from it, any images captured will have been 'seen' by the camera only. Putting into practice his recent photography lessons (Aisha says teaching helps her learn), he wonders how the aperture is set; he'd have it bring in the balcony beneath the windows, and the pools with their algae of rose petals glowing in the reflected sunlight, and the long valley, exquisitely terraced, mottled with adobe shacks and fruit trees below. His own vision is flat and filmy right now. It's the nerves. He peers at the camera and tries to deep-focus. The camera looks agape. He thinks at it, staring down it, trying to relax, 'Hey buddy. It's cool that you're squat. I like how those concentric circles of yours draw me through your domed hemispheres clear to your reflective blacks, beyond whose impenetrability (he can't even see them!) your pupil waits. He limpens his wig with his palms and takes another deep breath. Try to get that blur circle right in my left retina….'

The interviewer settles into a folding chair and scoots it out of frame. He pulls a small tape recorder from his coat pocket. "Mister Krizan," he officiously commences, in what sounds almost like a put-on accent, proceeding toward the record, suggesting that things need a nudge after all, pressing 'Record' with the one hand while encompassing the room in miniature flourish with the other, "I understand that you were requested to perform here only yesterday. Paradigm International Signature Resorts owes you a debt of gratitude for accepting their request on such short notice. Allow me to thank you personally, for also agreeing to this interview, and on even shorter notice."

"My pleasure," Avery frowns.

"Mine as well. So tell me... what has led you to this place?"

Avery's eyes bounce between camera and interviewer, focusing on neither. "We're starting?"

"Is okay?"

"Okay. Should I–" He puts down his toy ukulele, with its crudely painted beach scene and rainbow-lettered 'Maui', and sighs hard. "What led me?" If he didn't know any better (and he doesn't) he'd call the question leading. Worded like that, there's only one honest answer he can give. "It's a long story...."

The interviewer nods. "Yes. There are many long stories around here. And truths, yes. And tall tales, no? Tell me; speaking of tall...." The interviewer leans forward and gestures at Avery's knee with the camera button, with a refinement suggesting anointment, "What is it you call these?"

"These?"

"Your pants, the way they are..."

They are navy blue cords with sticky vinyl patches on the inside at the knees; they tickle Avery's ankle knobs when he walks, and ride up to mid-calf when he sits. "High waters?"

"High waters..."

"Floods?"

"Yes. Floods. I'm afraid you won't see many of those around here."

"No." Avery smiles honestly for the first time today. "I wouldn't think so." The camera emits a near-ultrasonic whine and vanishes behind a light field, taking the rest of the room with it. It hits Avery like an electric shock. He holds his squint a little longer than necessary, to let the interviewer know.

"The flash, it bothers you?"

"I can move out of the shadow if that helps..."

"You want details," the interviewer declares, as a way of telling Avery not to worry, that he knows already what he wants. "Also depth of field." Avery nods and stands up. The interviewer backs up a step. "You will have to sit more still."

"I'll try. Feel free to give me a heads up though."

The interviewer smiles that he might, but won't necessarily do that. He motions for Avery to sit back down. Avery reframes himself stiffly on the flat-backed couch. The interviewer leans back, gives the camera lens a blow and takes his seat. He wraps his thumb and forefinger around his chin, uses the knuckle of his middle finger to press his lower lip, turns his head and gazes into the middle distance. His intention seems to be to show a cost/benefit analysis being run in his head in real time, but it comes across more as the reflection of a decision already made. "Yes, okay." He pulls the cassette from the recorder, examines it in the sunlight, replaces it and presses Rewind. He faces back toward Avery and hits the button. "So. You say you have a long and interesting story to tell."

"I said long. I never said interesting."

"Mmm. I also like details, Mister Krizan. To say that there are lots of stories around here is not the same as to say one hears them, yes?" The machinery groans to a halt. The interviewer lowers his voice to a whisper. "I'll tell you a secret. It is my perception that people come to places like this precisely to focus on that which is not themselves. I think this is perfectly reasonable." Addressing the confusion on Avery's face, he adds, "the maintaining of one's own story is the most domestic of chores, yes? And does it not give rise to all the others? So. In sympathy with the... implicit demands of our clientèle, would you do us the favor...?"

Avery pictures a glossy hotel rag. Along with the ads and 'Things to do and see' is a photo of himself, sitting on this couch like a ventriloquist's dummy. Instead of a simple, direct Q and A session, there's the story of what led him to this place. Just the story he was hoping to avoid. He feels heavy. "That's understandable."

"As you must imagine, my subjects generally wish to discuss only what they wish to sell. I don't get that sense from you. So," releasing the pause button, "as they say in the casinos, let the chips fall where they may...."

The cleaning chemical smell gets stronger. "What has led me...?" Avery wriggles. His mind's a boiling blank. Semi-rehearsed bio-snippets sink like stones to the bottom of a big black puddle. He looks down at the sour pants he made himself wear this morning. And the blown-out shoes. "Okay. I don't know how this is going to come off..." The friendly face he tries to make feels like a grimace. This is probably a mistake, he thinks. "Someone once told me that stories are like... the land, in that... in that... though we like to think of them as, like, we're their masters, it's really the other way around..." Now what?

"If that is the case," the interviewer suggests after a short, clammy silence, "perhaps you might describe your master?"

Avery studies the interviewer's crooked mustache and heavy-lidded eyes. The stories, he means? That's a weird way to put it. "I'm not sure I—"

"From his shoes..." the interviewer points at Avery's busted creepers with his eyes and at the recorder with his brow, before rolling his head toward the ceiling, "and work your way up, yes?"

"Since you put it that way..." Avery clears his throat. He doesn't know where to start. His thoughts lie formless on the crust of his mind. But some elements have slipped through. He thinks of the stone Aisha carries now; he imagines stories as stones, sinking beneath his mental mantle to merge like magma, and emerge transformed...

* * * *

...Kwéte is waiting in the long grass by the wash. At his feet there rests a stone. The boy knows by looking that this stone has traveled from high up on the mountain to come to rest at his feet. At Toibi he learned about Chungichnish and Chehooit and Coyote and the stories of the land and how it danced into being, and how it dances, and how it must be kept dancing. And this stone has danced from the *mountaintop to meet him here. The boy lifts up the stone. It's smooth and cool and solid and heavy.*

At Toibi he was taught things he has since learned to recognize in human (even rahwah'nat) behavior. But too many things he hadn't learned; there were further recitations of the same stories he was not yet old enough to hear. He'd long known the name of Toibipet, The Devil Woman Who Was There, for whom his village was named, but had no idea Who was this Devil Woman, or why she Was There, or what she did when she Was There. If he were at Toibi he would know by now. If he were at Toibi still, he would be a man by now.

The sunlight descending from the top of round, grey Yoát has yet to reach the foothills. The light moves slowly down the mountain, the boy thinks, though not as slowly as did this round, grey stone. The sunlight will move down from the foothills; it will strike the campanário of the great edifice of the fortress of the hanging man; the bells will strike seven times before the sun reaches into the shallow ravine to touch this stone.

Kwéte had come across the brother two summers ago while foraging along the path that runs along the base of the foothills. He couldn't eat the oak seeds he'd been gathering, and he was hungry. Though he'd heard stories about the rahwah'nat, he'd never seen one up close. This one was nibbling on a corn fritter. He called the boy over to him and handed him the fritter, almost as if he'd heard the rumbling in his stomach. "Torreja," he said. The boy pulled off a piece and put it in his mouth. "Torreja." It was good. The man was dressed from neck to wrists and ankles in heavy grey cloth, and had a hacking cough. He pulled another fritter from a pouch, pointed with it toward the small, grassy hill rising up in front of them, and began walking in the direction of his shadow. The boy followed several paces behind the coughing man's eager lead, charmed at first, then out of curiosity, until they'd passed the hill. But the man kept walking. The boy made to slow down, which was to lead to his stopping and turning back, but the rahwah'nat would have none of it. He stood still and insisted that the boy catch up to him, then he placed his hand on the boy's shoulder and held it there, firmly but cheerfully as they walked, as if there was something marvelous in store for them both. They arrived at their destination just as the sun set in the far hills that in the boy's mind held the ocean.

It was this same fortress they came to then. He was given corn soup and a place to sleep. As he lay on a grass mat that first night he determined to leave early in the morning and gather all the way home. When the morning came he found his rahwah'nat walking and looking around, his hands knotted behind his back. He walked up to him and pointed toward the sun which rose in the direction of his village. The rahwah'nat smiled and waved. He placed his hand on Kwéte's shoulder like the day before, and began walking him very slowly around the dusty enclosure. First he showed him some fruits that were much larger than acorns or berries and could be eaten straight from the tree, and when the bells rang out and the boy shook fearfully, the rahwah'nat laughed and coughed and laughed again, pointed up and said "campanário." The bells. Seeing how the boy wondered at the bells the man brought him to a place where a large brown shell lay covered in ash. The boy touched the brown shell. It was very hard and clearly very heavy; heavier in fact than was sensible somehow, considering its size. The man leaned over, wheezed and slapped the thing with his hand. Kwéte did the same. The shell felt almost too solid, but it was empty inside. He didn't like how it felt. The rahwah'nat stood and pointed to the shell then lifted his hand to point at the campanário. The shell, the campanário, the shell, the campanário. The boy saw what the man was trying to say: that the thing in the ash heap was the same as those noisemakers in the sky. The man picked up a rock and struck the shell that would be a bell. It made a thick clicking sound. The man dropped the stone. He pointed back at the shell and waved his hand again so the boy would understand that the shell was a bad bell after all, and that this fact caused the man to have chest pain. The boy shook his head back at the man. The man began walking again, pointing out other things that were like the bell. Metal, he said, pointing. The boy had seen metal before, but never like this. It was everywhere. The man moved slowly, as if he were also heavier than was sensible. He called himself Español, and—seeing that the boy was curious, and a fast learner who paid proper attention to things—he told him in his heavy tongue about the fortress itself, which he called La Misión, and—proudly pointing out how this or that was built en el estilo de los Moros—that it was del sur, like himself. He ran a hand about himself, touching himself in spots. Muttering strange apologies, he made a motion the boy took to mean that everything around them either imposed itself or was imposed upon them from very, very far away.

They made their way to the rear of the building while the boy followed the walls-like-cliffs with his eyes and tried to figure how such a thing as massive and heavy as this could be moved at all, much less be brought from another world. Leaving its shade they walked to a terra cotta embankment that led to a ditch of flowing water. The man pointed to the water, then off to the distance. "Hondo." From beyond, the faraway motion again... to this field; beyond ... to this field. The boy turned toward the field and saw the people. It was as if they had been hiding in plain sight. They were stooped, and lined in rows, silently harvesting large berries from plants that were also lined in rows. Children his age, with misshapen bellies and limbs, worked alongside men, women, and old people. Kwéte immediately understood several things. He understood how these wheezing, slow-moving rahwah'nat managed to move all this stone and metal. He understood what the men at Toibi meant when they said the rahwah'nat steal people's souls and put their shadows to work. With a pain in his own abdomen, he understood that going home wasn't going to be as easy as he'd hoped.

He never did go back to Toibi, but he never had to toil in the bean fields like he'd feared on that first day, either. He had it easy. His first task at La Misión was simply to get accustomed to being there. Having his time ruled by those bells was difficult at first, but he learned ways to minimize their influence. One way was to use them for his own entertainment. In time he was able to predict the ringing so accurately that it felt as if he summoned the noise himself. Staring at bloody statues and paintings of corpses while the old Padre mumbled and held up his golden treasures was tedious, to say the least. In fact he found it so leaden that it became necessary to train himself not to think while inside the big room. But on the whole his days passed without much trouble. He liked the food. He learned to understand the rahwah'nat, and though he was never shown how to use their books it was clear from early on that he was being given an education. He was put to work making candles, for instance, with the understanding that his true task was to learn how the work should be done, and how it shouldn't be, and—underlying all, he suspected—the *importance of oversight in ensuring that things were properly tended toward the former. As was always the case, the candle making was a temporary job, then it was on to the next thing. He learned soap-making that way, and even something of blacksmithing, which he saw as fighting with the earth itself. He felt pity for the iron as it submitted to the fire, or suffered blows from the blacksmith's hammer. It didn't help that the blacksmith was a smelly, unpleasant man. He was bad enough all by himself, but he was worse in the company of the soldiers. Those men came to the shed every morning as if entranced, always pointing to some or other imaginary problem with their metal plates, weapons, or whatever else they might have on hand. The blacksmith kept a large clay jug behind the door. The soldiers would come in, one would close that door, and the other one would grab for the jug. The three men would stand there passing it around and around; the one whom the boy had nicknamed in his head Piyar would drink the most, but the other one—whom the boy did not nickname but in his head called hahmah'pe—would get as hot and red as the metal in the furnace, and would act more and more like a trapped animal than a man, until his thrashing seemed to derange the very air inside the shed. The boy would make sure never to look into that man's eyes when he was like that. He would busy himself with the hot bellows, while listening with one ear to the score of that one's daily plunges into senselessness and rage. Noting formal similarities from one day to the next, he came to think of the soldier's degenerative display as a sort of tortured anti-dance, a willful careening away from all notions of balance. Finally the soldiers would lurch out of the shed, each under their respective spell—the one slow, half-blind and thoughtless, the other simmering and fuming like a tanning vat, full of malicious intent—and wander off to teach the neófitos of the other visage—capricious, relentless, and criminally insane—of the spirit whose law undergirds and is made manifest by La Misión. Meanwhile, the blacksmith would shout and throw Kwéte and himself around the smithery for a bad spell before falling unconscious where he stood.*

Knowing how the soldiers treated the people, the boy felt painfully ashamed to see the neófitos brought in, gathered as he knew they were—like berries sometimes, like horses others—from the land. When their eyes met his he felt neither pride nor honor in his easier place. He'd felt this way long before the last Fiesta Día de la Inmaculada Concepción de la Santísima Virgen, though he never planned to do anything about it before that day. He was too well aware of how well La Misión worked. These were men who took everything by force. The metal for their bells and armor were taken from the unwilling stone. Water was taken the same way, diverted from ancient purposes to feed the awful bean fields and tanneries. The ritual warnings before the executed man, the bells, the high walls, the senseless undergirding all required people. They took people. From all appearances the rahwah'nat outcasts—which is what they must be, as troubled as they clearly were—were just troubled enough, and determined enough, that their war against the world might succeed.

At first he wondered why there were no rahwah'nat women. Sometimes he wondered whether this unnatural imbalance wasn't the cause of the bizarre and cruel hahmah'pe behavior; at other times he was sure that the unhappy rahwah'nat womanlessness resulted from their own cruelty, that these were men who had been banished from their birth nature. But there was one rahwah'nat woman.

La Santísima Virgen María madre de dios. María Virgen was a mother who never knew a man. The son conceived of himself. For a while the boy fought boredom by trying to figure this out, until finally he had to give up. He realized that there was no end to the confusion. The son was sacrificed, and he was not, and he floated away, and María madre floated away, and they all became statues. In contrast to the rest of La Misión, her statue was beautiful, but La Santísima represented *rahwah'nat* madness all the same, because she was not like a real woman. And if their only woman was not a real woman, then where again do these *rahwah'nat* come from? Kwéte learned to avoid the statue.

It was expected that he pay close attention to the workings of La Misión, and he did. He saw what happened when men and women tried to resist it. Sometimes it was the soldiers that did the whipping, but more often they'd give that job to the large, nameless boy-man who always smiled, even as he made examples of the proud or defiant men, handpicked by the soldiers for displaying those very qualities, by turning them into quivering collections of gashes. It was as if the beatings were simply a game he was good at, and which he found especially easy to play. The sight of one of them, and a stupid one at that, casually whipping their own kind was a spirit-breaking first impression for the *neófitos*. This was the lesson for the men. The women the soldiers preferred to handle themselves, teaching them by other methods.

On the last Fiesta Día de la Inmaculada Concepción he had seen them bring in his own Nãarotokón, his older sister, who'd been responsible for watching over him when he was young. She'd taught him many interesting things about the world; she told him all kinds of stories. He was there that morning when they brought the *neófitos* in for baptizing, and she was with them, and while the soldiers talked at the gate with the same brother who'd brought him there, who was also in charge of processing the neófitos, the bells struck. His Nãarotokón fell down just as he had, and the way that hahmah'pe treated her then, when she was so terrified... the memory burns his mind.

Kwéte looks at the stone. There is the finest vein of metal there. All the better. The soldiers will bring in their harvest of souls. He can hear them now, barking like roosters beyond the rise. He holds up the stone. The sun is half the way down the foothills and has reached the campanário. He stands. He sees the heads of the soldiers coming over now, now the bowed heads of the people. He sees that hahmah'pe grinning at the sun. Now the brother should be making his way around the inner wall to the outer enclosure to greet them.

He's running now, led by the stone; he's stumbling over damp, grassy clumps. The brother will be making his way now. The boy sees flecks glistening in the stone. Flecks of Yóat, brighter than Spanish gold. He is almost to the clearing now. That hahmah'pe is laughing... and there is a hum in the air. The bells should be ringing.

He will reach the clearing just as the hahmah'pe reaches the brother, and he will lift this stone, this long-traveled child of Yóat, and they will see him just as the bells ring seven, and if it is like his dream the hahmah'pe coward will soil his armor while the boy will bring the stone down onto the head of the brother, and before that one can think of giving chase the boy will be gone, and he will take this stone home to its home on the mountain, and the people will hear, and his Nãarotokón will hear.

But the hum is not the bells about to ring seven. Just as the boy reaches the clearing the hum becomes a great crashing *roar like all the thunder in the world breaking at once, and he is thrown to the ground, and the roaring ground slams up against his chest until he comes up to his knees, and from his knees he sees the earth lift up from beneath the fortress, lift up La Misión and drop it, and lift it up and drop it again, and he sees the soldiers crumple into piles of metal on the ground, the earth hammering up at them; the people are scattering; the brother vanishes from sight as the too-massive campanile with its too-heavy bells leaps from the fortress wall to fall silently amid all the roar until it meets the roaring ground with a sound from the rahwah'nat Hell, and explodes into dust.*

Still holding the stone, he looks again at Yóat. When the shaking stops and the noise fades he stands again and walks toward the fog of dust and earth. Nothing else moves. Even the dust fog is still. He can hear the hahmah'pe coward, shaking still. He lies in a heap by the inner gate, surrounded by the broken bells. Kwéte could bring the stone down on that one now, as easily as if he were a coiled snake. He looks down at the stone in his hand. It shimmers.

He doesn't want to bring it down now.

The earth rumbles again, moaning another great deep moan. Perhaps it was Yóat that made these wounds in the fortress walls. It might not be a stone's place, or a boy's or even a man's, to finish a mountain's business. Perhaps it was Toibipet, or Chehooit herself, coming down. He may not understand the stone's purpose, but there are several things he does understand. He understands that killing a soldier in this place, even a hahmah'pe coward, will bring nothing but harm to the people. If he flees they will all be blamed and punished. If he stays it will be him. Either way, two more cowards will come to fill this one's boots, each with *two boots of his own, and a boot is more important than a man to these men. He understands that he hadn't really expected to escape the killing of the brother. He was prepared to trade his life for them to know him. And now? Now they will not see, and even if they did see they would think him mad with terror.*

Besides, if he brings the stone down now it will never go back up.

There are two more things he understands: his incredible good fortune at his very point in time, and the need to act quickly. Just as he knows he hadn't really expected to bring the stone home to Yóat, that being a story to allow him to do the other thing, he knows that given the choice he would rather leave La Misión than kill and die here. And now this has happened. No one knows he is out here. He has time before anyone thinks to search for him, and more time while they search for his body. The boy looks through the dust to the glowing foothills. The dust is only beginning to settle. He starts to run. He can cut through the vineyard to the irrigation canal. The stone will not come down after all. It will lead him up that gutter to the river, and from there into the hills, and from there....

He reaches the vineyard and turns back. Seen or not, he must do more than just leave. That hahmah'pe coward is still sitting there by the gate. He approaches the dazed soldier. The soldier, upon seeing the silhouette of a man with a stone looming over him, decides that it would be best if he lay back down. Kwéte kneels over the man. Two days with a cobbler is more than enough time to learn how to remove a man's boots. He sets the stone down and in a single motion separates that hahmah'pe coward from his boots. By the time the soldier determines to sit back up, man, boots and stone are gone…

Avery taps the blown-out instep of a black suede creeper.

"It all started when I lost my boots."

* * * *

September 20

10:45 AM

Aisha Sandoval steps backward through the Mission-style bungalow's thick stucco arch and pulls the door closed in front of her. Inhaling the sweet-turning-savory air, she peeks absently through the tiny wrought iron bars of the peep window, checks the flintlock-trigger door handle thing with her thumb and locks the deadbolt. Bending over to pick up a doorknob flyer from the welcome mat, she runs her gaze once more up the cobweb-bunted cinderblocks to the blistered formica shelf and its knee-high lineup of plant kingdom hard cases. Years from now, when she recalls these hazy Los Angeles days, she would be surprised if those plants aren't the first things that come to mind. The way they persist on nothing but coffee slag and cigarette droppings. After four months of mornings, sitting out here feeding them ashes and reliving whatever menial crimes she'd committed the night before, she's come to see them as representative of one hard-truth strategy for coping with the local milieu. They tell her that minimizing unhelpful contrast between an organism and its environment may require said organism to become coarser than its ideal nature might dictate; it may even become necessary for the organism to sacrifice a portion of itself through atrophy or necrosis. In other words, you've got to learn to be kind of gross. Putting up with shit is central; it's an ethics unto itself. One must become one with the dirtiness. Because hey… that's lifestyle. Learn to enjoy being in on that secret about paradise. She stares at a grimy, puckered aloe. Psst. Hey Aisha. Know how you'd always wanted to go back and be unrecognizable, like you've escaped hometown physics or something? Keep bouncing between Edendale and your dad's lowball Garden Grove scene; keep resting on tomorrow's laurels while getting to better know Coop and Diamond Greg and the guy that lets himself be called Jigaboo (uh uh, no way you will call him that), dragging yourself up and down the Five for hours every other day like a bead crossing a skillet, adding your own thought-crime fantasies to a million others just like it? You've been spending more nights here than Candy has lately; maybe one day this all could become yours, like through osmosis or something, and your name can also not be on the lease like hers isn't. You can go back to visit your hometown and hear about how much you've changed; you can get irritated and impatient with your old friends' prematurely fading lives, and roll your eyes at their assertions that they could never live in L.A. You can go out for a smoke, knowing full well what they'll say when you don't come back. You can get behind the wheel of your aging sports coupe, check your reflection in the rearview mirror, not recognize it, and not care. Then you'll know where you belong. Then you'll *be* here.

Ah, but this is all another daydream. She still cares, she

still doesn't know, she's not really here. Four months isn't long enough. L.A. will wear off like a tan; she can tell that already. The thought of not changing is sad and comforting at the same time. She fishes in her purse for her sunglasses. There's one behavioral change she has undergone here: along with keys and cellphone, shades get accounted for before door gets pulled shut, always. But not today. She must have left them by the sink. She could go back in, but she'd rather suffer for the sake of poetic significance. She can be silly sometimes. Oh well. There are worse things to be. She runs her gaze down the hill, past where the trumpet vines and ivy are battling it out on the slope, past the curbed bay where Effie Street empties into Silver Lake Boulevard, down and back up to the Hollywood Hills in the distance. It's another gauzy L.A. morning. The sky's a huge frosted light bulb. Everything below floats in sun-charged vapors. In the foreground is her favorite piece of forgotten history: a grey-on-grey public storage complex that was once in fact (now a mere factoid, acknowledged only by the local graffiti artists, God bless 'em) the one and only Mack Sennett Studios. Keystone Cops were slapping sticks on this here hillock when Hollywoodland was just a mote in a marketer's eye, and long before old Mack himself first scalped that hill with the sign on it to make way for his ill-fated casbah. Chaplin, Arbuckle and Keaton, Normand, Swanson and Fields, and all those people behind the scenes were discovering a new language right here on Effie Street. Rules were eventually established and agreed upon, but codification couldn't have been the focus in those earliest days. The language wouldn't have been obliged to the past; it was not yet about its own history. Silent movies weren't even silent yet. And public expectations weren't so measured. Aisha takes the flyer out of her pocket and grabs a pen from her purse. She turns it over and writes, 'To be at the dawn is to marvel at the light.'

The canyons melt toward downtown, its skyscrapers like rock sugar in a cloudy jar. All the scattered mini downtowns, all the tired freeways in between are glazed, ghostly things, a world hovering over a fine, ever-settling silt. She adds: 'Let there be… a Kashmiri lake… a world…'

She picks up her small suitcase, bends the flyer around the galvanized-pipe handrail and steps off the porch. The concrete stairs are steep and irregular, wedged like an afterthought between two stucco cliffs. Like aggregate in a slurry, these cliff formations are remnants of the Los Angeles she imagined before she came out here, the one that existed before the human bomb went off. She skims the flyer weightlessly down the cold pipe, experiencing mild turbulence with each snag and imperfection. All things considered, she's proud of herself. She must have done something right to land this arrangement. Things could have been much worse. "Luminous anonymity," she stops to write. At this very moment there are countless edifices just as jarringly overexposed as the one she's descending now, on streets she will never know. She absorbs this matter-of-fact with equal parts gratitude and regret. She's paid attention; she's even had insight flashes here and there. But L.A.'s elusive all right. She's come to recognize a certain harshness, as if what gets absorbed most from all the lives played out within these vague city limits—radiating its negative in the same way color is presented to the senses, by which waves are rejected—is disenchantment. A sort of dream-vanishing. That makes sense though, doesn't it?

Sitting down on a step that the sun hasn't hit yet, she feels the cold from the concrete seep through her pants. She tugs at her newish bangs. 'Geography of fame imposed upon the terrain. A whirlpool scheme, all energy directed toward the middle. A light beam in a dark room, bombarded with synthetic dreams of starbirth.' She stares out at the almond-milky haze. 'Shadows on the streets, fighting to be cast, dream of becoming light,' She stands up, still writing. 'Dream-vanishing light. Dissolving dream-come-true. A smile turning to panic when held too long. A morning sky brooding with latent dusk. So long to the dream, vanishing.' So she can be corny sometimes. So what?

As if on cue, there's the exquisitely-timed rattling rasp of a seventies Porsche being forced uphill in the wrong gear. Candy's determined to drive it into the ground. It's trashy behavior, as Candy herself likes to point out. It's also superficial, as Aisha knows better. It's like an act. Like she'd bet Candy never slept with the Porsche guy.

For that month or so he moped around here, fawning and fretting over her, she hardly gave him the time of day. He made a weird play of resigning himself, though, didn't he? That air of feeble complaint, always sighing that 'buy the ticket take the ride' sigh like he was the unsung hero. It was also a performance. But that weird weak thrill she sensed behind the act? That was real. Candy knew it too. So she gave him the brushoff, and he gave her a Porsche. Aisha stuffs the flyer and pen into her purse and waves at the dog walker sneaking up the street toward the dead end, acting all devious. The woman pretends not to see her. What a funny place, she thinks, waving again when the woman tries to steal a backward glance. One of the first things she picked up on was how common the scorched-earth attitude is with girls around here. Maybe so they're not the only ones getting burned. Complicity in your own immolation is a form of agency, after all. Talk about roles! Way spookier are the ones who are only pretending to be pretending. But Candy's different. How many times has Aisha sat there while Candy exposed her photos? Her one leg on that stool in that dark blood-orange glow, that almost holy concentration of hers... it's intoxicating just to be near it. The photos are the real proof. There's something about them. They have... more. And it's not just her opinion. The rest is just Candy winking to herself. For the briefest, zillionth time, Aisha reflects on how they met. (She can run their whole relationship in her head like a movie, and often does. She mostly runs it super fast and chronologically, admiring its lines, but she also interposes sometimes, or she'll zoom in on a little moment and get just as much depth as in the wide view. It's like a mandelbrot of satisfaction like that.)

Right after she came out here, she bumped into a girl at the Norton Simon, and they got to talking. The girl invited her to a party out in Eagle Rock that night, and Aisha drove all the way back out there in Sandy's old Corolla. It was a pretty lame party. Too loud, too crowded, too predatory-leery, too fake-laughy. An ironic catering crew was serving-but-not-serving school-lunch style salisbury steak and boiled carrots. Candy was one of the "lunch ladies." She must've picked up Aisha's vibe from across the room, because she walked right over from her station, got in front of a giggly gaggle of CGI guys who'd converged to battle for Aisha's attention, backed them into the sloshy slipstream between bar and deck, did that face she likes to make, and said "hey". Aisha spent the rest of the night nursing a rum and coke that was supposed to be awful and was, and sticking close to her new friend. She never saw the museum girl again. She and Candy staked out an outsider position, observed, and commented on the festivities. They talked about Aisha's hard time finding a job, and Candy's hard time finding a job she liked, and their respective living situations, so it wasn't too out of left field that right when the thought of driving all the way back to Garden Grove hit, Candy, with what she calls her waitress timing, asked if Aisha wanted to crash at her place. Effie's been the closest thing to home pretty much ever since.

The Porsche jerks and stalls, startling the crows from their power line perches. Antique black against the silver sky, they circle the old movie studio in one big, lazy swoop, like synchronized extras on hidden wires.

"Ready Freddy?" Leaving the stalled car in gear, Candy yanks the emergency brake, removes the keys, jumps out and opens the hood. "D'jou say your farewells?"

"I did." Aisha takes one last look at the storage place as she throws her small suitcase in the luggage compartment. Her eyes move to those other arches across the street, the ones she's been o.c.d. about ever since she first noticed how they're fat where they should be skinny and vice versa, and their arches are all saggy and warped. Aisha once remarked to Candy how those warped arches sort of disturbed her. Candy—after first kindly acknowledging that she could totally see how those could be disturbing, and describing some generally related tics of her own—begged to differ. She said they reminded her of a de Chirico painting. Now, for the first time, Aisha sees it. Perfect timing. Comedic, even. Mr. Sennett would approve. Folding herself into the stalled car, she looks at but not through the windshield and lets the arches be her last impression of Effie Street.

* * * *

The interviewer crosses his legs at the shins, leans forward and draws the cross up above his knees with his hands. Should Avery describe the boots he lost? They were 1980s-issue Czechoslovak light-military; bulbous, inelegant, and almost indestructible. And what about his apartment at 421½ Trotter Drive, also doomed? He might describe how it stuck out from the side of that old duplex with its angles all mismatched, so that from certain angles it looked swollen... or how practically every surface was covered in a sticky micro-film of grease that attracted gnats and wouldn't let them go...

"There was a fire in my apartment building," he says. He thinks back to that afternoon, two weeks before he left. Black smoke rose almost freakishly gently above the rooftops as he lugged his laundry up the wide, empty street. When he arrived at the burning duplex, his studio had already been sacrificed. The upper-floor windows swallowed firehose water, and all that water filtered down through what used to be his apartment, picking up soot and bits of foul-smelling detritus along the way. It oozed out of what used to be his front door and flowed, foaming and black, into the steaming lake that had formed in the front yard. The fire was a shock, but the bigger surprise was the fact that it had nothing to do with Kyle, the tweaker building manager who lived in the apartment next door. Apparently it had originated at the Vongppandys, whose add-on apartment hung over his own. "These," he explains to the interviewer, indicating his creepers, with their thick soles split clear through, "and that," pointing to the toy ukulele lying string-side down on the table, "were basically all I could salvage. I had them in a plastic bag to go to the thrift store when the fire occurred. My prize possession at that time was a 1965 Martin acoustic guitar. It was a gift from my ex-girlfriend, and the last guitar I ever played. It wasn't in the best condition, but it played better than I ever did. It got lost in the fire, along with some other stuff I had... my boots, my computer, my phone, books and papers, personal stuff..."

"Did you have insurance?"

"Yeah. Well, the building did. The claims agent showed up even before the fire was put out."

"Did you get compensated for your losses?"

Avery scrutinizes the interviewer's face. "It's a long story."

The interviewer returns the scrutinizing look. "I see. Was that all that was lost?"

"Well... there was this sculpture my grandfather did, but—"

"Your grandfather was a sculptor? What was his name, your grandfather?"

"You wouldn't know him."

"I must tell you, Mr. Avery; I've long maintained an... interest in the arts. Might I insist?"

"Mika Krizan, but—"

"Of course I know him! He is a well-known Conceptual Brutalist!"

Avery moves his head back and forth like he's scraping at something in there. "No."

"No?"

"I mean you're thinking of someone else. My grandfather was a bowler, not a Brutalist."

"I see. Well, tell me about this sculpture your grandfather made. It must have meant a great deal to you."

Avery tries to see the sculpture as he saw it before the fire. Layers of meaning have been added since; things have merged and emerged, facts and details and more information about things like *Hull*, the other Mika Krizan's massive piece of public art, which Avery had seen in Berlin. He thinks, more or less:

Ayacucho: Obs. A ship-shaped object made of hammered tin, brass brads and wire, symbolically synonymous with his long-dead Grandpa... who never had a dime he didn't pay a quarter for but who was a man, and not to be confused with lesser specimen like the bastard who lost him his job over at Kaiser or any other echoes of that miserable company goon who cut Avery's great-grandmother down with a piece of rebar—it left those ridges, see...—during the Columbine Mine Massacre of '27 for trying to fetch him from the library so he could tend to things at home while his old man hacked himself to death with the black lung in the back room. It was in that old Serene library with all hell breaking loose outside, people making animal noises on the street, and then the worst dark and quiet until dawn, that he first read about the magnificent ship *Ayacucho* in a fine old leather-bound edition of *Two Years Before the Mast*. As Grandpa told Avery that long ago day, while trying to fix an old motor in his corkboard-paneled workshop and his 'sculpture' sat on the top shelf above the greasy coffee cans and tiny drawers and stenciled tool silhouettes like it always had (and always would, it seemed...), by sunrise that book's inside front cover had his own drawing of the schooner, a scroll with its name on it, and then his own name, Mika Krizan (not to take credit, but to take responsibility, because writing in library books was not allowed, see, and he'd been hiding all night...). He came home the next morning to find out that a coward in back of an armored truck had just turned his funny, affectionate mother mean, difficult and sad for the rest of her life. By the time Avery knew him, Grandpa was an old Californian with a 300 game ring, a garage, and a knack for hammering at whatever he had lying around. When he wondered aloud that morning in his workshop whatever happened to that old copy of *Two Years Before the Mast*, Avery imagined himself finding it someday, and bringing it to him.

"It was a ship, made out of metal scraps and wire." That's one answer, true enough. But it was more than that, wasn't it? It was also a question: 'If you hammer hard enough, can you transmute the past?' Now Grandpa's question has become his own. Did his commandeering of the tin ship's context manifest a qualitative shift in Grandpa's already completed actions, as a crime might reveal a previously hidden corruption? Did Grandpa become an accomplice, in the same way Elvis and Anne Frank posthumously became Mormons? And now? Had Avery made reparations? Does his own journey here represent a leap beyond the life-deferral of his forebears' working class struggle? Is it justification, or just a cheap flare, a wasted discharge of long-gathered and hard fought potential? Is he spending earned interest or draining principle? Is he an echo?

The interviewer nods toward the ukulele. "Tell me about your act."

"The Tiny Tim bit? Not much to tell, really." Avery taps one of his creepers. "These are what gave me the idea for it. It was never exactly an act; it was more of a whim. Nothing practiced or serious. In fact I only came up with it on the day I left. See, I had this job playing Top 40 songs at a convalescent home for old hippies, called the Love Inn—"

"Hippies?"

"Well, that was the idea. Anyway, it was about two weeks after I lost my boots in the fire. I'd been wearing the same tennis shoes every day since, and they needed a breather, so I dug these out of a salvage crate. On the walk to work I kept tripping on them. Not literally; I mean they made me feel top-heavy and out of proportion, particularly with the toy ukulele I was carrying."

"This is the day you left, you say?"

"Yeah."

"Good. Yes. Tell me about this day."

"Hmm... I'll try. Let's see. It's September 20th. I'm supposed to start work at noon, but I'm a few minutes late as usual. There's a phone call waiting for me when I walk in the door."

"An emergency?"

"It's from the insurance company."

"Ah."

"The point is, there's a little room right next the phone, where they keep the effects of recently deceased Inn Mates. I look up from my shoes and spot a bin containing the belongings of a friend of mine who had recently 'checked out', as they say. Knowing that this person had a thing for wigs, as soon as I get off the phone I decide to go in there and grab one. On a whim, like I said. I open the bin, and beneath the wigs there's a songbook for piano. By this point I'd about milked C and G dry, and the 'Lion'—" Avery waves his hands again, as if to erase the word from the air. "I open the book to a random page, which happens to be 'Livin' in the Sunlight, Lovin' in the Moonlight'. It even mentions Tiny Tim's ukulele version. It's another C G number, but whatever; I learn it real quick, grab a good wig, and get to work. So the room where I work... all right, to begin with," Avery swings his head around and pans the room with vacated eyes for effect, "they've taken the old cafeteria and converted it into a big parlor, with flocked velvet wallpaper, glow-in-the-dark outer space mural on the ceiling, heavy drapes covering all the windows, overstuffed couches scattered all over..." And little pill tables and lampshades, stained-glass domes, paper-and-bamboo spheres, Art-Nouveau-y cast-iron swing arms, silk-and-lace cones with the skeletal ribbing, and those improbably inviscid Victorian tassels... "The illuminarium? Illuminatorium? Anyway, they run this thing in there they call a light bath, that's basically a light show mixed with a slow strobe-effect type of thing that the guy in charge, who's actually named Doctor Love, believe it or not... that Doctor Love supposedly designed specifically to direct facial muscles upward and... smooth the—I was not to say the word *wrinkles* while on the premises, as per the agreement they had me sign when I took the job; nor was I to mention that while the 'light bath' was going you could hardly see your own nose in front of your face, and with all those pills going around, no wonder...." He was also not to critically assess any facility-produced tapestries and/or other handicrafts, or make any speculations as to their objective market values. "Speaking of pills…" There had already been grumbles from the pill gangs in back. They never wanted to hear the Top 40 stuff in the first place. But at that point his options were limited. He had to work in order to earn the money to replace his guitar, but he needed a guitar to fulfill his terms of employment, and he could only play so much on a toy. It was a classic catch-22 situation. At least that's what he told himself. "Never mind. Anyway, I get to work, but as soon as I start playing, in comes the doctor…" with his gas planet vibe, and his silver souffle of hair that jiggled when he talked. Avery softens his voice, slow and too soft, rounding out every syllable, "'Avery? A word, please?' He always put his hand on my shoulder, with his mouth touching my ear. And he'd squeeze, ever so passive-aggressively, and whisper. Something about the… something in his fingertips, like he's letting me in on some secret…"

"I take it you did not care for Dr. Love?"

"He was fine." It's like he would talk like you might imagine enlightenment is supposed to sound, or how the the next evolutionary phase after humans might talk. "He just bugged me." Avery tries the voice again. "Avery? It's been brought to my attention that you intend to regale us with nothing but falsetto today. Is that the case?

Avery?" There's no sense trying to look at him, with the light bath going on. "We can't have any more Lion Sleeps Tonight incidents," he says, muffling my strings with his thigh, which particularly annoys me, because I have a policy about stopping songs once I start them.

"Come on Brett," he replied with a petulance he was too old to be displaying, imagining the Doctor's face trying to harden, but only setting like custard, "if you'd've given me that advance we wouldn't even be having this conversation."

"We all sympathize with your situation," replied the doctor, with his thigh still pressing on the strings, and his hand still on Avery's shoulder, leaning in, " but we've been through this. Advances are verboten. Especially now. And Avery? There's no Brett here. Doctor Love—"

"Uh, uh! You can't put that on me, Brett. It's not my fault Mrs. Bostick's a psycho. That's on you. You let her in here. If you're looking for someone to blame, why don't you ask yourself what you all were thinking, letting her wear that ring in the first place?"

"I'm afraid I... we misinterpreted her."

"Well I'm no doctor, but... misinterpreted?"

"We assumed she was a rather ahhh... masculine... feminist...."

"And the neck tattoo? That didn't raise any freak flags for you?"

"She had her hair down during Inn Take. Stop it Avery. You're right; you're not a doctor. Frankly you're not much of a ukulele—"

"And Mrs. Goldenstein?"

"You saw her."

"I was in here, remember? But those kids got a show. I overheard some of their... impressions; no pun intended. Pretty graphic stuff."

"Yet it never occurred to you to stop playing."

"In the middle of the song? It wouldn't have made any difference anyway. Mrs. Bostick was quick. Before I knew it, the damage was done. So it's true what those kids were saying? About the welts?"

He could feel Doctor Love sag. "They saw those?"

"It wasn't like I had it in for him," Avery tells the interviewer, "but he was trying to slough responsibility off on me, and condescendingly at that—"

"Responsibility for what?"

Avery considers the question. He remembers how useless he felt when he first moved back home. He thinks about all those soul-crushing job interviews he went on in those dismal industrial parks, stinking with sweat after walking for miles. It's amazing, he thinks, the things a person can forget. The Love Inn was a bonafide plum gig. A paycheck for playing folk music and pop tunes for loaded old people? He couldn't believe his luck when he landed the job. He'd never even played live before, other than one open mic, and he was so drunk for that that it hardly counted. But it was his enthusiasm-bordering-on-desperation that won them over. No mystery there; he's always been good at summoning enthusiasm. They didn't even care that he wasn't that good; they were looking for family, and he fit right in. He remembers how happy he was when they called him, and how eagerly he signed that stupid agreement. He knew from the first call. He knew how bored he gets, how he tends to run…

"It happened in the Illumina-atrium the previous day, while I was singing 'The Lion Sleeps Tonight.' There's the usual heckling, no big deal… but then I hear these hard squishy sounds, and what I could swear is a big man's voice going off on this sped-up rant; next thing I know there's chairs sliding and lamps spilling, and more sloppy sounds, people grunting and smacking the ground—"

"What does this have to do with you?"

"At some point just after… after Mrs. Bostick's been subdued… the first time… she starts, like… singing in this fucked up voice, things like, "Where the fuck's that songbird!? Where are you, singer? Wait 'til I get my hands on you…"

"And what did you do?"

"I kept singing; like I said, I had a policy.… Meanwhile, poor Mrs. Goldenstein is laid out cold on the light bath floor. They drag her out to the hall, where a 5th grade class has gathered for a goodwill tour. They're the first to see the welts. Little '1%er' marks all over her face. Now I'm not aware of any of this at the time. By referring to what happened as the Lion Sleeps Tonight Incident, Doctor Love's trying to lay the blame exclusively on my falsetto. Maybe I should've stopped singing. But Doctor Love's light show was more of a crazy-making device than any legit form of therapy, and I'd been working in there ten days straight myself.…"

"The fact that '1%er' was reversed didn't seem odd to you?" he asked the doctor.

"Enough about the ring. As I've specifically specified-"

"You haven't told me how Mrs. Goldenstein is doing."

"She's fine. She'll be fine. You listen to me now. Your job is to play classic Top 40 hits and Top 40 hits only. That's what's in the agreement. No religion, no politics, and no falsettos. And this is absolutely the last time I want to hear you playing a—a toy. We simply cannot have it. Even our most... patient residents are showing signs of agitation-"

"Mrs. Love likes it."

"My mother—! Mrs. Love is a separate case, and none of your concern. She's ninety-five years old. Do the math."

"I don't know, Brett..."

"And don't I recall a certain 'Judy In Disguise' you were permitted to perform for our brother Thomas, despite the use of Eastern scales outside of Breathe Inn?"

"One time your Listen Inns actually did some good. You should be happy she spent her last days as who she really was."

"I've been under enormous pressure from the board as it is, Avery. This is a business, in spite of what you might like to think. It is not a commune."

"That's not what your ads say."

"That 'commune' is a verb."

"Clearly. Better than 'We Put The Jerry In Geriatric,' I'll give you that."

"Okay. That's enough. I never want to hear this thing here again. Is that clear enough for you? And the attitude can go too, because it's not going to fly. Do the job you were hired to do, or we'll have to make some major changes."

Avery asks himself what would have happened that morning had he not gotten the phone call. He's tempted to think he would have sucked it up for a while longer, that he'd have been wise enough at least to cross his bridges before torching them. But he was already running away. Being around all that cloistered Baby Boomer energy all the time was getting to him. The weird flirtations, offers of pills, off-color reminiscences of virility, conspiratorial winks (...how old these people are; not like you and I...); the snatching at whatever bits of currency he had on him. He'd go home feeling drained of blood. And it was even worse when he played stuff they liked. Still, The Lion Sleeps Tonight Incident had him pretty shaken up. He could have just bought a shitty acoustic and waited until the rest of his claim went through. Even after the phone call, he could have done that. But he didn't want to. He knew that call was coming sooner or later. He wanted to play toy. He needed the excuse.

"I start to remind him again how groovy it might be for him to cut me some slack, but my heart's not in it, so I suggest that he kindly take his creepy fucking hand off my shoulder, or words to that effect. And that was that."

* * * *

11:00 AM

Aisha groans. "And she's on that whole 'blessed' kick..."

"Ouch. Yeah, well... just take a month, you know? God, what's with the no traffic! Talk about blessings!" They're doing eighty-five on the 101. "What was I saying? Oh yeah. Take advantage," says Candy. "That's what I would do. Finish up school or whatever. Fuck it. Do what you got to do."

"Really?" Aisha stares straight ahead. Overpasses and interchanges curl like scrolls in her peripheral vision. So beautiful when you add speed; so ugly when you're sitting still. Why is that? "Like sell real estate?"

"You know what I mean."

"No; I do."

"You got the camera, right?"

"It's in my purse. Did I mention her boyfriend also flips houses? We'll be one big flipping blessed family—"

"That one's real good for shooting desert landscapes."

"And foreclosure zones."

"But of course." Candy cues 'The Passenger' from her phone (one of the Porsche's few updated features is its fully integrated sound system), but Aisha's not feeling it. She's thinking about how she and Candy will most likely never again be as close as they are now.

"That commercial kind of ruined this song for me, if you don't mind."

"No shit." Candy gives the volume knob a little smack for good measure. "Bastards."

"You mind if we just listen to the air? Thanks for the camera, Candy. And don't worry; I'll get a bag for it."

"I'm not worried. You'll put it to good use."

They roll down the windows. Freeway wind thrashes around inside the car. Aisha wonders if she'll remember this moment, the sports car and the trapped air, the bliss going bad in the pit of her stomach, the letdown acutely occurring. How can she possibly go back now? There's always the nuclear option; she could just jump out of the car at the next stop and wander away. Why doesn't she? "Heavy air today...."

"I don't have to tell you—shit—" Candy braking hard into mild congestion, "you'll be greatly missed 'round these parts."

"I'm going to—you have no idea. I wish—" Aisha can feel her eyes puffing. "Remember, if you're ever jonesing for some strip mall action…"

"I know just who to call."

"Yep," turning toward the open window, so Candy can't see her eyes. "It's who you know."

"So what are we getting at Shifty's, anyhow?"

"Just a couple of things. It should only take a minute. And say bye to my dad, if he's there."

"Cool."

The din settles back over them. Aisha never even unpacked at Sandy's. She almost says so but can't; just the thought of such a mundane little thing....

* * * *

Avery shifts his weight on the wooden couch. "Where were we?"

"You've just gotten yourself fired," the interviewer reminds him.

"That's right."

"Had you any money saved?"

"Not really..."

"But you had your insurance settlement."

"Did I mention an insurance settlement?"

The interviewer leans forward, clicks his chair legs on the floor like tap shoes, and leans back again. "Your words have an edge to them when you tell this Love Inn story," he says. "It's apparent from your telling that even when taking the effects of this light bath into consideration, you were unusually agitated at the time of this exchange with your boss. So forgive me if I get the sense that... was there something distasteful about the money that you were to collect? Something to do with the phone call, perhaps?"

Avery stiffens just as the shutter snaps. "Is this an interview or an interrogation?"

The interviewer lets out a brief chuckle. "You're quite right. I too get carried away sometimes. At any rate, you've left the Love Inn, yes? You are angry at yourself?"

"Not at all. Well... maybe a little. I'm outside the Inn, facing this cinderblock wall that bends around the entryway. It's one of those with concave diamonds centered in each block, so that when they're stacked they look like circles in squares. I can see through the wall. Across the street there's a bus stop; actually it's just a sign. There's a guy sitting on the curb beneath it, looking right at me."

"This man, he is someone you knew?"

"Total stranger."

"So you were startled that he was watching you?"

"I wouldn't say that. I was..."

"Uneasy?"

"Honestly, if he hadn't have been staring right at me, I wouldn't have given him a second thought. As it is—" The interviewer flashes a curious smile and holds the recorder up to Avery like a mirror. Avery narrows his eyes and shakes his head. "Sometimes when I try to explain things they turn to mush right before my... mouth. But here goes. Where I'm from there are lots of Mexicans—"

"Which is?" The shutter snaps.

"Which is what?"

"Where you are from?"

"Oh. East of L.A. A place called Primera."

"Yes. I have been. Route 66. It was part of Mexico once, yes?"

"Yeah. Then it was orange groves, harvested by Mexicans. So you got people there who are Californians from before there was a California, and Mexicans from before there was Mexico, who are native Americans, as in born and raised in the United States, but... but I'm not talking about them. I'm talking about people who cross over the border to work. Legally, they're not supposed to exist, so we let them do the shitty jobs and pretend they don't." A glare appears on the glass wall behind the interviewer. "When we were kids we used to call them wetbacks. Cholo kids would yell "la Migria!" at them during lunch to see if they'd jump. They just laid low and took it. Not much choice in the matter, I suppose...." Avery tugs the roof of his mouth with his tongue. "Most of the time they were in their own classes, you know? Segregated, I guess you could say. What they must've thought about us quote-unquote native Californians, who knows. In our imaginations there was a gigantic river out in the desert somewhere that they had to swim across just to get to where we just were... which we didn't think much of as a destination. It made them impressive, though. I'm sure I wasn't the only one who felt that way. We could only imagine what they'd had to do to get to where we were, but we knew it must have been intense. So we didn't know whether or not we could've done it ourselves. Mojado. That was another one..."

"The man at the bus stop?"

"Oh yeah. The point is, he's Mexican."

"Yes, I see."

"I'm kind of getting the feeling he's weighing something in his head, like he's about to make a decision. His eyes look... not wild, but very intense. He's got on kind of country-western clothes, and work boots. His skin looks like iron ore. It contrasts with his white eyes, giving them part of that intense look. Of course that's my own eyes seeing all that. But his hair is as black as your camera lens there, and cut straight across the front like a kid's haircut. He's sitting up straight, arms straight down at his sides. I'm like, where do I get off griping about my right to be understood, walking around in a wig, when some people got to be invisible—?"

"You felt guilty?"

"It's more like, when I was standing there in that office, looking at my dead friend's stuff all crammed into a bin... I don't know. I hadn't been putting enough effort into things." He hadn't looked up any of his old friends. He didn't even have a phone. "I'd just moved from L.A. about four months earlier, after breaking up with my girlfriend. Primera's where I grew up. For the five years I lived in L.A., I avoided it like the plague. But for some reason—"

"You came back."

After Lisa got her job at the Reality Channel, he's the one who changed, isn't he; even though he managed to convince her otherwise. Complaining all the time about his lame temp jobs, and refusing to go out with her work friends because he hated telling them what he did. He freaked out when she told a colleague he was a writer (she just said it, she said; she had no idea...), saying she was just embarrassed of him, that she was changing, becoming more superficial, less honest. Deciding to become a writer, if that's what would please her (and to protect his integrity now that she'd thrown it out there, he said), even though he hadn't written anything since high school. He had nothing better to do. After checking out a few examples online, he tried his hand at writing for television. He dared Lisa to be unwilling to show his scripts to anyone she worked with, until, against her better judgement, she gave one of them to the guy she PA-ed for. His response, addressed to Lisa and cc-ed to Avery, stated that after having read the script, he had some professional advice for them both. To Lisa, "let's not make a habit of this." Avery's was "don't quit your day job." Then she did start to change.... "Things weren't panning out."

"I see. So, there you are..."

"Staring at the street. An old lady creeps up to the intersection in a big yellow Oldsmobile..."

Standing there on the street corner, he had one of his

daydreams. In his daydream the old woman's name was Doris Chin, and she wore a little heart-shaped charm on her wheel-hand wrist that said *Slammin'* on it. The pickup truck behind her (it was really there) was making impatient little jerks toward her. In his imagination, one of the jerks tapped her bumper:

"Learn how to drive!" *the driver shouted. You drive no good."*

"No?" Slammin' Doris leaned back and let a couple of seconds pass before sticking her head out of the window. "Maybe you would like to teach me," she said, sweet-as-can-be.

"Huh?" The driver turned to his passenger. "Fuck's that supposed to mean?" The passenger shrugged. The driver threw the truck into reverse, peeled around the Olds, swung violently into the right hand lane and chirped to a stop beside her.

"Speak English!" he yelled. "Maybe I what?" Their light was green. So was the next one up, and its quanta of traffic was gaining on them.

"I say maybe you take me on, hot shot! You want to try?" She lifted her hand to the open window and fanned out her driver's license and registration with a magician's flourish. "Come on. You hold mine."

"Oh shit," the passenger wheezed into his cupped hands. He was laughing.

The driver laughed too, but his was more like a bronchial spasm. The passenger pantomimed a steering wheel. He twiddled his fingers, alerting his partner to the fact that the old lady's, with its clunky array of inlaid toggles and knobs, was appointed in the same simulated hardwood as was her dash unit. An association at best distantly related to this observation led the driver to a snap judgment. As of yet unaware of the more salient fact that the console wheel steered an even cherrier 442 W-30 complete with the virtually-unheard-of forced-air, four-speed-manual-transmission combo, the driver smirked at it one last time. "That for this? You fucking crazy?" He looked into her eyes, hoping to see crazy there. He was disappointed.

Doris flicked two toggles in quick succession. "Give me yours," pushing her papers out again. "Make it snappy."

The driver hesitated. The passenger reached into his glove compartment, grabbed his registration and handed it to the driver, who handed it over to Doris. "You're fucking crazy," he murmured.

"License too, tough guy."

"Suspended," the driver replied weakly.

"Say again?"

"It's suspended."

"Oohh. Outlaw, huh? Okay. Just the car then, Clyde." She smiled. "Can't have everything, right?" She scanned her rearview mirror, the nails of her right hand dangling from her cherrywood stick shift like spring blossoms. "Okay, here's how we go. Through the second light, no stopping for reds; no funny business," she dictated mechanically, watching behind them, wagging her finger playfully. "On yellow."

Avery thought, maybe it will happen...

"She's giving me this weird look." What's he going to say; that he likes to think he can control the world with his thoughts? Besides, it was the same prejudice fueling his imagination, just inverted to make himself look better in his own eyes. "Then I remember what I must look like. The bus stop guy's still staring at me. I nod at him, without knowing why. He nods back, stands up and brushes off his pants. Meanwhile, another woman has pushed her grocery cart down the crosswalk ramp right next to where I'm standing. A little girl is holding onto the cart." The woman's lips moved slightly, like she was trying to commit something to memory. She idled like a car, standing totally still and staring straight ahead. She was short, with dull black hair pulled up under a scarf. Her blouse was too small for her. Another poor Mexican. His eye was drawn to her midriff, which was at the same height as the little girl's eyes. "Now what happens next is going to be difficult to explain. I can tell by looking at the girl that her gaze is fixed at a point in space a few feet in front of her. And I've been standing there long enough to be sort of aware that the light is about to change. I can also tell… I can sense, I should say, that the driver of the car that's pulling out of the parking lot is also aware that the light will be turning soon, and in his determination to beat it he plans on accelerating the last thirty or so feet between driveway and intersection and cut in front of us to make his turn. A half-beat ahead of the little girl I step into the crosswalk and grab at what isn't yet there, so when she does step out—just another half-beat before a bumper, a hood, and the driver's dread-filled gape blurs by—it's right into my arms. A split second later the woman falls into me, like by some weird gravity. We stagger. The woman looks at me, out-of-phase terror and blame-response flaring in her eyes. The girl's fingers stick to the cart like candy canes. I see that the bus stop guy is almost crossed over to my side of the street. I'm feeling a headache coming on, and my mouth has become extremely dry. I take a couple of steps away from the crosswalk to let him by. He walks a few paces past me, slows down, turns around and jerks his chin in the direction of the grocery store. Oh, of course, I think. Duh. I've bestowed upon a stranger a dignity of purpose that's purely of my own making. This guy just wants booze. I crouch behind a magazine rack to count my money while he walks over to an abandoned photo developing kiosk in the middle of the parking lot. I go into the market, still shaking from what just happened. I grab a water, a toothbrush, and a big plastic bottle of cheap tequila. There's no line, so I head to the cashier and hand him my I.D.

"Name?"

"Avery K—"

"Says here Steven."

"Avery's my middle name, as you can see." While he searches for the thing to take the plastic collar off the liquor bottle, I'm hit with a familiar scent. In my peripheral vision, a neat hand is neatly arranging groceries on the conveyor belt."

Avery pauses.

"I mentioned that I'd been living with my girlfriend in L.A., right? Well her folks were serious people, and they had money. They were pleasant enough, but they had this way of making me feel like I was a safety pin through their daughter's lip, if you know what I mean. I could tell they had their fingers crossed when it came to me. Like please don't be too permanent. Anyway, I look up and my ex-girlfriend's mom is standing in line behind me, staring at the tequila."

"Having a party?"

Meanwhile, Steven is saying something about my "costume," and "coming in here like that."

"No," I say, aware of the pity peeking from behind her flippancy, "it's just me." Having clearly fallen in his estimation from interrogate-able to questionable, I doff my wig at the check-out guy, whose name tag says Steven.

"Well," she says, "Lisa said we might be seeing you back in town. I'm glad to see you've been... enjoying yourself."

Avery placed the smell. It was the same laundry detergent Lisa used. Something must have been written on his face, because her mom's smile changed. She looked him up and down, held up one finger like 'shhh' while her other hand snuck into her pocketbook. "You're the holdup here, man," he said to the checker, turning back to face Lisa's mom already shaking his head no no please no, while wishing she'd come closer, with that fragrance....

"I tell her the truth; more or less. I tell her I'm buying the booze for some guy outside. I explain about the ukulele and the getup and the job, but not about the fire or the getting fired." And he told her how good it was to see her. Surprisingly good, he even said. She kept her eyes on his, and wanted to say something... "I rush out of the store without getting a bag, but when I get back outside the guy's gone. I'm left standing in the middle of the parking lot with a toy ukulele and a big plastic bottle of liquor, and nowhere to go." Avery turns around and watches through the window as a tiny, fuse-like line lengthens way off in the distance. A farmer, plowing up dust. "You know that feeling, like you're in a place, but the place itself is no place? And part of you feels almost like it's your duty to do something about it? Like in order to exist, you must also will your place into existence? That's how I felt then."

He felt that autumnal shift toward the red, the falling away that gets repeated and mirrored by the foliage, the light like a memory of life…

The shutter clicks.

* * * *

11:15 AM

The marine layer is burning off. The sky looks faded and dingy, like a sky-blue toy that's been left outside too long. Aisha watches the Los Angeles skyline shrink in the side-view mirror.

"I didn't want the 710, did I?" Candy asks.

"You could've, but this way is better."

"Stay on the 5?"

"When there's no traffic, the quickest is the 5 to the 605 to the 405. That way you don't have to backtrack."

"Spoken like a true local."

Candy's phone skitters around the rim of the cup holder. Before Candy can pick up or not, a trippy female voice starts relaying her text message aloud, while Candy spins the bypassed volume knob.

"Hey Candace going 2 NV after all leaving 2night. Get 2gether b4? Zane."

"Zane?" Sometimes Aisha inadvertently uses the same exact voice as Candy; it's obvious, and embarrassing.

"He's a guy I met at work. Nice young man. You'd like him."

"So that's where you've been...."

"Where what?"

"Nothing. What's that about Nevada?"

"I don't know. Some work thing he's got going on."

"Are you going with?"

"God, no."

"Why, what's he do?"

Candy smiles. "You'll laugh. I know I did."

"Really? Tell me!"

"He's a gamer."

"Eww... Like poker?"

"Like video games. He plays them for a living."

"Does he live in—"

"And he doesn't live in his mom's garage, either. He's apparently some sort of celebrity. Like, thousands of people watch him battle it out online. He gets endorsement deals and everything."

"I've never seen any of that stuff."

"'Well, you've got a life."

"Ha ha. Seriously, how do you get that good at video games, you know?"

Candy starts thumbing through screens.

"The road—"

"I got it." She holds the phone so Aisha can see it. "Does he look like a shut-in to you?"

Aisha glances, keeping one eye on the cars ahead. "He looks like a cop."

"Oh God; don't say that. My brother's a cop." Candy takes a look. "Ha! You're right. He does, in this picture."

Aisha gets another tug in her stomach. "You meeting him later?"

"Don't know. Depends."

"Ah."

The freeway passes over the Southern Pacific yards. Aisha squints at the light ricocheting off the light-industrial rooftops. It's like a huge silvered mosaic table with the sun at its head. It echoes off her retinas when she blinks and drifts in her vision after she turns away. In the opposite distance Orange County sprawls like a huge marsh all the way to the ocean. Four months in L.A. and she never once went to the beach. Even now her cells are straining in the other direction. That's the feeling in her stomach, too, like it's trying to pull her back in time, as if there remains a channel between here and there. What she really ought to do is just stop thinking about it. She should have been much more prepared. But you can't be ready if you don't know what for. But she did know, didn't she? Why did she never insist on taking art classes or music lessons? Because the name of the game back then was her mom's struggle. There was no room for Aisha to indulge herself in that play. It wouldn't have matched.

In college, she focused on business administration like her mom wanted. At first she told herself she'd explore other avenues when her schedule got more flexible. At the same time she felt like it was already too late. She developed a nagging conviction that her environment was conspiring to keep what she was meant to do a secret. But her mom was right about one thing; L.A. is tough enough if you know what you want to do, and it's a downright nasty place to start from scratch. She's just not enough of a hustler for the gig economy. She applied for a dozen jobs she would have considered beneath her back home, and never got calls back. It was Candy who encouraged her to start writing on whatever she had on hand. That's been a cool thing. The combination of freedom and discipline required, how each one helps the other to build self-trust; it's taught her something for sure. But mom knew. They agreed on three months; it's been four. She made the same offer she made before, and this time Aisha had to take it. Even without the so-called free house, it really would be stupid to walk away from her degree at this point. L.A.'s taught her that much. Now the wheels are rolling; that's all. The wheels are rolling, and she's getting motion sickness. Would it do any good if she told Candy how she felt? Not at this point, other than to garner pity. The time for all that is passed. Besides, who's she kidding? Candy's not stupid. She knows. Nope, nothing to do now but shut up and get shuttled around.

* * * *

The interviewer sets the tape recorder on the table. "Tell me about Primera, then."

Avery turns from the window to face him. He picks up a stack of coasters embossed with the Kasbah Kandisha logo from the tabletop and places one near its edge. "Okay... so north is the mountains. They run east to west because of the San Andreas Fault...," pointing with his finger... "out here. It's unusual, actually. East is the high desert." He places a couple of coasters on the table. "West is L.A. and south is what... Orange County. The Pacific Ocean is here." He points toward the far corner of the table. "A long alluvial plain slopes down from northeast to southwest. Like sedimentation, homes tend to decrease in size and value the lower you go. Ghetto here, barrio here. Prison here. Money flows uphill here, and trickles down here." He stands up, walks around the table, and places the last coaster. "So test sites, bombing ranges and all that out here... towns as good as any for straight meanness. Excesses of speed, offensive defensiveness, paranoia. If you imagine an electromagnetic field between L.A. and the exploding desert, Primera occupies the zone between attraction and repulsion. The relationship between people and places is a mystery, don't you think? Sometimes I think places can determine which stories can be told there, and which can't."

Avery sits back down. There was a blimp bobbing around in the Primera sky that day, dark against the bright haze, rolling and pitching in that slow motion way blimps do. It had a big ad on its side that it kept dipping at everyone below. 'VODKA'. That's all it said. He walked past a whitewashed former fast food building that had been repurposed as a church. The preacher's voice came through the telecom speaker on the old drive-thru menu board. So this is what it comes down to, he thought as the VODKA blimp came back into view. No brand, even. Next door was a big field full of weeds and litter. He wandered into the field. The traffic noise mellowed to a hum; he could hear grasshoppers and flies and bees, and lizards slithering in crackling weeds. There was a breeze high up in a sycamore tree beyond the fence, and the swirling swish of a jet overhead. Some places are like old cassettes that've been recorded over too many times, he thought. Degradation becomes a component of the sound.

He looked to the south, toward where he grew up. He hadn't been down there in years. He had no more family there, and his few childhood friends were also long gone. The old neighborhood had distilled in his memory to a mystery he never solved, clues left in oil stains or written in the shiny black creosote tar on telephone poles, mysterious as obsidian, smelling deliciously of poison, promising profound revelation but only leading to cool places to daydream while the other kids fought and strutted in the sun. Those places, so sweet with the future, he was no longer allowed to visit.

An old soul song played from a radio somewhere. As he listened it ceded its place in the mix to a slow, low voice sweet-talking the name of a financial services company and its tag-line before accelerating into an enumeration of amenities, returns and risks-of-return. Meanwhile the song played on meekly in the background, as if ashamed of itself. He wondered how he already got himself so stuck, how he found himself so lost, so soon, when he thought he'd been paying attention.

So he deflected. He shifted the blame. There's meaning in meandering, he insisted to himself defensively. We nurture the world with the attention we pay, and no one is paying enough!

He felt proud and daring at that moment, like he was

part of a secret resistance. It was all so clear. The same way bees produce honey, humans produce meaning, and apply it to the world, and the world absorbs it, and trees become tall, oceans become vast, and mountains majestic. But it also is channelled, hoarded, withheld, and doled out. He asked himself what was worse: expending whatever charge he'd gathered over a hopeful youth in disinterestedly spinning his wheels, or being reckless with his future by grabbing at change that, while it certainly will demand his attention, will surely also call for a measure of shame, if not legal trouble? Again he could have just bought a cheap guitar, asked for his job back, and made some long-term plans. But he took the easier route, as usual. He lashed out. Attention must be paid! he silently declared. That's how mountains rise, right mountains? Not on credit, and not for free. I'm paying attention!' He looked past the trees and foothills to the mountains. Mount Baldy floated above the torn-paper hills like a granite chess king behind its pawns, telling him in no uncertain terms that he was full of shit. Still thinking about the little girl at the intersection, he started keeping an eye out for other situations in which to heroically intervene. He minded that the more purity he pretended to, the more rotten it was all bound to get. Was he harmful to others? No. He was a nice guy, wasn't he? He didn't aim ill will, did—Wrong! You don't have to aim a grenade. His self-righteousness was self-serving. Just who was he trying to kid?

"I'd planned to turn right at the intersection," he continues, leaning forward to talk into the tape recorder, "but there's a guy further up the street, squatting against a wall, with another guy standing over him. I'm thinking maybe one of them is the man from the bus stop. But when I get closer I see that the squatter is wearing a business suit, and is out of his mind on something. The other guy is scolding him. "You're a dinosaur...—" he's in the middle of saying when I walk up to them. "'Sup, holmes," he interrupts himself, greeting me with a 'you're in *my* world' inflection, before turning back to the squatter. He's probably in his early twenties. He wears woven pants rolled up over his calves, matted hair spilling from the top of his head like a fountain, and boots almost identical to the ones I'd just lost in the fire. There's something about him—his aggressive posture, the crocodilian cut of his jaw, the predatory glint in his eyes—that makes me uncomfortable. It feels incongruous, like a wolf peeking through sheep's clothing. He was holding a coffee grinder. 'We've had enough of the likes of you.'

'It's the love, man...' the seated man moans.

'What do you know about love?' He winks at me, 'It's the love, he says.'

The seated guy still hasn't looked up. He has a bald spot and some grey in his hair, so my first guess is he's in his mid-forties. His dark blue suit's smudged with concrete dust from the sidewalk. He makes a sweeping gesture, signifying everything, still without raising his head. 'Little roaster loves to roast. Big roaster knows you love to grind.'

'Chsh. You and your corporate swill.'

The suited man looks up with a dense, damp sadness in his bloated eyes. He's thirty-five, tops. It's hard to look at his face; the horror on it is almost obscene. 'I'm trying to... say something,' he practically begs us both;

'the ones... sold you the grinder... know about your... are aware of your...'

'Listen to you, all incapable of human speech. All you can do is croak.'

'Exuberance. They're aware of your... exuberance. It's their... life's blood. The little roaster is just like you... s-subject to the same...' He lowers his head. 'She wants to give you...,' he coughs, '... it's the love. She wants to love. So you... you go... you go—flickering in and out of coherence , 'you... feeling... feeling... you say... what? Swill... corporate swill... Here's some love. I need love. And you get it and you... grind... grind it into powder, and p-pour the powder... into the maker... and it's never as good...'

'Look at him. Hey, Droolio!'

'... because love isn't good enough. To know how you do... we... but I don't—' He stares, transfixed, like he's watching his train of thought fall into an abyss. He inhales deeply from the paper bag he's holding. '... just because we're...' he's gurgling, eyes red-ringed, chemically yellow, '... that we do not value...' there are pools in his eyes, '... the love...'

'You make-a no sense, bra,' says the other guy in triumph, winking again. 'Keep hitting that shit.'

It's not exactly the intervention I'm on the lookout for. My instinct might have been to nod in solidarity at the nonconformist, but when he starts mocking the suited guy for crying, and openly ridiculing him when he clearly isn't up to the task of defending himself, I find myself compelled to intercede on behalf of the scoldee.

'Dude, it's a coffee grinder,' I tell the scolder.

The scolder looks hard at me, while pointing his coffee grinder at the suited man, who gurgles something about just wanting to be a good father. The grinder cord sweeps back and forth over the pavement, the plug swinging and dragging like a hopeless little man trying to hold down a VODKA blimp in a stiff breeze. 'G motherfucking E.'

'Yeah? And?'

'And guess who made this?'

'Umm... G motherfucking E?'

'Ding ding! The media...' holding up one finger, 'the fucking military...' holding up another, 'the fucking banks...'

'So you're taking it out on this guy.'

'Ayyy, bruddah," in a bad Jamaican accent, dangling the little cord man, 'what you stepping like dat fuh?'

'I'm sorry...,' I'm thinking, an honest man might tell you you can't trust him for shit. A liar can even have your back. But this guy is something else. 'Did I stutter?' To the other guy, 'How you doing, man? You need some help?'

The suited man looks at me blankly, searching himself clumsily while holding the paper bag where it's stalled a few inches from his face, and after an almost absurdly long time produces an old business card that has been rolled into a tube more than once, by the feel of it. He drops the card and can't pick it back up. His hand keeps missing the mark. I pick up the card and read it. It says GE. 'No... I'm good,' the man mumbles, lifting the bag up to his mouth.

'Ramble on, Frankystein,' says the scolder.

'Yeah,' I smile. 'Keep fighting the good fight.'

'Fuck you.'

I back away with my fist held in a sarcastic solidarity salute. Keeping the axe-grinding grinder man in front of me until I'm out of sucker-punch range, I turn around, and tensely walk away, my comfortably abstract defiance replaced with anger and a vague but visceral sense of frustration."

* * * *

Kwéte reaches the foothills without stopping for breath. After some hard climbing he enters a rugged red landscape of live oak, yucca and manzanita. Exhausted, and safely out of reach of the heavy rahwah'nat for the time being, he finds an abandoned bobcat den and stops there for a rest. The dugout is cool, soft, and concealed by the white skeleton of an ancient madrone. Below him a narrow clearing allows him to look down over part of the valley. There is La Misión, neatly framed by the bonelike branches. He can make out a teeming, a shimmering simmer in the smoky haze, that's people and Spaniards scrambling like ground bees around a kicked nest. He watches the large wooden cross get dragged from inside the wounded fortress and propped against the courtyard well. The cross is as straight and square as ever. But the hanging man is nowhere to be seen. Kwéte draws himself deeper into the den and listens. His senses have never been as keen as they are now, and the world has slowed down as if to talk to him alone, and he is not alone. He is not alone. What if the hanging man escaped after all, like the Padre said he would? Maybe he has followed him up this hill. An achy chill runs through him. He sees himself as the hanging man, just as the Padre said men should. It's winter in his vision, and very cold. He sees damp greens, clay reds and milky browns beneath a colorless sky, all the colors of La Misión but in stronger values, as if making up in vibrancy for their lack of variety. He is surrounded by grey people, but they are not Spaniards. There is invisible panic in the air. He hears groans. The people have been given a beginning, but not an end. It is too much for them. They are falling apart.

The vision frightens him, so he opens his eyes. A large red brown bear heaves like a bellows just outside the den. Kwéte is relieved to see the bear. He doesn't move, other than to look directly into its eyes. They are a deep, reflective black.

* * * *

11:30 AM

"So we're expecting to see Shifty today?" That's Candy's nickname for Aisha's dad, Sandy, stemming from his apartment at the Ha' Penny Arms being a crash pad for the midnight-to-dawn crowd at the Lucky Pueblo Card Room up the street. (Sandy was birth-named Junior, after his father, Junior Sr., whom he never met. But people just called him Sandy.) Candy's nickname is funny to Aisha because her mom used to call Sandy shiftless when he was late with his child support. He's a good dad as far as shiftless, shifty, shitty dads go, even decent in his way, because he's always treated her with respect. In return, she cuts him endless slack. He works as a claims adjustor for a big insurance company. All she knows is what he told her once when he was feeling particularly good about himself, which is that he's not just an agent. He makes real money, whatever that means. Not that you'd know it from his apartment. The only decor is an empty CD tower in the corner behind the TV. So weird. But who knows; he might be a big shot over at the Pueblo. He acts like it all right, and his sketchy friends sure let him. She hasn't been over there to find out. And his car –

"I don't see his car." They pull into the Ha' Penny's parking lot. Aisha reaches into her purse then remembers about her sunglasses. Clomping up the cast-iron stairs, they can see that the apartment door is open. The TV can be heard from the landing.

"Getting an early start today," Candy whispers as they approach. Aisha lifts her eyebrows and grins. They step inside to find Coop and the guy she will not call Jigaboo lying each on his own couch, smoking and facing the figure skating blaring from the television.

"That was the luckiest flip I ever seen."

"Yeah he was."

"Aaaaaaahh!"

On the table is an ashtray, a mess of what looks like burrito in IHOP wrappers, and a Greek ruin of Bud tallboys. Two heads bend in mirror symmetry to face them.

"Hey Ish," Coop says. "Oh, hello there... I'm sorry, I forgot your name..."

"Candace."

"What, no Candy today?"

"You forgot, remember?"

"So you don't go by Candy no more?"

"Is my dad here?" Turning to the other man, Aisha adds, "Hey..."

"Hey foxy."

"Don't 'foxy' her, man, Jig," says Coop. "That's Sandy's little girl."

"Man, I know who she is. Shit. You got no class is your problem." After turning from Coop in his own exaggerated disgust, Jig nods at Aisha and Candy. "Pardon him. How you ladies doing?"

"Fine."

"Looking for your dad?"

"Mmm... sort of. He said he'd be here this morning."

"He's at work, ain't that right Coop?"

"Fuck yourself, Boo."

"What do you need him for? We can give him a message, huh Coop?"

"He's supposed to... ahh, don't worry about it. He knows. I'm going back to Arizona tonight."

"No shit. L.A.'s not doing it for you?"

"I don't know. We'll see. I might be back. My dad didn't mention anything?"

"I'm sure he did and we just forgot. Right Coop?"

"Well um... I'm just going to grab a few things, um...—"

"Call me Boo."

"No offense, but I'd rather not."

"It's my real name, girl. Fuck the dumb shit. Fuck the dumb shit you hear around here; ain't that right, Man-day Coo-pah?" Boo gets a bird flown from Coop.

"Thanks," Aisha says. She heads to the bathroom. Candy gags at Coop and follows. Aisha grabs some things from the bathroom before moving to the back bedroom. She checks the dresser. She finds one pair of pants in the bottom drawer, folded next to a small, empty tote bag. She balls up the pants and drops them and her toiletries into the bag. She thinks about leaving a note but decides against it. Coop and Boo are still arguing when Aisha and Candy make their way back through.

"It's gambling. Gambling is lying."

"What do you know about it?"

"Look at the motherfucking bailout—"

"Look at your motherfucking—"

"All righty then!" Aisha shouts, waving good riddance.

Boo gives her a concerned look. "You don't want to wait for your old man?"

"No, that's alright. Just tell him I'll call when I get there, if you wouldn't mind."

"Don't worry, I'll tell his ass."

"Don't—it's all right. I've known… I've known Sandy a long time."

"Yeah you have. Well, you travel safe."

"Yeah, you be safe," Coop chimes in. "And ay. Ay. Ay—"

"What?"

"Don't let 'em see you coming."

"Right."

"And ay. It was a pleasure making your acquaintance, Miss Candace."

"Nice stain there, Mandy."

Coop looks down at his shirt. "What the—"

"Man, just shut your ass up! You'll have to excuse Mr. Cooper here, he can't—"

"Know what, Jig? How's about you take your fucking—"

"Bye!"

"Okay then!"

"Be good!"

* * * *

"I get off off the busy street and enter a residential neighborhood," Avery continues. "It's shady and cooler there. No more ads or traffic noise, only sporadic domestic sounds like twitches in a nap. Yellow leaves drift from the gum trees, flickering like gold flakes in the early-autumn sun. Squirrels and birds scurry around the leaf-speckled yards, gathering and stashing food for the rainy season. For two blocks my sole purpose is to keep leaves crackling underfoot. Finally I come to a big stone house on the corner, where a poet lives. Theodora Gibbs is the poet's name. Supposedly she has lived in that same house her whole life. She walks around the neighborhood in an old moth-eaten trenchcoat and dusty bouffant, muttering to herself. People think she's nuts. Anyway, practically buried in her wild backyard is this old carriage house. I broke in there once in the seventh grade with a friend from school. I don't think those doors had been opened in years even then. It was like a tomb full of old books."

"Books?"

"Yeah. Old ones. I peek through some vines and see stacks of books outside, their dark colors camouflaged by the overgrown undergrowth. By this time I've almost forgotten about the bus stop guy, but as soon as the next armload of books emerges from the shed, even before I see the face, I know it's him. I remember the tequila and wonder whether I should show it to him now or wait until I can be more discreet. He puts down the books and his eyes lock onto mine again, just like before through the wall, but through the vines this time. He nods like he's been expecting me, bends his elbow, points at his arm, points back at me and nods again. He points at my bag, then at a spot on the ground in the yard, then toward the carriage house. I try to show him the bottle but my wig flops out instead. He goes back inside without seeming to notice. I stand up thinking, what am I doing? But I climb through the vines anyway. I stash the bag in the ivy and step inside the carriage house.

It takes my eyes a minute to adjust to the light in there. At first all I can see is a tiny sash window and a single floating light bulb, both covered in a dark, moldy film. But a jaundiced light eventually starts to fill the little room. I see three people to begin with. There's the guy from the bus stop, reaching for another armload of books. His name is Paco, by the way. But I don't learn that until later. There's Theodora Gibbs, leaning against the wall with the sun behind her, surrounded by little cracks of light where the slats have separated. There's a middle aged guy in a tweed jacket, squatting in the center of the room with a book in his lap. He and Theodora are in the middle of a conversation. They don't appear to notice me at first. As my eyes adjust some more I see that what I thought was a shadow is a woman, sitting Indian-style in the dimmest corner of the room. I can't see her eyes, but I feel them on me.

'... it has liquid properties and solid ones,' Theodora's saying. 'They flow, and they are granular. Like sand. Liquid and solid both. What else...?' She starts to answer her own question but changes her mind. 'In Kyoto—'

'Words are solids?'

Paco points toward the corner of the room that's being emptied first. After surveying the stacks, I grab a greasy stack of books and follow him back out into the sun. The pad directly in front of the doors is full, so Paco leads me through a long vine tunnel to another concrete pad even further back in the yard. The concrete of this pad is rotting away. It's enclosed by a sort of hut made of grape and berry vines, ivies and spider grasses and who knows what all else. We start a new pile in the least rotten part of the pad. Paco gives me a nod that's just on the friendly side of ambivalent, and we head back to the carriage house for another load. I walk inside and again my eyes take a few seconds to adjust again; again I can't see the person in the corner.

'Are phalli phallic, or just tools... hold that thought. Young man?' Jamming her hand into the pocket of her trench coat, Theodora stares at me intently as she pulls out an eyepatch, tangled up with some old medals and shoelaces. 'Speaking of tools,' she separates the eyepatch and shoves the rest back into her pocket, 'put this over your eye.' I stare at her like an idiot. 'Either one,' not mocking so much as gruffly acknowledging my confusion. I nod dumbly and put the patch over my left eye, wondering whether I'm being made a fool of, or even punished for my youthful transgression. 'When you come back inside, you switch it on over to your other eye. See?' The lack of depth perception takes some getting used to at first, but when I go back inside for another load and switch eyes, I can see just fine.

Who was it, said we should be careful who we pretend to be?' Theodora gives me a wink.

'That one with the suit. And the mustache.'

'Well he was onto something there.' I gather up a load of Vedas and start to head out when a voice stops me in my tracks.

'What do you think, young man? Are books silent?'

The voice is deep and female. Caught off guard, I dumbly wait for someone else to answer.

'Me?' I ask finally, attempting to point at myself through the Vedas. 'D-do I hear someone reading in my head, you mean?' Not a peep. 'Honestly? I honestly don't n-know, though uh… I've sure wondered about stuff like that…' I stall, to give my mind more time to wrap itself around the question. 'I think it might be different when you're, like, paying attention? Like, quantum physics… what you were saying about liquids and solids? If you look at it… Like what you were saying, right…?'

'Yes. I quite agree.'

'You said it.'

'I did?'

'He said it.'

'My name is Ursula,' the seated woman says, looking

right through me. 'What's your name again?'

'Avery Krizan.'

'Oh. Then you must be related to Mika Krizan.'

Before I can answer, a tall stack of books spills into the middle of the room. With old paper slapping the floor, and spines wrenching all around us, Theodora Gibbs slowly puts her finger to her lips.

'Silent,' she says through the clamor. 'Like the dead silent. Like the dead suspicious. The dead like the living once trust is earned, introduce one another.' Looking at me, she raises an imaginary glass, 'To the life of the party.'

So I go back and forth between this sort of talk and the growing piles of silent books on the pad, switching Theodora's eye patch on every trip. I'm starting to linger, getting drawn into the conversation. The whole time Paco doesn't say a word, and hardly pauses in his work."

* * * *

11:45 AM

They're back on the road. Candy gives Aisha a long look. "Are you pissed?"

"I should be."

"I would be."

"Yeah, well...." Aisha looks down from the elevated freeway at a sea of gently sloping suburban rooftops. They remind her of playing Monopoly with her parents when they were still together. She always volunteered to put away the board after the game. She liked to slide all the houses and hotels into one corner of the box, to see what sort of village they made. "What city are we in?"

"Beats me."

She'd said yes over the phone when dad offered to take her to the station, but she doesn't mention this fact to Candy. Why not? She can convince herself that deep down she always knew Sandy would blow her off, and she wouldn't be lying. But the truer truth is she never wanted to spend her last day here with him. She was always going to play it by ear, though; if he was particularly insistent then she was prepared to leave with a Garden Grove taste in her mouth, but otherwise she had private plans to spend the day with Candy. Naturally she's a little bummed and maybe a little hurt that he flaked, but it's not like that changes anything between them. It's par for the course, actually. And she didn't have to make the choice herself, so in that sense he's actually done her a favor. She won't be mentioning this fact either, so she can't let herself mope. That would be dishonest.

"What time's your train?"

"Seven-forty."

"Oh." Is that a note of irritation? "What do you want to do in the meantime?"

"Hmm..."

"Hmm..."

"Well... we could go downtown and get something to eat, maybe wander around by the train station." This was the plan she'd planned on suggesting to Sandy, had he kept their date.

Candy bites her lip and purses her eyebrows. "There's not much to do around there."

"Really?"

"Hmm."

"I'm sure it's all lame and touristy, but I haven't been to Olvera Street."

"Hmm…"

"But you know, whatever—"

"You know what? That actually sounds kind of fun. Let's go be tourists."

* * * *

"What do you think of cock, Avery?"

"I beg your pardon?"

"As a word."

"Ah." He was a little stunned by the question. "It's just a word, right?"

"Indeed. And a very effective one."

"Very physical—"

"Mm hmm."

"Active."

"Very strong indeed."

"Agreed."

"You must really use your throat to properly pro—'"

"Actions speak louder than words," he ventured, but got head shakes all around.

"Mmm…"

"Actions are words."

"Oh. I—"

"Drone attack to send a message," the tweedy guy said, addressing him directly for the first time. "And what language might that be, pray tell?"

"'That's what I call a bad word,'" Theodora agreed.

"You can say that again. Just how does one pronounce crimes that everyone knows were committed, but for which no one will ever pay? We all know this word. What's your name again?"

"Avery."

"Dave Edwards, at your service. So why don't we hear a mantra of that, hey Avery? We got drones—"

"Uh oh."

"Here comes the drone drone drone drone."

"You can say that again."

"They'll be coming after all the good words soon enough.'"

"'You think? Which they's this, now?"

"Theys that process and package what we like to call reality these days. You know."

"Oh, yes. Them."

On his next trip, Dave Edwards followed Avery outside to finish a point that the others had apparently heard already. By that time stacks of books were scattered all over the pad.

"Take the growth of the modern city," he said, moving

books from stack to stack to illustrate; "you've got your market, right, scaled for human interaction. The shopper and the merchant, all on same level. On the level, get it? Then you get your first blistering of the shopkeeper's quarters, and pretty soon you got elephantiasis... empty conference rooms by the cubic mile... but that's not the point, is it? No; that is the point. The invisible hand needs space, you follow? Like God needs His church. It ain't for usss. We ain't in its image." It was just a slight slur, but enough to show that Mr. Edwards was less sober than he was letting on. "'We like to say it's evolution, but we all know it's going too goddamn fast to call it that. You know what I'm talking about. I prefer the term necrotic metastasis."

He laid flat on his back in the midst of the book towers. "Have you ever been to Manhattan? Glass beams shooting—'Fieeww! Fieeww!—beyond the peripheral. The only way to see the damned things is to turn from humanity entirely. Might as well be outer space up there. Nothing but silicates and steel. Pondering what other eyes might espy you from behind those mirrors is a hell of an exercise, believe you me. You'll see. It's not for us anymore, is the point...." He closed his eyes and was silent for a long time. "'Mannahatta,'" he recited in a low, sober voice, "'My city's fit and noble name resumed... Choice aboriginal name, with marvelous beauty, meaning, a rocky-founded island shores... where ever gayly dash the coming, hurrying sea waves.' You a Whitman man, by chance?"

"I don't really know too much of his work, but—" Avery felt young; he was being given stories and advice and attention. With a pang of sadness, he looked down at his tutor. It won't always be this way; not even this way...

"No, of course not. Who has time for leaves of grass anymore?" The slight slur was back. "That's just my point. We've built an enormous inorganism, haven't we? A thing like that... and we think we can tell it what to do! Ha! Us? Look at Wall Street—" he tries to gesture toward one of the towers but hits it instead, causing it to rock in two places at once, and just barely spring back, "—look at the speed of transactions. We're talking microseconds! Good luck with that, people! Get it? It controls the stock market! It already tells us what it wants, and we jump! It's machine on machine love from here on out. We're becoming obsolete; most of us already are. You noticed that? Well... what did we esspect, for shit's sake? I mean come on! Let's hurry up and get relegated to conditional status in a holographic representation of an algorithm, everybody! That's who-what you'll be working for, if you're not careful. Ahhch. Well. You're welcome." Avery felt another pang of dread for his own future as he watched middle-aged Mr. Edwards try so hard, and come up so short. "Now I'm not one of those conspiracy theorists," Mr. Edwards confided, laying on the ground with his eyes closed, "but when those people took down those towers, what happened?" He opened his eyes. "Lots of people got killed by machines, am I right? Now ask yourself: what proof do we have that the revenge principle is exclusive to carbon-based multicellular organisms? If you start thinking in terms of struggle against inorganic ascendence..." He stumbled to his feet, plucking that same book stack again, laughed and patted Avery on the back. "Hey, we writers got to throw things out there... huh? Right?"

After the work was finished, Avery entered the carriage house once more. Mr. Edwards and Ursula stood around while Theodora scraped the dust, scattered leaves, rat and raccoon droppings toward the center of the room with the back of a rock rake.

"...take hair off—"

"Yes. Take care of your work, whatever you do," Mr. Edwards blurted.

"I will."

"Take hair off a wooden leg, is what I was going to say." Theodora shuddered.

"We're talking about your bag," Ursula told Avery, her eyes full on him. "Te-kill-ya, huh?"

"Yes; take—take my last novel, *The Uncorruptible*..."

Snoring sounds.

"Here comes the clone drone drone..."

"Listen to this. Original title for was *The Uncoöptible*. Bastard publisher tells me—" Dave dropped into a whiny, nasal voice, '—but there's no such word. We don't feel like making up a new one.' Yeah, right! We got no use for the concept is what they were really saying. Because they know it's true. That was the whole point—"

"They made it into a movie," Theodora added helpfully.

"The indigestible."

"Mmm..."

"You know what's the worst part?"

"What?"

"Uncorruptible is less of a word than uncoöptible. How do you like that? Hell, I wanted the cover left blank, if you really want to know. Oh, but they got their kicks. And the word is incorruptible, in case you were wondering."

"Apparently not," Avery replied. He could tell by Mr. Edwards' wounded expression that he didn't get the joke. "I mean, the word is apparently not incorruptible," he backpedaled. "You said the word is—"

"Incorruptibility is self-mummification, failure to decompose. A hell of a way to become a saint. Not what my book was about, mind you, but I'd have lived with it."

"You must have some made money."

"Money? Yes. And too many speaking engagements to speak of. Speaking of which," he reaches into his pocket and starts rooting around like Theodora had just done for the patch, "see that Sunbeam parked in the driveway?" He produced a set of keys. "Tell you what. Go grab the tan envelope from the glove compartment."

Avery had to push aside two half-drunk half-pints of Jim Beam to find it. He brought it back and handed it to the writer.

"Business class. All yours. Take 'em."

"But—"

"Go on; take 'em!"

"But what am I going to do with—"

"... thought I had a way out, but they curled it back in on me with that one, dinn they… like an ingrown hair, ha ha! Only juuuust slightly more prot—profitable…"

"But—"

"Easy Dave," said Ursula. "Didn't you made it a bit too fun for them? If I preyed on the willing all day long, I might want something with some fight in it too."

The writer's eyes twinkled. "Madam, I have come to the conclusion that common to all language are signifiers and stoof—stupefiers. Uncorruptible is clearly a stupefier. I have another category;—just occurred to me." He looked up at Theodora, his eyes glistening. "Hey Ted. Commodifier. From the French, pardon my French, root word shit. There's that language medium you were looking for, Ted! Solid and liquid both! You're quite right," he agreed with Ursula. "I was asking for it. The point being—'"

'So many points around here—'

"Just—don't let them see you coming."

"I can do that. But if you could have lived with it, why didn't you settle for... the first name?"

"'*The Incorruptibles*' was already taken. Some kid out in the Midwest, writes dystopian comedies. If we didn't share a publisher I—"

"Dystopian comedies?"

"Did I say comedies? I meant comics. Graphic novels, if you insist. But that's just the poi—"

"Dave?"

"I gave them the ingredients and the formula; they just had to do a bit of tweaking, and that's all he wrote. Ha! Put that in your pocket."

"But—"

"Which them's this now, Dave?"

"They, it… what difference does it make? So resistance is not even futile, it's functional. Lovely."

Avery tried to tell them about his earlier fit of defiance, thinking it might fit the conversation, but Mr. Edwards was on a roll.

"Any writer who's worth a damn just shows the reader what's already in them,' he barreled on obliviously. 'The buried braveries. That's what they're afraid of, you know. That we can show ourselves who we are. They'd have us tweeting like birds instead."

"Dave?"

"But books take so long to eat. Another matter entirely, eh?"

"Let's save some of the matter for later, shall we?"

"I got plenty for later, Ted. Besides, he's with me. Am I right, Avery?"

"Dave?"

"Better if we're gross, so we'll eat another doublebaconcheeseburger gha! Am I right?"

"Yes, we should stop aspiring to become gross," Ted agreed. "It doesn't become us very well."

Turning to Avery, "Don't hide who you are. Deal? That's not where it's at. We writers got to stick together. We come up with their ideas, remember. Otherwise they'd have to regurgitate their own vomit even more than they already do. They need us. Don't you ever forget it. And another thing—"

"But I—"

"You'll never convince them that yours is the better way. Okay? Unless you got an answer for the real problem, and you don't. That's the problem. That's where we always... if we got to die, in the meantime we all prefer a world we're good at. That's the thing. It's not that they're unaware. And it's blasted astonishing, how accommodating reality is. Up to a point. That's the point, isn't it? That's the—all the more reason to just be yourself. Just remember—"

"But I never said I was a writer."

Dave smiled wetly. "Who breaks and enters for an old book but a writer? Isn't that right, Ted?"

Avery tasted copper until she winked at him. "Love follows its own laws."

"Avery Krizan," Ursula repeated. "So you must be related to Mika Krizan."

"Not *that* Mika—"

"I hear he was quite the bowler."

"Eventually Paco and I empty out the entire carriage house," Avery tells the interviewer, to keep a long story short.

* * * *

12:00 PM

Back at the Ha' Penny Arms, Coop and Boo are taking turns throwing playing cards into the air one at a time when Sandy throws open the door and jogs past them.

"Gentlemen," he greets them over his shoulder.

"Sandyman."

"Mandy-san!"

"Aw man..."

"Sandy—Oh, not—Shit!" They're in for a buck a toss, and Boo's on a losing streak.

"You want in?" Coop asks. "Up or down, Sandy?"

"In and out." Sandy heads toward the back room. Several drawer slams later he comes back shaking, wielding a flashlight like a club.

"All right. Which one of you thieving pricks went in my bedroom?"

"What?"

"Hey man, that reminds me—"

"Do I look like I give a fuck, Jig? Huh?"

"Nope."

"Yo Sandyman, what crawled up your ass?"

Sandy gets in Coop's face. "And do I look like I'm fucking kidding to you, fuckwad? What's up my ass? How's about who's been in my fucking dresser before I crawl this up—"

"Hey, San-day!"

Sandy looks at Boo, his face unrecognizable with rage. "'What do you want, you goddamn jungle bunny?"

Boo doesn't flinch. "That was Aisha went in there. Shit." He makes a face like he just swallowed something rotten. "They left a few minutes ago, her and her friend. She said you were supposed to be here to see her off." He spits out an imaginary bad seed. "She waited a hour for your ass too. Huh Coop?" Sandy pales. His eyes go blank. He starts shaking his head back and forth like he's having a fit.

"Jig's right," Coop admits. "What's with you, Sandyman?"

But Sandy's in his own world, and it's spinning too fast for him to do anything but shake his head at it. "Goddamn it. They say where they're going?"

"You don't remember? Back to Arizona, man. She said you were supposed to—"

"Oh, Christ. You've got to be kidding me. You've got to be fucking kidding me." He said he'd drive her to the station. "When?"

"When was that, Coop? Ten minutes ago? Fifteen, maybe?"

"Something like that."

Sandy pulls out his phone and calls Aisha's number. He nearly throws it against the wall when there's no answer, but he stops himself and waits for the beep. "Hey mija. Hey. It's your poppy. Hey, uh.... I'm home now. I guess I just missed you. I wasn't expecting you so early, Ish. But I need—I want to see you before you leave though, okay? So call me from wherever you are. I'll come get you. Don't forget. Call me when you get this, okay mija? Mwooah. Don't forget." He slips on a playing card on his way to the door and kicks at the sprawling pile. "Clean this shit up, you fucking losers. Respect a man's home."

He lurches blindly down the stairs, climbs into his '95 LeBaron and slams his forehead against the steering wheel. "Let me take care of things." That's what he told Avery Krizan after the fire. "Give me signatory power and I think I can get you some real money." And Superior Life Insurance Co. claims agent Sandy Sandoval took care of things, all right. First, he fixed the paperwork to reflect that claimant Avery Krizan did indeed possess an authentic, one-of-a-kind Mika Krizan original, insured for market value. In the claim documents, he placed the market value of the sculpture at a cool $90,000. Then he put $15,000 on a hook and dangled in in front of Avery. Avery bit.

Next thing Sandy did was use the I.D. and Social Security card copies he had on file to set up a fake email account in Avery's name, then to use this email account to create an electronic back-and-forth between increasingly belligerent claimant Krizan and loyal company man Sandoval. The fake A.K. kept demanding his $90,000 as patient Sandy repeatedly (and traceably) explained that it was impossible, unheard-of, etc. He also set up a bank account, also in Avery's name, and also unbeknownst to his client (that was the stickiest moment of the operation up to then, as it required him to go to the bank in person, armed only with his signatory authority and the electronic trail of A.K.'s erratic behavior). Meanwhile he maintained all correspondence between himself and the real Avery Krizan by telephone, which is how they discussed the fifteen grand. He had reason to believe it would fly on the S.L.I.C. end, and it did. He had only to work out how to safely withdraw the rest of the money from fake A.K.'s bank account, which would likely be a simple matter of obtaining a fake I.D. Now he's lost possession of both the fifteen grand and the incriminating paperwork. Luck, schmuck. How could he be so stupid?

He tries Aisha again. There's no answer. If he knew

which station she's leaving from he could just meet her there. She's been staying with that Candy girl somewhere in the valley. Or is it Pasadena? If he rode the train himself he could find Ish wherever she gets on, get his bag, travel on with her to Tucson for some father-daughter time, have breakfast at the station, and head home... maybe hit a casino on the way back. Not bad. But his gut is telling him that this mishap is a reminder that showing his face at the bank isn't the only weak spot in his plan. The thought of the real Avery Krizan inadvertently or otherwise fucking up the whole deal won't leave his head. The guy's too soft to be trusted. Maybe Sandy should just drive out to wherever the hell Krizan lives, pay him the fifteen grand from his own money, and catch the train from somewhere out there. Then he can find Aisha, get the bag, giver her a squeeze, wish her good luck with her mother and that Evangelical she's been shacking up with, get off at the next station, and take a cab back to his car. He'll buy Ish a nice, fancy new bag; that's what he'll do. He'll tell her it's a going away present. That'll explain both the phone calls and why he wasn't at the apartment without him having to say a thing. A much better plan. Besides, he's got shit to do tomorrow.

He calls Amtrak and gets some good news. The train stops in Primera. He tries to reach Krizan at the motel they've got him put up at, but his call gets bounced back to the front desk. He hangs up without leaving a message and starts to call Aisha again, then he remembers that Krizan works at a convalescent home near his motel. Something to do with love. Free love? Make love...? Love shack? Love in? That's it! The Love Inn. He calls the Love Inn, but Krizan isn't there either. The receptionist says he's late for work, but that's nothing unusual, he's usually late but only a little bit, he should be there any minute. Would Sandy rather call back or leave a message? He tells her it's very important, he'd rather hold the line if possible. Suit yourself, she says. Two minutes later, Sandy—in his dryest, most matter-of-factly this-shit's-totally-normal voice—is filling his client/co-conspirator Avery M'man in on the super-sweet, very short-term cash-availability mushroom of a window just popped opened to them deal but thing is he's leaving for a two-week vacation train trip sort of—huh? oh, uh, Vegas, and he'd better get packing, but listen, the reason for the call, how about what if they met at the Primera train station tonight and he delivered the settlement in person on the way out of town as a favor? How would that be, huh? Pretty sweet right?

Done and done. Judging by the voice on the other end, he's made the right call. The sooner he can get himself in Avery Krizan's rear view mirror, the better.

2

It's a lovely, sunny late-September day in Oakland, but it's like a graveyard inside the DarkArk warehouse. Steadying a cup of matcha tea with both hands, CAMEL tiptoes through a wax-encrusted grotto of ceremonial objects collecting damp street grime on the warehouse floor and peers through one of the small, wire-gridded windows that run the length of the 61st-street-facing wall. There's new activity going on out there. A bunch of young tech dudes are chatting on the sidewalk in their tucked-in shirts and sneakers, while a couple of Mexican laborers on ladders level their new burnished metal sign over their obliviously level heads. *Studio 61*, the sign says. 'Goodbye artists, hello creatives', is how CAMEL reads it. He bends down, catches a glimpse of graying stubble in his scrying mirror, and dusts off an old Exquisite Corpse, transcribed in red nail polish in Ala's every-line's-a-spiral script, now flaking away on the concrete floor, darkened like old blood but still legible beneath her signature light bulb skull:

* * * * * *

Man-Machine is its own light
Project and projector
Process and processor
Transubstantial
Beyond our reach
Clouds store our souls
Leaving us loaded and empty
Withdrawal sick
And behind
Hassled by the Man-Machine
In an endless
Nightless
Dreamless
Police world

Jesus. They really had been drifting into negative-land, hadn't they?

CAMEL's thoughts turn to laBlab, as they too often do these days. Freaking laBlab! Once considered wannabees (not to mention slavish DarkArk imitators), they have managed over time to completely take over the scene. But the straw that broke CAMEL's back was last spring, when laBlab hosted a mega-gathering in the shadow of El Templo Ehécatl at Tolum. Distilling the neo-tribal spirit for mass consumption under day-glo "Shamanic Convergence" banners, laBlab made use of an elaborate gifting system that gave substance to a mountain of cash for them and their new parent company, Trance'n'Dance Ltd, the eye at the top of the pyramid scheme.

Those who attended the Shamanic Convergence (or Sham Con, as CAMEL calls it) looking for a once-in-a-lifetime communion with the likes of OENNES (the traitor!) and the Janus Brothers were shit out of luck, because anyone without a VIP wristband—a *wristband!*—couldn't get anywhere near the temple. CAMEL even has it that the T'n'Ders, the self-important louts, had themselves separated from the hoi polloi by way of three pristine Airstreams arranged in a U formation, with velvet-ropes spanning the open end, where they spent the Convergence entertaining deep-pocketed Hollywood Scientologists. While he and Ala stayed in California, every other member of the tribe attended the fateful event. Worse yet, they had a great time (Dark-Ark's own twentieth-anniversary equinoctial celebration—held on the same night, naturally—wasn't much of one). Sure, some of the cash went to hauling in speaker trailers and sound tents and scaffolded light arrays and portable bathroom oases and windsock figures and gardens of exotic statuary, and some went to establishing flash relationships with the local players and insurance 'partners', but CAMEL knows for a fact that those Airstreams weren't rented. They were purchased with g[r]ifted money and driven from the Yucatan to laBlab's East Oakland compound, where last he heard they were in the process of being integrated into some fancy architect's vision of urban dispossession chic. Silicon Valley money is involved, and from what he's been told the project's rails have been greased by City Hall. And he's the bad guy? He's the power elite? After all the suffering of leadership that he's had to endure over the years, when all he's ever wanted to do was open their eyes to the fact that there's another way, that if they all work together they can have their own village; they can become craftspeople and sell their wares to outsiders? He looks around the cluttered, lonely warehouse. True, the DarkArk consists primarily of his and Ala's own objects now (the fruits of their travels, freely shared), and they may have given the directives, but it was hardly a freaking dictatorship... and being real for a minute, where would they be without him anyway, some of them? Panhandling their parents' friends back in the suburbs?

He's starting to sound like Ala, NZYME would doubtless say. But even NZYME's never fully appreciated the sacrifices Ala's made for the tribe. Who ended up tending to the children during the climaxes? It seemed that at every gathering there were more and more kids running around. She's worked way too hard creating their community to be its babysitter. Ala is a goddess, not a governess. So she can be a little harsh at times. Sometimes goddesses have to be harsh. NZYME's had it made; he's gotten to just kick back and be Mr. Groovy Magus. Now it's up to CAMEL to come up with something.

Oh, Bhuvaneshwari! The being he helped give birth to is in mortal danger! What's a world-creator to do? Avoid these mental traps, for one thing. Tap into the old tap roots; try to summon the way it was before DarkArk staged their first gathering, their first tribal celebration. Before *this*. He's been looking back more and more often, and each time he's more astonished at how naive he was to assume they could actually stay invisible until a time of their choosing. He always told himself he was out to change the establishment, to bring them around as it were, but the truth is he always felt more comfortable with their contempt than any of their attempts at 'getting' what his trip was all about. He would have preferred to maintain a grace-state of mutually assured ignorance than merge with their deadly mainstream.

Lately, though, when he allows himself to lie awake with his thoughts, he wonders if the corporate sharks weren't secretly cheering him on the whole time, all the while letting him believe he was beyond their reach. So even if you take it as far as he has, it's not far enough. Now they're cashing in on his labor of love, and he's left with the sick suspicion that he's been one of their novelty pushers all along. There's too much negativity around here, the old tribe said; laBlab gatherings just feel... happier. It's not their fault, though. They're simply blind to the fact that laBlab is switched bait. At times he can hear the sharks snicker, "What did you think, trickster? You were trance-scending your birth function? Ho ho. Au contraire, mon frere. Your efforts only magnified it. Don't you see? You're an American, for Christ's sake! All for one and one for all! Have a dollar." But even if that's true now, that doesn't make it true then. If he kept himself ignorant of his own latent betrayal, it was only because there was so much to do, so much active dream-spinning taking place! Because that shit they're selling reproductions of now? That shit really happened. The sharks weren't there for that part. They never are. Should he thank them for that? Or should he say what do I owe you? Because dreams were manifested, he's here to testify. And what dreams! Those glorious, holy fyresides; those untold myths created from whole cloth while he led the chants! It all came from dreams.

And now? Now it's just him and Ala and NZYME, when N–'s even around. CAMEL's well aware that shamanism doesn't come with a 401-K, but he always banked on other currencies, trusted in securities that didn't involve them and their death machinery. He thought the tribe was on board, but… No! Stop! These thoughts spring from inaction, he must remember! Truth is ageless when the stories are being told (even if he is starting to hate the smell of his own sweat, and the lamentable poetry)! He himself taught himself that once.

CAMEL has an idea, but he's reluctant to bring it up with Ala. He's made passing comments, like "releasing ourselves from the thing-trap wouldn't be a bad idea," or "maybe the gnostics had it right," but with an escape hatch flipped open, just in case. He knows how important their treasures are to her (more and more so, it seems). They represent nothing less than validation and vindication in her eyes. And yes he's aware that these symbols are chained to outmoded concepts of success, but them's the facts.

They can open a pop-up store just by rolling up the warehouse door on weekends. They wouldn't have to sell everything, of course, just enough to pay for the gathering. That's right. They will pay for it all, and send out personalized invitations. The others will have only to get themselves there. They'll show laBlab how it's really done, for once and for all. The real deal at a real deal. Once they've gathered again, there will be time to discuss the future as a tribe. New gods may come and go, but the tribe will endure. And his words will again create myths.

* * * *

October 3

Kalila Scott usually takes the 53 bus up Woodward from the Detroit School of Arts, transfers to the 14 at Warren Ave., gets off at the Poletown stop and walks from there, except for when she's got some theme or character development to think on, or a plot puzzle to work out, or on those days when everything pops, and the world is beautiful and crisp, and even the trash and junk looks clean. On those kinds of days she walks the whole way. Today is both kinds of day. And she may have solved the guilt problem that's been pestering her plot line. The future-humans-we-only-think-are-aliens will be precisely as indifferent to our species' fate as any generic alien or robot race would be. Their vestigial humanity is expressed in a knack for keeping the buck moving. ("We'd rather not have to kill you all, but if it's between that and looking bad at the performance review, well...") So far it's a good day's progress. The trick now is to hold it like a soap bubble until she gets home, where she can get it written down and illustrated. She cuts through an open field, crosses the railroad tracks, and speed-walks the last two blocks to her house. She opens the busted screen door, steps over the chewed-up threshold and drops her book bag on a pile of shoes and slippers. She hears a toilet flush, then familiar footsteps and straining floorboards overhead.

"Mama?"

"Kalila!" Kendra Scott leans over the guardrail at the top of the stairs, flashing her cell phone like a badge.

"Hi Mama. Sorry I'm late. I'm going to get right to work, okay?"

"Didn't I tell you to call me if you're going to be walking home from school?"

"I left my phone in my locker. Sorry."

"You couldn't find a phone booth?"

"Not one with a phone in it."

"Don't get smart with me."

"I'm not being smart, I'm being serious."

"From now on you leave your phone at school you don't get to walk home. You hear me?"

"Yeah."

"What?"

"Yes."

"Yes what?"

"Yes, I heard you."

"So you're working on something?"

"Yeah. Yes."

"The Uncorruptibles?"

"The Incorruptibles. They stoled—"

"Stole."

"The company that bought Mynabird made that movie called *The Uncorruptible*."

"We didn't see that, did we?"

"No, we didn't see the movie. I read the book it was based on, though. Some of it. All I got was a bunch of… dystopian self-righteousness."

"Sounds great. You'll have to let me borrow it one of these days. Oh yeah. There's some mail on the dining room table for you."

"From the Y.W.W.O.A.?"

"It's an invitation to one of those comic book conventions, I think."

Kalila rushes into the dining room and picks up the envelope. "You opened it!"

"Don't yell at me! And what, you think I'm not allowed to open mail addressed to my own kid? Think again, Miss Fancy Pants. As long as you're under my roof, I'm the gatemaster or whatever you want to call it."

"This is a weird invitation." Kalila stares at the tickets. "Not cheap."

"I thought the same thing. How come they don't ever skip the party part and just send you some money? Or is that against the law?"

"I don't know, Mama."

Kendra gives Kalila a look of consternation, a ripple on the surface of a deep well of pride. Her daughter the starving artist. The extra little tilt of her head is meant to be wistful, only this time it doesn't look sad at all. "Well, some money would be nice…"

"You know Morocco is in Africa, right Mama? You're always talking about wanting to go to Africa."

"Of course I know where Morocco is! Let me see that invite."

Kalila hands her the invitation. "Can we go? We can pretend they paid me, and this is what we did with the money."

"That's what you always say."

"Then what do you always say?"

"I'll think about it."

****

For Marty Symanski it's just another day. For the first year or so after she came back to Fall River, she was given a wide berth. "Take your time getting into the swing of things, Marty," they said. "Go back to school when you're ready, Marty. You decide, Marty. Hell, after the shit you must've went through…" Yeah yeah. But it's been four years, and she's not back anywhere anymore. She's just here, living by the power plant, working this wicked-boring security guard job. Bill gives her good assignments, at least; at least she's not out guarding some Pawtucket ATM all damn day like some people. Downside is it's going nowhere, and that's not about to change any time soon. But Marty doesn't feel sorry for herself, for the same reason she doesn't allow herself to feel lots of other things. Shit's shitty enough without all that shit.

But a letter with her name on it, care of the Brockton office of Prevent! Integrated Security Resources, makes her wonder. Bill hands her the letter along with her check and schedule. A suspicious bastard, he gives her a good long look. "Not sure why you'd wanna give anybody our address, Marty," he says.

Marty gives his look right back to him. "Sure don't know what you're talking about, Bill."

"Funny cancellation on that stamp, there." Bill reaches out and taps the envelope. "Let me make you a suggestion. You got a secret, you get a p.o. box."

"I got no secrets. And besides, forget the cancelled stamp; there ain't even an address on this envelope. Someone must've dropped it in the box by hand. Come to think of it, Bill, I don't even know the address of this dump myself. It ain't on the building, and it ain't even on the goddamn check—"

"Sounds like you got yourself a mystery, I'd say."

"Hell."

As soon as she's out of Bill's sight she checks her schedule. It's fine; two more weeks of straight nine-to-five at the folk museum out in Duxbury, making sure nobody makes off with the lute, ha ha. Easy peasy. Bill's all right, the lousy son of a bitch. He's an old vet too. But an insult is an insult. Secrets her ass. She opens the mystery envelope and her stomach drops a thousand feet. Manifest the what? What the fuck is this? Tickets? And a flight voucher? It must be some kind of joke, like maybe somebody from the old crew, Tremont maybe, trying to be funny. Not letting her forget. Maybe he can't forget either. Instinctively, she reaches into her purse for her pills.

Back in '08 Marty, Tremont, and the old crew were dropping 500-pound JDAMS on insurgent strongholds in Diyala Province; now she's dropping Prazosin four-or-five at a time three times a day, in addition to whatever serotonin reuptake inhibitors they got her on at any given time, and does all of her remembering first thing in the morning. She hasn't been anywhere near a plane since she came back. But airplane tickets aren't the only fucked up thing about this. There's this 'Manifest the Casbah' on the invitation. The fuck if she knows what that's supposed to mean, except they used to play that old disco song "Rock the Casbah" during bombing runs. Made it their own. A couple of times they even timed the payload release to the singer's choked stutter: "... ji-i-i-i-i-i-i-ve!", like 'Geronimo-o-o-o!'. Good times. At least they told themselves it was good times they were having up there, above and beyond good and evil, doing their jobs. Now that she's finally almost gotten used to lousy civilian life again, she gets this fucking thing. No return address; nothing. Could it be a reunion? She takes the bottle from her purse, pops it open, drops five Prazosin and swallows them dry. The fuck if she knows; it could be anything.

* * * *

"Ala!" CAMEL shouts.

"Just a second!"

"Ala!"

Ala Adi Shakti chose to include her birth name in her totemic agname. Not only is it quasi-metronymic, as her mother changed her own name to Ala immediately after naming her daughter, its pronunciation contains an intriguing velar fricative, à la 'Xala'. Right now, though, it's getting on her nerves.

"I said hold on!" she yells from the bathroom.

"Well, when you get done dotting your eyebrows, I want to—"

The bathroom door shuts hard. CAMEL (short for CAMEL/EON, signifying earth/stars and/or the two faces of the Trickster) winces. Nice timing, dummy.

Ala emerges with an elegant semicircle of circles drawn over one eye, and a dark arc of eyebrow pencil smeared over the other. "Look what you made me do." CAMEL looks up from the laptop that's scalding the exposed flesh of his thighs. A Craigslist ad is displayed on the screen.

Ala peers down at the monitor for several seconds, first in confusion, then with alarm. "Are those... your priapic objects?"

"Babe, listen. It's the only choice we—"

"Are you high?"

"No. What's that got to—"

"Whose choice, Cameron?"

"Please don't call me that."

"Don't 'babe' me then, with... whatever this is. And what makes you think you can just sell our stuff without even discussing it with me?"

"They're my own talismanic endowments."

"Oh, I see. So now they're your endowments. That's just great. Fuck the balance we've worked so hard to achieve, huh?"

"We have to do something."

"CAMEL," leaning over the chair lip and using the sing-songy mommy voice she knows drives him up the wall, "I'm sorry to be the one to have to tell you, but this idea of yours? It isn't exactly the best one you've ever had. Okay? So why don't you do us both a favor and use that cybernetic prowess of yours to conjure the real world for once. You know our landlord's going to jack up the rent when that fucking designer office furnishings place opens up. But who wants to think about that, right? Another start-up is taking over Compound Fracture's old space; were you aware of that?"

"I saw it. The freaking grid, man. What do graphic artists need warehouses for?"

"See? There you go. It doesn't matter if they need them! What matters is they want them, and they have the money to get them. What matters is we'll be living in a shipping container out in bum fuck Egypt, eating dandelions—"

"The real world? Look around, Ala. It's just us and NZYME, when he's even around, surrounded by all this junk. We're like a couple of Citizen Kanes up in here. You know?"

"So now it's junk."

"It's not... you know what I—... what's in it for us? Everything's in it for us, Ala."

"Oh Jesus," Ala groans. "Tell me you didn't just say that." She pushes herself away from the papasan chair. "I swear; if this is your idea of a midlife crisis? Powering down? Well power down then, you jerk. There's obviously nothing I can do to stop you."

"I'm not powering... Ala, you'll thank me—"

"I don't want to hear it. I'm going to go throw my javelin. That's *my* javelin, Cameron, so don't go fucking selling it."

* * * *

October 2

Monsignor Tsing still receives his personal mail at St. Viviana's Parish, where he feels at home, rather than at the Chancery offices, where he is still something of an outsider. He retrieves a stack of envelopes from the tray marked *incoming*, leaves another stack in the tray marked *outgoing*, and steps toward the window. Having second thoughts about one envelope in particular, he fishes it from the out box and puts it in his pocket, making a mental note to drop it into the next street box he finds. He glances down to find his own face smiling up at him from a CD on the desk. He enjoys singing opera, and just before leaving charge of the parish to Father Richards he'd co-produced a number of duets with the widow Leona Bello for the March of Dimes. He picks up the case. The collaboration, he has come to admit, has made him undeniably aware that after a lifetime given to Church business, his untried manhood is waning. The true lover of God must also love his own dying; he knows this. But to sing the great duet of creation, if only once! How the thought has bedeviled his mind. He glances at Leona's face beneath the jewel case, gazing at his own so beatifically. What a voice. What lung capacity! He often catches himself envisioning her on stage, her noble bearing enhanced by a backing choir, a Viking breast-plate over her ample bosom... and thanks God for his unhappy promotion.

He tries to turn his attention back to the mail. Sliding a letter opener into the top envelope, what he feels now is certainly not Nietzsche's impotency, with its promise of future satisfaction (why did he ever let himself read that damned lunatic?), but that of the spectator. He looks out of the office window. There's Father Richards, coaching the JV basketball team. Msr. Tsing imagines white bb's of spittle forming on the corners of Fr. Richards' lips. He can hear him now, telling the squad about that new Xbox game waiting for them at the rectory if they 'really hustle'. But God knows there is potency in words, and the Monsignor prays that those in his pocket possess agency enough to convince the diocese to keep an eye on his successor. Meanwhile, he pulls an unaddressed invitation and set of tickets from the stack he's holding, glances at it briefly, briefly thinks 'where did this come from?' and shuffles it to the bottom of the stack. His thoughts turn to the new wine bar down the street (he seems to remember a mailbox out front, doesn't he?), while his hands move on to the next envelope.

****

Conversations over three minutes have been shown to cause oxygen deprivation, light-headedness, and even loss of consciousness. Panic attacks are frequent and can be unpleasant, particularly at the period of onset. Breathing is suck, blow, suck, blow; endlessly. Gil Aragon is sick and tired. He's been sick and tired for a long, long time. Nothing comes easy; not even waking up. He takes a gut-hit of air, opens his eyes and... yep, there it is again, right off the bat, reminding him he's just a dumb bunch of proteins operating an increasingly obsolete and unenthusiastic machine, and that it's mere blind need that drives these cells of his to persist. Why do they even bother at this point?

Deconstruction, destroyer of mystery and mocker of motivation. Gil's secret nemesis. Back when these things might have mattered, it was like, 'Like her? Let's break her down into an unappealing set of biological processes, then, shall we?' Nowadays it's more along the lines of, 'Appreciate that act of kindness, do you? Let's see if we can't show it to be just that, then; an act...' Rubble-maker of summer sublimities. Poisoner of springs. The Devil's own attorney. Gil wonders how it hasn't eaten through his skull by now. But the doctors tell him he's in sterling health, despite his brain's persistent efforts to convince the rest of him otherwise. Adding real insult to psychosomatic injury, his own debilitating eccentricities withstanding, Gil's in high demand. A lifetime of practice in getting the uttermost uttered before the swoon hits, coupled with the misanthropic tone of his voice, has furnished him with the perfect skill set for verbalizing fine print, delivering terms and conditions, disclaimers, copyright legalese, eligibility requirements, side effects, etc. at breakneck speed, without sacrificing the self-superior contempt for the target consumer that so resonates in today's voiceover echo-chamber. Playing boss, droppin' the Mom Bomb (the idea being if target/child/consumer hates hearing your goddamn voice enough they will *willfully* not listen to your words). Make them complicit, and they'll do the work. Shamespeak, he calls it; crappy words for good money (not to mention mantras for a self-loathing hypochondriac; but who better to emcee their S&M party?) He gets excellent medical too, the kinky bastards. And he takes every penny and perk. He forces out another spent breath, aware as always that things can always get worse, that time chews away at what feeble positives there are. What else is new? Turns out his youthful philosophy of 'live fast while you can, so you can dwell in the past when the future gets ugly' was based on the erroneous assumption that his past would cooperate. It literally, physically pains him now to remember it, particularly (and most cruelly) the best parts. He can't even look at his old photos, or listen to his old music. Each warmly approaching reminiscence quickly induces in him the thoroughly unpleasant sensation that he's a stranger in his own body, or, even worse, that he has no body, and only persists as an unhappy vapor wafting through the wastes of time. These episodes are generally followed by periods of listlessness, malaise and headaches that linger for days. The past is no ally.

But Gil is determined to see the damn thing through to its natural conclusion. Those are his terms. The reason for his fortitude is neither cowardice nor bravery. Simply put, his grim endurance is Gil's own show of love for his family. Gil has seen too many of his own kind climb down the drain and let go, so to speak. But he knows other stories too, of brave and decent Aragons gone by, and he may as well not let them down. It might be the bleakest life-affirmation in the world, but there it is. And he loves his living loved ones too, as much as it might surprise them to hear it. And he detests anything that smacks of evangelism. And he hates lies. The one thing that makes his fast-talking bearable is the fact that he gets to tell people the truth; whether or not anyone listens is another story. So he keeps sucking and talking, talking and sucking.

Today is his 55th birthday. It's also a Sunday. He retrieves his mail on Sundays, first thing in the morning. He prefers to avoid his neighbors, not to mention the earthquake tourists and skateboarders lately attracted to his damaged cul-de-sac, but he nurtures a special dread of running into the mailman. The mailman isn't exactly a ray of sunshine himself, and their encounters tend to be fraught occasions for both parties. Now that his stance, as it were, has been made clear by the weekly accumulations in his mailbox, his mail-borne anxiety has only gotten worse.

He gets out of bed, slips his feet partway into his shoes,

steps outside and tiptoes to the curb. It's a loud, windy day; a small gift. Reaching the curb, he turns stiffly from the street and gives his ostensibly undivided attention to the mailbox. With the usual flush of panic at what awaits him, he lowers the drawbridge. Along with the bills and coupons and junk, he sees a square envelope. It's the kind that usually carries a card. For years, the only birthday cards his mailbox has held have been from the vet, all because he made the mistake of giving his own birthday as Dog's date-of-birth on some form. Dog's been dead three years now, and Gil still gets the birthday cards. His family no longer bothers with cards, probably because they see him as an antisocial asshole who's getting along just fine as such. And they'd be right. He hasn't sent a card himself in ages.

He shoves the mail under his armpit and makes a beeline for the front door. Once he's safely inside, he tosses the new mail to mix with the old. Usually he doesn't even bother reading it, preferring to let it age until it's old enough to disregard, while paying God knows how much on late fees and service restoration charges for the luxury. But the pile is unsound today, and a slide washes the square envelope onto the floor. He picks it up, almost wanting the card inside to read "We're licensed veterinarians who send birthday cards to dogs! Even dead ones! p.s. Gil, in case you forgot—Dog is dead." But it is not addressed from the vet. The stamp is unusually shaped, and far too florid to be USPS. There's no return address. Squatting down on his kitchen floor, he opens it.

* * * *

The lunch truck is parked in front of the DarkArk

again, blocking all the sunlight, but CAMEL's not eating in the dark today. "You know what?" He sets his soggy plate of tempeh tacos and wilted styrofoam cup of vegan menudo on the antique Burmese lamp stand and turns on the light. "You're a table, aren't you?" he says to the lamp stand. He's not eating on the floor today.

"Agh...." He gets up, turns off the lamp, lights a candle, sets the food on a stool and grabs a cushion. Outside, the creatives are lining up; he can hear them prattling on about their angel investors and the lenses they want to get onto everybody's eyeballs when the big backing comes in (speaking of backing, if they rattle the roll-up door one more time he's going to fire up the International Harvester and smoke them out!). It's been a long time since he's felt anger like this, and he can't seem to shake it. It's not like he hasn't tried to be neighborly. Last weekend the Studio 61 guys came up and asked him if he'd be in some video they're producing for some tech convention. He agreed to play himself, as local color. For free. For street cred for them to turn into 'backing'. But as soon as he tried to mention the gathering, they called it a wrap. This morning he opens his front door and there they are, filming the same scene he was in, but with an actor. Playing him! The nerve, man! And there's been a bewildering lack of online interest in his priapic objects. To make matters even worse, when word got out that he was monetizing his endowments, he received hella social media flak from the old tribe. But he expected that. CAMEL/EON might be a trickster, but he's no fool. Even so, the fact remains; their plan has to work now.

Ala's come around some. She's even been willing to part

with a few of her own objects. She's still not happy with certain aspects of the idea, but she admits that they do have to try something. Ala's no fool either. She's extracted some compromises, too, so, although the original plan was not to sell tickets at all, they'll sell tickets, only not to the people they already know, but to strangers on the internet. They'll promote the gathering as a workshop, a week-long immersive experience for those souls who harbor a desire to know what it gives-and-takes to build a trance village from scratch, yet have for whatever reasons failed to join an existing tribal community. Sort of like one of those Rock Star Camps businessmen are into, but deeper, realer, and way more profound on so many levels. For the right people, it will be the ultimate resort. A ticket will include food, water, and self-built accommodations for the two-to-three days of supervised manifesting, followed by four or five days of music, magic and myth-making. And the best part? At five hundred dollars a pop, not including transportation to Marrakech (though there may be a shuttle to and from the gorge, if Tripsy agrees…), each five or six tickets sold could mean a free trip for one member of the old tribe.

So far they've put a small deposit on three hectares of picturesque farmland near Dadès Valley, and have made tentative arrangements to ship a few of the heavier temple objects and interiors to Marrakech. They've also set up an online entity and a tagline: 'Manifest the Casbah—build you and the world will come'. They have sent feelers to the most mind-blowing performers, gurus, musicians and body artists they know, even offering to cover travel expenses in some cases. They've got a probably from DJ Beforehead, and Tripsy Gitano has agreed to drive all the sound equipment down from Granada in his dope dump truck slash mobile DJ stage.

Speaking of trucks, the freaking taco truck blocks their freight entrance every day now, so they can't set up shop here. They have to pay for a stall at the flea market. The good news is that NZYME's back. He even paid Facebook to promote a ManifestU page (keywords 'spas' and 'witchcraft') with some of the money he made trimming plants up in Humboldt. N—also thinks (at least he hopes) that CAMEL's idea could spell a new dawn for the three of them. And the land will be rented for a month, so when the week-trippers go home they'll have it all to themselves for a while. It's a fine plan, if they can afford it. In the meantime, at least they're getting free tacos.

* * * *

October 1

The adjunct professor sways over his standing desk in his cozy-yet-airy Mid-Century Modern study overlooking the reservoir, enjoying (that's called a euphemism, class) another tall glass of his homemade honey brew. It's his weekday off, and Hope has taken Oeddy and Rex to Dog Day At The Gym At The Tennis Club Day or whatever the hell it is, over at the horse and tennis club. Speaking of euphemisms, here's one his wife made up, though she credits it to him: "doing some research" means "drinking that alcohol syrup you like to call mead and throwing hissy fits on that Greek tragedy chat room you claim to hate so much." But somebody's got to do it. After all, aren't there enough e-holes for the bozos to nincompoop in? Do they have to blow their bong rips all over æ.net?

Where do these experts come from? One half-baked 'aha' moment and they're Bob Graves. And it *is* research, blast it, in that it's always good to know what sort of idiocy is parading itself around as substance on any given day. So here he is again, having to put another clown in his place:

—Sorry to butt in here, *papasnbeer*. Glad you liked that "part", though technically it's not "epic." Tell me, how did it become okay to have Medea float up there in front of everyone like that? How could Euripides do such a thing?... she committed *filicide* for Christ's sake!

—JC same deal. Ironic much?

—A-and for that she gets a ride on Helios' chariot? Huh? Proto-feminist my *kolos*. Euripides wanted to do something different with the old *mechane*, if you ask me. First attack of the spectacle. You should check out Debord.

—Nah.

—And fantasy projects... wha? Somebody's idea of what isn't but in our imaginations? Do tell. Obviously, the way to imagine is not to settle for what is not here, but to imbue what is here with every possibility. Your man Euripides chopped down the plant to get at the flower!

—Ya okay. U drunk?

The adjunct professor might be a little tight. Maybe he'll step away from the monitor and go work on the roses. They could use some trimming, and it wouldn't hurt him to get away from the time bandit for a while. Make time for all the gods, as he has been known to say.

He goes outside, where it doesn't take him long to recognize that rose bushes don't forgive mead buzzes any better than wives do. He'll forget about the stupid plants for now, and just bring in the mail. Besides, this goddamn sun's giving him a headache.

Five minutes and two shots later, as he searches the mail for 'juice'—as he likes to call the increasingly infrequent requests to sit on a panel and mumble, or bullshit to another shiny batch of kids just before they're dumped into the ol' cesspool along with their dreams, or—Ahp—...? What's this? Toward the bottom... yessiree; here's something, hand addressed the old-fashioned way. How quaint. He opens the envelope and finds a set of tickets inside. No mention of topic or fee. This just may be the most oddly-worded invitation to a speaking engagement he's ever received. His fortified interest piqued, he pins the note and tickets to the fridge with his favorite rare-earth magnet.

* * * *

"Hey Handcar! Can you c'mere a minute?" It's the last day of the 58th annual Hobo Days convention, and Henrietta Hancock, aka Handcar Hancock, aka Hank Henry, lifelong rail-rider and the convention's resident humorist slash labor historian is relaxing on a picnic table, face up, watching hay dust float into the sky.

"Who's calling me?" Handcar barks, not wishing to be bothered just now.

"Here." Here would be Wyatt Timmon, the kiddie train owner/operator and a newcomer to the convention. Hank pulls herself up, puts her hands in the suspenders of her overalls and ambles over.

"What's going on Mr. Wyatt?"

"Sorry to bother you."

"Aw, you're not that bad, usually. How's business?"

Wyatt doffs his engineer's cap. "Good. Say, you wouldn't happen to know anybody who's in the market for a Lil' Puffer?"

Hank gives him a funny look. "I thought you just recently acquired this here choo choo."

"One season's enough for me, thanks, as thoroughly enjoyable as this one's been. I'm what you'd call a dabbler. It's time I try my hand at something else."

"A dabbler, huh? Well! More power to you, I suppose. But I know you didn't disturb my meditation to sell me a train set."

"Like you said, I'm not that bad, usually. No, look." He holds up a small stack of tickets. "A couple walks up to me yesterday," he says, flicking the stack with his thumb. It makes a little zipping noise. "They gave me these. I figure since you're the one who seems to know everybody, well, I—maybe you might want to hand them out to your hobo friends."

"Let me see those." Wyatt hands over the tickets, minus two. "I'll be doggone. This a tall fellow and a cute little brunette, inquiring about a couple of migrants?"

"Sounds about right."

Handcar spreads the tickets into a halo around her thumb. She glances at the topmost and fans herself with the stack. "Why you suppose they gave them to you?"

Wyatt shrugs. "They came up to my gate, I asked for their tickets, and they gave me those."

Handcar snorts. "You let 'em ride?"

"I offered."

"Good man. Yeah, I'll take these off your hands." Handcar pockets the stack. She points at the Lil' Puffer. "I can't think of anybody might be in the market for your rig here, off the top of my head. How much you want for her?"

"Three grand is what I paid. But, you know, I'll take what I can get…"

"Best offer?"

"If it's reasonable, I'm flexible."

"Fair enough. I'll ask around for you."

* * * *

In the week or so since the page went up, only two tickets have sold for sure, and maybe five people have expressed anything resembling genuine interest. All's quiet on the priapic front, but it's still hecka loud on the front of the warehouse front. The freaking creatives can't seem to get enough of those nasty truck tacos. The roll-up door has become their new lunch break hot spot. Every time one of them leans against it, it's like a machine gun going off in here. When he tries to tell them about the noise, they give him a bunch of condescending apologies and jivey thumbs-up like he's an old man yelling at them to get off his lawn, and go right on leaning. Still no word from any of the old tribe. They've got three weeks before they're supposed to mothball the warehouse and go lay the sacred groundwork, half their shit's for sale, and Ala's hardly speaking to him again. In desperation, he resorts to hitting up NZYME to hit up his grower friends.

"NZYME's not that kind of catalyst," NZYME tells him. "You know I got mad respect for you, but you know how busy those fools are. They're building shit all the time up there, yo, out of necessity."

"Not like what we build, N–."

"Without doubt, EON. But they don't want to be hearing that shit. They'll know…—they'll think we're trying to job 'em." Seeing the look on CAMEL's face, "You feel me, right?"

"I just—I'm running out of ideas, N–. It ain't happening."

"Don't trip so hard. It's only life."

"We need a plan—what is it now? We need a plan F, for freaking—"

"When was the last time you checked the web page?"

"Like a half hour ago. It's barren, man."

"What about the… fucking… Facebook thing?"

"I can't even look at that freaking… public embarrassment."

"Lemmeseeit." Without waiting for permission, NZYME grabs the laptop out of CAMEL's hands. He pulls up the Manifest the Casbah Facebook page. Another ad for advertising greets him straight away: 'We can help spread the word! Promotion is key to success!'

"Fuck it, N–. We're not buying another one."

"I'm doing it."

"No, don't! That just makes it worse!"

"You're tardy, bro. How long's it take to show up on here?"

"What show up? What's it say?"

"I don't know. It bounced me."

"Give me my damn computer back." CAMEL lunges but NZYME boxes him out.

"Hold up. I want to just check something real quick." NZYME does some hunting and pecking, reading the odd word or phrase semi-out loud. Suddenly his voice gets clear and deep. "Bro."

"What?"

"Whoa..."

"What?"

"Trip out..."

"Dude, just tell me!"

"How many tickets were left when you last looked?"

"We've sold two, so a hundred and forty-eight. Why?"

"Now it says one-ten. Op—there it—one-o-nine... one-o-eight—"

"Shut up, N–. Now you're just being a dick."

"Oh yeah?" NZYME hands the laptop back to CAMEL. CAMEL stares in disbelief at the growing column of bank-to-bank money transfer requests, and shrinking number of available tickets.

"No... freaking... way."

3

The Man leans against the counter in the tiny motel office. He watches the semi go by, that tiny binary star burning for hours in his rearview flashing supernovae to receding red mocktangle. He blinks once. "Pew pew pew." He blinks five times. The moon's a headlight coming at him at him at him; he's got a little bleed-through going on. Dark hours on straight roads, and the coke, natch, having a little fun with the cogs. No wonder. Reality's a pussy. It gets with the Program. He kicks the baseboard three times. The awning-dammed floodlight can't reach the counter, but it can brush the nickel nippletip of robotitty bell. He taps it, ding-g-g...g.......! Out of sight, long sticky snorts sharpen to short hacks. A light goes on behind a half-open door. Ding-g-g...g.......!

"Hold on." Troglodyte piles out of cave in a blanket, hugging a wastebasket, drags himself to the counter, switches on the desk lamp, rolls a phlegmball, "chhuuuuit...," shoots it hard "thhwoop!" onto the can lip half-in, half-out, rocking like a dirty weeble wipes chindangle half-civilized with rank blanket, frowns at the wall clock. Tapp-zzz-ta...-ta-tap! A moth taps against the lamp glass, gets its answer.

"Yeah?"

"Manager?"

"Tha'd be me."

The Man waits a beat, moth fails to figure out how it got itself into such a predicament. "Thought I'd drop by, Thad, and see how you're doing…"

"Huh?"

Nodding up or down with each word and speaking real slow, like to a child or retard, "I'd… like… a… roooom?"

"That's what I—" Manager takes a deep breath, his veiny pinkyellow eyes face-searching warily through viney grey brows, decides he'd best not… "Smoking or non?"

"Smoking."

"I'll just need a credit card and ID…"

"I'll pay cash."

"Dandy. I'll still be needing a card and ID."

"What for?"

"You'd be surprised."

"Hmm. I'll have to take your word for that. But perhaps…" The Man flips his wallet open, flicks out a card, fingersnaps three mint-fresh hundred dollar bills, "this just might could ass…wage your pertur…bations?"

Manager rubs the bills together. They swish like real fine grit sandpaper. He gives The Man a long look, brings the card under the light. "Might just at that." Moth fritzes, slams against the glass, looks like a sunspot. "Prometheus International… Strategic… Resources?" He hands the card back to The Man, palms the bills. "Military?"

"Sure. Say, how are your TVs?"

"They all work, if that's what you mean. New set in seven... result of one of them surprises I was talking about; preacher took a—"

"I'll take it."

"Seven? That one got the two queens; not sure you'll be—"

"More the merrier. Three Cs ought to get me two queens, I'd a-reckon. Speaking of..." rubbing the bell tip, "any action around here, like real local like?"

"This ain't one of those places, if that's what you're driving at." The Man shrugs. The manager pulls a key from the drawer and slides it across the counter. "Around the corner, first door. That your cruiser out there?"

"Thad, it is."

"You can pull it around or leave it where it is; it's up to you. Excuse me—" He loads another roll of phlegm, pumps it into the can, gets his hand ready on the lamp switch. "Checkout's at eleven."

"I'll be long gone."

"Either way."

"Hand me one of those paper towels, would you?"

"Help yourself." Manager tosses the roll (lamp goes out while it's in the air), scrapes himself back behind the door. The Man tears off a paper towel, picks up the keys with it, pulls out his phone, wipes it off, leaves the used towel on the counter, checks his texts on the thirteen-step stroll to matte maroon 2249cc Rocket Roadster with custom, XSKillaHaul-inspired accoutrements parked under the floodlight where everynobody can see it. It's good where it is. Because he dares them. Route confirmation/passcode/receipt of funds transferal received, phone back in pocket, he crouches beside the bike, clicks open sleek and sexy composite sidebag, pulls out black kevlar knapsack, closes compartment, slings knapsack over his shoulder, releases straps from behind the seat, lifts large artist's briefcase from rackback. "Alarm." Chirp chirp. Red light on instrument panel blinks from its minilight-years away, receding. The Man scans the roadscape, turns, and walks thirty-seven steps to tonight's headquarters.

He enters the motel room and turns on the light. He lays his case on the bed closest to the door. What's he got this time? Two fluffy queens flanked by nightstands. A bigger nightstand pressed between pressboard headboards with phone, phone book, lamp and rules card on it, beneath a print of a split-rail fence in eight shit-shades of brown. That print just won't do. And four is the brown of numbers. It won't do either. The Man removes the rules card from the middle nightstand and puts it—along with his wallet, his keys and his drugs—in the top left drawer of the dresser with the TV on it. But that makes four again, so rules card goes in the garbage can. He removes the offending print from the wall, turns on the TV and mutes it. He opens the large case, pulls a cord from its own special box, removes a dvd player from the custom-fit compartment, places it on the dresser, plugs the cord into the TV and dvd player, lifts the oversized laptop computer and portable hotspot from special compartments and sets them on the bed, sets the case next to the dresser, connects the player, hits play and is immediately treated to the quick killing of a sultan by a knight in armor.

The Man reaches behind the TV, feels for contrast

knobs, strips blue and yellow, cranks up red, takes off his pants, unzips a small travel case and removes vial, razor blade and black Bubba straw, opens the vial, dumps a pile of primo flake onto the nightstand, taps at it with the blade while he watches the tv. The knight is walking. Now he's at the Dutch door. Top part of the door is opened by a dark-eyed female in veil and hijab. The knight holds up the head of the sultan, the woman raises hand to veil, covers her eyes. Perspective shifts to hers; camera pans from knight's visor-covered face (level and contrasting with the sultan's naked death-grimace) down his armored torso to nickel hard-on rising majestically from his crux. Perspective shifts again. Woman gasps into the camera, her eyes moist with shock and awe. Bottom half of the door opens. Knight chucks sultan head over his shoulder like a half-eaten apple, steps inside. The Man runs the razor blade at an angle to the pile to make it longer. He does the same thing in the other direction. He splits the rail in half lengthwise, drags the blade along one of the halves, aims the straw, erases line with one nostril, mirrors the process on the other side, sucks white dash from the middle with a kiss, runs his fingertip over the filmy erasure, applies mix of local dust and coke residue to the tip of his tongue, and bam! The world shivers like a chick about to come. He claps three times. Bounces over to the computer bed, hooks up the wi-fi and gets online. If he waits too long he'll have to do the other bump.

Signing on as MecOne, he enters the waiting room of his nonpersistent-metagame-of-the-month, TrueCross V (ergo the vid, natch) to do some insomniacal trawling for Prometheus. It's all about conversion tonight. Ah look; Moslem bitch gots her hijab all in a bunch. Arms outstretched, fists clenched, getting big Jesus bigtime.

Mmmh! Huhc! Time to hit a battle arena.

MecOne annihilates all opponents in 43 seconds, visits another arena, wipes out bunch of novitards, visits another and does the same, then another, making four slaughters. Five's the charm, while Moslem bitch gets her First Communion. He leaps from the bed, restarts vid, dispatches another batch of barrelfish. Oh, not quite. Who's he got? Cycfrac, huh? Cycfrac has a bead on him. Well well well; where are you, Cyc—... and MecOne is dead. The Man waits for Cycfrac in the lobby, follows him into the next arena, finds a safe spot, watches Cycfrac wreak havoc until it's just the two of them again, types '—You bored?' into Cycfrac's text box, counts to five and kills Cycfrac.

He repeats this process three more times. Watch, ask, smite. On the fourth go-round he gets his response.

'—WTF?'

'—UR good. Want to play better game?' There's a long pause. There always is.

'—Who RU?'

'—Not creep. Paid Gamer. Want 2B12?' Another long pause.

'—?'

'—Follow me.' MecOne leads Cycfrac to a hidden corner of the MOBA. '—Cut and paste this code into your text box. Then I will ask you a question. Type YES. No period, all caps. U Savvy?' MecOne types a long line of code, containing characters not found on any standard keyboard setting. Another long pause. This is where he loses most of them, but Cycfrac takes the leap. Not long after the code is pasted, a box of general personal information on Cycfrac appears on The Man's monitor. Carla Conway, F, Cauc, 18 y.o., 2150 Horseshoe Rd. Terre Haute, IN, student, 3.9gpa. drawing, violin No a.r., no p.r.. Rel. affil. unspec.. etc. Somewhere a very smart computer speed-reads Carla's email, social media and browsing histories. No red flags. Yellow flags for interest in avant-garde music and literary fiction. Her photo shows a chubby, pasty Midwestern chick with moderate self-esteem issues. Not optimal, but doable.

'—AREYOUBORED?' Nothing. She's still connected, though. The knight's letting her have it again. Come on, Carla.

'—AREYOUBORED?'

'—??Name of the game?'

'—METOO (but U won't find it)' He waits patiently for her to search, to give up.

'—OK'

'—AREYOUBORED?'

'—YES'

'—METOO'

Their pixelated arena dissolves into a high-resolution black and white moving-image of an urban environment, looking straight down from a distance of about fifty feet. There is no sound. Their text box is intact, and identical to how it looked before the dissolve.

'—WTF M I looking at?'

'—METOO. Stands for Middle Eastern Theatre Of Operations. 'Flyalong program.'' Let Carla absorb that fact while he lays out another bump. Speaking of bumps, might as well restart vid...

'—U said game'

'—Watch.' The camera is hovering over a public square. There are many people milling around. At first nothing out of the ordinary seems to be happening. Suddenly people start running in all directions. The crowd flees until the square is empty. It doesn't take long.

The knight kills the sultan again. He's at the door again...

'This real?'

'Bir Asuwara, Libya, Carla Conway from Terre Haute, Indiana. Real time.' This is the fishing part; a light touch is of the essence. He lets her panic. Her reaction is not atypical; she tries to disconnect. No can do, natch.

'—What is this? Who are you?'

'—Oppor2nity. As much real or as much game as U want. I am an Indy e-warrior all-eyed with Xeedingly gener$ Prometheus Int'l Sec.Recs. (U won't find it)

'—I'm a pacifist.'

'—PISR = peace, Carla Conway from Terre Haute, Indiana'

'—Pls leave me alone.'

'—1st ask Cycfrac'

The dark-eyed woman gasps, lets the knight in again.

'—Cycfrac isn't real.'

'—Cycfrac as real as U want. But is he game?'

'—I'm calling the cops.'

'—1st ask if Cycfrac wants 2 know what real power looks like.' The Man lets her wrestle with that while he does some typing. The image changes from clear black and white to a bluer, grainier view of a modest Midwestern split-level, seen from above. '—Terre Haute PD feed. 2150 Horseshoe Rd. U recognize?'

The Man waits. A light goes off in the modest Midwestern split-level. Carla Conway is sweating down there, in real time. The Man tingles with satisfaction. This is what the Program's all about. He is the messenger, the face of the Interface. MecOne has just transcended the virtual battle arena. He has agency now. His game just got real.

'—Better turn the light back on and get dressed, Carla Conway. U have a long day ahead of U."

He does another bump. As thrilling as this trawling game is, it's still child's play compared to what tomorrow has in store for him. He's got himself a date with the Shitkicker Mafia. Prometheus has got a sexy new drone they want to show to a swishy African arms dealer, and they need a hot-shit pilot to demonstrate its capabilities. The Man can do that, all right. That's his function. His hand on the joystick can make a drone come. Tomorrow, his game is going to get very, very real indeed.

The Man waits. He knows Carla will get with the Program. She has no choice. Tomorrow, the swishy arms dealer will get with the Program. The Man can afford to wait. He's the face of the Interface; he has all the time in the world.

* * * *

Half a world away, guests are arriving at the Kasbah

Kandisha on the afternoon mules. From time to time one or two will peek into the meeting room and duck away.

"So Paco, Ursula and I leave Theodora's place together," Avery continues. 'The city's making her fumigate,' Ursula tells me, as if reading my mind about Theodora and her books. 'She'll leave them outside for a few days, let them have some fresh air. Allow a few to escape too, I'm sure.'

'Escape?' I ask.

'You know, she's too kind sometimes. Tell me, are you still a thief?'

The interviewer leans forward. "And what did you tell her then?"

"I don't know."

"You don't remember?"

"I said I don't know. To her."

"Ah. And what of your friend Paco?"

"He doesn't say anything. I'm starting to wonder if he might be deaf."

"I see."

"I tell Ursula how I read the book I stole, and that I learned a lot from it. I tell her about the fire, and that, although the book is in a pretty sorry state after being soaked by fire hoses, I still have it.

'Fire and water,' she says mysteriously. 'Where are you headed now?'

"I might have lied to her, if I could have come up with anything else to say. 'See those palm trees?'

'That's interesting,' she says. 'That just so happens to be where I'm headed. In fact, we should really hurry. I have someone waiting for me.'

I stare into my bag, wondering what the two of them might be up to. Who are they, really? 'What do you want?'

She laughs. 'What do *I* want? So it's true what they say, that to the thief, everyone is a thief.'

We walk briskly, with me sandwiched between the two of them like a convicted man, unable to extricate myself in any casual or dignified way.

'Who are you?' I ask.

By then the palm trees are as much above as in front of us. Behind them a pair of police helicopters lean forward as if catching an invisible wave, their tail booms pricking upward like twin scorpion stingers. I'm starting to feel more than a little creepy hanging out with strangers in the middle of the afternoon.

Ursula points at the trees. 'Washingtonia filifera,' she says; 'the only palm native to California. The ones you're looking at were planted over a hundred years ago on the grounds of La Casa Segundo, the oldest building in Primera. That's where we're headed.'

'Why?'

'I'm the Historical Display and Exhibit curator there. I also help keep the adobe grounds. I can't speak for you.'

'Oh. So that's why you were looking at those books back there?'

'That's right. Theodora has some excellent volumes on California's Mexican period. Treasures, really. She donates to our little museum from time to time.'

'I didn't mean to assume you were—'

'It is quite the coincidence, I'll admit. Would you like to meet the trees?'

'Um… sure.'

We arrive at the adobe grounds. Ursula leads Paco and me to a massive oak tree that dominates the main approach to the house. Gnarled, branches thick as human torsos splay out in all directions. She leans against the monumental trunk and motions for us to join her. 'This one's been hit by lightning a half-dozen times that we know of,' she says, gazing familiarly up at its muscular-looking branches. 'Did you know that oaks are more prone to lightning strikes than other similar-sized trees? Are you hungry?' An orange tree glows in a patch of sunlight, obscene with fruit. Although much smaller than the oak, it's almost as old and gnarly looking. She walks over to the tree and picks a few oranges. 'Best oranges in the valley right here,' she says, giving us each two. 'Nothing better after a good walk.' I eat one right away. It's delicious. Paco puts his in his pocket. Ursula walks toward the adobe. It's a whitewashed mud-brick structure dating from the 1830s, with a wide, sagging porch and broad eaves that wrap around the whole place, and tiny windows set deep in its thick, spreading walls. It looks like a giant cupcake that's been dropped in the dirt, icing side down. I start up the porch steps but she motions for me to follow her around the side. I give the adobe wall a good smack and follow her. We make our way around to the back of the building, where a fire pit has been dug in the hardpan and lined with river rocks. The pit is surrounded on three sides by wooden benches, which in turn are semi-encircled by that ring of Washingtonia palms. It's also where they hide the port-a-potties.

You could tell this was a fine field trip destination at one time, but not so much anymore. Beyond a small expanse of foxtails and rusted iron, a dry, stone-lined gutter runs along the edge of the property. An old woman kneels in the middle of the gutter, collecting branches and twigs and piling them on a piece of cloth she has spread on the ground. I'm reminded of the woman from the crosswalk, and how I never said a word to her even after the incident with the car. I smile at the woman but she doesn't smile back. She has the air of someone who's throwing a dinner party, and the first guests have arrived at a critical moment in the preparations. She doesn't seem surprised to see us."

"Were you introduced to this woman?" the interviewer asks.

"Not at first, because she's over by the back fence, and we're by the benches. I see that some kindling has been arranged in the fire pit. I sit down and start pulling gravel from my soles, while Paco goes over and stands next to the woman. Ursula sits down next to me, facing the two of them.

'Have you ever heard of William Mulholland?' she asks casually.

'Sure. He built the aqueduct.'

'And the Saint Francis dam. We mustn't forget—'

'And he was involved with that whole Chinatown thing too, wasn't he?'

'Which whole Chinatown thing is that?'

'You know, the one in the movie? With the water?'

'Yes, that Chinatown thing. Because you know, another

Chinatown thing happened right down the street from here, but with fire.' I shake my head. She nods. 'It's true. There was once a little Chinatown where First Street crosses the railroad tracks. During the time the aqueduct was being built, the good citizens of Primera burned it to the ground.'

'Whoa.'

'But we were discussing Mulholland, weren't we? Did you know that when he was a young man, Mulholland cut his teeth right here in this valley? It's true. He was divining for artesian wells. See that little ditch over there?' She points to the dry wash. 'That was once part of a much larger irrigation network, quite sophisticated for its time, that brought water down from the canyons to irrigate this valley.'

'Mulholland built it?'

'Oh, no. It is much older than that. He studied the network it belonged to, though, I'm sure. Think; you may be looking at the genesis of modern California, right there in that old gutter.' I think back to the washed-out-place vibe I felt earlier, while she points from the ditch toward the foothills. 'Speaking of currents, did you know that at the same time as Mulholland is poking around here for water, Westinghouse is using Tesla's designs to send the very first long-distance high-voltage transmission down an arroyo from those very hills? Fire, flowing like water. Albert Michelson was up there too, with his mirror, measuring the speed of light between here and L.A. Before rush hour, of course… ha ha. But seriously, it is important to remember…' All during this impromptu history lesson, I'm racking my brain trying to place the other woman. I know I know her, but I can't put my finger on from where. Then I remember that she was in the same bowling league as my grandparents when I was a little kid. Back then her purse seemed to hold an endless supply of those dum-dum suckers, which she'd hand out to the children while we roamed around the arcade, mooching money to play video games. That must be how Ursula knew my grandpa was a bowler. The woman's face hasn't changed much at all, but her clothes have. Back then they weren't so... earthy. She didn't come across as particularly Native American back then either, so to see her after all those years in those sandals and fabrics, bending over an old stone ditch to gather sticks is kind of a trip. A couple of her twigs slide out from the back of her bundle as she walks over to where we are. Paco picks them up and follows. She places the bundle next to the pit and Paco adds the droppings. She stands over us for several seconds, gazing down at the pit. I get the feeling she's trying to place me too, but I don't bring up the bowling alley, and neither does she.

'Well...,' she says to Ursula, patting her hands, 'I think we're ready.'

'Thank you, Lilian,' Ursula says, then she introduces us. Now I have to say, at this point my mind is already a little blown. After a pretty odd morning—"

"The phone call?" the interviewer asks.

Avery grunts. "I was thinking more about the getting fired, and the thing with the little girl, and my aiming for some random palms trees leading me to Paco and the books, and now the fire pit and the company of these people. And yeah, the phone call.

'Along with our local history, Lilian and I have been

keeping these grounds alive together for quite some time,' Ursula says quietly, 'and over the years we've come to realize that it's not only the plants that need fertilizer around here.' I shake my head while she points to the fire pit, where Lilian is constructing a cone of twigs. "This pit, for instance.' She and Lilian nod at each other with their eyes. 'It likes stories.'

The interviewer leans back and smiles.

"I thought the same thing," Avery says. "But these women are, like... regular people. There's nothing even remotely flaky about them. Lilian stands up and does one of these—" He holds out his hand and lets it hang from his wrist as he touches his forefinger to his thumb, so making an upside-down teardrop that he swings back and forth, "—while Ursula pulls a set of keys from her pocket, and tosses them over. "

'I'll be right back,' Lilian says, and disappears through the adobe's back door.

'Speaking of stories,' Ursula continues, pointing back toward the foothills, 'do you know anything about Webber Canyon?'

'What about it?"'

'You ever go up there?'

'It's been a while, but yeah. It's got a great view of the valley.'

'It sure does. Ever wonder why they don't build houses up there?'

'Not really, honestly. I don't usually think about real estate when I'm in nature.'

'Good for you.' She looks me squarely in the eyes. 'Do

you know about Don Palomar?' She makes a sweeping, encompassing arm gesture. 'The man to whom all this real estate once belonged?'

'Sure.' After some more consideration I add, 'a little bit.'

'Let me tell you something about old Don Palomar. He came through here with his buddy Vallar just after Mexico won independence from Spain. They were soldiers-for land, those two. They came upon this valley that had for centuries been the home of the Tongva, and decided to declare it their own. They went down to Mexico and found an official with authority from their brand-new country to sign his name on a piece of paper granting this land to them. Then they split up their grant, with Palomar taking the better uplands, where most of the artesian springs were, and Vallar taking the drier lowlands to the south. At that time there was a big creek that came down from the mountains. It ran from where the dam is now, all the way down through the valley. It marked the eastern boundary of Palomar's property, where the county line is today. At that time, though, there was a large Tongva village on the banks of that creek. But old Don Palomar had visions. When he looked out over his newly acquired land, he saw things which were out of line with his visions. So he bought in more soldiers to help him manifest his destiny, so to speak. Imagine those soldiers being out on the frontier, so far removed from the civilization they represented, charged with all of its power and authority and none of its constraints. It's hard for someone like me to see them as anything but violent, opportunistic criminals, but I'll let you be your own judge. As I said, the only authority in those days belonged to Don Palomar's visions. So under his orders, those... I hesitate to call them men, but of course they very much were... those men murdered every living thing in the village. They killed an entire world. They were strangers to whom the Tongva were little more than—' she makes another motion with her arm to encompass not just the property as it is but as it once was, 'chaparral to be cleared. Those murdered Tongva are still buried up there in Webber Canyon.'

'Jesus.'

'Have you ever heard that story?' I shake my head again. 'And you grew up here?' I nod. 'If the past is so past, then why haven't you heard this history? Could it be because the crime is still in progress? There's a reason why stories are suppressed, you know. They play.'

'They play? You mean like play out?'

'I mean they play like children. And when they play, we're powerless to stop them. The stories tell us—'

Lilian returns with some long matches, a milk jug with the top cut off, and a shot glass. She motions for us to not mind her.

'So you know what he did then?' Ursula asks.

'What?'

'The reason he needed to clear them off that land,' she says in a low voice, pointing back at the gutter, 'was so he could start digging La Zanja Madre; the mother ditch, that this once fed from. Some things... ' She nods toward Lilian, who is kneeling next to the pit. 'Maybe Lilian can tell you about what else may have come down from these mountains. Something not so easily harnessed as electricity, or water.'

'Bandits?'

'No; those came from the east.'

'She means Toibipet,' Lilian says. 'The Devil Woman Who Was There. An old Tongva myth. We'll see.' She takes one of the long matches and strikes it on a rock. She shoves the lit match deep into the small cone-shaped cavity at the center of the structure. The fire quickly makes its way from there to the point of the cone, where Lilian waits with a cigarette. She lights the smoke and picks up the shot glass.

'Let me see that tequila.' I hand her the bag. She examines the plastic bottle. 'Good enough.' I glance at Ursula. She smiles curiously. I look at Paco. He doesn't seem to be paying any attention to our conversation. Lilian stands up again, carefully balancing the shot glass that she's just filled to the rim. She bends down and places it on the spot where she had just been kneeling, without spilling any of the liquid. She sticks the cigarette in her mouth, picks up the empty milk jug and the nearly full bottle of tequila, and turns toward the dry wash. She takes a handful of something from her skirt and tosses it into the flames. Whatever it is hits the fire and blooms into a billion tiny sparks. She walks away with the bottle, while Ursula and I join Paco in staring at the sparkling fire. There are some green twigs sizzling in there, flaring from their ends, and the fire is giving off an intense odor, like a mix of herbs and urine. Ursula takes a deep whiff.

'Smell is important,' she says. 'It helps us to remember.' We sit silently for a few seconds, breathing, smelling, trying to remember. 'This place is dense with stories, generations upon generations upon generations of them, buried by a catastrophe that isn't even past. Cruel memories, memories that burn the teller with the telling. Those are the crucial stories. They are happening now. They are staggering—'

'We are still staggering.' Lilian has returned. The tequila bottle is empty and the milk jug is full of water. She tosses her cigarette butt into the fire, bends over and carefully lifts the glass of tequila from the ground. 'The ashes rise. What happened to the Tongva? We became Mexicans in your eyes. But we are here. We endure.' She pours the tequila into the fire. It goes up in a quick puff of steam. Lilian urges me to breathe it in. 'Think; not the handful of generations boasted of by those descendants of the pioneers, the so-called first families; not four or five or even ten, but a hundred generations, growing up and dying as a part of this place. Our history, which is us, has been entombed in myth. We're banished from your time, in case you haven't noticed. Our history is just another dark sea for your ships to sail upon.' I lean over the pit. The tequila has turned the fire's heart bright red. Plasmatic fire whips around within the filamental charcoal shapes like a demon in a trap. One formerly green branch is an incandescent fibula that collapses into sublime untouchability. 'The good thing about being out of time is the perspective it gives.' Lilian leans over to where her head almost touches mine, and pours the jugful of water onto the fire. Another, great big steam cloud goes up—'Wwhooosh!', and—and we're right in the middle of it." Avery turns to the window to gather his thoughts. More loaded mules are making their way up the switchbacks. "Okay," he says finally, "This is where it gets strange."

The camera clicks. The interviewer smiles.

"So, you could say the steam cloud passes through us, although it feels more like we pass through it. On the other side—"

"The other side?"

"I don't know if it was just me, but... you know how we sort of feel time creep forward, like a slow moving stream? That's what it normally feels like to me, anyway."

"But this was different?"

"Imagine that time stream overflowing its banks and spreading like a flood, so instead of just moving a given distance in one direction, it moves the same distance in all directions."

"Into the past?"

"Except there is no past. Everything's happening at once."

"What you describe sounds like a sensory collapse. Certain chemicals have this effect on the brain."

"But it doesn't feel like a collapse. If anything, it feels more like an expansion. There's plenty of space."

* * * *

2:15 PM

Candy and Aisha wander into the old city plaza. A few feet in front of them a man who looks like John Brown is fast asleep on a bench covered with little metal spikes to prevent people from sleeping on it. Candy faces the gazebo stage in the center of the plaza, where an old woman performs interpretive dancercises while her cardboard-collection cart wobbles toward her, as if being drawn in by the performance. Next to the gazebo a young corporate-type guy sits on a bench back with his shiny leather shoes on the seat. He looks up from his phone, points in their direction and winks. Aisha looks behind her.

"Is he waving at us?"

"Yuck," Candy spits. She looks around for something else to present itself. Her enthusiasm is fading. "Who cares. Let's get out of here before we catch narcolepsy."

"You want a churro?" Aisha asks, nodding toward the push-cart on the other side of the square.

Candy chuckles. "No. I'm good."

"Hmm… I wonder what that old church is about." Aisha points to a small adobe chapel across the street. Candy shields her eyes and peers into the glare.

"I don't know." Candy used to love checking out L.A.'s historic places. But it's such a hassle just to get anywhere around here, and when you do make the effort, too often it ends up being like meeting an aging celebrity; it's all too shiny, it's had too much work done, there's too much self-referential frippery been added for good taste. When the strangeness of time is stripped away, the strangeness of life is too, and the matter no longer does its mattering.

There are always exceptions, of course. She takes a long look around, considers their options, calculates pleasure over driving-involved, and comes up short. "You want to go look, don't you?"

"It's right here. Might as well. We've got plenty of time."

****

"'The river is presented first,' Ursula speaks into the steam cloud.

With these words the gutter is at once a gutter, a spring, a creek, a bloody first and last ditch, and an aqueduct. Electricity pours down the canyon to flood the plain, while the plain drains of water. The currents combine into moving images of missiles and microchips as a dusty, pixelated chorus of neo-proto-flappers warble, 'Hey Big Data! Don't you get me wrong…' I'm clearly hallucinating, but I don't feel drugged.

'The river, not the view of it from land. Those spots are not so real from that double distance. No shimmering on the water is there, is there?' From what I can tell, no one is talking. The words are either coming from my brain, or from the fire pit itself. 'Your refracted images precede you. You are far more intricate in your beauty when you are alone. Evanescence is essential. We become less beautiful as our poses proliferate. They contaminate.'

'They do?'

'Like lies to the truth. Like corpses to a stream.'

'Oh… whoa…' It's the drought year of 1824, and also the plague year of 1868; the grounds are both bustling and avoided. The gutter is a thousand funerals, all leading downstream.

'We have no word for the river, but we have names for its every bend and bank.' It's 1883. Me and Lilian and the last free Indian on Indian Hill sit watching a Krakatoa sunset blaze beyond the railhead. A smoky fog gathers in the valley. 'Two hundred years is but a stage, a temporal clearing in a vast, timeless, inhabited forest. The forest speaks in designs, rhyming patterns of untold, told and retold...'

'There is rivers,' the brave says to a young Mulholland, who holds a divining rod and a look of confusion.

'A rippling sea is like a carpet of shadows. Still water holds the day, by refusing the light.'

'Ted?'

'Those ships that set sail yet sail.'

'Tesla?'

'On strange currents... ahem...; who is cursing?"' The Mexican Vallar, who lost his land grant to Palomar and his new American friends when Primera was founded, raises his hand. He's followed by the pox-ridden Tongva of '68, and '36 and '16 and '77. A village of Chinese laborers stands up to be counted. There are many more. The last, earliest curser is too dim to be seen; she speaks a language even the Tongva don't recognize, yet as soon as her curse is uttered it's clear that the others are mere echoes.

'Angel, curse and namesake.' Lilian? 'Toibipet—' Ted again, interrupting by nodding her head at Tesla, who is in the middle of a grand Victorian rant: '... this is why a lens cannot be molded but must be ground, little by little, by applying successively finer sands and powders and pastes. I daresay, any object that acts upon time must itself contain time. Time must go into it. Time and refinement. They must be infused, contained within; informed; natural processes without; finer and finer. Work the time in! Yes! Yes! Da! Da!'

The trees join in. The tall Washingtonia palms, nodding on their stretched necks, whisper amongst themselves like a Greek chorus. A scarred old oak tree, still sore from a 100-year-old lightning strike, in an umber rumble grumbles, 'we can't be expected to keep track of your skitterings. Yet once every so often, when we're alone together and you slow down, some attention can be paid...'

'As language, it is a medium.' It's Theodora again. 'It has liquid properties. Words flow. Granular. Like sand. Sand flows. What else? What does it describe? Mostly itself. Liquid properties—'

'See that deciduous gang over there, with the new leaves?' asks the oak. 'They stay up all winter long, and sleep all summer. They'll end up as driftwood; mark my words.'

'Who asked you, pops?'

'You see? There's something rotten about them.'

'Get struck, old wood.'

(In the midst of all this, Avery recalled the conversation with his claims adjustor when he first filed his report:

"So," Mr. Sandoval said, his words loaded with persuasive confidence, "I am to understand that the *original Krizan* you had was an *authentic sculpture*? This is good news. You follow, I assume?"

"I'm afraid I-"

"I can work some magic here, but I'll need your cooperation. How would fifteen thousand sit with you?"

"Dollars? That sits... well...."

"Good. Then... great. Great then. I'll be sending you a simple form letter giving me signatory power in this particular… particular. You submitted a 1099 last year, correct? That's good, that makes you an independent contractor. So this shouldn't be a problem."

"I'm sorry; what might be a problem?"

"Did I say problem? There is no problem. This is only to allow me to approve certain legal documents on your behalf."

"Certain—on my—"

"Trust me, Mr. Krizan; the less you and I let ourselves get bogged down in the back and forth here, the better. You don't want to overthink things. The paperwork in these cases is complicated; let's leave it at that. Once we start factoring things in, which we're going to want to do in this case…"

"Once we—"

"Just how much do you want to understand, Mr. Krizan?")

'The old oak is right,' the tallest palm whispers at me. 'You're too far in the weeds to see what's quite clear to us. We're all time processors. You, me, the mayflowers and the mayflies… so many varieties of time surround you. When you see like this, all becomes inseparable.'

'Like you know from separable,' heckles the leader of the deciduous gang.

'Saw it, kid.'

'Why, you've never worked a day in your life,' the oak ribs, in support of the palm. 'Why, you're so green—'

'Yeah, and synthesizing winter sunlight is easy? Knot!'

'So many impossible things to say! Hidden aesthetics,

symbiotic relativities, inorganic ascendancies—'

'Mr. Edwards?'

'Yesh,' the author from back at the carriage house falls out of nowhere, stinking drunk, wearing Doctor Love's hair, 'the point being—'

'Something akin to ecosystems, perhaps... chronosystems?'

'Chronosystems it is! And what's a sphere of Chronosystems do?'

'Give me a minute.'

'Yes!'

'A visionary must take things into account.' It's Ursula. She's wearing a bear suit. 'Everything is brought to bear.' And just like that it's over. The fire clarifies beneath me. The same steam cloud that rose before still rises.

'So what do you think of our trees?' It's Ursula's real voice.

'Huh?'

She points up at the tops of the palm trees, slowly swaying high above our heads. I look up. The steam cloud curls in the middle of the semicircle like a smoke ring, then vanishes.

'Pretty impressive.'

'Before you go, let me show you something...' Ursula proceeds to demonstrate the Tongva bear dance, explaining how it rotates like the sun and all the cosmos, and how it circles to a point beyond the beginning and not a point so much as a field to be orbited. 'Then and only then do they invite their ancestors, in the guise of their ancient dance partner the bear, to aid in a corrective or rebalancing ritual that can take place only within this timeless center/centerless time. After all cosmic adjustments have been made, the dance circles in the opposite direction as before, and runs the new story forward to the newly-fortified now.'

I point at the soggy fire pit. 'What just happened here? What did we just do?'

'In our dreams things matter so much,' Ursula replies, as if I'd asked something else entirely. She sits back down. 'We must get it right. But when we wake we tell ourselves, maybe things don't matter so much.' Paco and I rise to leave. Lilian stands up, while Ursula remains seated. 'Thank you,' Lilian says to Paco and me. She produces two dum-dums; a purple one and a brown one. 'Things do matter,' she says, handing Paco the purple and me the brown, 'and matter does things.' I nod, staring with surprising disappointment at the brown dum-dum."

* * * *

2:30 PM

The old chapel is sure different from the airy, well-lit church Aisha's mom goes to. Old women shuffle down the center aisle in lapping waves, bowing, genuflecting, and retreating without turning their backs to the altar. Two newish banners flank the altar. One reads 'Lord of Lords'; the other, 'King of Kings'. Aisha imagines an actual king or lord sitting under that elongated crucifix that looks like a sword, and the vision strikes her as funny. She's sorry, God—no she's not; she can't help it.

Her eyes sweep the perimeter of the small nave. Hanging there in a line are some grisly Stations of the Cross, dark visions darkened further by years of grime in a weirdly successful collaboration between time and mortification. No euphemisms here. Jesus' anguished face is candy-striped with blood; a rivulet runs from every single thorn, the course of each rivulet faithfully, even obsessively rendered. Gloomy supporting figures struggle to differentiate themselves from the murk, except for Mary, whose spore-green flesh seems to glow in the dark. The paintings also strike Aisha as silly. Violently silly. So grim! It's like a house of horrors in here. Her question is whether it consumes fear or produces it, via some hidden transubstantiation. Just how beautiful is it, really (isn't she also afraid)? But it is beautiful. She turns around. A wedding couple poses outside, smiling into the blinding sunlight with pained eyes. She turns back toward the altar, half-heartedly crosses herself for her grandma's sake, and backs out. She finds Candy squeezing happy little yelps from a street musician's accordion while he tries to show her where to put her fingers. She looks up and raises her eyebrows critically.

"I couldn't be in there anymore."

"Me neither."

Candy stands up. "So it's almost three o'clock..."

"Really?"

"I mean... " Candy hands the guy back his accordion, gives him a high-five and a buck and looks at Aisha. Her phone rings. She turns it off without looking at it. "I don't know what you want to do, but..."

"What were you thinking?" Aisha already senses the

answer.

"Honestly? I think I'm done with this scene." Aisha's cell phone rings. She also silences hers without finding out who's calling.

"Okay…"

"I mean… I don't know. You're welcome to—…, well, actually…," as if she's thinking it through, "how's that going to work…?"

"Don't worry about it, Candy. Let me just get my stuff out of your car—"

"You know we'll just end up sitting in traffic, and then what—"

"I totally get it. It's pretty boring around here. You got better things to do, people to see…"

"It's not that."

"No, I know. I'll get a magazine or something. I'm going to be on that train for a while, anyway," Aisha says sagging slightly at the prospect, truly without meaning to, "I might as well get used to it."

"You sure? I mean, this is okay, you know, whatever, but it's like, I don't know, *The Long Goodbye* or something. After a while, it's like I—"

"Totally get it."

"You sure, Aisha?"

"Totally sure."

"I can help you carry your stuff."

"Please, don't worry about it."

"I feel bad now."

"Candy, don't—you're—you've been awesome. Are you kidding? You've done so much. I can't thank you enough. I just wish...—"

"Watch; you'll be back soon enough."

"We'll see. I should probably get my stuff before traffic gets too bad."

"It's not that."

"I know. I get it. But still."

* * * *

Kwéte watches. The bear paces in front of the den, making smaller and smaller circles in the clay until it spins in place. With a long, low hum, it sits down like a man and starts to inspect itself. The sky is gathering the ripe, fragrant, golden day, gently lifting it up from the earth. Soon the sun will be low, and the great gate at Ahmutskupiangna will open, and the day's eastern migration will begin. Kwéte stands up tall. He will follow the day. If he must hide from the rahwah'nat, he will face the bear. He walks out of the den with the stone in his hand. The bear looks up, grunts its assent, and returns to its grooming.

When Avery and Paco reached the sidewalk Paco nodded curtly, turned and walked away toward the sun, leaning into it like a sea captain and shading his eyes from it with his hand. The sidewalk was a harsh yellow beam spreading toward them from the direction of the train station. Avery felt dizzy. Buildings, trees and telephone poles pitched in his vision. Watching Paco walk away, he also felt conflicted. A very strange thing had just happened back there at the fire pit, it seemed to him, and he would very much have liked to hear Paco's take on it. But Paco wasn't talking, and had walked away once already. Not to mention the fact that following a mute stranger around was just a weird thing for him to be doing. Was he that lonely, or scared? Or what? It was getting late; the yellow sunlight was getting redder. It would be dark soon, and then…? The orange light reminded him of the ceiling of Union Station back in L.A. He couldn't even visualize the inside of the Primera station, but he imagined himself there anyway, meeting the insurance agent.

"So I'm sort of following Paco down the street again," he tells the interviewer. "Not on purpose, really. We're… we both seem to be headed downtown."

The 'exclusive retail experience' is buzzing with activity. One particular couple catches Avery's attention. They look familiar, but he can't quite place them. The interviewer yawns. Avery feels a bit sorry for him. But what can he say? It was the fire. He moved along like he was on a ride, finishing the chocolate dum-dum, softening the stick, whittling it with his teeth, twisting it free like an apple stem, rolling the shrinking barbell around in his mouth until it was nothing but a sticky bit, and swallowing it…. "So…" Avery holds his breath to absorb a fresh wave-set of nerves. He keeps his eyes on the interviewer's face. "I'm sort of supposed to meet someone at the train station."

"Yes…"

"It had to do with the phone call."

"Yes."

The sun was directly behind Paco, who never turned

around. Avery must've still been hallucinating, because time was still all out of whack. He was twelve years old, walking down the same street, imagining himself as Holden Caulfield from *Catcher in the Rye*. When he was twelve even the past belonged to the future. As he walked he imagined himself older, wiser, and more damaged… like seventeen.

I'm twenty-six, he had to remind himself. The only number between a square and a cube. And…? It had turned out that he was no different from anyone else. When he was twelve he thought that he might be being tested. He no longer thought that. If a visitation was going to happen, it would have happened already. It would have happened when he was better than he'd become.

"I'm still dazed from whatever just happened at the fire pit…" He felt the late-afternoon sun of a picture-perfect, long-forgotten day. What to do with the aftertaste of the future? Twenty-six, staring down at the same sidewalks so much like they'd always been, only in a baffling reverse-negative. Those long, airy afternoons, so full of expectation, had become vapors. He tried to hold his moments then; he tried to squeeze them into permanence. His grip was much tighter in those days, and it had failed. His grip had since become infinitely looser,. He was less intent anymore. The years were accumulating behind him like silt. But still, the silted river flowed. It still slipped through his hands. Even examining it to the point of panic would do nothing to help him hold on. Admitting it was painful. But not admitting it was worse, wasn't it? That's what turned people into sad clowns. That's what killed. No, he'd never given twenty-six much thought while growing up. He didn't know what to make of it. And yet it also slipped by. Nothing (not even insanity, Holden!) would slow it down.

Once upon a time he'd tended a sort of imaginary time garden. He knew it by heart. He could visit the Era of the Buried Treasure Game Box any time he wanted, or the Days of the Sprinkler in the Olive Tree, or the Age of the Best Pencil Ever. But a couple of years ago the garden started getting too overgrown for him to take proper care of, so he abandoned it.

He'd let practical matters drift while other people navigated just fine. What was wrong with him? He'd told himself a million times to get a move on, but he never took his own advice. Twenty-six. Shit. Already. How many immortal names had been made by that age? How many careers were peaking; how many had or were about to receive the great "yes, you are legit" sacrament of confirmation because of effort, discipline, persistence already invested and channelled into useful accomplishment? If he was a theoretical physicist he'd most likely have done his best work already. How ridiculous was he, by contrast? He was still unwilling to scratch theoretical physicist off his list of possibilities! So what had he been working so hard at? Smelling the roses? Swimming upstream? Procrastinating and fretting? Was it too late to go with the flow? What once made diamonds will soon make paste. And those countless promises he made long ago, unremembered but never quite forgotten? Look at us now, he thought pitifully at his twelve-year-old self; we're a grown man following a stranger down the street, on our way to involve Grandpa in a posthumous fraud. Had he forgotten his story? Or was this his story? 'In your dreams things matter so much. You must get it right. But when you're awake, you tell yourself 'maybe things don't matter so much...'

"Avery?"

"Sorry; I lost my train of thought. So Paco and I come to a zone of drive-thrus, gas stations and chain motels all crammed around a large freeway overpass. Paco catches the light and disappears beneath the overpass, but I have to wait. Next to me a car full of teenage girls sip Big Gulps, dressed for a night out west. I can smell their perfume. 'We're so weird,' I hear one of them say from the back seat, and they all start laughing. The passenger looks at me, rolls up her window, turns around, and they start laughing again. After seeing my reflection in her window, I have to agree. The best part is the getting away. The light turns green, the girls take off, and I slouch toward the big concrete slab of freeway. A sustained howl meets me at the entrance, with thumps, whines, shrieks, rising and falling sounds, chain rattles and slams from above. Street-level noises slosh off the walls, coming back all weirdly filtered and amplified. Concrete seems to heave at me from all sides... then I'm back in the open, back in the sun. A pickup truck pulls up to the corner and the driver looks at me like I've just insulted him, like he's considering whether or not to pull over and kick my ass. Then he peels out, leaving me standing in a cloud of burned rubber and exhaust. It's the wig, I figure. And he was probably right to take it personal. Since leaving the adobe, I'd been taking turns ordering myself to take it off and refusing the self-directive. Now I feel more determined than ever to do both things. I start to wonder whether being back in Primera isn't giving rise to some mutated regression to adolescence." Avery pulls an imaginary screw from the side of his head and looks at the interviewer. "I pick up my bag and keep walking."

* * * *

3:15 PM

Candy's Porsche backing up traffic in Union Station's palm-lined drop-off zone. Amber-lit skyscraper windows and sunlight flashing from windshields. Warm asphalt, car horns, bus exhaust, khaki canyons, a thin dusty glaze over everything. The smell of her neck. Light and cheerful goodbye, almost giddy with noise and rush. These will be her last impressions of Los Angeles.

Pantomiming determination, Aisha turns and marches through the main doors… and just like that she's back, alone again in the station's cool, cavernous Mission Revival concourse, with bags in hand and shoe squeaks slapping back over acres of super-polished terracotta. It's like nothing ever happened. It's even the same time of day as when she arrived in Los Angeles. She feels weightless, like a scrap of litter caught in an updraft. But she resists that feeling. It's time to relax and get comfortable with her own company. She chooses to wait in line for a human agent instead of using one of the available electronic ticket terminals. A sense of anonymity washes over her in warm, almost cozy waves. She savors the sensation, and the way it's enhanced by the station's solemn air of purpose. If only she were going somewhere new. She gets her ticket and scans the room for ways to kill some time. She peeks through the frosted glass doors of an upscale restaurant that's gone way too far, in her humble opinion, with the whole Orient Express aesthetic to be excellent in its own right. It sort of reminds her of an '80s TV detective show, in eatery form. Turning her attention to other diversions, she spies a small transept containing a bank of lockers and a newsstand slash micro convenience store. She walks over to the store and buys a water, a canvas notebook and a National Geographic with a long article on desert photography in it. She's putting her debit card away when her phone vibrates. She stuffs her purchases in her bag before looking at her phone. It's her dad again. Again she lets it go to voicemail. He leaves another message. She ignores it while she checks out the courtyard, and bums what she tells herself will be her last cigarette. She's between worlds; she'd rather not think about Sandy or anything else right now. But after she finishes the smoke, with not much else to occupy her time, she relents.

"Hey Mija, it's me again. I don't know if you're getting these things but hey, I really really need to see you before you go. Like I already said if you listened to my other messages, I want to say goodbye to my daughter in person too, okay? And I got something for you. And also, hey; I think you might have took something of mine by accident, so please do your poppy a favor and—"

Sorry, dad, she thinks, hitting End. Too late.

****

Avery walked. No sedimentary pasts or metamorphic stories or lost holdings or shady windfalls or granite mountains or cryptic futures or heroic interventions or posthumous frauds; no self-conscious focus or vaporous blurs...; just long, shadeless blocks of car lots, 99cent stores, tropical fish shops, medical clinics and funeral parlors, with the sun burning his forehead and sweat burning his eyes, and Paco far up ahead. He got honked at again, and gave it no thought. After a while he stopped under the rotten awning of an old TV repair shop. In the shop window, displayed among the yellowing boxes of capacitors and transformers, grimy tubes and patinated antennae, was an old green-walnut console TV. The set was turned on. The picture, bleached to a glaze by the direct sunlight, showed a bald eagle being released into a stadium full of sports fans. The camera cut to a soldier choir singing, from what he could lipread, "God Bless America." A scroll ran along the bottom of the screen: ...Challenger the Living Symbol of Freedom Challenger the Living Symbol of Freedom Challenger... He watched as Challenger—now a speck above the crowd, now lost in its human static, now above it all again—flew rings around the stadium. Thirty seconds or so after the soldiers' lips had stopped moving, the eagle kept circling. Higher and higher it went. The camera panned the crowd, who seemed thrilled that the eagle had ignored its cue. A cheer rose up, and so did the bird. Avery really wanted Challenger to make a break for it. But it didn't happen. It took a while, but Challenger eventually spiraled back down to earth, perched on the handler's arm, and was quickly restrained and hustled out of sight.

"I take a left and cut through a parking lot." The sun was low in the sky by then, and the way it was getting lost among the thick trees and heavy old homes gave the neighborhood an aura of premature twilight. "I spot

Paco on the next block, sitting on the steps of a padlocked church."

From the window of a small cottage next door he could hear a Bach sonata and two male voices.

"A red herring," the first voice said.

"A red herring?" the other voice echoed, in a foreign accent and an astonished tone. "Are you... mocking me? I'm trying to talk to you."

"I used to like our talks. As for your red herring, I never asked for it, and it would be presumptuous of you to think I don't know what to ask for. Or that it's yours to give. You have your opera..."

Someone changed the record. He heard a scratch, then the sonata was replaced by an upright piano and a nasal howl, the dusky *del Gesù* by *Black Night*.

"You have the ability to do what is right. You have agency."

"Oh, God, please!" the first man shouted, before containing himself more or less, "I beg you. Listen, damn it. Desperate, hopeless... bliss! Do you hear? Love-in-despair. Isn't it something? Not holy, you say? And who are you to say? God?"

"I'm not God."

"I'm not talking to you!"

"*...black night just keeps on falling keeps on falling... oh how I hate to be alone....*"

The sun dipped below the rooftops across the street. Crows began to caw. Late-working bees rose from their flowers and headed for home. A dog barked nearby, and was joined by another, then another. We take from what's here, he thought (the thought arrived so casually amid the canine chorus, thoughtlessly even...); we string horsehair onto twigs and catgut onto wooden boxes and rub them together to express what must already be there to express. It's for beauty to recognize itself. Bach and bees dance differently, but for each other, with each other nonetheless.

He passed the neglected front yard of a run-down apartment complex. But the dandelion puffs that glowed in the setting sun did not look like weeds. After all, they were also fed by the sun's steady gaze. And at that moment, they seemed to be getting its special attention. And what does the sun get out of the deal? Maybe what the sun gets out of the deal is the realization of an idea.

"The sun starts to set." He thought, to the sun the dandelion puff is a dream-come-true, like *'someday I will go...'*. Someday I will go, and that will mean the end of *'someday I will go...'*. And in time all three things—the dream, the dream-come-true and the memory—will merge.

It's gotten louder at the Kasbah Kandisha. Chatty voice-clusters compete with vies for employee attention. Luggage is being dragged and wheeled and dropped and hoisted; shoe soles click on the varnished cobblestones. A sweaty handprint on the glass wall catches and holds the afternoon sun. Avery and the interviewer share a look of mild surprise at the small commotion outside. They pinch their chins in unison, as if the same curious thought has just struck them both.

"Before I can catch up to him, Paco starts walking again," Avery says. By that point his skin was sticky with dried sweat. His stomach ached. He could almost feel the Earth creaking as it turned from the sun. The breeze that had been in the trees all day wafted down to earth like an old birthday balloon, bringing the scents of eucalyptus and honeysuckle down with it. "We're approaching Spadra Boulevard, the main east-west thoroughfare through town. Some of the signs have been turned on for the night, although there's still plenty of light left in the sky."

He looked at the signs and let his mind wander. — *Sell everything!* roared an imaginary cartoon capitalist. *—And anything that values itself you sell extra hard, you hear? Why? Don't you pay attention, son? Like that shitfaced writer says... we commodify. It's what wee doo...*

"I'm getting hungry. Spadra Boulevard sprawls out in front of me like a dry riverbed." Back in his grandpa's day, Spadra's wide lanes, big plate glass windows and shadeless parking lots were the future. But the future came and went like a flash flood, leaving behind that broad asphalt wash and a few shallow commercial puddles. "Paco's sitting at another bus stop across the street, beneath a hand-painted sign offering the entire strip mall attached to it for lease with the words 'Avalable Commercal' above a 1-999 number. He's looking at me just like before. Between us two huge funerals pass, moving in opposite directions. Following the hearses are limousines, horse-drawn carriages, choppers, lowriders, cops on dirtbikes and Segways, people carrying candles, sparklers, flowers, torches, horns, drums, swords and rifles, and a sky blue Sherman tank. One funeral crawls toward the growing night, twi-lit and festive-looking, while the other heads toward the setting sun, becoming negative space against a field of burnt-orange. In the middle, bits of sodium light arc and flare over a thousand polished surfaces. The sky is clear, all reds and oranges in the west, pinks and yellows, and that uncertain green…" He's drifting again, procrastinating with the telling. "Speaking of having a hard time getting across, I've just watched Paco cut through both processions like a laser, without once changing pace or direction. Somehow no one seemed to notice him, but people are looking at me like I'm a ghoul. It's no wonder. I'm still wearing the makeshift Tiny Tim costume from the Love Inn, and I'm still holding a toy ukulele. And my wig is crooked. It could just be hunger, but some of their looks seem like dares. I try, but I can't bring myself to cross the street after him. Paco's disappeared again.

"I'm actually relieved to see the empty bus stop bench. It's like I've just snapped out of a trance. Suddenly the whole idea of following some day-laborer around, or pretending to or whatever I'd been doing, seems totally crazy. I take off the wig and start to turn away from the funerals, figuring I'll go grab something to eat and decide where to go from there, when I hear a fire engine siren start winding up nearby. I look instinctively in the direction of my old apartment, which happens to be just a couple blocks north of where I'm standing. For some reason I'm not surprised to see a brown cauliflower of smoke blooming from that same block. The engine is flying toward Spadra Boulevard now, with its lights, sirens, bells and whistles going full blast. For the next several seconds the intersection is like a kicked anthill. The funerals scramble. Horse carriages and lowriders trying to hop curbs, choppers pirouetting, cops conglomerating, bottling themselves into corners and straddling their Segways like hobby horses. The fire engine hits the scene like a seizure and passes in a pandemonic flash of red, metal and light, leaving a weird dissonant afterglow and the siren's exaggerated doppler descent in its wake. The unmolested portions of the processions have continued on, leaving our little zone of confusion to sort itself out. As the last pedestrians wash up onto the sidewalk, I step into the near-empty intersection. Cops start peeling off around me and speeding away in pairs. A few stunned mourners remain in the intersection, spinning in circles and muttering to themselves. I give one last look to the empty strip mall. It's dark and shadowy, except for the gas station at the far end. I see a figure standing between the rear of the station and a narrow strip of hardpan extending a couple blocks in the direction of the train tracks.

"Forgetting my plan from a minute ago, I walk into the abandoned lot toward a figure I'm sure is Paco. My feet are starting to hurt from walking around on blown-out soles all day. I'm hungry, and tired, and it's getting dark. When I get closer, the figure I'm following turns and starts toward me. There's no one else around. I don't get a look at him until we're just a few feet apart. When he lunges forward I can see sores and rotting sutures covering his face. He starts yelling 'You you you you you you you you you you!' I stumble backwards, but when he starts running toward me, I turn and run too. I see an arm waving at me from the gas station bathroom. I run toward the arm, with the guy chasing me, gurgling and grasping practically on my heels. I squeeze in and Paco shoves himself against the door just in time to catch the guy's fist. It splays open and a pastel explosion of pills goes ricocheting all over the walls and floor. The guy lets out a miserable squeal and pulls his hand away. Paco gets the door bolted. I crouch beneath the sink and hit my head on a pipe. The guy outside starts alternating between making garbled, wounded pleas for mercy and throwing himself with horrific force against the door. Practically right in front of me, a woman is sitting on the floor with her legs crossed, brushing her hair. Her hair is arrow-straight, jet black, and very long. Her left arm moves slowly, gently, and the comb in her hand moves through it effortlessly, like fingers down a waterfall. She sits up very slightly as she reaches the end of each stroke, bringing her hair up and folding it like a wing before letting it curl into her lap, where two oranges sit like eggs in a nest.

"'Crazy Bob,' she says. Her accent is hard to pin down. Somewhere south of the border; equatorial, maybe. 'And he is. It's good for you that my twin brother was watching.' She seems to choose her words very carefully. Her voice is round and soft, but her enunciation is brittle and crisp; the combined effect is a head-tingling clicking purr. 'My name is Mara,' she says, nodding curtly. 'I think you have met my brother Paco.'

"I shake my head, meaning to nod. Paco nods without taking his eyes off the door. 'And who are you?" I tell her my name, and about helping Paco with the books. I leave out the part about the tequila and the adobe. 'Yes,' she says. 'My brother cannot speak.'

"'I had a feeling,' I say, still looking at him, 'but I didn't know for sure.'

"'He has no tongue.' She smiles gravely. 'I was more fortunate in that regard.' I nod along stupidly. 'Paco and I have lived on and around freight trains since we were children.' Paco turns from the door to join the conversation. 'We take care of each other… as best we can.' I notice the grey in her skin, and the look of hard acceptance in her large eyes. Paco nods absently. 'And you?' I tell them about the fire, and how I've been renting a room down the street. I tell them about how I grew up not far from here, and how I moved away for a while, but things didn't work out. Then something snaps in me. I tell them how I couldn't get anything going at all; I tell them about splitting up with my girlfriend, and how after that I stopped seeing the point of all the hustling or much of anything else for that matter. I tell them I don't know why I'm telling them all this.

"Mara knits her brow. 'This is not the end, you know.'

"'I know,' I agree sharply, feeling my eyes start to well up.

"'What you have so far is the beginning of many wonderful stories, you know. Your past is alive; it changes as it grows.' She stares at the tiles in front of her. Her eyes follow their pattern.

"'I've been thinking that all day long,' I admit, feeling a wave of lightheadedness coming on. My stomach growls loudly. 'That's the problem.'"

* * * *

After her third tour of the station, patios, and courtyards, Aisha squeaks back to the center of the main waiting room. It's like an oversized, toy version of the church she was in earlier, only with a kiosk and a schedule board in the middle instead of an altar and a weaponized crucifix. The big oak benches all face the board, just like pews. Horizontal beams of setting sunlight come in through the western windows and cross the room over her head. A couple of people even seem to genuflect at the schedule board. She takes a seat, folds her hands and stares straight ahead. She's reminded of the silver St. Christopher medal Nana Sandoval gave her when she was little. *For safe travels*, Nana said; *take good care of him and he will take good care of you.* Aisha took great care of that medal, too, for what seemed like a lifetime. But it was only a childhood. She kept it in her top drawer with a $50 savings bond and a lock of baby hair for all those long years. And then what happened to it? She gets an aftertaste of that bittersweet old feeling of outgrowing a favorite toy, and the accompanying realization of what once seemed impossible, that somehow you can learn to love things less. How strange that she can't remember how she lost that medal.

A placid thoughtlessness sets in. Aisha stares at the clock until it becomes an abstraction. When the boarding announcement is finally made, she's the first one on the train, and for a few minutes she has an entire car to herself. She picks a seat, drops her bag on it, and stows her luggage in the overhead rack. Her phone vibrates again. Fuck off, dad, she thinks at it angrily, again. I'm not doing you any favors right now, get it? She sits down and puts the bag on her lap. She looks at the bag. He can't be calling about this, can he? There's nothing special about this thing… is there?

* * * *

"I tell them about the phone call and the impending meeting. I tell them how I'm pretty certain I'm participating in some sort of insurance fraud, but I don't know for sure, because I made sure not to ask, but there's no way my grandfather's sculpture was worth $15,000. I say it would be one thing if Grandpa's Ayacucho story, which I also tell them, wasn't really about living with dignity. We've got to be better than the bastards, he would say, or else we're much worse. I tell them about the other Mika Krizan, and how I suspected my claims agent of purposeful misattribution of my grandfather's work to the famous artist, which not only erases my grandfather's name and work in a sense, but transforms his creation into a counterfeit object. For cash. All because I get too bored, too easily dissatisfied. I tell them Crazy Bob is right. It is me. I know I'm going to meet the man. I know I am, because if I don't I'm fucked. I've got nothing going for me, and nothing's on the horizon. How did I end up here, hiding in a fucking gas station bathroom...

'You think you are stuck,' she repeats. 'But you are only confused.'

Avery squints at his shoes. He was going to say to her, *that's easy for you to say*. He's so glad he didn't.

The interviewer leans in. "And then?"

If he said Mara eyed him for an eternity, how would that sound? He felt Paco gesturing behind him. And then? Then things really went off the rails. That's when she told him about a sort of hidden society to which she and Paco belonged. Most of those moments have blurred in his mind, but he clearly remembers her eyes at that instant, her starting to tell him, and Paco nodding along as if to say he'd been trying to say so all day, and him being terrified of them both, and horrified at himself at the same time, for exhibiting symptoms of their disease. When she described the noble outcasts who wander the world's streets and railways, blending into the background and hiding in plain sight, he gaped at her sitting on the piss-sticky tiles and was sick to his stomach. A borderless network, she called it, possessing in its totality a profound knowledge of the world's vast and interdependent commodity-transport systems, its members sharing an unwritten moral code that is as deeply understood and more firmly adhered to than scripture. She began braiding her hair. Could he imagine? He began to nod. Every member has some knowledge of the larger features of these systems, she said, but it is up to each individual or member-unit to become intimate with a locality. If he didn't believe her then, he started to want to. They use no money when dealing with one another, she said, but are rarely more than a day without a meal and a place to sleep. Some 'arteries' could boast decades or longer of continuous flow. They also regularly benefit from arrangements operating within the realm of enlightened coincidence, she added without elaborating. At least it's a friendly insanity, he thought. He relaxed, and they sat in silence for a while. She and Paco were west of where they'd planned to be, she said, as if reading his mind. They were returning from a doctor's appointment up north. She was tired. Life is too valuable to be easy, she said. But you must make do. And she had had some thinking to do.

He asked her about the doctor. Her voice was like fine craquelure when she told him about the appointment, held in a municipal water tank outside of Oxnard. "We have experts in many fields." He asked her how one became a member of their society. "A strict process of self-initiation." If it's secret, then why was she telling him? "To illustrate the point that you only think you are lost."

"Then she says, 'I'll tell you what I know about secrets. A true secret can only be said to exist.' She points to my ukulele and asks me to play something. I play 'The Lion Sleeps Tonight' for them, real slow, in my own voice. It sounds corny, but it's not. It's nice." Avery stands up. "Can we take five? I need to use the bathroom."

4

Aisha looks at the luggage in the seat next to her, then at the bag on her lap. So she should feel lucky. That's what Candy was getting at. She asks herself whether she feels lucky. She does not; not at all. She opens the small bag and pulls out her ticket. She takes the bottle of water and the magazine and a bag of trail mix and stashes them in the seat-back pouch in front of her. The train jerks, and the platform starts to drift slowly across her window.

True, not everyone gets offered a down payment on a house in exchange for completing college. She gets that. Maybe Candy really would jump at the chance like she says; her not having a mom to be smothered by definitely adds weight to her assertion. But Candy would never have set out to get a business degree she never wanted in the first place. She's not that weak-kneed. And while a free down payment might sound fabulous in the abstract, it's the fine print Candy doesn't understand. The issue isn't the fact that the down payment will be for a depressing tract home in some treeless foreclosure zone her mom's trying to hustle back to viability, or that Aisha will be expected to parlay it into something better, real estate-wise. It's more how Aisha has to struggle for every free thought whenever she's around her mom. That's really the crux. It's like she can't breathe. It all stems from those lean early years, when her mom needed respect and admiration. And Aisha supplied it, not just because her mom deserved it (and she did), but because even then Aisha knew those things were what kept everything else from falling apart.

And things got better over time. Her mom finished school and started making a little money, and even managed to sock some away for Aisha's college tuition. But the old dynamic didn't go the way of the old desperation. It mutated. As her mom got more and more confident in her own capabilities, the us-against-the-world thing became more of a follow-me thing. Aisha only chose business school in the first place to acquiesce to her mom's implicit plans to establish a mother-daughter real estate enterprise. To be part of her mom's dream, forever. "That could be you and me up there?" she'd say during Aisha's high school years, when they'd drive past a competing agent's billboard. "Solid gold." Things like that. She was kidding at first, and Aisha would just tease her for it, then she became less jokey, and Aisha stopped teasing. She began to suspect that her mom was using the old compact for purposes for which it was never intended. Worse, she sensed that her mom knew what she was doing was wrong, but she kept doing it anyway. It took her long enough, but that's why Aisha quit business school. She'd hit a wall. Of course she never told her mom the real reason for her quitting. Now she's supposed to make herself believe that the wall wasn't a wall after all, but was something wispy, frivolous and insubstantial, like a beaded partition.

Aisha sighs and stares, idly feeling around inside the bag for a hidden pocket or something. A bump in the bottom of the bag grabs her attention. She pokes around what feels like a small accordion folder, cut to fit the bottom of the bag and concealed by a flap of fabric with a wraparound zipper. She touches the underlying bulge for several seconds before unzipping the flap. Although they've never met one before, her fingers know they're feeling a stack of cash right away. Her head, on the other hand, doesn't fully register the fact until she looks inside the folder. A weird weightless feeling comes over her at first, but she recovers her senses soon enough. After taking a glance around the train car to make sure she's not being watched, she flips through the money. It must be several thousand dollars. She finds a small set of documents folded beneath the bills and skims through those, flipping them sideways with her fingertips like index cards. She takes one with Avery Krizan's photo ID on it and inserts it into the National Geographic, so she can access it without having to reopen the pocket. She pulls out her phone. A fresh flush of anger courses through her as she plays Sandy's earlier messages.

"Mija, it's your papa…"

"Mija, it's very important to me…"

"Nice, dad," she mutters out loud. He could have just told her he needed the stupid bag instead of sweet-talking her like a sucker. She considers what to do next. The last thing she feels like doing is calling him. She tries to stay pissed, but the self-pity calms her down. She knows it's a shame that she's not more hurt. That sort of numbness spreads. But it is what it is. Right now she's more curious than anything. There were some large sums of money mentioned in those documents. That must be what she has. Apparently Sandy is overseeing some account for this Avery Krizan guy? That's weird. Then what's the cash for? And the printed emails? Judging by those, Avery Krizan is either a total nut job or he and Sandy are in cahoots. Judging by her dad's cagey voice-mails, she'll assume it's the latter. If it was on the up and up, why not just tell her the truth?

She spends the next few minutes playing at convincing herself to take this Avery dude's money and this train all the way to New Orleans. Wouldn't that be something? That would blow Sandy's mind, all right. She has come to the last of his messages. She listens to his plan to meet her train in a place called Primera. He also says he's got a gift for her. If he's planning on meeting her there, then it can't be too far. She takes a route map from the seat-back pouch and confirms her hunch. It's the next station stop.

* * * *

The interviewer waits for Avery to resume his story. Avery arches his back and yawns. "Where was I?"

"You were in a gas station bathroom, I believe."

"Yes, of course. So we end up hanging out in that bathroom for a long time after the kicking stops. Finally Paco opens the door a sliver. He motions for me to join him. Crazy Bob is still bobbing crazily on one of the light post islands about fifty feet away. I look at Mara sitting on that cold tile floor, surrounded by glossy peach-colored enamel, soap scum and graffiti. I want badly to tell her something, but I don't know what to say.

'There's a working phone booth where First Street

meets the Southern Pacific tracks,' she says, looking at Paco and smiling a sad, interested smile. 'if you are still inclined to meet the train at your appointed time, you could make sure it's on schedule. While you're at it, you could call your insurance agency and confirm your appointment. The tracks can be a dangerous place at night.' I nod, but I don't think she sees me. 'Paco?' Paco turns toward her but she doesn't say another word. They just look at each other."

The afternoon rush at the Kasbah Kandisha has subsided. Most of the guests have been seen to their rooms. The interviewer is checking his phone with increasing frequency, neglecting the tape recorder, which is still paused from their last break. "The phone booth is where Mara said it would be," Avery says, watching the paused machine work against itself, draining its batteries in tense inactivity. "But I knew that already." For as long as he could remember that phone booth had stood in that field, chained to the foundation of a building that burned down long ago. "I climb into the booth and pick up the receiver." The booth reeked of urine, the buttons were greasy, and the receiver smelled like sour milk. "There's a dial tone." That was a genuine surprise. They must have neglected to decommission this one with the rest of Primera's phone booths, he figured. "I hold the receiver and stare at the corner of the old foundation it's chained to." It stood right where Ursula told him that Chinatown used to be. He looked up and envisioned a couple of dusty alleys in mild bustle, in a palette of browns and blacks with bits of yellow and deep crimson, grey-washed by a screen of kettle steam. He turned to the right, where Americans were spilling, drunk, foul-mouthed and righteous, from a saloon. "I make the call."

"To the insurance agency?"

"Yes. Meanwhile Paco has crossed the field in the direction of the tracks. My agent isn't in the office, so I ask the guy who answers if there's any official record of my appointment. He says no... but that that doesn't necessarily mean anything. I can't think of anything else to ask him, so I say thanks and hang up. I put the wig back on and head toward the tracks. It's less than an hour until the train comes in, and we're still a ways away from the station. Ever since we left the bathroom, Paco's been on his guard, staying out in the open, crossing through the middles of the fields and streets. Now he climbs the small gravel embankment and starts walking on the tracks."

Avery looks behind him. The valley is in shadow now; the interviewer's reflection is forming like a film on the window. Aisha should be back soon.

"This story you've been telling me is quite long, yes?" the interviewer asks hurriedly, as if an alarm has just gone off somewhere.

"Is that a problem?"

"I only mention because it is six-thirty now. I asked you how you came to be here, and we are within walking distance from where you began, and I believe The Berber Room likes to start their dinner shows promptly at eight. Have you seen the venue?"

"It's more like a bar and grill, isn't it? If you'd like, we can skip ahead."

"No, no," the interviewer insists, with a fling of his free hand. "Please continue..."

****

From a shadowy corner of the RTD lot, Sandy Sandoval watched the train station. He'd gotten four calls from the office already; two kiss-ass requests for a chit chat from his boy Donny over at Internal Affairs, and two hang-ups. Donny's last message mentioned Avery Krizan by name. They were on to him. And Superior wasn't going to wake up hungover and embarrassed like some asshole and let bygones be bygones. The thought—and it occurred about twice a minute—hit his logic center like an electric shock. It caused his vision to blur, and gave him a nasty jolt of vertigo. Normally he was laser-focused under pressure; there was almost a bright, straight line he could follow that would shoot him out ahead of any situation. He could kick back, cover his ass, get comfortable, and wait. But those were mere teases. A bitterly funny thought occurred to him. He conned the fuck out of himself, didn't he? He allowed himself to win some easy ones, get comfortable, then cocky, then Wham! As soon as he bets big. Fuck! What had he done?

Say what you want about him, but Sandy always tried to keep Aisha clear of his sketchy bullshit. God must have one fucked up sense of humor, he bet, because he'd left her literally holding the literal fucking bag. And just when he could use some sharp, clear edges to focus on, it all turned to jello on him. Black jello. Lasers were no good in that stuff.

He was getting softer, too. He'd never really noticed that before. He'd gotten used to his idea of the good life. Even when he was growing up in the barrio, and 'the law' was a thing to be feared, he never once dreamed that he would end up in prison. It just wasn't in his cards. He was too smart for that. Cold sweat came with the thought of it now. In an effort to avoid the new fever dream death of his freedom, he held his poker face and repeated to himself, 'they're on to me; but...'. Because he still had options at that point, but they would require clarity of thought, which would require relaxation. He was almost relaxed when at precisely 8:15, two police sedans—one marked and one unmarked—pulled up to the station, and his thought-loop fried like film in a busted projector. He slid from the trunk to the bumper as a matching pair of cops exited into the turnabout, and a detective-type exited curbside. The final, fatal blow to his defiant delusion landed when old Donny Endlicher, along with Barbara 'Cuda Guzman from Fraud emerged from the second, unmarked car. They followed the detective into the station while the uniforms pretended to scan the perimeter. The cops made a big show of looking for something, but he could tell by their floodlit faces that they couldn't see jack shit. For the time being, at least, he was safe. But what if they made Avery Krizan? That'll be the end of the line for old Junior Jr. They had the file by then; they already knew better than he did what the kid looked like. His phone buzzed. Shit! What if they tracked him there? And what about Ish, whom he'd been calling all fucking day? They couldn't possibly know she was on the train, could they? Oh, for fuck's sake... Sandy lowered his head and thought about the dad he never knew. Prison. He found himself praying that Ish kept on ignoring him like she'd been doing, for all those good reasons she's got. He took the battery out of his cell phone, climbed into his Chrysler LeBaron, tossed the bag he bought for Ish in the back seat, and rolled the fuck out of Dodge.

* * * *

Avery speaks a little faster. "All right. So now Paco and I are both walking along the train tracks. The station's a pool of yellow light in the distance. Behind me, the rails are twin blue streaks stretching all the way to New Orleans. Ties pass beneath my aching feet like frames of an old film strip. We're in a wide corridor of derelict industrial buildings and decaying warehouses." They walked in and out of overlapping light cones and compound shadows. Chain-link fences and high cinder-block walls screened massive black piles of obsolescent machinery, the grimy effects left behind by those dead factories whose carcasses still lined the tracks, protected by the curses of asbestos and soil toxicity. "The ties are raised from the level of the gravel, and I've got to pay attention to keep from tripping. I keep my eyes down while keeping Paco in my peripheral vision. We're less than a quarter mile from the station when a light appears in the distance. It's small, but growing. I pick up the pace, then—with a sick feeling in my stomach about it—I start running toward it. Paco doesn't seem to notice at first, but just before I catch up to him he stops and holds out his arm like a semaphore. I stop. He crouches. Now his whole being is trained on the tracks. I'm still trying to figure out what he's tripping on. At first I see nothing but the light, then I make out two police sedans and a couple of cops loafing around out front. Meanwhile the light keeps getting brighter. Paco lays flat on his stomach and puts his ear to the rail. He looks up in the air, then at me. There's a confused look on his face. He puts his ear to the rail again and listens even more intently, like a doctor with a stethoscope. He stays like this until after the train reaches the station. I just stand there. It's like I'm watching a silent movie. I'm totally perplexed. What's he listening for? And should I keep listening to him? I can see the train now that it's not moving. On the one hand I'm thinking, there's no way those cops are there for me. That's absurd. On the other hand I'm thinking, of course they are. It's absurd to think otherwise. Paco keeps his ear on that rail the entire time. At the station, meanwhile, two men and a lady have just walked outside and are talking to the cops. Judging by their suits and body language, I'm guessing they're working together. They stop talking after a minute, and just stand there. Now no one's moving, and if I don't get a move on, I know the money will likely be gone. I clench my muscles and get that weak, just-woke-up feeling, and am reminded of how hungry I am." And how unemployed he was, and how broke. "But I don't move. I try to tell myself that it's better this way; that the more this whole process developed, the more the prospect of big, pure change had fooled me into believing that anything is better than the sleepwalking I'd been doing since I'd returned to Primera. It strikes me clear as a bell that I hadn't been thinking straight about things. I'll be all right. I have another month-and-a-half's rent paid for by the insurance company. I've committed no crime. I just have to step up my game. I have my last check from the Love Inn, a little bit of money in the bank, and the insurance company owes me a few hundred bucks, at least...—"

"But you—"

"Yes. I totally would have done it if Paco hadn't stopped me. But what happens next...—I'll try and tell it to you exactly the way I remember it—or don't remember it, to be more accurate. I have a vague image of Paco getting up and moving quickly away from the station. Now I'm on my feet, and turning the same way, when Paco turns around again toward me. He's got a brain-sized rock in his hand, and he starts jogging with it in the direction of the train. Before I know it I'm running alongside him. Meanwhile the light has grown a lot larger, and is getting brighter fast. Even with our own chaotic locomotion toward it, and with one eye on my feet, there's no doubt that the train is accelerating. I stop, but Paco keeps going. I yell, but he either ignores me or doesn't hear. I can feel the train picking up speed, and the light is getting really bright. I yell again, as loud as I can, but it's drowned out by the engine noise. By the time it blares its whistle the train is practically on top of us. I leap off the tracks, but Paco doesn't. He turns around, and with the train howling over him like a huge wave about to crash, heaves the rock at me..." Avery stops.

"And then?"

"Then I'm in the air. And there's the light. Then a blur–"

* * * *

Endlicher and Guzman manage to keep the train and the "less than enthused" detective sergeant at the station for an extra five minutes. Guzman covers the doorway between the platform and the waiting room while Endlicher checks both sides of the train and platform, and the detective gets coffee. No one matching the descriptions of Sandy Sandoval or Avery Krizan either boards or disembarks from the train, no one matching either man's description is spotted loitering on or near the platform, and no one is seen lurking around the parking lot. Without authority to search the train, and having endured the sergeant's impatient body language long enough, the investigators are forced to cut their losses.

Bells clanged and lights flashed as they watch the Sunset Limited ease into motion from their respective vehicles. Up the street, the crossing gates had just start falling when it hits.

* * * *

Avery smiles apologetically at the interviewer.

"Just as I hit the ground, it gets yanked out from under me. Before I know it I'm flat on my back. I slide down the gravel embankment, while the train skids to a halt and sloshes backwards like a huge bucket of water just a few feet away.

Then everything gets real slow and dreamy. I can hear steel springs creaking, pneumatic hisses and compression grunts. A dog starts barking. A car alarm goes off in the distance. I just lay there and breathe, and listen. A buried bug rattles a pebble next to my ear. I turn my head and see the rock Paco threw, laying in the gravel beneath the train. I crawl under the train and grab the rock. I lie still for what feels like a very long time, holding the rock, breathing in the heavy gear oil and diesel smells from the train, and the mildly sulphuric odor of the rail ties. Finally I hear the gasp of a door opening directly above my head. A bright yellow stool drops onto the gravel in front of me. The combination of my state of mind and worm's-eye perspective turns the stool into a lunar landing craft. I slide my head closer to the edge of the car as two patent-leather walking shoes and the bottoms of two navy blue pant legs touch down on its surface, and the moon lander becomes the base of a Colossus. The doubleclick of a flashlight button and the Colossus becomes a silhouette of a heavy-set Amtrak conductor. The conductor starts walking toward the front of a train.

Soon more feet start dropping from above. It's the smokers. They form a pack and start lighting up while I pick up the rock and roll out from under the train, away from the group. You know that old truism that nothing draws a crowd like a crowd? Well, by the time the second conductor shows up, more passengers are jumping out of the train. I'm sort of half-kneeling near the back of the crowd, faking like I'm tying my shoe. No one seems to notice me. The second conductor yells for everybody to get back on the train and stomps off after the first conductor. I jog over to the spot where I last saw Paco, which at this point is directly beneath the cafe car. A little kid's got his face pressed against the window and is watching me. Luckily for me, an unseen parental force sucks him from the glass, and I'm able to take a quick look. There's no sign of Paco whatsoever, thank God. I back away from the car just as two flashlight beams point in my general direction.

'Let's go, people!'

'All aboard!'

"When I get low blood sugar I can't think straight. I could have been in some shock, too, I guess. Who knows. But there was no good reason for me to get on that train. I'm supposed to meet the guy at the station, not on the train."

"But you would have—"

"I know. I'm just saying. I could have... anyway, when the conductors finally herd the smokers back on board, I join them."

* * * *

The diagonal lurching subsides. "What the hell was that?"

"Earthquake," the driver answers.

"You think?"

"Ma'am?"

"Nothing." Inv. Guzman rolls down her window. They sit for a minute or two, listening to the car alarms and freaked-out dogs, until Endlicher breaks the silence.

"Gonna be a fun day at the office."

"Heard that."

5

October 11

In the days after the unbelievable windfall fell into their laps, tension inside the DarkArk warehouse achieved nucleosynthesis. What started off small and prickly to the touch soon ballooned, developed its own atmosphere, increased in density, and began emitting a steady stream of ulcer pulsars capable of traveling through walls, over water, and into their dreams.

$74,000 out of nowhere made for one crazy high. At first they could hardly think straight, they were so ecstatic. Not only would they be able to host their gathering, Manifest the Casbah—also called the Ultimate Resort, or UR (you are) and in darker moments, Last Resort—exactly as their wills desired, they would also be able to bring the DarkArk warehouse up to code, and renegotiate their lease with the landlord. It was a dream come true.

But as with any rush, theirs soon came to bust. The surge of baffled giddiness they'd been riding was replaced by a thickening fog of anxiety. All of the tickets were purchased by one individual, a mysterious Mr. Avery Krizan (like the artist). The tickets were to be packaged together and sent to Mr. Krizan, care of a place called the Freed Seed in Kansas City, MO. They were urged not to contact the Freed Seed under any circumstances. So they had a name, the address of a seed bank and a request for privacy. That was it. They buzzed around the warehouse in the dark, asking themselves and each other over and over and over again, 'who the hell, what the hell...?' But they were afraid to find out, as if that might break the spell.

NZYME was first to snap out of it. For NZYME, the fact remained that whatever shade their windfall was made of, they'd be on their way to manifesting a catastrophe if not for it. What was it, three tickets total they'd sold to the old crowd? It was a gift from the fates, like it or not, that they'd be cosmically remiss to refuse. They shouldn't approach it fearfully. So, having gotten his fill of manifestering (as he'd come to call what they'd been doing), he decided to disregard their benefactor's request for privacy and do some due diligence.

The first thing he did was call the telephone number Mr. Krizan provided with his order. It was answered by a lady at a life insurance company. When NZYME asked to speak to Avery Krizan, she didn't say anything for like a minute. Then she asked him in a totally aggro voice who he was and why he was calling, so he hung up on her. Not an auspicious start, for sure. Suspicious, maybe. Then he snuck onto CAMEL's laptop and found a guy in So Cal with the same name, but he dismissed it, reasoning that anybody with a street address of 421½ in a shithole like Primera wasn't likely to be giving $74,000 to strangers. He looked for Avery Krizan on Facebook, with no luck. As a last resort, he traced the IP address from the online order to the Sleepee Teepee Motel in Tucumcari, New Mexico. The IP address was registered to The Echo Fund, an investment firm based in Hong Kong. Weird shit, indeed. Avery Krizan was turning out to be one slick character. He was all over the place and nowhere at the same time. NZYME considered contacting the bank, but decided against it. NZYME and banks operated on opposite psysic wavelengths (as in, coming into contact with theirs usually did something to cancel his out). He didn't want to press their luck.

The next day, CAMEL received an email from Superior Life Insurance Company's fraud department, inquiring as to the nature of their online enquiries. The insurance agency wanted detailed accounts of any conversations, communications, etc. between them and this Avery Krizan guy, and practically demanded that CAMEL contact them as soon as possible. But that tactic only drove the trio further underground. They holed themselves up in the Dark Ark and cranked the manifestering up to eleven. Adding speed to the equation probably wasn't the best idea. Specious speculations proliferated like spores. (CAMEL's tended to circle back to U.S. government involvement, while Ala held to her mob/landlord/Whole Foods theory.) For the next three days they used the computer only for a few seconds at a time, and then only to check CAMEL's inbox. At the end of each day they would visit a different ATM machine to check the balance, fully expecting that their bonanza would end up being a case of easy come, uneasy go.

Then a strange thing happened. After that single intimidating missive, CAMEL didn't receive another email from Superior Life. Far more surprisingly, the money stayed in their account, even after they finally dared to start spending it. So the edge dulled a bit, but the sword still hung over their heads.

Now Manifest the Casbah is coming up fast. They still have no idea who their mystery Manifesters might be. A thought has begun to keep CAMEL up even later than usual. Normally he could be pretty sure that any strangers at the gatherings were at least friends of friends, fellow travelers in the same psysical (from psysic, their portmanteau of psychic and physics, signifying the extra-sensitive form/source common to all manifestations) orbits, who understood more or less what to expect, and what not to expect. It requires a certain willingness, a suspension of disbelief, even, to participate in their brand of world-building. What if these people are not willing? What if they don't give him the power?

* * * *

It's been three weeks since the evening of September 20, when Superior Life internal affairs agent Don Endlicher answered Avery Krizan's phone call. Avery Krizan had said he was calling to inquire about a claim settlement that was to be delivered to him in cash later on that night at the train station. He sounded worried. Punching up the file, Don saw that the claim originated from Primera, and that it was handled by Sandy S. (there were two Sandys at Superior then; Sandy S. and Sandy R., the Ice Queen of Azusa/Glendora, who wouldn't even hand him the creamer that time...) Don liked Sandy S. He even got invited to one of Sandy's infamous poker tournaments, where he proved that you can know who the sucker is and still be it. It was fun, though. They strung him along long enough for him to get his buy-in's worth.

Don knew that the agency had recently flagged Sandy S. as a PERV (Potential Ethics Rules Violator, probably for his gambling) and he himself could identify several glaring irregularities within the claim documents, but the first thing he did was to try and reach Sandy on his cell, as a professional courtesy. Sure, he was looking for a reason to forget about the call, and he wasn't looking to be picky about what the reason might be. But it didn't matter. His call went straight to Sandy's voice mail. So Don left a short message and told himself to forget it. But he couldn't. After consulting the clock again, and trying Sandy again, he puckered up and passed the call details (such as they were) and file contents to his superior at Superior Life, Barbara Guzman, head of in-house fraud investigations. Unfortunately for Don, Investigator Guzman—due to the time-sensitive nature of the situation, in combination with the sizable sums of money involved—was compelled to take more aggressive action than he was looking to engage in at that particular time. First she got on the horn to Enforcement, who got her the two rookie cops. Then she called Don back and asked him to accompany her out to Primera train station, where she'd hoped to intercept Sandy.

That bust turned out to be a bust all right, as they were unable to locate either Avery Krizan or Sandy Sandoval. Back at Superior Life Insurance Company's West Covina office in the days following Sandy Sandoval's disappearance, Investigator Guzman came up with another plan. While the agency execs agreed to her approach "in principle," they were less than committal about committing additional resources to it. More disappointed than surprised, she went ahead and left a personal message on Mr. Sandoval's voice mail elucidating the portions of her theory that she hoped would appeal to his paternal instincts. Running with a lead she got from Amtrak, she informed Mr. Sandoval that as his fugitive client was now the prime suspect in their case, and as his own daughter was last seen in his client's company, the agency had no choice but to consider her as having been complicit in the scheme from its inception (one of Amtrak's car attendants had made note of a couple that fit their descriptions, after the male claimed to have lost his ticket during a smoking stop. What aroused the attendant's suspicion was how willing he was to buy another one. And while there was no record of Avery Krizan having bought a ticket for that train, there was such a record for Aisha Sandoval).

The day after she left the message, she got a call from a vacation rental in Bullhead City, Arizona, just over the border from the gambling town of Laughlin, Nevada. Junior Sandoval babbled semi-coherently about secret societies and men in high places for several minutes, before abruptly changing his tune. It was all his doing, he suddenly declared; come and get him. Although she told him that she believed his confused confession to be a blatant attempt at minimizing the complicity of his daughter Aisha (and, by extension, of Avery Krizan), Guzman contacted the Bullhead City authorities and had Sandy detained. Then she contacted every casino in Laughlin in order to ascertain just what kind of money he'd been throwing around out there. She received a single facial-recognition match, courtesy of the Laughlin Lava Rock Resort's surveillance division.

It wasn't much to go on. For roughly two hours on the morning of September 23rd (03:49—05:43 to be exact) Mr. Sandoval played one-on-one blackjack with the dealer at a five-dollar table. He ordered a single drink, tipped and sipped conservatively, lost one hundred and twenty-five dollars, cashed in a couple hundred dollars worth of chips, and exited the casino.

Three weeks have gone by, and still all Guzman's got is Junior Sandoval, who refuses to talk to her. The agency's lawyers have taken over everything. All internal records pertaining to Junior's embezzlement scheme have been sealed tight, even from her. Her complaints about that have fallen on deaf ears. But they don't call her 'Cuda for nothing. Even without the agency's help, she has been able to verify the existence of the ninety thousand dollars referenced on the claim documents she and Don Endlicher saw before they were sealed, but not before the bulk of that money is laundered through some neo-pagan art cult in an arrangement that still has her guessing (she'd've had the pagans dead-to-rights, though, if not for more narcoleptic follow-through on the part of Enforcement). There have been no recent sightings of Mister Krizan or Miss Sandoval. To top it all off, last week both she and Don Endlicher received an Executive Directive directing them to pivot their energies toward more actionable concerns, if they had not already done so.

Don Endlicher had already done so. The recent earthquake has been keeping everybody at the office busy and on edge, including Don. So he is genuinely surprised when he gets a flimsy European-style envelope addressed to him, care of the agency's fraud department. Noting the Southampton postmark, and the fact that he's been involved in exactly one fraud case lately, he invites Barbara Guzman to his office so they might open the envelope and examine its contents together.

"What do you make of this, Barbara?" he asks, after they've both seen the Manifest the Casbah invitations.

"It's too good to be true."

"They looks real enough to me."

"I'm sure they're real." Barbara Guzman pulls out her Blackberry and starts typing. "All the more reason…"

"Hmm. I see your point." He has no idea what she's talking about. But circumstances keep conspiring to make them a team, and he's a team player. Her truths are a smidge too self-evident for his taste; he'll just leave it at that. "I'm sure I don't need to mention that this is the only active lead…"

"No you don't." Softening her voice, she adds, "but whatever this is, I'm sure we'll be able to use it to our advantage." Sensing he's got a soft spot for female attention, she flashes him a sweet smile. "Let's keep this development between the two of us for now. I'd like to take these to my office, if you have no objections…" she says, already gathering up the envelope and its contents, "make some calls, see what I can find out?"

"Be my guest." Endlicher walks Guzman to the door. "But hey, uh… Barbara? Umm uh…"

"Spit it out, Don."

"I was thinking… since we've gone this far… together… you know… if we deem it necessary to investigate this lead… in person…"

"You would like to tag along."

"Well...." Mr. Endlicher shrugs. It's been too long since he's been asked to do anything interesting. "I wouldn't mind..."

* * * *

Three weeks ago Avery Krizan snuck aboard a train and left Primera. Now he stands on top of Mika Krizan's *Hull*, bracing himself against the sharp Berlin wind, while Aisha Sandoval takes pictures of him from a nearby bench. He doesn't know what else to do, so he contrasts the two ships, this sculpture by Krizan and the one his grandfather made. This one is made of war debris, while his grandfather's was made of hammered tin and wire. His grandfather's was a light and fragile vessel in full sail, and this one is a solid brick-and-concrete prow that plunges twenty feet into the Kreuzberg mud. From above ground all that can be seen is a flat, bell-shaped pad the size of a small stage. It looks almost like a fallen wall of some church or synagogue, but apparently it's a cross section, an amidship slice.

Not that he was expecting hovering jewels waiting to be plucked from thin air, but he feels vaguely disappointed. There's a mild buzz of foreignness surrounding him, but not even much of that. Here is the thing that is this in a place that is here; that's all he's getting. How come? This is the one and only Berlin. Why doesn't it feel like it?

He looks around. Just like in L.A., dogged young professionals shove their stylish baby carriages along similar stroller paths, while similarly monkish runners tug at their similarly sweaty shorts. Even the squirrels scurry similarly. The world is the same place after all, it all suggests; a place that dreams of other places. So much for the differences.

What about the similarities, then? There's the subject matter, of course. And the name Mika Krizan. And both pieces were created in 1968. Could they be two perspectives on the same thing? No. Grandpa wasn't an art guy; he would have given no more thought to what some Serbo-Swiss-German Conceptual Brutalist was up to than the famous artist would have looked to some anonymous Croatian-American tinkerer for inspiration. On second thought, what difference does it make? They're connected now, thanks to him.

He looks down at the pad. It's art, he reminds himself; he's supposed to meet it halfway. But where's that? He sets his feet and tries to feel the thing beneath him. Some kind of bomb, is it? Some postmodern geo-pornographic penetration of Berlin by California culture? An Unexplosion? Is it like rebar hammered into foil, an escape from guilt? No, that's more projecting. He raises his head and lets his eyes rest among the leaf-beaded cords of a willow tree until the beads blend with their shadows into a boil of late-lingering summer golds, autumn rusts and deep early-winter greens. A cryptic compound fragrance of cool, dense stone, canal water and old coal dust hovers in the chilly shade. Readers shift similarly in their sunny patches. In the distance, old Communist housing blocks float in a hazy, cloudless sky.

A peasant woman wafts up from the depths of his imagination. She warns him to stop asking the world for meaning. He protests (to himself, as her); what does she think he's been trying to do? The phantasm, now more teacher than peasant, and more holier than-thou in aspect, gently scolds him: *'Now you see? You're creating too much mental clutter. We'll have to start all over.'* But hey, he asks, how come you don't count as clutter? The vision, no longer peasant or female or teacher-like, but mannered, almost foppish, replies, *'Right you are! Do you like riddles? I just made one up. What bookends every absurd journey? A pair o' docks!'* Oh, brother. He's getting nowhere.

"What do you want to do now?" he asks Aisha.

"You're done already?"

"Yeah, well…"

"That was quick."

"What am I supposed to do?"

Aisha puts down her camera and gives Avery her undivided attention. "Lighten up," she tells him. "You trying too hard. Go with the flow."

"Easy for you to say. Speaking of flow, there's also that water tower where he had his studio…"

"Is it walking distance from here?"

"I don't know. Where's Prenzlauer?"

Aisha consults their laminated tourist map. "It's across town, in the old East Berlin. Looks like we'll have to take the U-Bahn."

"Ooh boy. Another train ride."

"Avery?"

"Hmm?"

Aisha roll her knuckles over her cheekbones and frowns.

Avery holds his breath. Yes, he's pouting. He's the one who picked Berlin in the first place. "I know, I know. Alright; let's go check it out."

* * * *

In Prenzlauer, on the sunny sidewalk outside of the Café Liebling, Wieland Verrückte holds a table for four. Running his fingers through his dirty blonde hair, he stares unsteadily at the dark brick water tower across the street and tries to ignore the rosaceatic midget fanning his smoking Opel at the curb in front of him. Is he in a Fellini scene or what?

Thick Hermann, they call it. The tower, that is. It could be a thousand years old; it is so fat somehow that it gives the impression of having once been thin, and eons of holding all that water have stoutened it up. There is a Thin Hermann not far from here, but Wieland has not yet seen that one. He prefers to know that there's an antipode or counterpoint to this Thick Hermann for him to see someday. Meanwhile, thick-headed Wieland has himself one *furchtbaren Katzenjammer* this morning. So thick tower for Wieland's thick head! Thick bread for Wieland's thick head! Truly, he hopes that the bread will do the trick, because they must get the cargo van ready, gather their equipment, and drive all the way to Plzeň for Reggae an der Wassergraben. For the *Zerstreuungskreis*, it will be the first out-of-town assignment.

It would be very nice if they could find an American to shoot. Then they could ask The Drones for a progress payment. Being Americans, the band is so enamored of Murnau's grainy contrasts that they can't imagine filming a music video in Berlin without them.

Wieland cradles his 16mm Paillard Bolex. It should give them what they want. The Drones also wish to evoke the Berlin of the early Cold War in their music video; they want it to have some of that menace and ruin they know from their Hollywood movies. But Wieland's not much fascinated by the poor Germans of those days. He was born tired of them. No, the *Hauptdarsteller* of Wieland's postwar Berlin-video is an American G.I.. He is a little too tall, with some Montgomery Clift in his posture but without the sense of doom. This is why Wieland needs an American for their video. No German he knows could pull off the slouch he envisions. What he, what they need is –

"Entschuldigung?"

Wieland looks up into the sun, rubs his temples, "Please," talking before coffee, who...? "I'm sorry?"

"Sprechen Sie English?"

It can't be! And a girl? Camera bags, tape recorder, notebooks in silhouette...; a photographer? Can that be a U.S. Army jacket? Wieland, you are charmed for sure. "Yes, of course? A little bit. Join us for a coffee?"

A barrel-chested, bleach-blonde, baby-faced young man balancing a large urn of coffee in one hand and a tall stack of tiny, cone-shaped paper cups in the other, emerges from the café by rotating a fellow patron like a turnstile..

"Uwe!" Wieland yells. "*Hier drüben!*" The blonde guy skips over to Wieland with a big grin on his face. The reproving patron turns toward them, hands on hips, when a flurry of "Pardon me—Yes beg your—Ach—Quite, yes-yeses; just—Mmm—Watch those hands!—Ooh! Mmm—Pardon—"s drives him back inside the café. The commotion is coming from a man and a woman. The man wears a cavernous hoodie, and the woman's face is veiled by a thick, loose bob of curly auburn hair. She juggles some croissants briefly, tossing one high in the air. It spins, curls out of its arc as if by its own volition, and bends toward Wieland.

"Oh, no, Karina," he moans. "Where's my thick bread?"

"Bread is behind a paywall," she replies in German.

Wieland smiles weakly, understanding this to mean that the croissants are *gratis*. Uwe flicks little cups all around. Avery and Aisha get cups and, for the next few minutes, everyone takes turns squirting shots of coffee and downing them. The cups pile up fast. Uwe lifts the urn and pumps straight into his mouth.

First they introduce themselves individually, then Wieland introduces himself, Karina (the juggler), Zafer (the hoodie), and Uwe (the maniac) together as the *Zerstreuungskreis,* an up-and-coming, cutting edge filmmaking crew. Karina asks Aisha if she might see her camera, and takes a photo of Avery with it. Avery asks Wieland about the tower, and whether Mika Krizan still uses it.

"I have seen him once," Wieland tells him. "He is well known in this neighborhood. But around here he is not Mika, he is called by his birth name, Ljubomir."

"Ljubomir. Got it."

"So... you are interested in art?" Wieland asks. He and Karina share a look, then he asks Avery if he would like to appear in the music video the crew are making.

"When?"

"Now."

Before Avery can answer, the patron steps outside again, this time with the barista in tow. Uwe motions them over to him. He leads them to the Opel, opens the carafe and pours the remainder of the coffee into the car's radiator. "Alles besser!" He pats the confused midget on the back, hands the carafe to the steaming patron, nods seriously at the mystified employee, and walks away.

* * * *

"Would you like a hypnosis?" They're just about to begin shooting. Avery smokes without inhaling while Uwe double-checks the equipment and Zafer and Wieland finish setting up the shot. Aisha is across the street, writing a postcard to Candy. High-waters tucked into Uwe's bulbous combat boots: check. Camel straights protruding from a chest pocket of his own Vietnam-era army jacket, a bit too obviously: check. Porkpie hat that a friend of Zafer's picked up for Wieland in Brooklyn, New York: check. A fashionable passerby's aviator shades and he's good to go.

"You mean," Avery's not sure who's joking, "you hypnotize me?"

"For relaxation. For reduces the number of takes. You should try. You need, I think."

"Walk, stop, light a cigarette, look around, wolf-whistle but not too aggressively, walk; I think I got it. Besides, I don't hypnotize. I mean, people have tried, but it doesn't work on me."

"No? I think I could do." Karina steps up to him slowly, her body language both fluid and precise, until her face is about a foot from his. She slowly extends both of her arms and, with the same fluid precision, wraps them around his neck, bringing her face even closer. With her fingertips rubbing gently at the base of his skull, she stares into his eyes and relaxes her own facial muscles. Slowly (roundly, fully...), she breathes in a tidal whisper. Her concentration is crystal-dense and delicate as she holds his gaze. She brings her fingers around his head, letting her knuckles slide along the hat brim, then she sweeps them lightly along the contours of his eye sockets and rests them there briefly before slowly pulling them across the shrinking gap to touch her own temples. Avery stares at her eyes, transfixed. They're a shimmering brown-mixed-with-blue, like cool rivers pouring into warm lakes. Beneath their tiny surface facets a darker current flows. She lets out another long, slow breath. "Follow me." The fore and index fingers of her left hand drift down her cheek to her lips. She pauses then lifts them, one fingertip catching her lower lip for a peek of pearlescent lower teeth. Her fingers alight on her earlobe. They start drifting again, pausing this time at her jugular vein. She holds them there and lets her fingertips rise and fall with the swells of her pulse. He can feel her eyes watching his as he watches her fingers. Moving her chin upward, and barely to the right, she slides them down her neckline to her collarbone, then slowly follows its ridge to the base of her throat. They stall there until he thinks she might be finished, then they start falling again. Hooking their tips so slightly on her v-neck sweater-blouse that it could conceivably be accidental, she tugs to where the light just touches the perfect valley between her breasts, a golden dawn...-, "see how I breathe? In...," her breast swells heaving against her lace bra edging, "out...." She lets go of her sweater-blouse and her fingers drift another inch or two down her breastbone before reaching over, running a hand over Avery's shoulder and tapping the pack of Camels into a more believable position.

"There."

* * * *

At this same moment in Oakland, Ala lies face-up on the DarkArk floor. She holds her hands fingertip to fingertip in front of her face, inflates them into an ovum with each in-breath, collapses them into a birth canal with each out-breath, and attempts to manifest clarity. They could sure use some right about now. They've been unable to learn anything else about their mysterious Mr. Krizan. They have managed, on the other hand, to gather a small amount of intel on a few of their ticket holders. But rather than giving them a better angle to work from, somehow the new information only makes the unknowns even murkier and more unnerving. Ala gets the funny feeling that their invitees are just as in the dark as she is, and not in a good way. The first three were full-on carnies. Then there was the fake prince, the rescore band, the Hiroshima dude and his nurse, the single mother from Detroit and her kid, the migrant worker, the fine art lawyer, the oil explorer, and the ex-priest. It's a veritable fucking freak scene. Fucking scary, really. The questions they've been asked online have basically all been varieties of "what the hell is this, and who are you people?" They're at a loss to explain themselves to these bewilderingly ignorant people. So CAMEL responds to their inquiries with that mystifying word paste of his ('... we gather to render us one in wonder, s[trip]ped naked of spirit beyond the beasts and flesh of Bou Tharar, to dance along the fertile bleeding edge of night As One Blood holy and wholly, we will-to follow fallow furrows to hallowed hollows of the wadi of Amejgag, bidden there to drink of labor and LOVE and lightless fyre, blah blah blah...') and the snowball of confusion keeps rolling along.

So Ala tries to clear her mind. She holds her hands, fingertip to fingertip in front of her face, inflates them into an ovum with each in-breath, collapses them into a birth canal with each out-breath, and attempts to manifest clarity. In... out... In... Out...

* * * *

"What's *Zerstreuungskreis* mean, anyway?"

"It's... how do you say... a circle of confusion? You see, in a camera lens (Wieland apologizing to Aisha with a tilt of his head, for stating the obvious), light is focused; it is bent toward a point. Okay. But this focal point is really no point at all. I mean to say, it is more of a tiny disk that cannot be focused, a blurry circle at the very center of every image. It was Uwe came up with the name."

"Hm." Aisha nods. She vaguely recalls Candy talking about something similar once.

"After some, ahem, democratic debates, we are determined not to limit ourselves to... how do you say... post-Freudian Surrealism—?" The shoot is done. Avery's performance, everyone agrees, was *swag*.

"So you say he's still up there?"

"Mika?" Wieland points at a tiny window way up at the top of the tower. "He has an anechoic chamber—you know this word, anechoic?" Wieland is quite beside himself over the crew's good fortune. He also speaks remarkably good English. Karina, on the other hand, is (being?) difficult for Avery to decipher. It's almost like she's mangling her English on purpose, just for with him to fuck. Then she'll just stare at him, her face framed by her loose amber bob, or she'll frame him with her thumbs and forefingers. And when she speaks to him in German, it's like she's daring him to know what she's talking about. She seems to get annoyed when he doesn't. In either language, she's giving him conflicting signals for sure. She's from Saxony, Wieland said, as if that explains it; she doesn't trust Americans. Wieland also said she understands English much better than she speaks it. Uwe and Zafer fall somewhere between the other two in the English department, it seems. Of course, apart from a few disembodied phrases, neither Avery nor Aisha speak any German at all.

"I'm not sure... anech—"

"Okay; it's a little room, yes. And no sound can get in the little room. So Mika can think. An anechoic chamber, I think, it is called in English."

"Ah. Anechoic. Yeah, yeah," Avery says. Aisha shoots him a 'you're so full of shit' look. "And he still uses it? I thought he lived somewhere in the Alps these days. I had no idea."

"Yes. He no longer uses the studio, I don't think so; although he owns it still. But the anechoic chamber, yes;

I think he uses."

"So Wieland; if Uwe and Zafer cover the technical ends of things, and Karina directs—"

"Yes, Wieland?" Zafer teases, kicking shut the door to the cargo van Uwe's just pulled onto the sidewalk. "What do you do?"

"I get ideas. I set up shots and direct secondary photography. And of course Karina and I will edit together the films."

"How many music videos have you guys made?"

"Let me see… one… this is to be our second. Plzeň will be our third. And a fourth is in the works, as you say."

"So you're kind of just getting going."

"You could say, yes. We have all worked on projects for others, of course. I have assisted on many commercial projects. So has Karina. By the way," Wieland pretends to whisper, "I shouldn't use this term 'music videos' around her if I were you. Karina much prefers the term, how you say in English, 'scored shorts?' We also are working on a medium-length film; produced and directed by the four of us together. We are in preproduction—"

"It will be sick," Zafer puts in.

"Do you know what the film's about?"

"It's about so many, many things right now," Wieland is quick to answer. "It's hard to say simply. So far we are maximalists. But we hope to…" he looks at Karina, "narrow it down, I think? This reminds me. We've also been meaning to ask you something. It is very intriguing to the four of us. You and Aisha have come all the way from California to Berlin only to visit Mika Krizan's tower studio?"

"Not even."

"And now you will go home?"

"Not exactly. We're thinking of making our way south... southwest from here."

"This is perfect then!" Wieland exclaims. "Plzeň is south... southwest from here."

Uwe and Zafer take off in the crew's van to pick up supplies, while the rest of them walk the few blocks to Karina's apartment. "While he may come on strong like a wild man," Wieland explains, "Uwe is simply driven by contempt for what comes easily to him. When he was a boy, he was counseled that he might make a fine engineer one day, if he focused his talents in that direction. But the thought of becoming an engineer did not interest him. He says engineering is only a matter of making the new thing fit in, to have it work in the same obvious way as everything else that works obviously works. He had begun to suffer from a tremendous boredom, and a fear that there are no more surprises in this world. For this problem, he reasoned, reason was no solution. Aesthetic fitness, that secret answer to all questions, was itself far too settled a question. So *Kurz gesagt*, he declared with gusto, he should prefer to inhabit a world in which there are surprises! Sensible distinctions were put aside in favor of chaos. When his reason revolted, he plied it with chemical matter-over-mind. By training himself to appreciate, understand, and finally to assimilate it into his deepest thought processes, he began to become one with the *hirnfick*."

It was around this time that Wieland met him (luckily

for them both, Uwe's determined absurdism meshed well with Wieland's own admittedly slushy notions of thought revolution, if not his also admittedly dopey Americanophilia.) Avery and Aisha sense a bit of hero worship going on in Wieland's narration.

Uwe lives in the *Zerstreuungskreis*' van, and earns its maintenance money by dispensing from its back doors his own 'meow meow' blend of six parts mephedrone and one part secret ingredient to the pulse moths who line up every weekend to get inside whatever is the cool dance club of the moment. He admits to finding a certain elegance in his illicit existence; according to Wieland, he says there's only the one risk to internalize in criminal behavior, rather than the constant breathing an atmosphere of lawful hassles. His pointless-of-view has also grown more political over time. But now that Uwe's failed to fail at becoming an artist, he's at a loss. Whereas Wieland wants to change the world into some better version of itself, Uwe would say there can only be the one, with only changes in moods, or another entirely, impossible from here, so preferable to attempt to attain. Artists are only possible.

They arrive at a sea-green, five-story Wilhelmine tenement in a neighborhood of five-story Wilhelmine tenements. They pass beneath its restored façade by way of a large, chilly concrete barrel vault, and emerge into a treeless courtyard. They cross the small expanse of packed earth and broken pavement to an arched doorway with a heavy door. Karina opens the door and they enter another medieval-looking passage leading to another courtyard, larger but darker than the first. Scars from Soviet bullets still mark the unpainted, soot-stained walls. It smells like ages. Aisha thinks; stone and iron, dark and industrial. They cross this courtyard, Karina opens more heavy doors, and they walk up three flights of iron-railed stairs to her flat.

The flat consists of one small room with a coal-burning heater and a stove the size of a lamp table, and a tiny bathroom. There is one image on the wall: a curling magazine cutout of a man holding a strange skull. A large pile of blankets, sheets and pillows takes up half the room. There's a shelf containing a few spices and dry goods, some filmmaking books in German, Russian and French, and one English book entitled *On Canadian Agitprop*. A table and two chairs sit beneath the fogged-up window. Sharing the table with filmic odds and ends are a small editing machine and an old Pentacon movie camera. Karina disappears into her closet-sized bathroom to shower. Wieland flops onto the pile of blankets, sniffs at them, and invites Aisha and Avery to join him. They decline. Avery stares out the window at the innermost courtyard, where a one-legged pigeon is hopping around. It seems to be looking for something but not finding it.

Aisha points at the clipping. "Who is that?"

"Eisenstein." Wieland tells them about Karina's influences, her admiration of Buñuel and (with an amused look in Avery's direction) her fascination with mesmerism. They hold these positions, listening to the sink and cabinet noises coming from the bathroom, until Karina emerges, emanating focus and humidity. She walks directly to the table, sits down and starts messing with the Pentacon.

Fifteen minutes later she's still working intently, while the rest of them have fallen into various states of abstraction. Wieland gasps when Zafer and Uwe throw the door half-open and fall inside, dangling large, steaming sacks of food from all hands. With the six of them it's laying room only, so Avery and Aisha take places on the bed while Karina gets up and clears some space on the floor. Zafer passes out the food and they start eating.

"Tell me," Karina asks Aisha over what is hands down the best falafel sandwich she's ever tasted (courtesy of Zafer's brother, who runs an imbiß stand in Charlottenberg, as a *gute reise* for their first traveling assignment), "where do you stay now you are in Berlin?"

"We have a hotel in Mitte."

Looking into her eyes, "Oh, a hotel in Mitte? Yes Mitte is nice. Very pretty. But would be better for you to come to Plzeň, I think. Mitte is for old people. Too many tourist. Is boring for a photographer, I think?"

* * * *

"So what else has he got in that tower?"

They're on their way to Plzeň, rolling through a stretch of flat, hedged farmland punctuated by ghostly orchards of wind turbines. Uwe's behind the wheel, mumbling along to Lou Reed live in Berlin in 1976: *"…on a gray pig clip of ship, sailing from this and into that…"*

"You mean Krizan?" Zafer peers up from Avery's ukulele, which he's using to hold up his chin while he pretends to play. "If the story is true he has a type—I mean to say he has a page of type containing an accidental design: from corner to corner a perfect diagonal white line formed by blank spaces between words. They say he was studying a book in his chamber and wishing he had room to write on the margins when the thought occurred to him that were he just to increase the right hand margin of the page he was reading by less than one centimeter, the line it would appear. Can you imagine? What kind of person thinks like this?"

"What do you think?" Wieland asks.

"About what?"

"If we create a system based only on art, would everybody become an artist? I say yes."

"*I say... no, no, no!*" Uwe sings.

"And anyone can be artist like you?"

"They don't have to be like me, Karina. "

"No? Then who are you, if not artist?"

"I would be myself; the same—"

"As those who are not like you? Wieland, you dream yourself out of existence!"

"Further proof that I am an artist."

"What do you say, Aisha?" asks Karina. "Is art *verdächtig?*"

"Suspicious," Zafer translates.

"Continue please, wasting your menial lives," Uwe trills with exaggerated British-accented vibrato, "I'll just be over here, turning them into the Stuffs of Beauty. That means no dirty work for me. What? You don't see the beauty? Ach so, pity for you! I'm afraid that wasting your menial life as you have done, it is become impossible for you to recognize the sublime. Go back to work, then! You will never understand."

"Let me see if I do," Aisha chimes in. "You mean like a hypothetical economy with artistic creation as its primary medium of value," turning to Karina, "and you're suggesting that not everybody would really become artists, but that artistic creation, by virtue of its exalted position, would attract enough people for whom pursuit of the sublime is just a means to other ends that art as we know it now would cease to exist? Well that's not so hard to imagine. It's happening now. But the artists in your hypothetical… and by 'artists,' I assume you mean 'people who would follow their muse no matter where it leads'; I think they'd find a different way. I think there's a relationship-to-society component to the whole artist thing that I don't see changing, though I do agree that there'd be more opportunities for self-expression among those who might not otherwise—"

Uwe bounces his palm against the steering wheel. "That's it!"

"What is it?"

He turns off the music. "We must stop making art!"

"Not again."

"We should start to make art first, please?"

"No," Uwe insists, as if this is the first time he's thought it, "we must stop feeding him. A worldwide *détournement*, only—"

"But for that to mean anything, Uwe, please, we have to be *stopping* something."

"The only thing for us is to making good movies."

Uwe shakes his head wildly. "No, Karina!" He turns far enough around in his seat that everyone else points involuntarily at the road ahead. "A preemptive strike!"

"Oh..." Karina palms her forehead. "*Du auch?*"

"What do we do, then?"

"It does not matter," Karina says, shaking her head. "They have struck already everything. Stop pretending." To Avery, "you Americans will never let another People's art movement happening, with your *ficken überwachung* and your microwaves. Ideas are no match for you." To everyone, she adds, "I can only pretend to be warrior, or try to making better movies. This is all."

"Speaking of which," says Wieland, artfully steering the subject just enough (it's a long drive, after all, and they haven't even reached the mountains), "what is the plan?"

"It is bearing on us, from all sides," Karina says, her voice soft and dissonant, like she's waking from a dream, "like a *schwarzes loch*." Firmly, at Avery again, "a sucking. It is the same for everyone, rich and poor, I am sure. We all feel it, yes?" Avery isn't quite sure why, but he nods in agreement.

Wieland claps his hands. "On that note...!"

A little later, Zafer shows Avery and Aisha a video recording of a film projection. The film shows a rush of words moving from right to left, with the camera occasionally panning up to take in an arrow-straight horizon backstopped by steep mountains. "Check it out. My homeboy found them in a...," Zafer spreads his arms wide, "how you say... *müllcontainer?*"

"A dumpster."

"Yes! A dumpster, yes, in Brooklyn New York. Look

through the viewer. There right there; do you see them? Scratched into the sand?" Outside the cargo van, the heavily forested mountain scenery constantly opens and divides itself in the windshield, bends, and rushes past the side windows in twin blurs. "The words are in English, so we think it is the American desert."

"Looks like it," Avery says.

"I have a friend who would love this," Aisha says.

"Do you know this place?"

"Hard to say, Zafer. The desert's pretty big."

"Too big."

"It will be the central motif."

"For your movie?"

"The mysterious center."

Avery watches the screen in silence for a minute or so. "It just goes on like this?"

"For one hour and five minutes."

"Hmm?"

"For reals, though; how do you travel around staying at hotels like in Mitte?"

Pretending not to hear Zafer's question, Avery addresses Uwe. "Did you know that heroin was once a brand name? Came out at the same time as aspirin. Hero, aspire—"

"You sell drugs?"

"Huh? No, God no. We're not... I got some money from an insurance settlement, that's all. We're using it to wander around Europe. Since Aisha does photography, and I guess you could say I write—"

"You are rich," Karina says.

"I do." Uwe says.

"I'm sorry? No. Actually we haven't... our money is... it's an anomaly. It was unexpected. You do what, Uwe?"

"You are rich," Karina repeats.

"You do what?" Avery repeats.

"The rich are despicable, the well-off are irritating, the middling are abhorrent and the poor are frightening," says Uwe. "Isn't this the way? Someday we must deny the existence of money. I sell drugs."

"Oh."

"Don't worry," Karina winks, tapping her chest, referring no doubt to the cowhide grouch bag hanging under Avery's shirt. "We won't ask how much."

"Why would—do I look worried?"

"You look guilty."

* * * *

Reggae an der Wassergraben ends up being a less *Filmisch* event than the *Zerstreuungskreis* crew had hoped. Only twenty-five or thirty people show up, musicians included. The moat water is ugly and uninteresting. A steady, scraping wind sound befouls the mic mix. Most vexing of all, the Potsdam-based space-dub outfit they'd been commissioned to film blows off the engagement entirely, leaving the crew with nothing much to do. So they make do; almost all night is spent shooting Avery and Aisha in Plzeň's ancient town square. Avery is Der Leser: The Reader. Walking slowly and in an inward-flowing, clockwise spiral, he pretends to read a German-language copy of *The Magic Mountain*. Aisha is Der Schütze: The Shooter. She starts at the far corner of the square and also works her way to the center, but counterclockwise, taking actual photographs as she goes. They meet twice during each contracting revolution, paying a bit more attention to one another at each pass. By the time they get to the middle they're doing a sort of dance, with Avery reading directly into Aisha's camera, until there is room enough for neither camera nor book between them. Karina shoots all four views of the scene: one from the bushes, another from behind Aisha's shoulder, a third from behind Avery's shoulder, and a final close-up, filmed with the three of them pressed tightly together and rotating as one.

No one sleeps that night. Just before dawn, while everyone is sitting around the van with blank, exhausted looks on their faces, Avery's mind wanders to a strange place. He's at a café. He has an old paperback opened in front of him. The book is thick, soft, and dense. He has the sense that the tactility of the book matches the feel of the words, but when he looks down to verify his hunch the type is too small to read. He is interrupted by a young woman bursting through the door of the café and shouting at him from across the room. He's not too concerned. He knows her. He looks down at the page again, and the words are big again, and the scene he is in 'in real life' is also what is on the page. So in double ways the woman reaches his table and sits down. She produces a pocket watch and starts swinging it back and forth in front of him. She tells him to keep watching the watch, but she swings it so close to his face that it's hard for him to focus on it. It just blurs his vision. In a thick German accent, she proceeds to explain the advantages of film over digital, while wrapping her legs around one of his. "Ein; the frame is a heartbeat," moving her chair forward, "zwei; each contains time, and mass." Sliding, squeezing, inching, "it is not a lonely point but a wrapped pulse," closer, warmer, warmer, until his knee has nowhere to go, still pressing; "follow me."

Suddenly they're surrounded by people, all asking questions at once. The woman doesn't skip a beat. Without losing her accent, she answers in over-elaborate but otherwise perfectly good English, "yes, it is not either-or. No, this is two bodies circling one another until they're wrapped around a point that exists only between them, and their mutual struggle to balance gravitational attraction with dissociative directional radiation creates a dance. This creates the pulse we see; it is the true focus of their struggle. As long as they occupy differing parts of the pulse, and so slightly different positions in time, they can never come together...."

"What's this all got to do with film?" he asks, becoming one of the crowd.

"I told you, each frame is heartbeat. Feel that? And every film is vessel." She stops swinging the watch and looks him straight in the eyes. Her presence is as deep and warm as raw blood. "There are seas to sail, Avery Krizan; there are dark and concealed places to explore. There is a film to be made. A vessel. It will take us. I want you forever inside my film. You must trust me—"

"Isn't that... manipulation?"

"You poor, stupid American. Are you so afraid to be touched?" She surges, engulfing him like a wave. "You must be brave. The seas are not only theirs...."

He looks up to find Karina framing him with her thumbs and forefingers again. It might be the first time he's ever seen her smile.

* * * *

It's early the next morning. They're all freshly loaded with phone numbers, email addresses and soft plans. Uwe leans against Plzeň's Plague Column. He speaks shyly. It's a different side of him from the ones Aisha and Avery have become accustomed to. "Against the middle our common nature is set," he says. "Consciousness, lens, or *schwarzes loch*; they are all the same. It is the blind spot that allows the rest to be seen." A church bell rings. He points to the sky. "Like a bell."

"A bell?"

"Hmm. It hangs from the middle, yes, and rings from the center. I don't know. To ring truest, it would have to float."

"Okay."

"Believe me. I don't know."

Wieland walks up and puts his arm around Uwe's shoulder. "Let's hit the road, partner. Zafer and Karina are waiting in the van." Addressing Avery and Aisha, "he's a softie, but everything he says is a lie."

"Not everything. Only every other thing."

"Thanks, you guys," Aisha says. "It was really fun."

"Maybe we will see you later?"

"We hope so."

"It could be. Karina maybe thinks we should go to where you are going and film. It would take several days to drive, of course. We will have to see."

"Does she?" Avery asks. He hasn't seen Karina all morning. "Yeah, well; you're more than welcome."

"Yes, good. *Viel glück* on your absurd journey then, for sure. She won't say, but Karina thanks you too, I know."

* * * *

In the end, CAMEL/EON, Ala, and NZYME agree that there's nothing to do besides what they'd hoped they'd be doing in the first place. So they advance-procure building supplies for the village manifestation, set up, break down and pack the great-yurt and sacred spaces, praxis their tabla, tantriyoga, target-shooting et cetera, figure out the food situation as far as what they'll need to ship, and start shipping to Tripsy. CAMEL and Ala will fly ahead to meet the stuff while NZYME sews things up on the Oakland end. Ala's dark star has burned itself out, but events of the past few weeks have hardened her facial muscles into more of a scowl than she'd like to see, so she's particularly looking forward to getting some restorative squinting in. Similarly, CAMEL's beard has been turning grey before his eyes; the sooner he can get a shemagh around it, the better. NZYME is firing on all cylinders. He's even been practicing his scoring esperanto on a couple of friends of acquaintances from the low countries, and may have gotten a line on some premium party favors out of The Hague.

It hurts that no one from the old tribe ever offered to participate in the gathering. Of course if any of them have looked at the website in the past couple of weeks, they must know that Manifest the Casbah has sold out. Who knows what sorts of rumors are floating around the laBlab about that! CAMEL worries that they won't have enough English-speaking manual labor, so he picks up a couple of hitchhikers and asks them if they'd like to barter some elbow grease for the experience of a lifetime.

Dewey and Flyball, fresh up from Fresno, display a base-velocity somewhere on the low end.

"Unkay," Dewey grunts.

"Yuh," Flyball agrees.

Their final days in Oakland are a blur of activity. After all the idle fretting and paranoia, there's hardly time to think. They exhaust themselves in tying up loose ends. On their last night in town, NZYME tries to give his traditional interpretive offering, but his heart's not quite in it. The motions he goes through are impressive nonetheless. Afterward, CAMEL runs the plan through his head one more time. Get to Marrakech, chill for a day or so, rent a truck, hire some local labor and make the first trip to the valley. Get a feel for the place. Source and gather local supplies. Return to Marrakech, get tattoos, wait for Tripsy and the shipment and N—with the drugs, caravan with them back to the valley, draw the ley lines, begin building the altars, work out the sanitation issues, make sure the water tanks are filled and there's plenty of gas for Generator X, procure plenty of wood for the fyre, and will-to the best possible outcome....

6

Aisha twines her dry fingers over her damp hairline. Her bangs are growing out. That's fine.

She'd rather not think too much right now, with the sun hot on her brow, and the warm, dry wind brushing her skin. This is as real as things get. She doesn't ask if she could ever have imagined herself here. She doesn't think about all the effort involved in doing what each situation has required of them these last several weeks; all the seeing-through of fragile, see-through plans, the slogging through muddy non-plans, the coincidence-rides and impossible kindnesses that have brought her to this oddly familiar place. You drink where you find water. You let most of it run through your fingers, and catch what you can. You don't build a dam to make it linger.

She can see the back side of the Kasbah Kandisha from here. She can't say whether the tingle she feels is from the spot essentially deeming itself as such, or from her having finally come to her own decision slash realization slash whatever about where the spot is. She doesn't want to say. Now is *so* not the time. This is the spot; that's all. It's a stone-scattered platform overlooking a small ravine, located a few feet from the barren crest of a steep, chalky cliff. The valley floor looks very narrow from up here, and she can't see any water, but the cliffs tell her that the river was once much larger and livelier than it is today. A thin green ribbon coils down the red valley like a calligraphic flourish. Staring down from the spot, Aisha can't help but reflect on how all those trees and plants she sees flow with water too, so even though she can't see it, the river is still there. She's holding the same bag she found the money in. Now it holds the river rock Avery boarded the train with that same rock; he said his hobo friend threw it at him. He asked her to leave it somewhere out here. She reaches into the bag, takes out the stone, crouches down and places it in the dust, like she's performing a ritual that she's making up on the spot. She doesn't quite understand why Avery doesn't want to know where the stone ends up, but that's okay. She's happy enough to oblige.

While she's bending down, another, smaller stone catches her eye. She picks up this new stone, turns it over in her hand and holds it in front of the sun. It's very different from the granite and quartzite river rock she just placed, but similar in that it is clearly not from around here. Pale cream in color, and honeycombed with countless little holes and tunnels, it's like something from a Chinese rockery or landscape painting. Something for Candy's aloe plant, maybe. She puts it in her bag and wonders what Candy would she say if she were here. She still misses Candy terribly. She should drop her another postcard. The last one must have blown her mind. She closes and opens and closes and opens her eyes, takes a couple of warm, deep, dry breaths and takes in the view one more time. She nods to herself, stands up straight, drops the new stone into her bag and walks to the lip of the platform. She cranes her neck over the lip, being careful not to get too close to the edge. Far below, she sees a group of children playing in what looks to be an orchard. One of the children sees her, points, and waves. She waves back. The other children look up and wave. Aisha notices what look like two ship's prows emerging from the opposing cliffs and heading right at each other.

She's thirsty, and she's out of water. She's spent most of the hike up here thinking about what's going to happen to her and Avery when they go home. She's still pretty sure that the willful atomization of $74,000, even if it wasn't technically their fraud to begin with (it wasn't their money either; so, so much for innocence...) is bound to create some real, solid problems for them down the line. Soon enough they'll be facing the music, whatever that will be. And from here every direction leads home to face it. There'll be no going back to how things were. Her life will be different from here on out. It has a shape now. She can work with it. An adult runaway is what she felt like at first, but not anymore. She's made herself at home in the world. How cool is that? Even if she goes to jail, which she honestly doubts, it might not be intolerable if they allow cameras. Even if they don't, she'll sneak one in. She knows this now. She is getting a decent eye too, if she says so herself. She can even sense a style developing in her approach. Candy would be proud. Aisha the photographer. Aisha the international outlaw! The money bag is filling up with rolls of unprocessed film. Considering some of the places she's been these last few weeks, some of the shots are bound to be interesting, at the very least. Some of them will be good. So who's to say what the future will bring? At least it's hers; she can finally feel it. But enough of all that. Too much thinking can be corrosive to some things. She takes one more deep breath and starts her descent.

* * * *

"I've made four in a row!"

"That was only your third!"

"You weren't watching."

"I didn't see four either."

"So?"

"So do it again."

"Fine. I don't think I will miss any more. My arm knows what to do now."

"Oh! Hello Asulil's arm. Would you like to know what I would do if I were you?"

"Go!"

"Go!"

"Stop distracting me!"

At the far end of the small canyon, two homes have been built into the base of a narrow gorge. Each dwelling is a perfect cube, and each is oriented on a diagonal, so that one corner seems to plow several meters into its respective cliff. They face one another this way, corner to corner, each line parallel to its opposite, but offset just perceptibly, as if to allow for grout. A bowing strip of land separates the two buildings. It contains a mixed orchard of apricot and fig trees, with several large poplars to break up the wind. A stone-lined irrigation system laces through the orchard, circulating water among the terraced vegetable beds and ornamental patches before releasing it to join the big valley system some four kilometers to the north.

The homes were designed by and built for two sets of male-female siblings—Ali and Nadi Guessous, and Ibd and Eden Guennoun, namely—who, despite envy-fed insinuations of opportunism made by others in their profession, happened to fall in love with and marry their opposite number (that is to say, the homes' adult occupants are the married couples Ali and Eden Guessous, and Ibd and Nadi Guennoun, respectively). Ali and Eden Guessous, and Ibd and Nadi Guennoun are Zelij artists, renowned in Morocco and Southern Spain for the intricacy and sophistication of their designs. Their tile work can be found adorning many of the local resorts. They are also considered (to a degree that serves to enhance rather than detract from their collective commercial status) to be somewhat eccentric. While initially they came upon their reflective public images by twin accidents of true love, they have since taken the enigmatic, overlapping symmetries of their art and self-promotingly applied them to their personal and professional lives. Some say Eden and Nadi even timed their pregnancies to run concurrently. When they gave birth less than three days apart, Nadi and Ibd named their son Asulil, meaning rock, while Eden and Ali named their daughter Rahiq, meaning nectar. Two years later the process repeated itself, only this time it was Eden who gave birth to a boy, whom she named Aghbalu, meaning spring, while Nadi had the girl, whom she named Shula, meaning flame. Ten years later, and the two older children are inseparable, as are the two younger children. All four children are close.

The children have each gathered a bunch of apricot pits that they take turns trying to throw into a terra cotta jar they've set in the clearing between the groves. Their friend Usem (meaning lightning, though he was named after his grandfather) bolts into the clearing from the fig orchard.

"Mule trains of Americans are arriving at the Kasbah Kandisha," he gasps, his hands on his knees.

"How can you tell?" Rahiq asks.

He shrugs. "They look like it."

Aghbalu laughs. "So they must be."

"I think so," Usem agrees.

"Let's go see," Asulil suggests.

Usem puts his arms over his head and takes a deep breath in preparation for more running. He raises his head to the sky and sees the figure of a young woman, leaning over a high ledge and peering down at them. "Look," he says. He points to her and waves. "There's one."

* * * *

It takes Aisha several minutes to descend from the dusty, rocky outcropping to the orchard below. It must be twenty degrees cooler here, she thinks, as she's met at the bottom by a fragrant gustlet of breeze. A boy of ten or so emerges from a smaller, wilder path than the one she's on, holding what looks like one delicious-looking glass of pink grapefruit juice.

"Ayyuz!" he says, and hands her the glass. It's ice cold.

The condensation tempts her to lick it.

"Ayyuz!" she echoes without hesitating, and takes a big swig of the juice. It's not grapefruit, but it's sweet and thirst-quenching. She finishes it off in a giant gulp. Meanwhile the other children she saw from her aerie have gathered around her. They giggle and wave and gently push each other at her. She waves at them all.

"Hello."

"Hello."

"My name is Aisha." She points at herself. "Aisha. What are yours?" The children whisper at each other and laugh out loud when the one who gave her the juice pretends to spit. Aisha is startled by the boy's pantomime, and the reaction it gets from the other children. Just this morning she'd gotten a similar greeting from a man she met while walking along the main road, but that man looked genuinely alarmed when she told him her name, and he spat for real. She stops smiling and looks curiously at the boy, who takes a tiny step backwards.

"Why did you just spit like that?" He stares at her, smiling but not as widely as before, then turns and says something to the other children. Aisha doesn't understand a word of it. She tries again, this time smiling herself to let them know she's not unfriendly, just curious. She pretends to spit and asks, "why?" The boy continues to stare. Aisha tries a third time. She holds up a finger. "Aisha," she says. Then she spits. Then she holds her palms out like she's carrying a giant platter in her arms, smiles, and shakes her head. "Why?"

The children brighten with dawning comprehension.

"Yes," the younger girl says, pointing at Aisha. "Aisha,"

she says again, moving her finger from Aisha to the spot where she'd just descended from. "Aicha Qandisha," she says. "Devil... Devil woman."

"Devil woman?!" They nod eagerly, playfully. "Well!" Aisha gasps, pretending to be offended.

"Man," the older girl says, looking at Aisha with a sort of admiration, and pretending to spit. The children lead Aisha to the edge of an irrigation ditch. The oldest girl reaches down and runs her hand back and forth in the stream. "Aicha Qandisha."

"She's in the water?" The children all nod. Aisha stands up and points in the direction of the resort where she started out this morning, and where Avery is now. "Kasbah Kandisha?" she asks. The children nod again. "Aicha Qandisha," they repeat in unison, while the spitting boy points again to her spot up on the cliff.

Aisha grabs her canvas notebook and a pen from her bag to write that down. She sits cross-legged on the ground. She'll just jot down two or three general impressions of this orchard while she's at it, as well as anything else she might be able to glean from the children, in particular about the peculiar twin houses. But the children want to know what she's writing before she even knows herself. She's ready to cut her losses when the older girl gestures whether she may write something in the notebook. Aisha finds a blank page and hands the pen and notebook to the girl. The girl writes her own name of Rahiq, followed by four other names, pointing at their owners. She thumbs through the notebook. Aisha doesn't mind this at first, but when Rahiq writes: 'May I read?' she shakes her head.

"Oh, no. it's private," she explains, gently taking back the notebook. But after seeing the look on the girl's face, she decides to search for a compromise. With embarrassment surely showing on her own face, she reopens the journal and starts skimming.

page 1

Leaving L.A.
train rocking slowly through poor backyards
Pacific sunset is pink platinum. Will miss for sure.
Man must've boarded drunk, drinking something clear
   from water bottle, clearly not water:
—*what's your story kiddo?*
—*nothing much*
—*know what's just so good about trains?*
looking at me, n-o-d-d-i-n-g
-*it's so easy to start a conversation. Where you headed?*
   Where you coming from? See? All the way wherever…
   none of that fuggin… bullshit. My real namezzzRon. I
   got a couple hours till this here catches up with me.
(Swirling liquid in plastic cup)
—*So you know what I mean? So where you coming from?*
   You got a story, help me enjoy this little buzz uh mine?
zzzRon LV blackjack dealer, Civil War buff
Man sways with the train.
Gathers his name from the floor.
Says my real namezzzRon

The rest of the page is left blank. The blank space was its own private message. She'd put her notebook away as the train was approaching Primera. It was supposed to be a smoking stop. They wouldn't let anyone off the train, though, so she had to look through the window.

She wanted not to even look, but she ended up looking anyway. Sandy's last voice message told her not to worry if he wasn't there, which he wasn't that she could see. There was a delay at the station that she didn't think much of at the time. She was thinking about what might have happened to her dad. She didn't think much about the train stopping so abruptly just after they pulled out of the station, either. She'd taken Amtrak out to California from Arizona, so she knew that sudden stops—particularly while approaching or leaving a station—were no use paying attention to. Actually it was best not to, as they generally led to open-ended periods of not-moving. Likewise with the extra swaying; she never even noticed it.

page 4

Zzzron, to crazy guy(?) in wig, w/ rock in one hand, ukulele in the other:
—*What's with the rock, Alice?*
Crazy guy (Alice?) passes it to Zzzron, who passes it to me. Ordinary river rock with quartz flecks and a thin vein of gold:
—*Don't know, man.*
—*You don't know why you're carrying a rock?*
—*No.*
Zzzron gives A—long wet look. A—looks scared.
—*So long as you're not planning to brain nnnybody with it...*
—*I'm not.*
A—sits looking at the rock. A—looks familiar, but from where?
Zzzron, to me: This one over here...
Zzzron, to A-: You all right over there, kemosabe?

*A—says he's not sure. Says he's trying to straighten
something out in his head...*
Zzzron: Lemme help you out."
—All right.
—That there?
—Yeah?
—What you're holding?
—Yeah...
—It's a rock.
—Yeah.

The next page is missing. She'd torn it out and thrown it away. Along with some cringeworthy sentiments about Candy, it had contained an account of her first recognizing Avery when he took off the wig, and how she immediately pulled the paper from the magazine, checked his face against the one on the photocopied I.D., and saw that Avery Krizan lived in Primera. She'd also mentioned Sandy by name several times, and wrote down a couple of theories to explain Avery's presence on the train, one of which turned out to be very close to the truth.

page 5
*Zzzron's passed out. I ask A—what he was doing at the
station. He looks at me funny, says he was there to pick
up something else... but he picked up the rock instead.
Seems confused. In shock? Ticket lady wants to see his
ticket. A—super nervous. Zzzron wakes up, tries to
say he remembers A—boarding in Alhambra. I say
he must've lost his ticket when he got off in Primera.
Ticket lady breathes Zzzron's atmosphere, says cool it
or he'll be joining A—on the next platform. I tell her
A—'s my boyfriend, that we got on together in L.A.*

She says prove it. I say how about we just buy another ticket, and file a complaint when we get off in Tucson. She says we can be her guest. Zzzron asks her why we stopped the train in Primera. She shrugs. None of our business, I guess.
A—white as a ghost, has been since getting on.

page 6

>> lunar architecture & the interstate highway system:
A-: = one enormous structure!
his friend disappeared where we stopped.
Also tells me about not meeting man at station
I take A—to cafe car, show him papers
Not surprised (still in shock?)
2:24AM
Sunset Ltd, ?, AZ
A—quite the talker once he gets going.
Says has nowhere to go, doesn't know what/where. lost
    laptop, phone in apt. fire
Talk about things in common (L.A.)
similar but different…
underachievement ?? traps?
A—doesn't care about the $$(?!) Jokes we should spend
    together, like outlaws. Travel around and give away to
    poor. Sounds tempting
who decides who's poor? Does poor = cool?
A—'s self-absorbed / spacy combo could get annoying.

page 7

Tucson AZ, 6AM
dawn
metallic mist floating over pale AZ sage
Headline of Daily Star found in parlor car: Earthquake
    Rattles Windows and Nerves over much of the Inland

Empire... some damage to older brick structures... several minor injuries reported...'
>> 8:45pm, as we were pulling out of the Primera station. Didn't notice. Another L.A. experience missed. 5.2 on the Richter scale, epicenter near Cajon Pass. Opened old artesian wells, with reports of water flowing in Mexican-era irrigation ditches 1st time in over a century.
A—They're calling it the Devil's Punchbowl Quake. Logo's next.
A—wandering around the station, looking for a secret a hobo told him about (?)
A—on another trip. Whiny but ok, harmless.

page 8

A—says is serious about traveling idea.
we got as much right to $$ as anyone, maybe do something cool?
— We?
— You found it.
— That's pretty weak logic.
— I know. Well who should get it then?
— Send back?
— There's some interesting stuff in these docs. Not so sure it's in x's best interest for me to come clean.
— Not following
— If my hunch is correct, x has their own reasons for keeping this 'in house'. But they'll get to S—soon, if they haven't already.
—Why?
The phone call he made to x
— You don't know S—.
— Fine. But let's say everybody's got a little something to

hide. If I were a big insurance company with a little
 something to hide, I'd make sure some charges get filed
 somewhere, so some gag orders can get put in place,
 maybe.
— But what have they got to hide?
Tempting but how crazy would I have to be? A—is a
 preener. Soft, as Sandy would say. Could get annoying.
 But harmless. I'm tempted. idk...
8:30AM
I must be crazy.
This is where I'm supposed to rent a car and make my way
 up to Laveen.
Instead I'm about to leave the station on foot.

 The first thing they agreed to do together that morning in Tucson was get a decent breakfast and some coffee. During the walk from the station, Aisha pointed out points of interest or places she'd known, and Avery asked touristy questions about them. They kept more serious thoughts to themselves. They settled on a diner near the university, called Desperado's. Avery ordered the Pancho Villa and she got the Black Bart. That neither was looking for apocalyptic blazes of glory was firmly established from the get-go. Aisha's voice message to her mother made it sound like she was just taking a little road trip with a friend before coming home. She told her mom not to worry. She also told her mom to tell Sandy not to worry; that she'd met his guy for him.

 They agreed that the 'real money' in fake Avery's account should stay put, as it would be stupid for them to get too involved with that whole mess. Avery was already intent on blowing the fifteen thousand, though. He said it was the right thing to do. Privately, Aisha wasn't so sure he wasn't being a bit delusional on that count. Either way, he was determined, and she couldn't exactly ask for the money back. After all, it was more his than hers. Deep down she knew her choice was either to go with him or end up turning him in. There was no way she was going to be able to lie to the cops. She was a terrible liar. They'd probably get her to tell about Sandy too. She didn't see any other way things could play out. Avery also insisted on keeping her name clean no matter what, so she could go back to school when the spring semester started. Her gut told her to trust him. They agreed not to tell anyone anything. But neither would they hide their identities. Why should they? They agreed on a simple plan. With frugality as their watchword, they'd take turns picking destinations, starting with Avery, since his was personal, directly related to the money, and relatively (but not too) local. They got separate hotel rooms that night, and first thing the next morning they bought a dry-rotten Toyota Corona with a leaky head gasket and no back seat for two hundred dollars cash, no questions asked, filled its tank with gas, loaded its trunk with quarts of oil and its back seat with rolls of 35mm film and headed for Serene, Colorado, the site of the Columbine Mine Massacre of 1927. Avery was hoping to find the copy of *Two Years Before The Mast* that his grandfather had illustrated so long ago. But when they got to where the town of Serene was supposed to be, all they found was a county landfill. Not only was there no book, there was no library. The entire town had been buried. They might have given up right then and there had a scavenger they met not suggested they try the municipal library in nearby Trinidad, New Mexico. It wasn't there either, so they spent half a day in that library's records room, zeroing in at last on a defunct Army barracks a day's drive to the west, where several local books had been sent during the early days of the Cold War. They had no luck finding the book, but some crude directions scrawled into the sand on the old mess hall floor, along with some very lucky guesses of their own, led them the next day to the hidden town of Wovoka.

Wovoka is not found on any map (at least none outside of that mess hall, and they've looked at plenty). It can only be 'circled in on', with the primitive dirt road that leads to it constantly splitting off into false curls and circle-backs as it spirals through the Iron Hills. But they guessed right, every time. The Corona emitted a strange blue smoke for the last few miles and seized up immediately upon their mid-afternoon arrival in the dead center of town. They lurched to a stop and found themselves surrounded by a small group of buildings, all fronted in thin tin sheets stamped to look like masonry.

"Uh oh."

"Well. I think that's that."

"I feel like we're being frisked," Avery said as they exited the vehicle. Every window in town seemed to face them, and the windows looked like eyes.

"Yeah."

"Does your phone work yet?"

Aisha checked. "Still no signal."

"Where is everyone?"

There wasn't a soul in sight, other than a few dirty brown horses grazing on top of a flat hill behind the town. "Yeah."

"Doesn't look like a ghost town."

"Not... exactly."

"No cars."

"I noticed that too."

They walked up to the largest building in town. Heavy iron storm shutters covered its doorway and lower windows. It was locked. So was the next building.

"There must be more to it that we're not seeing here," Aisha said.

"Where?" A landscape of olive-drab scrubland and squat, barren hills spread out in every direction. A storm was condensing in the sky behind the flat hill. "This place is literally a dead end."

"Good thing we bought those tortillas back in Beclabito..."

"No. There's got to be somebody around here. It's too well maintained."

"Let's see what's over that hill."

"Couldn't hurt."

They walked around the last building and checked its back door. It was locked. They started to climb the hill, the top of which was about level with the highest rooftop in town. The dirty brown horses stopped eating to watch them approach.

"I think those horses are tame," Avery whispered.

"Of course they are. What did you think they were?"

"I don't know."

"See their leads?"

"Those ropes, you mean?"

"Yeah. It's strange...."

They'd reached the top of the hill. There was a gentle but steady breeze blowing, not strong so much as big.

"Um…" The horses had gathered around to face them. Aisha walked up to one of the horses and scratched it behind its ear. Its neighbor nuzzled her shoulder, and she petted its cheek. Avery tried to do the same thing to the big horse in front of him but it turned away… and rather arrogantly, it seemed to him. He was ready to climb back down the hill. "You see anything?"

"It's not normal for their leads to be on them when no one's around," Aisha said, to the horses as much as to Avery. "They could get injured that way."

"I should have guessed you'd know your way around horses."

"A little bit. I take it you don't?"

"I've never been on a horse in my life."

She looked at him like he was from outer space. "Seriously?"

"Heighhh," he whinnied. "I grew up in civilizeighhhtion."

"Hey, you should use that voice. It's less whiny than your regular one."

"Nice."

The big horse pushed by Avery to get its ear scratched by Aisha. She talked to them all in a voice he hadn't heard her use before, while he saw what he thought might be a tiny building way off in the distance. But there were no other signs of humanity in that direction. He turned around. Dark grey was spreading in the sky like ink water on wet paper. It cast a huge shadow over the far hills. "Shit." Avery looked at Aisha with worry on his face. "I don't know…"

"Hey, do we have any apples left?" she asked.

"A couple. Why?"

"Come on."

"You're hungry?"

"Not for us, silly."

"Shouldn't we save those, Aisha? I mean, we might be here for a while. We should probably find some water. And a telephone." He looked down at the town. "No phone lines. Shit…"

"Trust me."

Less than an hour later they were standing on the side of highway 191. The same crow's-flight distance had taken them twice as long by car. But as soon as they reached the highway the horses refused to go further. "You did pretty good, considering," Aisha told Avery when he slid off the big horse with a grunt and a curse. Riding bareback isn't easy for anyone, she said, when he complained about how much his thighs hurt; but when he tried to complain about his horse's attitude, she said he was lucky he didn't get tossed, the way he was holding onto it. They still had no car, and the sun was going down. The horses had already disappeared back into the hills. A long time went by. The sun set. A heavy rain started suddenly, drenched them, then stopped. The moon came out briefly. Another storm drifted by, drenching them again. Just after the second downpour stopped, a set of big, high-set headlights crept around the long bend. A big truck slowed and stopped. The driver reached over and opened the passenger-side door. The passenger seat was full of bags, maps and road junk, so they climbed in the crew cab. The driver asked what they were doing out there, and where they were headed. They told him they were ghost town tourists, and their car broke down in the hills.

"You didn't find it, did you?" Without asking what he meant by the question, they told him no. "Good." He told them there was a sort of a ghost town a couple of hours away. Used to be a library there, he added, without them asking. Later on during the drive he told them he almost didn't pick them up. "For fear you was skinwalkers. That's why they changed the highway name. This here used to be Route 666, you know." They asked him what a skinwalker was. "You don't even want to know," he said, before telling them about some local Navajo medicine men who were hung for witchcraft around here back in the nineteen teens. "It's them bastards, if it's anybody. All's I know is I'm glad you two come along. See, if you got a empty seat they like to ride—." The driver was silent for the rest of the ride.

A stormy, awkward four hours later they were unceremoniously dropped off in tiny Jicarilla, located at the junction of the old highway 191, an even older stagecoach road, and a dead rail line. All that was left of the place was a derelict post office and the front half of an old general store. The post office was barely larger than a ticket booth. There was a man bent over a desk in the tiny room. He waved them over and introduced himself as the former postmaster (he comes to work every day, he told them, and splits his time between keeping the town's forgotten records, taking apart the old general store brick by brick, and selling the bricks to a rich Californian who comes by every so often). In the former postmaster's desk drawer was a written record of where every one of the library's books went when the town died (he knew they'd come in handy some day, he said). It was there, in the faded ink of a nearly forgotten past, that they found the small handwritten receipt that led them to Sessy Lu.

page 18

St. George, UT
Night scenery = 95% darkness.

You pass something that's lit—a refinery or a factory or the porch of an isolated farmhouse; and you see every bolt thread and gravel pebble and paint peel. Like islands in time, for that instant those random groupings become your whole world. It's as if you've worked thirty years in this refinery, or you've raised a family in that farmhouse. Time and memory emanates from these big, solitary lanterns. You can smell it through the glass. And just like that it's gone forever, except for a dim afterimage imposed on the blackness until the next beacon appears.

Dawn
Colfax Park
CO

Some days are also like lanterns.

Shedding grey veils, greenblack shrouds, revealing red roses, bluepink, orangepink flecked with bits of night. Constant, thinnest washes of light. The things drink it in. Absorb absorb, absorb absorb. A shadowless coming-on. Hard to hold. Shadows forming like pools, indistinct. The shadows *are the last part, now too much to be absorbed by the things. Shadows forming like reservoirs, not absences but abundances.*

When the sun rises that red you thought was red ignites. The greens become incandescent gems. The world glows like a kiln and the sun's a laughing bellows. There's your color!

Even in the middle of nowhere, Paco's disappearance left Avery with a shock and determination that still echoed in him. So far there hadn't been much for him to be encouraged by on the hidden society front. They'd gone out of their way to search rail yards and train stations for signs of its existence, but it wasn't the sort of subject one easily brings up in the course of casual conversation. Avery did get word of two fairly-reliable Paco sightings: one from a couple of hoboes he talked to in the Superstition Hills, and another from a truck stop cashier in the Sangre de Cristos. The cashier also said she saw someone who fit Mara's description. She looked very ill, she said. While he kept on his lookout, Aisha took pictures. Sometimes Avery entertained the probability that Mara was braiding a yarn in that bathroom, along with her hair. But even if she made it up, he'd say, he knew she was telling him something true. Being on the run was good exercise, and beat the hell out of dissolving into his hometown.

Aisha thought about Candy all the time, but out of consideration for Avery she tried not to imagine her out here instead of him. She considered him a real friend by then. She also knew that he was a little confused about the nature of their relationship. Sometimes his compliments (he'd suddenly be blown away by her quiet capability, or her personal charm, or the smell of her hair...) had timid little feelers on them. But on some level he received and registered her signals, because he never pushed it. Since the moment they met, they had encountered a remarkable succession of people together, many of whom had been peculiarly willing to share their stories. Avery started writing the encounters down on the backs of the photocopies, but they read like fossilized events, he said, so he decided he was better off letting the stories accrue and commingle in his head for a while without him getting in the way. But he did maintain a list of the remarkable assortment of books, pamphlets, manuscripts, etc. they encountered, along with brief descriptions of their custodians. There was the hotel clerk in Globe who, before a single word was spoken, pulled what he swore was Hemingway's own heavily notated copy of *Absalom! Absalom!* from the magazine rack right next to the front door; and the roadkill collector, also named Avery K., whom they happened upon while he was washing death-smell from his flatbed Thing at a rest stop outside of Silver City, who showed them a large, duct tape-fortified pad of graph paper that he kept behind the driver's seat, every other page of which was crammed with wild diagrams and illustrations, bacterial microprint and bizarre script combinations, that the man suspected just might be the key to his mother's 1985 coffee table edition of the Voynich manuscript, most likely decoded by himself during one particularly eye-opening ephedrine hayride back in the nineties, but that even he "cain't make head nor tail of nuh more..."; and Nancy the octogenarian carhop at the Sonic Burger off the old Spanish Trail, who showed off a napkin soaked with the blurred, splotchy same-ink autographs of S. Kubrick, T. R. Pynchon, and J. A. McCone that she claimed had been crumpled in her purse since 1964; and Joaquin, who not only claimed that he could recite *El Ingenioso Hidalgo don Quijote de la Mancha* in its entirety, in Navajo (that was at least partly true), but who also insisted on having been told the story by an old drifter who claimed that it originated with his own Native American ancestors, and had been passed down orally for centuries before being stolen, locked in an empty chest marked 'Oro', stowed in the hold of the slave ship *Madre de Deus*, sailed across the Atlantic to Portugal, loaded onto a wine cart, walked to Spain, ingested by the Spanish imagination and further distilled through the mind of Cervantes before returning to America as the quest for El Dorado. There was Doctor Border, whose outwardly-tidy shotgun shack contained floor-to-ceiling shelves of manifestos, ranging from the celebrated to the wildly obscure, which he dreamed of one day synthesizing into a single, one-stop online metafesto, though he was being kept busy enough for the time being with his more scope-limited MyManifesto website ('Mix 'n' Match!'), which had been getting some serious traffic lately.

But it was Sessy who cast the largest shadow on those days.

Echo 'Sessy' Lu was a semi-retired hedge fund manager. She was raised in a series of Hong Kong high-rises each higher than the last, and had an Oxford education. Her current residence was a cluster of nine squat stucco tee pees off Route 40, near where the town of Tucumcari dissolves into the high plains.

Avery and Aisha arrived in Tucumcari just before dusk, on a charter bus of sketchy Mormons headed for the Texas Riviera, and in the alleged aftermath of a shootout between the justice of the peace and a local dipsomaniac. According to the officer who met them all there at the gas slash bus station, the ruckus had just took place not fifteen minutes before they arrived, and right just about where they was standing. The officer—who evidently preferred apprehensive strangers to apprehending locals—kidded-them-not about the odious miscreant-at-large like he was telling a ghost story. After a short walking tour of Tucumcari's yard dogs and biker bars, they headed east, and reached Sessy's well after dark.

The ex-postmaster in Jicarillo had told them that he'd email ahead on their behalf, but they had no way of knowing whether he followed through on his promise or not. Half-prepared to be chased back into town by a survivalist wildwoman, they approached carefully. But the postmaster had kept his word, and Sessy proved to be nothing if not welcoming. She'd even prepared a special spread of medicinal teas and finger foods for their arrival. She made quite a first impression. Though she was only in her early fifties, and otherwise quite young-looking, her exquisitely bobbed hair was completely, shockingly white. Her outfit (of which she has many, she said, all identical) consisted of a snow white cotton-waffle robe worn high-cinched like a kimono, and white hotel slippers.

"I am so pleased to see you!" she greeted them, like they were old friends. "I have prepared a nice room for you." She looked at Aisha. "Two rooms."

The teepees were originally built as a Route 66 courtyard motel, she explained as she showed them their quarters, but their layout held exquisite feng-shui. She gave them some time and space to relax while she set the teas and edibles on a small table beneath a small wisteria arbor. A few minutes later, while Aisha and Avery washed up at the outdoor sink, Sessy disappeared into another teepee. She emerged a couple minutes later with a large hide-bound book in her hands.

"It was the illustrations that first drew me to your volume," she explained through a bite of khaki-colored madeleine, after carefully placing the book on the table, "such depth for a child's hand! After hearing your story, I understand just that little bit more. Thank you so much!"

Avery pointed at the book. The cover was old and blank; the title had been worn away long ago.

"May I see it?"

"Yes of course!" Holding the cover with her fingertips, Sessy balanced the book on its spine. She spread her fingers and it flopped open more or less to the middle. "Only you mustn't touch it."

"Why? Is it fragile? Oh—" Avery frowned. The book was written in Chinese.

"Your volume is waiting for you in your room. Whether you take it with you or leave it here is up to you. This is another volume, and another story entirely. It is ancient, but not fragile. I thought you might like to see it."

"If it's so sturdy," the madeleine buzz effecting in Aisha an odd bluntness that came across almost as rudeness, though she hardly meant it that way, "then why can't we touch it?"

"This is a handwritten copy of Fù Zé Rèn. It predates the first official printing by several years, and is likely the only copy to contain chapter fifty-three."

"So...?"

"So there is a legend referred to in the preface of the 1675 printing. According to the legend, the book's original author, who remains to this day anonymous, presented a copy of his work to a rich and powerful man, who had murdered the author's father many years earlier. Just as the story unfolding from the book's pages gradually exposed its reader as a murderer, the author had also added to each leaf a bit of a kind of poison that accumulates in the nervous system, so by the time the rich and powerful man finished the damning novel, he was on his own deathbed."

"Wow."

"And you think this is that book?"

Sessy ran a long finger through her hair. "I've read chapter fifty-three."

The next morning, while relaxing inside the mirror-lined Eternity Teepee, Aisha and Avery determined to find out what a 'real' Mika Krizan might be worth. Using Sessy's laptop and wi-fi, they were not surprised to discover (confirm, really) that it was quite a bit more than fifteen thousand dollars. Avery reread the policy language in his bogus claim and noticed that some of it had been lifted directly from the attached umbrella policy belonging to a fraternal organization called the Knights of Califa, which was apparently the legal owner of the building. That policy was also handled by Sandy, who'd kept a copy of it in the bag with the money and rest of the papers. There were some interesting details in those documents. The Knights of Califa had a Valuable Items policy attached to their blanket coverage. There was a long list of items listed on that policy, from old ceremonial objects like ebony thrones and gold candelabras, to decidedly nonceremonial objects, like a 1966 Shelby Cobra and a matching set of Mark Rothko paintings. Avery had sure never seen any objects like those anywhere near the building. He also discovered that he was not supposed to even be living there. There was a clause in the policy stipulating that the building was not to be used as a rental property. There was an exception made for the building manager, Kyle Bland. That must be Kyle, the tweaker who Avery had assumed was the cause of the fire. He must have been running his own landlord business on the sly. So that's why Avery paid his rent in cash!

They did a quick Google search and learned that a Junior Sandoval had recently been arrested in Arizona on unnamed charges. There was no mention of accomplices. They did a search of their own names and came up clean. Avery looked up fake Avery's bank account. The money was still there. They concluded that it would not only be stupid but unjust of them to throw themselves at the mercy of Superior's leagues of attorneys. They would just be feeding themselves to the wolves. Playing wronged innocents would only be adding insult to inevitable injury.

That's when they decided to blow the whole situation sky high, by raiding the bank account money and tossing it to the four winds. Superior's lawyers could spend all the time and insurance company cash they wanted to in sorting it out, while Avery and Aisha would just keep doing what they had been doing. While they would have liked to pick a worthy charity or something, they decided that that would be too personal; the less they personally knew about who benefitted, they determined, the less they themselves would benefit, and the less chance anyone innocent could be held accountable. They were of one mind in suspecting that any innocence of their own wouldn't be tolerated anyway, but more likely would get rolled into the tons of complicity the situation already contained. Of course there was always the possibility that the agency would find their solution equitable enough, and leave it at that. You never know, they told themselves. It would make some sense.

"I feel so American," Aisha said, while surfing the internet for recipients of the ill-gotten money.

"What do you mean?"

"Power tripping with money like this. We're like angel investors."

"Don't enjoy it too much."

"Hey, look at this."

"What do you got?"

"These guys in Oakland are selling tickets for what looks like some burning-man-type-thing in Morocco. 'Only' a hundred and forty-eight tickets are still available, it says."

"Let me see."

"I say we buy them all."

"Really? That's a lot of money."

"That's the idea, isn't it?"

"What would we do with all those tickets?"

"We can just give them away. What's more random

than that?"

"I don't know. How would we actually get them?"

"Maybe can have them Fed-Exed here. Then we could mail some from the road, leave some for strangers to find…"

"Hmm…"

"It couldn't hurt to ask."

They explained their situation to their hostess, who was only too happy to engage in a spot of monkeywrenching, as long as no one got hurt. She asked where they were headed. Aisha had already chosen New York City as their next and quite possibly last destination, so rather than have them wait around in Tucumcari, Sessy got a hold of a former client at a seed bank in Kansas City and asked her to accept a package (containing nothing illegal, she assured her), to be picked up by her friends Avery and Aisha, who would be coming through on their way east. She even dealt with the bank to confirm the transaction.

page 19

Maybe it doesn't stop. Maybe you have to hold on the whole time.

Sessy says acquaintances are like short spells, and full of aware, *which is a Japanese word meaning 'sighing for love of the transience of things'. She says we can never meet again as we are. This meeting, the way we are and the way we are together now is made of a rare element, and that is affirmation.*

"Leave part of yourselves here, as you are, to live among these books," Sessy told them just before they left. "You'll be safe here. And go too, and change, and take us all with you to those places you'll go, so we can change too. You will go and you will stay. We look forward to re-making your acquaintance."

They left the book in Sessy's possession.

* * * *

Aisha folds the notebook to the last page and hands it to Rahiq. She'd more or less stopped writing when they bought the film, but still she thought she'd written more. Bouncing up and down and grinning between words, the girl reads out loud while Aisha winces with embarrassment. The girl pronounces the words slowly and with eager determination, making it clear that she enjoys this type of challenge. From time to time she makes an Amazigh aside to the other children. When she reaches a word or phrase she doesn't understand, she slows down her enunciation and shrugs.

When the girl asks what Aisha is doing wandering around on cliffs in Morocco, she tells them about the gathering that she and Avery are planning to attend the next day. Aisha asks about the twin houses, and about the children's hobbies. They show her the game they've been playing, and she joins in for a few tosses before returning to the Kasbah Kandisha.

7

Avery saved three small souvenirs from those strange first days on the road with Aisha. They are in his pockets as he talks to the interviewer.

There's the stem cap, acquired when he and she were walking up that long incline into Tuba City and that tire came bouncing over the rise, with nothing else around it for miles, and came to rest like a hula hoop at their feet. They moved the tire to the side of the red road, and Avery pocketed the cap.

There's the fork. What a day that was. Another empty stretch of road, pine country, high elevation. They had come to an unmarked fork in the road that morning, which led Aisha to share something her dad used to say: "I came to a fork in the road, and I took it." Later on that same day, while walking on a plank sidewalk in Silver City's charming little downtown, he spotted a little silver fork lying smack dab in the middle of the road, and took it.

The third trinket is a little diamond-shaped piece of popsicle stick. It was late-afternoon in Durango. The sidewalk and most of the street was already in shadow, but late sun still gold-leafed the trees on the other side.

As they passed one white-blossomed bush, a tiny white butterfly flew away from it like a petal blown from its parent flower. The sun was hitting the blossom just right. The flower was as white and bright as anything he'd ever seen, until the sun hit the butterfly, and it became, for an instant, even brighter than the flower. Avery was inspired to muse out loud about butterflies and flowers being tertiary aspects of another… but Aisha shook her head: not this time.

They were in front of a coin-op laundromat. Strands of music reached them from the wall-mounted speakers inside. Aisha sat down on the curb. "I love this song," she said. It was the old Blondie song, *I'm Always Touched (By Your Presence Dear)*. Avery sat down next to her. Avery let his eyes relax in the breeze-tossed branches and their shifting shadows, and they listened in silence. Almost abruptly, Aisha slid toward Avery and put her arm around him. They'd embraced before, but always with a sort of clumsy ironic barrier between them. There was no irony on this occasion. Avery turned to her, wondering what he should do next. "Don't do anything." She pulled his arm over her shoulder and laid her head on his chest, and they sat like that until well after the song ended, both of them watching the big blue shadow slowly drive the mountain sunlight up the laundromat's whitewashed wall. When they finally got up to leave, Avery found the popsicle stick nib laying next to a tannish streak on the curb where he'd been sitting, where some kid must've been grinding it to a point.

Avery slaps his pockets with his palms. "What time is it?" Outside, the guests who'd arrived red-faced and dusty during the afternoon are reemerging, cleaner and darker-attired, for pre-dinner drinks. There aren't as many as there were earlier, but their conversation is louder. Avery can make out the sounds of buss carts shuttling to restaurants, lounges and bars & grills. He had intended to end the story at the point when he met Aisha, but time's been flying faster and faster and the show, which he's managed not to think about for a few hours, is suddenly looming large.

"But what happened to the money?" The interviewer seems somewhat taken aback. "And your friend; what happened to him? Did you never find out where he went?"

"I never saw him again, but I heard stories that he'd moved up to the mountains. Living off the land."

"That would be fitting. And you, you came out to Morocco."

"Yeah, it seemed like the right thing to do. We're all motivated by our own..."

"Helloo?" Aisha cranes her neck around the doorway to the meeting room, air-knock morphing into a wave when she sees Avery.

"There you are!" Avery chirps. "Perfect timing." He motions for her to join them. "I'd like you to meet my partner in crime," he says to the interviewer, who looks like he's just hit a traffic jam in the middle of nowhere. "Aisha, this is my intrepid interviewer, uh... I'm sorry..."

"Call me Al." Al stands up, sending the tape recorder skittering in a tense slo-mo across the room. All three of them wince as the machine clatters brittly to rest at Aisha's feet. She picks it up and shuts its sprung cassette door.

"How do you do." Aisha recognizes the look on his face. She's made it herself, she bets (like when that guy in front of her in line let like ten of his late buddies cut in front of him, and gave her that 'oopsie' look…).

"Fine, thanks," she replies just as graciously. "Here you are." They perform a half-handshake, half-'here's your tape recorder back/thanks' greeting. She gives Avery a querying thumbs-up, raises her eyebrows and looks up at him with the same question. "How did it go?"

"Pretty good, I'd say." Avery glances at Al, whose name he'd failed to remember all afternoon. It's kind of ironic; by trying to be evasive, he ended up only telling Al the stuff he was worried about bringing up in the first place. "I was about to tell Al about how we met, but we ran out of time. I'm not sure if he got what he was looking for, but I couldn't have asked for a more patient interviewer."

Al nods nonchalantly, lifting the camera to his eye and pointing it at the two of them. He doesn't shoot. "I asked you for a story. You gave me one. Whether or not it will work is… another story.…"

"I thought it was fun. It's not often I get to talk about myself—" He looks sheepishly at Aisha, who rolls her eyes at Al, "—in that much detail."

"It was a long afternoon."

"I warned you."

"Yes, you warned me."

"Well thanks, doc," Avery jokes, sort of. "I feel much better now."

"My pleasure," Al frowns.

"If you've got nothing better to do, I go on at eight-thirty." Avery puts out his hand but Al doesn't take it right away. "Or not."

"Perhaps," Al replies with a wink, catching Avery's hand on its way down.

Aisha tugs Avery's sleeve. "Oh, hey! Guess what? You remember Peregrine?"

"Nahhturally. The Eeaarll." He starts to tell Al about Perry, but changes his mind. Enough long stories for one day.

"He's here."

"What do you mean?"

"I just saw him, just now, in the lobby."

"Nuh uh!"

"Yuh huh. And he's wearing a full-on safari suit. My walk went well, by the way. I found the spot. I met some local kids. They might be going to the thing tomorrow, with their parents—" They both look at Al, who appears not to be listening.

"What time is it?" Avery asks himself out loud again, craning his neck to check for clocks outside the room, "I'd better go change my shirt…"

* * * *

Only a few miles from the Kasbah Kandisha as the crow flies, but much farther in other ways, NZYME stares at a makeshift sundial. Why's it say that? he wonders. Ohh… because that's not the sun, remember? Man…

…Why's it not—? Oh yeah… not the sun… remember? Man…

NZYME's brain's a quasar; it blinks in sync with his pulse. *Jhoomp.* Thoughts come *jhoomping* around the black spherewithinosphere, and when they do NZYME feels he should be able to reverse-engineer his present condition...; spin the quasar in reverse, to figure out just what's in a Dutch Dewdrop, but *jhoomp.* Seems like for*ever* it's been spinning. If it was yesterday, or an hour ago even, he'd be *jhoomp.* But he could've just now taken it for all he knows, in which case he's looking at here it comes... *jhoomp.* Forget it. Too many variables at this point. But as long as it's not tomorrow already, he's good.

* * * *

It's 8:29. Avery stares himself down in the mirror, buttons the top button of his jacket, pins a paper tulip to its lapel, and hitches up his high-waters. Keep your feet together, he coaches himself. Sashay your hips, roll your eyes around in your head like you're swooning. Remember, it helps to imagine a Marx Brothers coquette twittering on a settee. Remember to breathe. Play the tunes. Don't stop in the middle of a song, no matter what.

Last night, Avery watched some old TV footage on the internet to get a sense of Tiny Tim's schtick. But the more he tried to imitate it, the more he preferred his original approach of just winging it. He never worried about his falsetto before comparing it to Tiny's trills, but he does now. Still, he guesses he'd rather careen than stall. Maybe he'll do both. He didn't even know he'd be playing until yesterday, when the concierge stopped him in the lobby and asked about his ukulele. The Kasbah Kandisha is expecting unseasonably robust activity this weekend, the concierge apologetically confided, and it seems they've found themselves somewhat shy of entertainment offerings. Would he possibly consider performing, perhaps in exchange for complimentary accommodations? He waffled at first, but agreed at last. It was a well-paying gig, after all. Late that night, when Al called his room to request a special biographical portrait, he wondered briefly whether it might be a bad idea, but decided he was just being paranoid, and agreed to that as well. "I'm no resort act," he warned the concierge and Al both. And he wasn't lying. And now, in less than a minute he's going to step onto a platform specifically designed to take and hold the attention of strangers, put his blown-out creeper soles together and start falsetto-ing. A deal's a deal. He'll do his best. Like they say, let the chips fall where they may.

Avery steps out of the dressing room slash employee lounge, walks through the kitchen, squeezes past the line for the bathroom and climbs onto the stage. There's a spotlight already waiting for him, so he heads for it. He feels dense; his mind is so blank he's surprised he can walk. He hoists his toy ukulele to lung level and stares out into a huge smoky shadow. The spotlight he's centered in sucks the rest of the light from the room. He's in the blur circle now. He looks straight into the light. It's a train headlamp (blinding, spellbinding…). His eyes swim in and out of it, and into and out of the blackness beyond it, exaggerating both uncompromising extremes. He launches into 'Tip Toe…' and next thing he knows he's already at the end of 'Livin' in the Sunlight', having in the enchanted thirty-minute meantime slipped into a vocal polyphony that he never knew *existed* (he sang "Livin'…" to the main melody and "Lovin'…"

to a countermelody, simultaneously). The house lights come on and he returns to his body. He can finally see the room. There are tables and chairs directly in front of and slightly below the stage, and a small, elevated dining area in the back of the room. A stylized mural of dunes, palm trees and camels covers the walls. Most of the chairs have people in them. He stands there staring out at the people, feeling at first like he's just traveled a great distance very fast, and then like an eternity has passed since he last moved. The crowd is presenting him with a solidly confused round of applause. The first faces he sees look as out of it as he feels, and their hands stop moving as soon as their eyes make contact with his. It's a respectable ovation, but eventually it dies away, and people start turning their attention to other things. Many people leave their seats for the nearby bar, and most of the others pick up menus or return to eating, but one guest hasn't stopped clapping. Avery holds up his hand and peers to the back of the room to see who it is. It's Al, the interviewer. Avery is surprised at how happy he is that Al seems pleased (and equally surprised that Al seems pleased, after the way the interview ended). Al is seated between a lady in a grey business suit who glares at his cupped, clapping hands like she'd like to shove them somewhere bad, and a big chunky blonde man with a flushed forehead and laboring sport coat buttons that strike Avery as oddly cartoon-diaperish. More oddly, it's not an entirely negative impression. Avery does a doubletake, and realizes that it's the same couple he saw during the afternoon rush. They looked vaguely familiar then, and they do still now. He strongly suspects that they're American. They don't look like tourists, even though the blonde guy keeps winking at two women in headscarves who seem to be actively ignoring him. Avery scans the room some more as the rest of his senses return to him like air into a vacuum. There are a few drunks arguing by the bar, and an elegant-looking old guy and a much younger woman in the far corner by the restaurant proper. Where's Aisha? There she is, talking to a—robot? No, that's Wieland's old box camera—Wieland? So those arms gesturing wildly and too close to the cocktail chef must be Uwe! Avery leaves the stage and walks over to Aisha and Wieland, wearing a pleased "well *that* just happened" look on his face.

"Hey!" Wieland greets him with a high-five.

"No way! You guys made it!"

"That was super, man! Really swag."

"Really? You could hear okay? Because—"

"We could hear everything. I took several photos."

"Oh yeah? Because it was hard to tell. There are no monitors up there, so I couldn't hear a—"

"Avery, I must tell you; the most dreadful thing about shooting live performances is this being asked immediately afterward to articulate my critical opinion as a reass—"

"Say no more."

"We will talk later, I'm sure."

"Don't sweat it. I just saw Uwe over by the bar. Is... Karina here?"

"She and Zafer stayed below to explore the area. This place we are going, have you seen it yet?"

"Not yet. It's a drive from here."

"Ah. Speaking of driving, you will never guess who we met on the road."

Avery holds up a finger. "I'm sorry, man. Can you excuse me for just a second?" He wants to make sure to say hi to Al and his company (ostensibly to fish for compliments, mostly to see who those other two are) before they split. But they're no longer in their seats, and he doesn't spot them in the bar, where a small crowd has gathered around Uwe, who is either holding court or making a scene. Aisha nods at him and looks toward the door. "I'm sorry," he repeats, turning back to face Wieland, "I need to go talk to somebody. It'll just take a second."

"We will talk in the morning."

"I'll be right—"

"No, no," Wieland insists; "it's good. You go talk to your fanatics, man. In this overpriced *drecksloch* I can no longer breathe. Uwe feels the same way, I'm sure, but he can be forgetful sometimes. Besides, it will take us almost one hour to walk back to the van. This is why I brought only the Zeiss."

"But how did you—"

"This Casbah Manifestation is not even mentioned in local tourism sites, you know. But there was a listing for 'Tiny Tim interpreter'. How many could there be? When we saw the photo, we knew."

"Photo?"

"But you must go." Wieland pats Avery on the shoulder. "We will see you two later." He gives them high-fives. "*Fröhlich und früh!* We will find you. Bye bye."

Avery and Aisha wander off in the direction of the bar, leaving Wieland focused on his camera.

"Hey, nice work tonight," Aisha says. She takes Avery's face in her hands and plants him a big friendly kiss.

"Well!"

"You looking forward to tomorrow?"

"Yeah, I guess. In a way, not. Why—"

"What a trip, huh?"

"Hmm? Yeah..." There's no sign of Al or the other two. "God, I got to say, though; that was so weird, what happened tonight."

"What?"

"My singing."

"Yeah, you were kind of great. I had no idea you could do that."

"That's the weird thing. Neither did I."

They check the bathrooms, the foyer and the smoking closet, the bar again, and the grill. Mutually satisfied that Al and his friends are no longer on the premises, they exit the Berber Room into the wide, overly bright perimeter hallway. Around the corner and just out of view is the 'exclusive retail experience', polished up and waiting for tomorrow's arrivals.

"So those people your interviewer was talking to..."

"Yeah? There's something—"

"Well, I didn't want to say anything in there, but I've met that guy before."

Avery stops in his tracks. "Nuh uh!"

"I'm serious. My—"

"I thought they looked familiar! So I was right. Where did we meet them?"

"You weren't there."

"What do you mean? I *know*—"

"He was at a poker game my dad hosted on the night I arrived from Arizona."

Avery shakes his head. "Nice."

"I know, right? I remember showing up and thinking, whoa, what have I myself gotten into? There were all these middle-aged men there, and that guy was one of them. I remember him because he busted first, but hung out for a while to watch."

"Did you talk to him?"

"A little."

Avery rattles his head "I—I don't even—"

"I know."

"Your dad's not, like... connected, is he?"

"You mean, like, in the mob? I seriously doubt it. No, he's—I'm pretty sure they worked together at Superior Life."

Endlicher. That was how he answered the phone when Avery called that night. "Endlicher..." starting high and falling, like he was calling a dog. His was one of only a few pairs of tickets that weren't randomly addressed, or just left somewhere to be found by whomever. The two of them had just arrived in England and were in a brassy mood that day. It seemed like a good idea to let the agency know they weren't hiding. But they didn't think they would be here themselves then, much less that Endlicher would make the trip. But why do they look familiar to Avery? "He must have recognized you, right?"

"I couldn't tell for sure. Judging by the way he was looking at me, I'd say no. That lady he was with sure was giving me the stink-eye, though."

* * * *

Now Sandy can add his own name to the list of people he's suckered. If he had to get fucked, at least it took himself to do the job. And fucked he sure is. One thing has surprised him about that, though, it sure feels good to have the pressure off. They've made it as clear as possible that they'll go easy on him if he cooperates. His court-appointed attorney is tight with Superior's lead counsel, who's also tight with the lead prosecutor. As in, they're running the show together. They don't say squat to him directly. They just give him little crumbs and let him figure the rest out on his own. He takes it as a show of respect. In return, they don't got to tell him the definition of cooperate. He pleads guilty to one charge of embezzlement and they drop the fraud charges. Three years minimum security; he'll be out in two. No surprises. His lawyer treats it as established fact that he gambled away the money, and is saying shit like it would be best for all parties concerned if the case began and ended with him. Sandy knows a tipped hand when he sees one. So everybody knows everybody knows.

What he doesn't know is what the fuck is up with Ish. First, she has her mother tell him that she met his client and took care of things. Next thing he knows he's got

'Cuda Guzman from Fraud telling him she's gone off with fucking Avery Krizan! He didn't think she was even interested in men that way. He'd have laughed in 'Cuda's face if she hadn't showed him a picture of the two of them together on a fucking cruise ship, of all places! He's gone over it a zillion times. There's no way in hell she could have known him before that night.

But Ish's got a good honest head on her shoulders. He knows that in his bones. And knowing it helps him sleep at night. She's nothing like him in that department, thank the fucking Lord. Would she believe he never wanted her to get comfortable at his place in the first place? But what was he supposed to say? He was betting on her hating L.A., but she surprised him. He didn't expect her to basically move in with that Candy chick so quick, for one thing. What were the odds of that? Ish is a smart girl; maybe she's not so easy to read as he thought. It's even possible that Krizan isn't as clueless as he came across. Maybe he had his own scheme going the whole time. But there's no way he could have known about the seventy-five grand. Sandy made damn sure of that. He wanted to laugh when Guzman told him they already blew the cash. Smart money says that it went back where it came from. But why would Krizan tip off Superior, then steal the same money he was going to get anyway? That makes the least sense of all. Sandy might have slipped up, he might even be slipping, but one thing that's never let him down is his knowing damn well when the guy he's dealing with is out of his depth. Avery Krizan was out of his depth. Either way, no sense getting too worried about it. From the photo, it looks like she's having fun, whatever the fuck she's up to (what's up with homeboy's *floods* would be his question). At least she's not moving back to the hacienda with his ex and that Evangelical squeeze of hers. It was nice of Mel to visit him in prison, though. She looks damn good for her age. She said she got an interesting postcard from Spain. She sounded almost proud. She whispered it, like it's their little secret. She's probably scared shitless. But it ain't like Ish is a kid anymore. That's just what he said through the receiver, too. ("And what's that make us, Sandy?" was her reply.) And God knows (because Sandy sure does) that Mel's strong medicine to be taking every day.

Does he worry? Of course he fucking worries. Last thing he wants to see is Aisha getting a taste for bad decisions. But he'll just have to wait and see. He doesn't hold those cards. About all he's got right now is this situational leverage. If he plays that right (as in keep his story where they want it) he survives to fight another day, and they leave her the fuck alone. He has a sneaking suspicion he may even get his old job back after all this shit is said and done. Why isn't he panicking? Because what Aisha's got going for her is class. It doesn't matter how much money you got, you can't buy that. (*Not that they won't try, Mija. And what they can't buy they can get you to throw away, so nobody gets it!*). Class can take you places money alone can't go. Every sorry-ass loser up in here knows that.

8

The universe continues to separate itself from itself through NZYME. What's it *growing*?

Some amount of time must have elapsed. CAMEL/EON's gone with Tripsy to get gas for the generators, was it? Or was that-? Things happen for NZYME now in disassociated chunks, with indescribable in-betweens in between, and one in particular with the—are there cars? How'd they get through? They *grew...*? NZYME can parasense the pressure shift. Psysical barometer in free fall... no more centrifugal force... life forms are bleeding in from the edges... Wait, which who said DJ Beforehead never got on the plane? Ala? ... those hoboes? ... who? hobo nobodies, hobo hoboes with untattooable skins, bleeding in from the edges? Oh, no, hobo nobo-... bonobo ho... They're hungry? Who said that... Ala? Yeah, but Alalalalalala I can't tell anything apart right now... toootoootooo destructive. Huh? The food is still frozen? Not for long if they don't come back with the gas for the fridge. Tents are going up on the trance floor? They've found the drugs. Where's the nearest what... Shhhhh... I hear you, Ala! It must feel good to scream. I'm going to tootootooo...

Fine. I'm fine. Sorry? I'm sorry. Those are whose impossible cars? *Is* that is the sun, then? Whose impassable cars are those? Friends of these hobos? Is that *was* the sun?

As busy as he is, NZYME has managed to form the opinion that these people won't surrender to the sacred movements the way the trancers used to, or shed their artificial realities through intermediary guidance so easily. Perhaps these are the messengers of balance, if not the coming bliss.

* * * *

It's dark when Aisha, Avery and the *Zerstreuungskreis* set out from the Kasbah Kandisha and wind their way down the mule path to where the van is parked. On the Imaghran road, they drift through silent Skoura as the tourist hub still sleeps, and the rammed-earth Kasbah Amerdihl is only felt as a deeper, browner blackness—and head northeast with nothing beyond their headlight beams but a few lights floating slowly by in the distance. The landscape looks like the bottom of the ocean to Aisha, and outer space to Zafer, until Wieland first perceives a subtle saffron suggestion, like a low voltage being applied to a cathode tube of true neon, providing just enough ionization for the vacuum to seem expectant. The light becomes incrementally more declarative until it crests the far hills and they find themselves in the middle of what Karina describes, with a strange word, as *[a cacophony-scape, expressionistic in aspect, of jagged, exaggerated and conceivably malevolent spearlike forms]*. It's a psychedelisch prehistory, says Zafer, correct when he bets every last one of them was maybe not consciously but still expecting to see nothing but desert. It soon becomes clear that it's only a palm oasis they're driving, through, and a fine coincidence that it materialized when it did, because the landscape soon does become parched, and the cliffs bleached, and the trees scarcer than even on the road from Ouarzazate. The polarized light also reveals distant Kasbahs and flat-roofed Berber outcroppings. Bright green cultivated patches break up the bright, dusty monotony, and soothe their eyes. Uwe's meter-tall, 'meow meow'-lined bearskin busby lays cat-like on his lap. Zafer rides shotgun. Avery and Aisha ride on either side of the middle hump, while Wieland and Karina straddle equipment crates behind them. While passing the commune Ait Sedrate Sahl Gharbia, Aisha relates what the local children said about her name, and Avery's mind reels back to Toibipet, the Devil Woman Who Was There. They turn left up the Vallee des Roses road toward Ighil M'Goun and the gorges. With the bronze Assif M'Goun on their left and a wall of drab, stony cliffs just a few feet to their right, they follow the Rose Road through the smoke-tree-lined farms of Tabarkhachte and Agoulzi and up the narrow valley to blossom-roofed Bou Tharar, where the road narrows further. With an even muddier tributary now on their left, and lower, even dryer cliffs now on their right, they wind through aromatic Alemdoun and up to Amejgag at the northern extreme of the Valles to where the road forks again into twin unpaved paths. The right fork is marked with a precarious-looking pile of stones, so they choose that one. After another mile or so of slow going they come to a set of cairns festooned with sticks and festive bits of ribbon, directing them off the path and onto the wadi itself. They enter the riverbed and skid between tire tracks for several miles, with Uwe enthusiastically and expertly avoiding drifts, bars, ruts and slushy areas, until—in the middle of yet another blind bend, with the red cliffs still well beyond the brownish-grey hills up ahead—their makeshift road becomes a parking lot.

* * * *

Ala stands on the lumpy ridge that runs along the eastern edge of the plot. There's the crummy little alfalfa plot, the band-aid-colored stone hut that's locked and off limits to them, a whole lot of low thorny forest, some scattered palm trees, and the dry riverbed. The shower and water tanks are in order, the trance floor vibes as receptive, and the fyre circle's right where it should be, in the sand next to the water tank. It will extinguish beautifully, and the darkness will be magnificent. The tower looks great from here, and she can even see the light bulb skull she painted on its siding. Old Buzzard's tent is up and running, and the jamyurt is stocked with all kinds of musical instruments. Most of the local scrap has been de-nailed and cleaned up, and there are plenty of gloves to go around. The altar's got a good head of steam going. There's plenty of paint and fabrics and that kind of stuff. The cliffs are pretty killer to look at all lit up by the sun, with the valley still in shadow.

The wadi is surrounded by thicket. The only public access is the two cart paths leading to the road, and the riverbed itself. It sucks that the alfalfa plot is so useless to them, being furrowed and all. A trancefloor on that would be funny as hell though, wouldn't it? Good thing they've got the riverbed, or else they'd really be fucked. It's totally flat and basically level, and the sand makes for easy digging. It's nowhere near rainy season, so there's no real chance of flooding. This whole bear-claw-shaped mountain of mud she's on was inaccessible until she macheted a path through the gnarly vines at its base. Now it's to be the site of the sunrise tantriyoga workshop she will lead every morning at sunrise, starting tomorrow.

People are gathering, all right, trickling slowly but steadily up the wadi, some with packs on their backs, a few dragging supplies, and many carrying nothing at all. There's a much smaller trickle dripping in from the edge of the forest. They must be coming from town, she figures. The three or four people she's seen coming down the wadi from the direction of the cliffs can't be so easily explained, though, since as far as their maps are concerned there's nothing up there to be coming down from. More perplexing is the fact that with all the people showing up, not a single vehicle has arrived at the site since before dawn. What gives? With her field glasses held up to her eyes, she walks along the ridge line to beyond the bend where the people are coming up from. Eventually (starting from the center, and spreading across her field of vision) a bottle-shaped valley reveals itself. The bottle points in her direction, and at its neck is a carbonation of Citroëns, Renaults, Peugeots, a Škoda, a Laraki, and a homemade-looking 4x4. The stopped cork is Tripsy's dump truck, bogged down in the mud where a small side ravine joins the narrowing wadi. The 90° of skid-arc leading to its rear axle indicates that whoever was driving must have spun it perpendicular to the creek bed; now it's wedged in between two sand bars, with her ridge on one side and the dense rose thicket on the other. She can see from here that its tires are hopelessly cratered. People are leaving their cars behind and walking. A few bystanders stand around gesticulating at the truck. So that explains that, she guesses. Now what? She can only hope CAMEL and Tripsy were on their way back when they got stuck, because there's no driving out of here now. They can survive without recorded music if worse comes to worst, but they're sunk without gas. Food will spoil, people will freak. It took a near-meltdown for her to get the tents off the trance floor as it is. Look at them now, picking at the totem pyle like they're at a garage sale! Who knows what they're thinking down there? Crystallization is occurring, and crystallization without guidance is rarely a good idea. Look at the locals, strolling in without tickets like they own the place. Fucking relativity. Of all things not to take into account. Just because Amej-fucking-gag was so hard for *them* to get to; no one raised the possibility that they might have to run a door... and fucking *NZYME!* Where is he? Now is when their meta-will is supposed to manifest its own unique psysics into organic communal re-creation. But for that to work, people have got to be somewhat on board to begin with... or at least have some idea what the fuck's going on. And NZYME's normally the catalyst of that process, but he's primordially useless right now with his asinine refusal to tell things apart. Of all times to fucking become divine. She'll rip him apart when he comes down from whatever he took, but in the meantime somebody has to get this freakshow on the road. She lowers her binoculars just as the pale sunlight reaches the rose forest, and a pink cosmos sparkles into being. It's a sublime sight, and a good sign. She would love to just stay up here and let everything else sort itself out... but the shocking brilliance has already begun to die down...

On her way back up the ridge she sees a trio of local women, heads and shoulders piled high with hats, purses and parasols all covered with the same pink Damask roses that just glittered her valley view. They're descending the path she just cleared, and are clearly headed for the gathering. Ala lets them pass. Their roses ought to reflect well on her own brilliant white morning haik, and lend a touch of pageantry to her approach.

*****

Uwe leads the way, followed by Zafer with the Crew's new used Eclair 16mm and gear bag, and Wieland with his trusty H16, both only appearing to film the overexposed sandscape. Aisha carries Candy's camera and her own bag, while Avery carries his and Karina's totes and Aisha's suitcase, and Karina brings up the rear, stopping from time to time to transfer her observations to a tattered octavo notebook.

"I was half-hoping no one would be here," Avery whispers to Aisha, though they're in no danger of being overheard.

"So much for that."

They stop once to take pictures of a tricked-out dump truck stuck chassis-deep in wet sand, and once again to rest. Coming finally around the last bend, they catch sight of a twiggy cluster of structures, crudely painted in yellows and reds and arranged around a large, rug-covered clearing. A wooden tower provides some verticality to the scene. A gold dune buggy is parked just outside of the clearing. Lanterns, lights and prayer flags strung on poles mark a loose perimeter. Inside the perimeter a few more cars and tents are scattered around what looks to be a demolished building. People are milling around, generally looking mildly irritated. Aisha steps into the clearing just as a heavily-tattooed woman wearing white linen and a necklace of roses ascends a small cantilevered platform on top of the tower. Her hair glows like a cholla in the morning sun.

"Of Lakshmi!" the woman calls out, making a 'Y' with her arms. "Of Cerridwen and the Corn Mother, of Urd and Maeve, of Chasca and Tlalteutli, of Pachamama, Bastet, Nephthys and Aphrodite, of Inanna and Rhiannon... Welcome!" A small, groggy crowd tightens around the platform. Someone claps a few times, then stops.

"Of Evita," Aisha whispers.

"I don't recognize many of you, so I thought I'd begin by explaining who we are. And by we I will-to mean all of us... yourselves included. We are the fertilizer, the incubator of the coming age, when we will finally end our... self-imposed malignancy upon this living organism some of us call Earth. We here are charged with protecting the zygote of en-night-enment—"

"Did she just call us fertilizer?" someone asks.

"The what of en-what?!"

"What do I mean by en-night-enment, you ask? To put it simply, as modern people we're trapped in the electric will-projection of a speed freak who was afraid of the dark."

"A what?"

"We're here to turn from Edison's oppressive nightlight and learn to trust our own emanant states. In order to do that we must manifest darkness-in-darkness. This will require praxis, which we will exercise in the organic erection of our pop-up para—"

"Praxis? What's that, a pill?"

"This some sort of a joke?"

"Praxis. For exercizin' the organic erection—"

"—... we will build oases for thirsty shadows, and walls and ceilings to hold in the dark—"

"You mean keep out the light?"

"That's one way of looking at it, sir. The way you were taught to look."

"Now you tell me."

"I am telling you, if you will-to listen." She clears her throat. "Let's go deeper, shall we? We are all just dull matter. But what happens if enough dull matter accumulates?" A few scattered murmurs. "No one? Nucleosynthesis. Stardom. Stardom is our dream density. It is the light we seek, and we are its reflection. But what is the dream density of stars? What do they reflect?" Ala looks at Aisha. "There's a darkness at the center of every galaxy, and starlight is its projection. The darkness sets all else in motion." She glances at Weiland. "So, just as the body wills-to stardom, the star wills-to the darkness behind the light. It doesn't just will-to act. It wills-to be behind the camera. It wills-to direct." She looks at Aisha again. "The darkness directs a great, circling dance, a cosmic passion play." She spreads her arms again. "So we gather, we come together organically to manifest our own dream density from these discarded things. We will direct ourselves in the dark. We will remember what it is to fulfill the ancient need to apply our true strengths, and to encourage those of our sisters and brothers. We will dance and feel and play. This time can be so magical, if you will-to believe. Once we have built our Casbah, we will have four nights and days to organically, in darkness and as one, reap the rewards of our common labor, by going beyond—"

"You're kidding, right?"

Ala peers into the small crowd. What a batch this is! What are they fucking doing here? Do they even know? They're all over the map. Maybe the mysterious Mr. Krizan ran a scam on these people. Maybe he resold the tickets under false pretenses. On second thought, they do have something in common: they're not buying what she's selling. (But this is not the time for judgment, Ala. Besides, old people are famous for fatigue, confusion, and hostility…) "Excuse me?" she singsongs, trying but failing not to condescend to the overweight boomer lady in oversized t-shirt, "if you could kindly hold on one minute, ma'am, so I can finish? That would be helpful?"

The woman's forehead mimics the useless farm plot behind them. 'Ma'am?' it says; 'and just who do you think you're kidding, sister?' She flings an imaginary something in the direction of the tower. "Knock yourself out."

Ala more or less does just that. She freezes. Ah, but here comes CAMEL, slouching his way up the wadi covered in axle grease, looking beat to hell. She motions for him to join her *hurry please* just as a local man in a black and gold-embroidered djellaba, whom she'd already been sort of checking out (the way he leaned against the dune buggy, with his arms folded in front of him, a bearded Burt Reynolds with Bedouin eyes…), emerges from the crowd.

"You cannot build your settlement here," he says, his voice like warm caramel. Well, hello.

"Hello."

"Whoa," CAMEL climbs the ladder, waving his hand and shaking his head (how long have she and he been looking at each other?). "Hey now. We are so... not about settlement it's... I can't even..."

Ala sighs. Oh well. Let's hear some more of you, Burt.

"This is not the crusades!" a glassy, disembodied voice cracks. "They were a thing."

"NZYME?"

"You've misunderstood me," the local man's assurance dripping now like massage oil into Ala's receptive ear canals; "you can not easily see it, but the river is still here." He scuffs his sandal on the ground, describing a dark arc in the sand. "This sand flows beneath our feet. A dry wadi will dismantle your settlement," he winks, "as surely as will a wet one." CAMEL gives Ala a 'get a load of this guy' look, which she ignores. The man is pointing to the far side of the clearing, where the Manifestation is to take place. "Those materials you have gathered from the banks, do you know what they were once? Outbuildings built too close to the wadi's edge. It's true." He gives Ala a ruddy Valentino grin. "Now they act as flood breaks during the rains." He winks again. "You could say they manifest themselves organically where they are most needed."

CAMEL puts his hands up. "I thought we were doing you guys a favor—"

"Take it easy, my friend. You are free to use these things... we only ask that you replace them where you found them. Heh heh... I kid." He winks at CAMEL. "What you should be most immediately concerned with is where you've chosen to place your... how you say... water closets?"

"Oh...—Oh." In his preoccupation with aromatic concerns, CAMEL'd dug the pits in what seemed a nice isolated little spot by a salient of rose forest in the far northwest corner of their little stretch of wadi, directly upstream, or whatever, from their site.

"After a few days, you understand..."

"I get it. We—" CAMEL sighs bottomlessly, "we'll have to move them, then..."

"Then?"

"Now?"

"The sooner the better, do you not think? You are most welcome here. We like visitors. But dysentery? You understand..."

"I get it," CAMEL grumbles, thinking he could climb into a hole himself right about now.

"Dysentery's the *shit!*" erupts one of a quintet of heavy-lidded teenagers, all wearing black leather jackets decorated with feathers, embroidery, trading beads, safety pins and buttons. "Fugginn... *love* those guys!"

"But hey," mumbles another from behind long black dutch boy bangs, "we're here to dig some muhfugginn... *noise.*"

"Not muhfugginn...," from a third or the first again, kicking the sand with a steel-toed moccasin, "*outhouses.*"

"In the *desert*."

"Sorry, chief."

"That goes double for me… except for the noise part, I think?" A woman in pastel green pullover sweater smiles nervously at the rockers, who don't seem to see her. "To be honest, I'm having a hard time quite—… I was under the impression that I was attending a cybernetics retreat?" She gets thumbs-ups from a pair of grey-haired futurist prëenactors, and a tip-o-the-pith-helmet from a heavily mutton-chopped gentleman in citrine field jacket and seersucker plus-fours. Aisha waves, and the Earl strides over to where she and Avery are standing. Meanwhile the *Zerstreuungskreis* have separated themselves from the crowd and are scrambling up the hill to get a panoramic shot.

"I hold no position on most matters, but I am firmly antiseptic," Peregrine declares.

"Fancy meeting you here, His Lordship."

"Isn't it, though? I wouldn't normally go in for this sort of thing, you know;" Perry grins, "so dirty. Yet one must take the time to cultivate one's eccentricity, if one wishes to remain worthy of the epithet."

"Quite."

"I've been rather hoping to speak to you, my dear. Your photographs are quite exquisite, you know. I should say they've created quite the flutter among the flock."

"Did they? Oh, I'm so glad they turned out."

"And well you should be. You're a talent. We must talk about your future plans. I say, I know a man in Dover…"

It was Peregrine who secured them passage to England. They met him at the Museum of Natural History in New York, while Aisha was sitting on Avery's shoulders, taking pictures. They were in front of the Amazonia diorama when a man wearing jodhpurs and spats tapped her knee, introduced himself as Earl of Peregrine, and started asking her photography questions in an accent that had her leaning so far over trying to follow that she almost fell on him. He asked Avery "deah buouy" if he might also have a hoist, declared "all right pukka" the shot Aisha had taken and offered her a job on the spot, as official photographer for the Feathership of Odd Birders' quincentennial dinner and awards ceremony being held four days hence in the middle of the Atlantic Ocean, during the flock's return to Southampton aboard the *Lady Di*.

They were thinking more along the lines of checking out the Erie Canal and maybe popping over to Canada, but once the opportunity to travel by transatlantic oceanliner presented itself, they were fairly surprised that they hadn't thought of the idea themselves. They were halfway to England before they considered attending the gathering, but once that initial compromise with randomness was made, and with America long gone from their horizon, their self-imposed restriction began to loosen. Perry asked about their plans during the affiliated 'Orny Buggers' Birds and Bees dance and Aisha, half-drunk on sparkling wine and so a bit too sure he wouldn't remember, mentioned Manifest the Casbah. When they met for breakfast the next morning the Earl had already independently verified the gathering's existence, and expressed a keen interest in attending. And here he is now.

"Hey Perry."

The Earl extends his hand to Avery. "Hey sailor," he drawls, doing his most wretched John Wayne.

"Enchanté."

"The hell you on about?" They turn around to see a wiry, weatherbeaten man in a cowboy hat standing at the base of the tower, pointing his knobby index finger at the people up there like a stick. "Looky here," he shouts. "The little lady's right. We come a long way, now. Now come on down here and talk to us on the level. All this business about the darkness and what-have-ye, it's getting a mite awkward." Ala and CAMEL stare at the weatherbeaten cowboy. Reluctantly, CAMEL descends the ladder, while Ala lowers her mandrel and leans over the rail.

"So you all are from Cali, ain't yez?"

"Oakland," CAMEL replies, when they're eye to eye.

"Stedman." The man puts out his hand. "Rubottom. Russell Rubottom."

"CAMEL... EON."

Russell squints. "All right." They shake, each grasping with his free hand the backside of the other's, so making it a four-handed operation.

CAMEL notes that Russell is stronger than he looks. "I've never heard of Stedman," he says, when they're through shaking. "That up north?"

"Nope."

"South?"

"Nope."

"All righty…"

"So Chameleon, I'm guessing you didn't bring us all out here to listen to speeches."

"You guess right. And I don't mean to be rude, but… we didn't exactly bring you here. Where do you… what do you think this is, exactly?"

"What're ye asking me for? It's your blamed sweepstakes."

"Our what?"

"See, here's what I can't make out… whatever this here is, it must've cost you a pretty penny." He looks at Ala. "Ain't that right?" She nods warily. "So couldn't youz'a done this out in Barstow, say? Or Bakersfield, maybe? Lord knows you all got plenty of trash right there in Oakland."

Ala holds her ground. "We 'done this' in Bakersfield, sir," using finger quotes to illustrate, "on the ghost shore of the great Tulare Sea. And we done it in Barstow too, on the west bank of the Río de las Ánimas, where it flows due north from the narrows, in the spring—"

"What was that fella took all those people down to South America?" someone asks.

"Who said that?"

"Hitler?"

"Hey—"

"No…"

"Jim Jones?"

"That's him. This best not be one of them Jim Jones situations."

"I don't think you get the—"

"So where's the kool-aid?"

"Fuck the kool-aid; where's the beer?"

"If you let us just us finish—"

"Don't it get dark enough for yez in Cali?"

"I... It's sort of hard to explain when you're—"

"What the man's trying to say," explains a large black man in a black leather jacket with 'Oakland Vultures MC' embroidered on the back, "is we're not seeing no Casbah. Now you say we got to do what, now? Build it from junk? Now? For free?"

"Why, you ask?" CAMEL begins to spin wildly. "Brothers and sisters, my travels have taught me many things—"

"Oh, this should be good."

"One!—" yelling by accident, then resetting, settling, "... one thing I've learned is that putting my psy—my physical self in a foreign place is quite—it's almost like the opposite of seeing it on TV, right, or reading about it, or looking at it online or whatever, because, see, by physically putting myself somewhere I might normally consider like way-out exotic, what happens is the place stops being exotic. It becomes familiar, right. It's me that becomes exotic. In this way I literally become that which I desire. You see? Look around. Do you feel foreign? You are actually your true selves here; you're unmerged, unblended..." He's getting a few anticipatory winces already, but he keeps climbing, "when you become... exotic, every land sings the Earthsong, adding its own endemic harmony. Dilongs share lines with Dongfengs!

Just like... T. Rexes share lines with T-birds! It's true! But you can't see or hear Dilongs from... Bakersfield. Because it's like, we don't just know our lines... we are our lines! And speaking of lines, it's only by listening to the... variations that we can truly know the song; and if we really listen, we might even hear the Music of the Spheres... I'm talking visually, too...." CAMEL wills-to-believe what he is saying, even if self-consciously, and he's liking the sound of his flow. But he's still not feeling quite requited, and conflict always strikes him dumb sooner or later.

"Kill me now!"

CAMEL is struck dumb.

Avery does a double take. Old Mrs. Love? For a flash he accepts the virtual impossibility as fact.

Ala jumps back into the fray. "What the hell's that supposed to mean?"

"You people got nothing. You dragged us out here for not a goddamn thing. What a goddamn—."

"Uhmm, first of all," (Ala's had it...) "... first of all, we didn't 'drag you' (finger quotes again) anywhere. Hello? And if by 'nothing' you mean an attempt at genuine communion with our fellow beings, then yeah; guilty as charged. Crucify us, why don't you."

"I bet you'd like that, wouldn't you?"

"Lady, if you will please... fucking—"

"Ahh ha ha! Check out Jesus!" The voice again, familiar, yet different.

"*NZYME?!*" Again there's no answer. CAMEL spreads his arms and corkscrews like a fed-up dervish.

Avery glances over at Aisha, who's looking a little peaked.

She returns the glance, then walks up to CAMEL/EON.

"We'll help," she shouts, toggling two fingers back and forth between herself and Avery. "Right Mike?"

"Uh, sure," Avery says, as Perry, with a wink and a bow, suddenly, serendipitously espies that *Phylloscopus inornatus* he's been looking simply everywhere for. Antiseptic indeed.

"Really?" CAMEL hugs them together. "Oh! You guys are heroes!"

* * * *

"Can't be too aggressive, now," Endlicher says as he and Guzman trudge up the wadi. They follow the tire tracks on foot, with no idea how far it is from where the cab dropped them off to wherever it is they're going. One thing's for sure: they're getting warmer. And thirstier.

"Yes, Don."

"The quieter we are—."

"Yes, Don. And let's try not to repeat ourselves. Some of us have that habit—"

"Barb, listen; the only way they're going to accept the logic of our proposal is if we can get them by themselves, without… outside influences. Or interruptions. I've given this some thought. If we go barging into their party waving accusations around, we won't be very well received."

"Barb?"

"I, uh… it slipped out."

"Mm hm."

"Do you, uh... mind?"

"Just—give it a rest, Don. It's fine. We'll do it your way."

"We want them to cooperate..."

"Yes. Quit while you're ahead. And Don? Not too much fun, huh?"

"Aw, come on.. That was just a little dancing. Last night was a special case. Jet lag always messes with my—"

"Don."

"All right. I'll take it easy, if you... ease up a little. We'll blend in better if it looks like we're having fun."

Guzman spins an imaginary noisemaker next to Endlicher's face. "Woo hoo!"

"That's better."

* * * *

Turns out it's not a *Phylloscopus* Peregrine had spotted after all, but an even rarer subspecies of the African Yellow Warbler. There's a small colony of them living in the woods, undisturbed until the port-a-potty portage party of Avery, Aisha, CAMEL, Russell and Brother Benny flushes it out.

"Shit, Perry," Avery shouts amidst the avian panic. "You scared me!"

Apoplexiae silenti from the blind: "scared *you*?"

"What's that?"

"...!"

"All right, all right. I hear you."

Fortunately (particularly for anyone who may have found the sight of toilets being dragged out of site unexpectedly moving), the sandy clay in the next clearing shovels easily, and the work goes fast. In addition to that small stroke of luck is the practical miracle that no one made use of the facilities before they were uprooted. Barely an hour after breaking new ground, they've finished the job. In the spirit of commode-araderie, CAMEL has liberated himself to bitch to the crew.

"Basically, what it is, is a disaster. Those people out there could give a rat's ass about what we're about."

"So? They're here, ain't they?"

"Yeah Benny... they're here all right. Whoever bought all those tickets is one sick puppy, I'll tell you what..."

"You don't know that for sure," Avery offers.

"You heard them, Mike. Don't you think it would have been better for us to have fewer people, but a larger percentage who were actually somewhat privy to our trip? I mean fewer people, who—you know what I mean. It's not for everyone."

"But they're here, ain't they?"

"And some of those people are privy... no pun intended...."

"Sure. The ten of us can bliss out in the middle of a resource war."

But when they emerge from the woods they find the atmosphere not all that unpleasant. Tempering the air of complaint are some friendly conversations taking place on and around the trance floor.

"See, look—"

"So what about you guys, Mike?" CAMEL asks Avery in particular. "How'd you end up here? Some random invitation, like most everyone else?"

"We, I, um—"

"We got tickets online," Aisha replies as they reach the wadi's edge. "How else...?"

"So... did you like... know somebody, or...?

"— *Ye gaht yer peeker twicked in yer whipper, sonny?*"

"Huh?!"

"— *fools learn to pronounce it Pew-litzer—*"

"Where are all the rugs?"

"— *comedy of errors, am I right?*"

"— *just showed up in my post, it did—*"

"— *like when you click on bad news, you get that bonus strip of misery on the side bar there—*"

"— *good thing it was free—*"

"— *a sense of humor only genocide can—*"

"— *suicidal immortal—*"

"— *speaking of tetanus, this better—*"

The voices echo off the hills, compelling some people to speak louder.

"— *my point being—*"

"It could work still, CAMEL," Avery pleads amid the din.

"Huh?"

"— *eye-motion software's embedded in our proprietary glasses. depending on what the viewer chooses to focus on, she will be routed—*"

"Maybe tweak your message a bit? That stuff about gathering darkness in tents might be a little... specific?"

"— *if I was crazier, maybe I might—*"

"— *neighbor said she'd feed my geese, else there's no way—*"

"— *telling the text when it has sunk into the consciousness it's addressing—*"

"— *dropped my e-cig in the goddam john; had to fish it out by—*"

"— *even legal—?!*"

"— *told her don't get used to nothing you don't like—*"

"— *one of several different endings. You see, the interface is only—*"

"— *saw the cop throw that bottle with my—*"

"I have to find NZYME."

"— *summbitch come at me like—*"

"— *sshmanipulation—*"

"— *better have band-aids—*"

"We can help with whatever, right Ish?"

"— *you pull out a gun, he says? Says there's no way of knowing with you—*"

"— *shelf-manipu... litzer—*"

"— *should some institution take the credit? I mean fair is—*"

"— *stold a steak off the devil's plate—*"

"— *whoever said life—*"

"Of course. Totally."

"— *get them preblooming petallic husks,* —"

"— *he'd make a hell of a lawyer* —"

"— *now someone's said it, haven't* —"

"But back to my question. Seriously; did you guys know somebody, or…?"

"— *he'd make a hell of paradise* —"

"— *you guys into inclusiveness? How about we take off* —"

"— *stomach's a bubbling cauldron right about* —"

"Like I said, we were just surfing the web one night, and came across your site —"

"— *like the grail. On the one hand, it doesn't exist* —"

"— *took that crazy-ass Tizi n Tichka pass up to Ouarz* —"

"— *my life trying to prove myself wr-*"

"Really!? And you just said what the hell, let's go to Morocco? You guys millionaires or something?"

"— *old lady's handle is Tinkerbell, 'cause she* —"

"— *going to feed us or what?*"

"— *amounts of pain and cetera, people just pass theirs on to* —"

"— *reveal themselves only to the truly desperate. The holy hobos mark the* —"

"— *depends on the story you're in* —"

"— *mutiny of experimental subjects* —"

"— *Ariaal? That African?*"

"— *ever you do, never look directly at the cam* —"

"— *still kept secret, because—get this—the subjects continued the exp—*"

"Huh, Mike?"

"— *the color of brush water—*"

"— *starving—*"

"— *some hinge on seventeen, sure; others on the deathbed, or even—*"

"— *we are a nomadic people, so I'm afraid—*"

"— *pericope's a selection or extract from a—*"

"— *zone out in the middle of the Pacific where all those—*"

"Mike?"

"— *all those undigested mood elevators and anti-anxiety go—*"

"— *hmm? Change it to what?*"

"— *a ha ha! I love cured fish!*"

"— *portion of sacred writing read in a divine service; lesson; lection;—*"

"— *I suspect furthermore, and my body confirms, generally, if I am the blasphemer—*"

"CAMEL?"

"Yeah."

"My name's not Mike."

"I knew it!"

* * * *

Kalila Scott moves up a step to let the potty party

pass. She's sitting next to a large, framed section of plywood that's been propped up at the upper boundary of the weird junk village. She dumps a bunch of sand out of her shoes, puts them back on, stands up and looks around. Even if she hadn't made a point of taking the website language figuratively, she's not sure she would have envisioned this. A guy with his mustache going into the sides of his mouth and coming out of holes in his cheeks is talking about how this piece of outhouse is a living yǐngbì screen. He says it keeps out evil spirits because they don't like to go around ninety degree angles.

"How come?"

"How come what?"

"How come they don't like ninety degree angles? Seems like it would be the opposite." She pauses. "Why don't they they just go around?"

"Ha. Good question."

"But seriously," she persists, "if you were an evil spirit would you just line up in front of the wall like you were supposed to? I'd be coming in from the side."

"You're right. There should be a gate and a courtyard and all of that. We're going to do the best we can, okay?"

"I was just wondering."

"No worries. Why don't you keep watch? From what I can tell, you don't let nothing get past you…"

"Don't let anything. Nothing's invisible, same as evil spirits."

"Well you got me there. We'll just have to keep our fingers crossed, I suppose. In the meantime, why don't you grab a brush and join in the fun?"

Kalila pivots her torso back and forth between the panel and the art supplies. "That's okay. I'll just watch." She examines the bins that have been set out, mentally cataloguing the various paints, powdered pigments, pastes, fabric strips and magazine pages. Once she's satisfied with her inventory (could come in handy for her writing), she takes better stock of her strange company, starting with the (did he say ex?) priest gold-leafing a halo on an icon that looks a lot like his ladyfriend. There sure are lots of Americans here. We're like a colony or something, she thinks. There's a cop-looking American lady joking in Arabic with a guy in a big silk hat. Mama's laughing with some other American guy. Talk about a small world! Mama and the guy she's talking to know each other from the Wright Museum back in Detroit. Whew! She was just in a bad mood from having to tramp through all those brambles in her pantyhose, just to find out she was the only one who got dressed up again, after she was just talking about how she hates feeling like a fish out of water (not to mention how she hates messes, and hates hates hates farms, having heard too many of Grampa's stories by time she was Kalila's age to ever even want to set foot on one...). At least she didn't wear the high heels like she was going to. That would've been a real disaster. And unlike at some other functions they've attended together, there are other black people out here. But Kalila hasn't seen a single book. That's sure strange.

Speaking of strange, while the guy's chatting away with Mama, he's also using some art supplies to do magic tricks for a couple of homeless-looking people. To Kalila, there's something sleazy about magic. This guy's not changing her opinion on that, but the reappearing brush stroke trick is impressive, she has to admit. She stretches her neck and toys with the words 'strange', 'stranger', 'odd', 'odds', and 'odder', scrambling, stacking, and tying them together in her head. She was sure expecting more in the way of accommodations. Hopefully they weren't supposed to bring their own tent. The tribal priestess lady was talking about everybody building huts out of the piles of junk. Maybe they ought to be getting on that? She peers down toward the of the compound, where some people are dragging some junk from the big pile. Good. Way up behind them, she spots a shepherd and a bunch of sheep coming over the rise from the east. Looking closer, she spies some kids hiding among the sheep, popping up their heads here and there like whack-a-moles.

A man approaches her with a look on his face like he knows her. He does look familiar.

"Excuse me, miss?" His breath smells like cheap wine. Good. Mom's got her eye on him. "Might I ask your name?"

Kalila shakes her head.

"I just wanted to ask; does it happen to be Kalila Scott? "I'll be—"

"Can I help you?" Kendra has snuck up behind him.

"Oh—"

Kalila recognizes the stranger just as he crumples like a finger toy before her mom. "Mama!" she declares. "This is the guy who wrote that book."

Kendra isn't sure which book Kalila's talking about, but she's been starting to doubt whether all this has anything to do with books whatsoever.

"Good afternoon, ma'am. I... I'm David Edwards. And you," he says, turning to Kalila, "you are the girl from the midwest, who wrote that dystopian comedy—"

"Comic."

"Comic. Of course. *The Incorruptibles.*" Turning back to Kendra, he adds, "I must say I'm... uniquely familiar with your daughter's work. You see, we share the same publisher."

"Is that so?"

"In fact—"

"*Oh...*," Kendra laughs. "You must be the guy who wrote the uh, oh, the Incorrupt—"

"*Un*corruptible, Mama."

"Actually, young lady, your mother's nearly correct. 'Incorruptible' was to be my second title choice." He pauses, before adding (rather graciously, he feels, considering) "inane was my—*our* publisher's, so naturally we went with that." He smiles sadly. "I'm sure you understand the pain."

Receiving the nod from Kendra, Kalila nods and puts her hand out. She and David shake collegially.

"I figured I'd meet you someday," Kalila tells Mr Edwards. "I wouldn't have expected it to be here, though. Kind of... I don't know. Did Paradigm Press set this up? That would be pretty weird if they did. I haven't seen any books here, have you? Don't you think that's a little weird? I do. What are we supposed to be doing if we're not reading? Or are we reading? Or what?"

"We? Oh... I'm afraid I'm as in the dark as you are. I will say, I very much doubt that Paradigm had anything to do with this. If they did, they were smart not to tell me. My invitation was, shall we say... wanting in granularity?"

"Ours too!"

Starting from the top of the bearclaw-shaped hill, several children begin zigzagging more or less in Kalila's direction. She waves shyly to let them know she sees them before resuming her conversation with Mr. Edwards.

"This might sound like a weird question, but do you feel sometimes like, how narcissistic I must be to think I should be allowed to do this? I mean, like, writing, when other people got to work work?"

"And you are! We must have some narcissism to start with. But we work, don't we? I often wonder if my novels aren't in fact by-products of a process whereby my own narcissism is distilled into humility, my solipsism into empathy, and so forth, by my own ef—"

"So you end up with less of those things than you started with?"

"Ha! That, my dear, is an excellent question!"

"Because otherwise... otherwise, wouldn't you say we're kind of monstrous?"

"Indeed! Good point. Ah, yes; the monster. It's a gorgon, you know. You must know it's there, and describe it, but you mustn't look directly at it."

"The sun?"

"I mean the camera. The black mirror."

Kalila takes a step backward.

"I—no—you see," David Edwards backpedals, "I took

a speaking course some years back, after my little taste of success, to help me cope with all the dog-and-pony shows they had me performing at the time. One of the things I learned was never to look directly at the camera, or you'll lose yourself in it. You see? You become artificial, an imitation of self. So in that way it's like a gorgon. See my point?"

"Hmm. So when we get lost, where do we go?"

"Nowhere."

"We become not-human?"

"Yes!"

"So therefore monstrous?"

"Yes!"

"And with each photo taken, a frozen bit of us is stolen—"

"Yes!"

"While we feed our life-energy to inorganic forces, one selfie at a time, digitizing ourselves out of existence, becoming spent shells in the end?"

"Yes! Yes! It's like you read my mind!"

"I read your book."

"Oh. Aren't you cruel. Well." (He must remember he's talking to a child, of sorts...) "That's quite ambitious of you, isn't it? I mean, reading that at your age? But you are a writer, aren't you? And how did you find my prose, if I might be so bold?"

"In the dollar bin."

"Ha! I mean, what did you think of the book itself?"

"It got pretty heavy... after a while."

"As in—...?"

Kalila smiles. "Some of it I liked."

"The only reason I ask, going back to what you just thought my point was—"

"You mean the sun?"

"It's very much the same as my camera, is it not?"

"Yeah. You can't look at it directly."

"Indeed you cannot. And the sun is where your...—"

"Incorruptibles?"

"Thank you. Where your Incorruptibles hail from, yes?"

"So you read my books."

"Generally speaking, I don't read comics. But I made an exception in your case. You're quite sharp-witted, I'll grant you that. And you know how to erect a plot. And graphically speaking, I must say I never get tired of pointillism. We don't see enough of that particular technique anymore, if you ask me."

"Thanks."

"But yes, the similarities are rather uncanny. A bit of advice, if I may: whether it's raining existential crises or hailing solar superheroes, the point... the point of origin, if you will, if you to focus too directly upon it, will make you blind to everything but itself."

"So I should stick to the periphery?"

"Ha ha. Wouldn't that would be nice! But I'm afraid that won't work."

"So what's your advice then?"

"Just be careful. You don't want to end up like some people."

"You're okay."

At the opposite, downstream end of the plot, NZYME, tempered, clarified and invigorated by his dark light year of the soul, is seated in the padmāsana at the foot of the tower, tapping on a clay drum. "What NZYME means to say is a visionary's got to take things into account," he says. "We all co-opt. It's the only way to grow, yo; else your magic becomes too... like smoke." He pauses. "That's just NZYME talking, though." Turning to another questioner, he responds, "but then again, regarding your perceptions of conformity, are we talking about mobs of individualists, or isolated free-thinkers who believe theoretically in the collective spirit? See? The answer's not so clear." He pauses again. "At least to NZYME it isn't."

It's an open but unspoken secret between them; back when EON and Ala were calling the shots, N—was the one making them. That's cool by him, though. NZYME's down with his gifts of persuasion, even though the whole leader-follower trip is hella dubious to him. But he can't avoid it, so what's he going to do? He gets the irony that his reluctance to lead further legitimizes his authority, and yeah these things happen to him too often for his will-to not to be involved on some level. That level's an ego trip trap, for sure. Sometimes he partakes more than he should of the party favors just to take himself out of all that, leggo his ego a while, but that only works about half the time, and never for long enough. It's a conundrum for sure, tell N—about it. He'll use his talents for protection all day. He's been in a zillion sketchy situations over the years, and he's never felt himself in any danger from organic entities. If he could at least show his brothers and sisters how it's done, he'd be doing them a real solid; the thing is that requires mass exertion of influence for purposes of manipulation, and NZYME can't name one single time that sort of thing didn't devolve into a con. Bullshit highway is paved with honest answers, trancers. You got to know-how on your own, but you got to know how to know-how. Conundrum, conundrum, NZYME paradiddles. He's got to be extra careful. "Those were some epic gatherings, no doubt," he says to this beer-bloated Austrian sycophant, *con und drum* rolling around in his head, "but you learn different things as you get older. Don't sweat it though. You're young." To a local girl: "Petty? Doubtless. But we were part of a thing. A pretty cool thing, too. It worked way better for us than the dominant paradigm, for reals, and didn't bother anybody else. What more could you ask for? The Man left us alone for a long-ass time too. But then like, people started getting hip to what we were up to, and dug it, like, or their interpretations of what some of them maybe thought we were up to or some shit, they dug that, and then their ears or whatever, their snouts started smelling money, and, like, before we knew it our thing got turned into this other thing that was like, sort of our thing? Except it was smoother around the edges. Like a projection, as mothersister Ala always says. That's truth too, yo. Then like that projection became bigger than us, like a big money version of us that didn't even have us in it, which is a trip, right? And you might think maybe could be a good thing, right? But it wasn't. It was like a... flash flood flushed right through our tribe. Brothers and sisters cashed in, some of them cashed out.

The three of us were left high and dry. EON and Ala are beautiful people, no doubt, but they got egos. N— ain't gonna lie about that. They started getting a little negatory. Things got to be a lot less—the quality of the energy input went down; let NZYME put it that way. Shit got heavy. But if you ask NZYME some of those fools got soft, and started overreacting instead of just being understanding and cool. Some of them went to the light side, and sold out. And the projection gets bigger and bigger every day. Now you got like thousands of people coming together for a real experience in this fake-ass world, maybe some catharsis if they're lucky, and the whole thing's being put on by Google or some shit. You feel me? It hurts to watch that deal go down. We lost a lot. So brother EON was like, "hey—"

"We must go bigger and better too! How positively American!"

"You know what, comrade? N–'s calling bullshitpa on that noise. We're not conning anybody; we're just trying to make something cool happen. That's truth, yo. Maybe we are delusional, or running from whatever like you said, but at least we're fucking doing it... fucking... biodegradeably." He turns back to face the first questioner. "Either we go the entropic route, and end up as billions of fucking... mutually repellent particles; or we learn to connect through our differences, and get free." NZYME spreads his hands to encompass the wadi. "Figure out a way to value things. Like with water. You can look at it as whatever, either worthless, or like... real fucking valuable. But it takes value to know value. That's why we're here, yo. To create value in ourselves. You feel me now? It looks like a trick because it is. But check it; sometimes the insight's the illusion. Trip on that. Or don't. In NZYME's experience, the better we get at convincing the other guy that ours is the better way, the less we're convinced of it ourselves."

"I'm convinced!"

"You can disagree if you want to. Like that story with the two people who argue, right, and try so hard to convince the other that they end up fucking switching positions. It doesn't matter; we're all sharing the same mind. But some psysical strengths are developed through exercise. NZYME likes to think that refined psysical output is precious as fuck these days, and something we should all aim to increase. Alright. Now N–'s going to shut up. Thra-dum thra-dum thra-dum."

There may be no DJ Beforehead, but they still have Tripsy's twin T60s with heavy duty cartridges, a mixer, a few good mics, and his QSCs that don't fuck around. The dude with the dune buggy went to retrieve some vinyl from his place in town. Thra-dum thra-dum. CAMEL's being cool. He understands how it is. It can't be any other way with NZYME. Ala's still a little pissed, but she'll be all right. The important thing is they're playing by ear now, which is what he's been waiting for. It takes some chaos to get to where he needs to be. He'll help Tripsy set up the DJ booth in the back of the dump truck, run the PA, fire up Generator X and get everything ready for when the vinyl shows up.

When Tripsy's truck finally returned, it was followed in by a 4x4 containing a couple of vacationing Frente Polisario youth organizers named Tobi and Omar, and a soft exile from Mauretania named Saikou. They said they happened upon the scene by accident while off-roading down a side ravine. Saikou is one healthy-ass refugee. There he is now, with a local girl on one arm and a bottle of local wine in the other, singing the song they're dancing to. Meanwhile the leg humpers are closing in on NZYME. Happens every time.

"So there *is* a quantum spin inherent in action that's related to intent? Like I always knew that, but until just now I didn't know I knew, you know?"

"NZYME's just gonna chill—"

"Why can't there be a fish that walks on dry land that instead of fins and gills has long legs and a long neck for reaching branches, and instead of being covered in iridescent scales is has fur with markings that look like that cracked mud?"

"NZYME will have to get back to you on that, bro. Yo, CAMEL!"

"I still don't get it," CAMEL is saying, when he hears someone yelling his name. "Who's that?"

"Maybe we were selfish, but all we really did was accept your offer. You put the tickets out there. You took the money. If you wanted this to be so exclusive—"

"That's exactly what we didn't want."

"So what's the problem?"

"Well... if by exclusive you mean limited to people who are willing to make, like, a personal investment, based on some understanding of what we're trying to do? Then yeah. But the idea that we should've known that because of some insurance scam or whatever, a total stranger might give a bunch of other random people free trips to our gathering? And we—you fucked them too, you know. These people were probably expecting to have to ditch a time-share seminar, at worst. Look around."

"You don't know."

"I guarantee, most of these people have no idea what we're up to out here. If someone randomly sent you free tickets and airfare somewhere, would you honestly be expecting *this*?"

"Maybe not. But again, you made it possible. And personal investment? I don't know any of these people's reasons for coming any better than you do, but they're here, aren't they?" They've crossed to the kitchen zone, where Dewey and Flyball are busy building kabobs. Several people stand around eating, while many more wait patiently, sprawled out on the makeshift benches and tables.

"Yeah, but—"

"CAMEL/EON!"

CAMEL raises his hand. The Eye of Horus tattoo bisected through its retina by his Fate Line aligns with the middle of his forehead as it moves toward them parthenogenetically from his Sixth Chakra, before vanishing into a loose fist that itself vanishes as he turns (it's a move he praxised a lot when he was a younger trancer, but has long since become second-natural). He listens.

"CAMEL/EON!" It's Ala. Avery and Aisha follow him over to where Ala's manning the grill. She appears to be a lot more relaxed than when they first saw her.

"I could have sworn you were—"

"Tripsy showed up while you were gone," she says, adroitly flipping fragile ginger-lentil patties, turning tofu kebobs and color-checking the roasted sweet peppers she'll be incorporating into the aioli. Things are looking up, she explains; kinder vibrations have irradiated the wadi in his absence. After their introductory splash got canceled by that rancorous counter-wave he rode out on, the crowd sort of forgot about her, and started bickering amongst themselves. She hung out on the tower for a while and watched, and listened. She didn't consciously manifest a deeper understanding of the situation, it just came to her. These people were as tired and confused and far away from home as she was. They were justifiably mortified and pissed off, but they were still trying to hammer some sense into the situation, which meant they were trying not to succumb to the dreadful fear of the dark. Despite all their efforts to pre-establish place-context and plant the usual seeds of meta-will (stubbornly predicated on a certain like-mindedness in attendees), they hadn't reached out enough. It was stupid to greet their guests from the tower. There is no dominant paradigm here, she understood then.

So she snuck down from the tower (mostly to avoid NZYME, who was circling it *very* strangely...), hung back and listened some more. Then she manifested a big pitcher of lemonade with cardamom and rosewater in it and went around offering it to her thirsty guests. And she saw worry in people's eyes, but also sparks of will. Then people just started doing stuff. It started with some of the most down-and-out-looking individuals.

"It was kind of bizarre," she tells CAMEL, pointing behind her with the spatula. "You should have seen them. First they climbed up the trees and ran ropes, and wrapped them around some of the long posts from the pile, and tied the other ends to some pieces of scrap wood that they buried deep in the sand, packed tight and covered with rocks. Then they started lashing palm fronds together like pros, and sewing some sheets onto the rope matrix. It was like they'd practiced it a hundred times! I swear; they knew exactly what they were doing. Before I knew it, they built that! Go check it out. It's pretty sweet."

CAMEL watches a crew of what he'd assumed were bums drag the rugs from the trance floor into the shade beneath the long tent.

"They inspired me to get cooking," Ala tells him.

"Did I just hear NZYME?" he asks.

"Fuck if I know. Keep him away from me. But you should talk to those people, CAMEL. Seriously, I'm starting to think this can actually work."

CAMEL looks around nodding, then he turns back to Avery and Aisha. "Where were we?"

"You mentioned something about free airfare?"

"Airfare, train fare, you name it. Why do you ask? You know full well how they got here."

"We don't know, actually."

"Of course you do. You are Avery Krizan, aren't you?"

Aisha looks at Ala, who looks like she just walked into a glass door. "We're the ones who bought your tickets," she tells her. "But that's all we did."

Ala's mouth drops. She looks at Avery. "You did this?"

"Your ad just happened to be in the right place at the right time," Aisha answers, "or however you want to look at it. But if we didn't—"

CAMEL interrupts her. "It's stolen money, Ala."

"Not...—technically it's not—"

"It is."

"But we didn't want the money," Avery protests; "that's why we bought the tickets. We gave them away."

Ala narrows her eyes at Avery. "You did what?"

"We gave them away. To strangers, mostly. Most of them we left lying around train stations, or in museums. Motels..."

"Out in the desert..." Aisha adds.

"Out in the desert... We didn't... we didn't consider much beyond that, to be honest."

CAMEL waits for an explosion. But Ala seems more interested than upset. "You didn't consider much," she ponders out loud "Hmm. How's that work?"

"I don't know. It's a long story. We weren't even planning on coming here ourselves when we bought the tickets."

"And you never once considered how that would affect us?" CAMEL asks. "So it was all about the money."

"We took the money, CAMEL," Ala says to him, in not quite the mommy voice. CAMEL shakes his head stubbornly.

"But you said people got free transportation," Aisha reminds him, "and that wasn't us. If it wasn't us, and if it wasn't you...—"

"Okay," CAMEL admits, "we—or should I say whoever you stole the money from did kick down for a few tickets. Certain people had to be here. We wanted there to be a core group." CAMEL looks around. "And they're not even here, apparently."

"That wasn't going to be my question. My question is who—"

"Snap!"

"Fuck, NZYME!" CAMEL spins around. "Where'd you come from?"

"We told us apart, didn't we!" NZYME replies, ignoring the question.

"That's seriously not helpful, N–. You know who this is? This is the fucking dude who—"

"Of course I know who this is, bro. I've been right here this whole time."

"No you—" CAMEL beings to say, then lets it drift. "So, what? You're cool with it now?"

"So what *what*? I guess you're right. What this party needs is some violence. When should we start the beatings?"

"Man, that's not what—" turning to Avery and Aisha, "he's kidding—.... whatever. Overexaggerating." To NZYME, "Easy for you to say anyway, N–."

"Not really. But Ala's right. We spent that shit."

"NZYME's right," Ala says, while giving Aisha a long, slow look. "Let's not tell each other apart right now. There's too much to do."

From the top of the middle ridge, Kwéte can see the ocean. It is not a large lake like he'd imagined but a golden vein, brighter than the melting sun. He is amazed. Who knew the sun and the sea and the stone he holds were so related? But he has no time to ponder such things. It will be dark soon. The trip ahead will be difficult and dangerous. He will have to descend from the ridge twice to find water; in the close-walled ravines and arroyos he will be vulnerable to capture. The crest is dry and cold, and there is no hiding from the wind. Food and sleep will be in short supply. But there aren't enough rahwah'nat to trap him up here. Even if they were to spot him from below, he will see them long before they can reach him, and he has the advantages of size, speed and agility. Standing on the hill crest, looking down at their cattle grazing in empty Toibi, Kwéte can see the future. The rahwah'nat may be slow and heavy like a flood, but they are also steady and relentless like a flood. They will keep coming. Someday there will be enough of them. They have already infected the arteries of the land, and those of the people; the trails and rivers are already theirs. He has learned enough to know how these these things (floods and infection, ...) spread. He looks toward tahmingar'ro, and the golden floating peak of Akvág-na, equal of Yoát, guardian of the land of the Taaqtam. His destination will be as difficult and dangerous as his journey. Water is scarce in the *desert, and he may not know how to find it. He will be at the mercy of the Taaqtam, if he can find them. His people say they defy the rahwah'nat. In spite of the future he sees written in the land, he will try to join them in their defiance. But he has spent many seasons in his easy place at La Misión, and it will show. This crime could earn him death. As well, the Taaqtam could refuse him help, or cast him out if they think he is being followed. His best hope is that these rahwah'nat boots will bring him a first favor, and he will earn the rest. The golden light upon Akvág-na reddens, dims, loses its color; it becomes an image from his fateful old dreams, a dark white island in a deep, grey-blue sea.*

* * * *

Watch reads 0515. Computer monitor is still the brighter lightbox, but window is competing. Outside, contrast between arrow-shaped patch of floodlight on asphalt and surrounding darkness decreasing. One last bump and The Man will close his eyes for a few before hitting the road. A long and productive night of trawling was had; he harvested a couple e-souls, tugged on a couple of lines. He's fixed his demo target's coordinates and plotted his course. He closes his laptop and puts it in the case, unplugs dvd player (vid has been dormant for the last hour or so, but the TV's still emitting black illumination and electromagnetic dog whistle), turns off tube, lays out and rides another rail, hops over to the window. What's he got? Jackrabbits in the parking lot. Pixelated dew on matte maroon 2249cc Rocket Roadster with custom, XSKillaHaul-inspired accoutrements. Blue glass insulators sticking on fence posts along empty brown highway. Tule fog windshield sweat and slag heap silhouettes (grey, getting browner), a big corrugated metal shed, a couple of double-wides, a quonset hut and a chain-link fence corral on the far side. Exhaust pouring out of an old pickup in an off-yellow field. He should rest his eyes before it gets too bright. First just one more bump; a mighty mightay.

Ho boy. One bump over the line sweet Jesus, full speed into a wall. Pores succumb; arms, face and neck suddenly bloom with oily condensation. Heart is a pumping fist. Ho boy. Snowblind and leaking sweat, he staggers into the bathroom, throws cold water against his face, stares at the pulsating psychopath staring back at him from the mirror and waits, hand tamping heart, for the flood to crest. Oh no! He loves it! Oh shit! A hot minute, then things begin to subside. Breathe, see, check nostrils. He pinches, sucks hard, releases, flushes bitter air through his sinuses, swallows yum-m-mm! The sun shines full on, steam's rising from metal posts outside window. No rest for the wicked.

He eats a power bar in the shower, washes it down with milky showerhead water while he rinses off the sweat stink and coke funk. He gets dressed, chokes down a banana, slams a cup of what passes out here for coffee, and gathers up his shit. He double-checks his map. Three hours, give or take. Should arrive at oh nine hundred hours local time, commencement at oh ten, demo at nineteen hundred hours for a twilight zone show time, his favorite. But first things first... one more white line for the road...

* * * *

Several small clusters of people rest beneath the long

tent. Pillows, blankets, and sleeping bags have been brought into the shade for use as furniture. Blankets and rugs hang between the thicket and the awning to keep the bugs away. The clusters are connected by a few loose threads of conversation. Talk is casual and friendly, curious but reserved, like the patter of passengers on a long train journey. Several people sit silently, gazing past the sparsely populated trance floor to where a ring-like structure incorporating tents, tarps, wood scraps and rocks, with the fire pit in its center, is being erected. Meanwhile the sun is creeping in on their shady shore like a rising river. Soon it'll flood the tent along its length, and more sheets will have to be hung. Word has it that there will definitely be dancing to outdated Techno later, and a fire, and probably drugs; quieter scuttlebutt has chanting, more-exotic drugs, a ceremonial dousing-of-the-fire, and weird ritual shit in the dark. The kinkier whispers are mostly sarcastic. There is plenty of discomfort, disappointment and disbelief to go around, but there's also a growing anticipation. No one has lit out for pre-manifested accommodations yet. Even a few of the locals have settled in for a spell.

Wieland and Zafer have set up the Eclair in one of the open spaces between two rug walls. It's a good spot, cinematographically speaking; the floral geometry of the rugs juxtapose intelligently with the organic visual chaos of the wild roses behind them. Wieland holds for a four count, pans right out of the multi-patterned shadow and into the bleached monotony of the wadi, adjusts to the raw light now flooding the lens for a quick foreshortened crowd shot, pans right again, follows a path up the hill to where Uwe moves among the sheep herd like a big schwarzes Schaf bullseye, centers him, pulls in, and holds for an eight count. Judging it worthy of his limited film footage, Weiland resets to repeat the shot "rolling," but he's interrupted by Avery and Aisha entering the frame, accompanied by the guy who calls himself Camel Lion and another man who is being shadowed by a sleepwalking fellow he's seen somewhere else, He ends up using his precious footage on their approach instead, somewhat to his chagrin.

"Say hello to the camera please!"

"Hello camera."

"Aisha! Avery!" Zafer turns toward the couple laying next to him, holding his hand out like a display mannequin, "Meet your—"

"Waterloo?" CAMEL states the present level of philosophical diffraction.

"I've had worse," says someone off camera.

"Schnitt." Wieland puts down the Eclair.

"Yeah well," CAMEL says. "This is a ceremony; it's not just entertainment."

"Entertainment? Well! Have you had this to happen to you?" Wieland nods at Avery. "You are watching some music, and between the songs the singer starts to make excuses for his own performance, apologizing for things that did not bother you before? So then you become bothered by them? It is because you wish to live vicariously through the singer."

"What's your point?" asks CAMEL.

"How is your ceremony to be performed?"

"Focusing all these perspectives into something transcendent?" CAMEL shrugs. "Search me."

"You mean to say you don't know what you are to do? Splendid!" What is that accent? "Splendid!" the voice repeats, with a single hand clap for punctuation. "Marveloso!"

"Mm hm," CAMEL grunts. But there's a new note in his lament. He's starting to enjoy himself. "That's easy for you to say. You don't have a hundred random strangers to satisfy."

"Tsk tsk. Random strangers? Come come." The voice again. Avery turns around. It's the old guy who was sitting in the corner of the Berber Room last night. The same woman who was with him then is next to him now, whispering to Karina, whose eyes lock onto his like electromagnets. He tries to look away as CAMEL grouses.

"We got five, six days. If people don't get... on board, which I don't see happening, then I don't know what to say."

"I see. Is there nothing for which we might become more... on board, as you say?"

"Such as?"

"We might build a boat." The old man points to the wood pile. "From that."

"A boat. And why would we want to do that?"

Wieland, taking it as a cue, "Avery, I'd you to meet—"

"Like Noah Ark?" Karina says, a teasing skepticism showing through her accent. "Two by two?" She reaches over and tugs rough-playfully at the bottom of Avery's shirt, and wiggles two fingers at him when he looks down. If she's fucking with him, it's working.

"I had another vessel in mind," the old man says.

"Der Fitzcarraldo!"

"Not quite..."

"There once was a ship," someone says, "that had over the course of its many years afloat many repairs made. With each replacement the original piece or part was stored away in a warehouse. After the last piece of the original ship had been replaced, the warehoused parts were reassembled and put to sea..."

"Which is the true Piece of Shitteus," says some joker.

"Speaking of piles..." replies another.

"Chsh...."

"Why the hell not."

"Ship it is."

* * * *

For fifty-three minutes the highway makes a perfect T with the horizon line, with the sun firing light from directly above its vanishing point, so SmartVisor frames cubist crucifixion in business casual palette. The Man turns his wrist and the shoulders blur, but not the vanishing point. He cuts on the white line and it's too perfect, impossibly symmetrical, proof he's locked in. The face of the interface is he.

Face down, just; noon on his Tropic, sun-disc just out of frame, but close enough for synthetic—crepuscular pink-gold halo rays to dart down SmartVisor. To demonstrate is all that is necessary. The Program will play itself. They will be watching a screen. They will be aroused, natch, all the more fully present. They will experience the separation-pull at the horizon of the interface. They will understand that a reality-complex corresponds with what their eyes receive; these will merge and blend and bleed; they will feel the connection. And yet they will persist in distinguishing themselves substantially. They will not wrap their heads around their own entanglement. They never do. They will glimpse it, but they won't get it. They don't need to get it; for what is matter but a critical density of data? He is not in the cloud, for He is the Cloud; the Cloud Primordial, the Cloud Coalescing; the Program is the Bubble—the Bubble that grows inside the Bubble to become the Bubble. The Program will play itself, with or without them. Only a chosen few need to get it; the Bubble is virtually inevitable. The rest are to serve it. The Indians; they get it. Hindus that is. They see what it does but they don't know what it is. He's sure as fuck not going to tell them. Every client is Constantine; what happens on the screen should only plant dreams within him, from feel-good without and about him. Let the process unfold; yep, natch. The Program will play out and in and out and in and out—; today's reality-fucks are tomorrow's creation myths. Constantine shouldn't understand; he should only be impressed.

The point becomes a line separating, now falling in front of the horizon. Temporary exit, check. He gets on the frontage road that runs parallel to the highway. Highway plane lifts from the ground next to now above him like a canopy, becomes causeway as frontage road dips into ancient volcanic river-turned-flood plain. Flash of darkness as highway makes long right-angle right sweep to southwest, becomes one line again, same as before only smaller in his rearview, scrolling back to reset. Frontage road continues straight ahead; highway remerges with rearview horizon just as he reaches Two-thirds Road. Too perfect.

A doublepop from the bullet and he's flying high again. What's up, *g*? Mo' grams for the Program, that's what! Jshjhoooo! He drives three miles up Two-thirds to a steel gate in massive earthen ridge. Guard receives him, takes credentials and voice-code signature. "Follow me." Gate opens, guard climbs into waiting beige golf cart with blue awning (bizness caaj-, natch), leads them up narrow road toward helipad and solar array lying flat on the desert floor. Past helipad, ground drops beneath plane of solar panels, spirals into enormous circular depression. Caldera carcass, eroded to a shallow sunken ring, with a stillborn volcanic swelling at its center. Low-slung, solar-paneled buildings clustered around a domed radar tower, a giant blue mosaic robotitty swelling to gunmetal nippletip daring him, begging him, to get it up. He pulls over, powers down, releases electromagnet holding stipulated rearview mirror (srm), hands srm to guard, stipulates, stretches, snorts good and deep, reaches the reservoir. "Let's get a dawn...."

* * * *

"I might share a story?" the old man asks. Avery nods when the man's eyes meet his. He'd like to hear the man's story, but Karina keeps tugging his shirt. She has the cruelest timing.

"Shoot, gramps," the joker says.

"*Hvala*. It is a long story," the man tells them, "but I will try to make it short. When I was a young man, I did a grand thing. At least I like to think it was. I hitchhiked all the way from my hometown of Novi Sad through Serbia, Slavonia and Slovenia, and then I walked out of Communist Yugoslavia over the Kolovrat into the Veneto. In 1966 this should not have been so simple to do, but for me it was. I cannot explain why. Sometimes it is this way. From Trieste I crossed Italy, and sailed from Genoa to New York City aboard the *S.S. Michelangelo*. She was a good ship, but the voyage was difficult. We nearly sank. Sunk? Two people died. I suffered terribly from seasickness. When we landed in the United States I kissed the ground first, then went immediately to Greenwich Village, because at that age I was as impatient as I thought I had to be, and quite smitten with the American trends—or I should say my own wonderful misconceptions about them, dreamed up back home in Novi Sad. After one week in Manhattan I took the Super Chief to New Mexico, where I had relatives living at the time. Ah, what a lovely train trip that was! I enjoyed it very much, except but for one thing. You see, my birth name is Ljubomir Aristocles Vukosavljević. Ljubomir is a lovely name, you know. It means love's peace. Not bad, I think, but a mouthful for Americans to swallow. Aristocles was the name of my mother's favorite martyr. As a name, it should be unsurpassed, as it literally means 'well-named'. Aristocles was also the birth name of a man who, like myself, became far better known by another name. I am referring of course to the immortal Plato. This I find very funny. I will tell you why. I worked very hard to teach myself English in Yugoslavia, and I was eager to practice it in America. Yet during my train journey across America, conversations were most often a challenge. The challenge would consist of my new acquaintance attempting to repeat my name back to me, and myself being obliged to politely encourage their efforts and correct their mistakes. Once we had agreed on relative success or good effort, that would most often be the end of the conversation. It was okay, of course, but not what I wanted. So by the time I reached Kansas City, Missouri, I had decided that if I was to make any inroads into that country I so wished to experience meaningfully, I would first have to get off of my beach-head of a name. In other words, I would lie in my search for the truth. Of course I could not call myself John Smith...."

Avery watches Karina out of the corner of his eye. She's taken those two fingers, inverted them, and made a walking person. She "walks" from her midriff to his hip, and slips her fingertips into his pant waist. Aisha sees the enticement; she hoists her eyebrows and smiles familiarly. Avery's torn; he's not being allowed to pay attention to the story, but he wants to hear it.

"After several days in the barren plains of northern New Mexico, I decided to take a bus trip to the Taos Pueblo," the old man continues. "At the church next to the bus station there was being held a... rummage sale? It was a sunny autumn day, very much like today. I had no plans, so I stopped to have a look. There I came across an autobiographical tale of a young man who sailed around Cape Horn to California. The most wonderful thing about this volume was what I found when I opened it. On the inside cover was a drawing of a three-masted ship in full gale; a blossom of sails, beautifully rendered. It appeared to be the work of a talented child, in my estimation, as the hand was both light and unstudied. Yet there was something—a longing, perhaps; I cannot say—that gave to the drawing what I can best describe as *import*. That is, this ship seemed to urge me on. Beneath the drawing, in the far lower right-hand corner, was very carefully written the name *Mika Krizan*. The instant I read this, I knew I had found my new name. I liked it so much that I've kept it ever since, and it has served me very well. Perhaps it was the same for Plato. It's a pity that I did not purchase the book. I thought it would be too heavy to carry around."

"You're that artist dude," CAMEL says, genuinely impressed. Maybe he'd been underrating his clientele some after all. "I got your book at home. Talk about heavy; that thing is *brutal*."

"*Hvala*. Thank you. Yes. It was unauthorized, you know. I like it very much also, so much so that I sued the gentleman who published it, and assumed his debts."

"Cool. No wonder you want to build a ship."

Avery shakes his head in disbelief. "Wait a second. You mean—?"

"I was many times trying to tell you," Wieland whispers to him. While Avery is still actively struggling to process what he's just heard, Karina blows in his ear from a good three feet away. For a few seconds he forgets all about the fairly gargantuan fact that the famous Conceptual Brutalist whose shadow he and Aisha chased all over Berlin is standing right here, in this of all places, telling him that his grandfather has not only been a source of his inspiration, but is in fact the *real* Mika Krizan. So not only is she a hypnotist, he thinks instead, she's sort of a ventriloquist too. Her breath is soothing and intimidating at the same time, like the ocean. It's also very seductive.

"I will tell you," Ljubomir/Mika says, "this is a reason why I bury much of my work. My critics have supplied so many wonderful interpretations, of course, but never the true one. It's very good. And I understand that you are *the* Mika Krizan's very grandson. How remarkable! What a pleasure it is to meet you! My counsel," gesturing toward the woman sitting next to him, "informs me of any legal actions concerning my, or I should say, *your grandfather's* name. You might say it is a hobby of mine to know these things. When I learned that a deceased American named Mika Krizan was part of a fraud case involving my work, naturally I wished to investigate further. When I learned that the fraud concerned a lost sculpture of the *Ayacucho*, I knew that I had found my child illustrator from so long ago! I cannot express to you the delight I felt! I was reminded of the words of the poet Agathon: 'Of this power alone are even the Gods are deprived; to make undone what has been done.' I am here to test this assertion." But Avery can't respond right away, as Karina's leaning over him now, and sticking her tongue in his earhole. Her breath is hot, but cool on the wet part. Aisha looks at him. She looks amused, sympathetic, and also a little jealous. Of whom he can't tell.

David drones on. "It's all got to be so cheap now, huh," he says, looking at the sun. "All ram, no rom...; is that what you millenn..ualsssay?"

"Mmm..."

"Why do you think they're shtarving the artss?"

"I—"

"I'll tell you why. They don't want us to believe in ourselves anymore... the basstards."

Although she knows better, Kalila asks, "Who's they?" Lucky for her, he ignores the question. "Another reason I can't stand doing readings," he says, spinning off on another tangent, "you're exsspected to explain the whole... blashted thing in two minutes..."

"Uh huh."

"Huh? What? 'If there is a special hell for writers it would be in the forced contemplation of their own works.' You know Dosspassoss?"

"Uh uh."

"Ahch who cares. The book is the show, okay. I tell them, if there was a better way of getting the bloody point acrossss, I would not have bothered writing the— fucking thing in the first place, esscuse my Fraunch. You ever think about that?"

"Wha—hmp mm."

"What are you asking me for! Am I right or what? Right?"

"Uh."

"If you'd have bothered reading it, I tell them—"

"Hm?" Kalila is also having to split her attention , back ans forth between the increasingly belligerent writer and the kids who keep circling. Finally, one of the boys falls out of orbit. "Hi," Kalila says. He stops. "Hi," she repeats. He waves shyly, taking another step toward her.

The taller of of the two girls joins him. "American?"

Kalila nods. She holds a pretend steering wheel. "Detroit."

"Oh..." the boy looks at his partner, makes like he's

shooting a gun.

She shakes her head. "It's not that bad." Gesturing around herself at North Africa, "Just like most places."

"But don't think you're going to find out anything about that on the internet," Dave Edwards says contemptuously, as if being forced to speak an obscenity, oblivious to the children's fidgety esperanto. "They feed us a tidal fucking wave of useless information every god damn day. Burying all of the important shit where we can't—Where'di'go? It's too deep. You get my point?" Kalila nods absently. She and the other children have silently begun to formulate their escape plan. "Problem is, your generation won't even know what you're missing! Sorry! And mine? We've been twenty-nine for thirty fucking years. Don't look at us.... Talk about monsters." Mr. Edwards is a bit of a magician in his own right. He's getting drunker by the minute, but she hasn't seen him once produce a bottle. "First world problems, right?"

"Do you live around here?" Kalila asks the taller girl.

"There," she replies, pointing toward the muddy hills.

"Let's go."

"Well listen," David says to the retreating children, "I'm going to go... do it up." He leans in, almost falls over, steadies himself on Kalila's shoulder. His breath gives her a head rush. Kendra looks over and puffs her chest. "Remember what I told you," he reeks at her, "they don't have your imagination. Don't forget that. That's the thing, and there ain't a damn thing they can do but try to steal it. They're depending on you to imagine your own failure, to envision your own subjugation at their ssstupid hands, because they can't do it alone. I mean it.

Don't let the basstards—"

"It was nice to finally meet you, Mr. Edwards," Kalila says, already running. "Gotta go. See you."

David Edwards raises his eyes to the horizon and aims himself in its general direction, grunting over his shoulder as he pitches blindly into a group of trancers, "don't let 'em see you coming."

CAMEL/EON watches the writer slosh to the far side of the trance floor. "It should go there, where that guy is—or was. Let's clear the rest of these rugs out." NZYME is the first one on the job, followed by Tripsy, Tobi and Omar, Benny, Benny's biological brother Brother Kendall, and his fellow Vulture Brother Throater. It would seem that the Vultures received their what were supposed to be the laBlab's comp tickets by honest mistake (in one of his early spasms of passive-aggression, CAMEL must've stuffed the unaddressed envelope into the wrong mailbox), giving their presence here an extra degree of randomness (with the free airline tickets, reserved in their names being another matter entirely, in their case as well). Russell starts dragging planks of wood from the scrap pile and laying out the dimensions of a hull on the wadi floor.

"We can bury the walls and go from there." Sunlight floods the long-tent, but the sun is sinking fast. In another hour it will have dropped below the far hills, and they'll be working in the dark. A critical mass is reached. When someone suggests that they build a platform from which she might sing an aria, she is gladly accommodated; likewise, when someone suggests they turn the hull a couple degrees for better magnetoception, the answer is "naturally." This same attitude is taken toward all suggestions, a policy that proves, paralogically perhaps, to be a massive time-saver.

Russell and CAMEL, having reached the same long beam together, move to its opposite ends. "We don't want to be part of the mainstream," CAMEL tell him. "All that commercialism; sorry to sound all holier-than-thou but it's just so... shabby..."

"Shabby, huh? Appalled at the poor quality, are ye?" Russell jests across the charred-on-one-side beam as he lifts his end. "Too shitty for you? Not magic enough? Magic or no magic; don't mean talk ain't cheap. Shoot. Might be greedy bastards, but at least they keep it where their money's at. That's where it belongs, ain't it? Where everybody can see it? It's the folks what hide their greed who I worry about. You never know what you'll dig up with them—"

"It might not seem like a big deal to you, but that's just what we weren't trying to do! It's not that they've coopted our future, Russ, they've coopted our past. It works for them now. That means we've been working for them all along! See? No?"

"So what're ye giving 'em that much power for?"

"What are you, a life coach?"

"I'm a Coyotaje."

"A what?"

A couple of Vultures burst through the bushes from the direction of the toilets. "That's what I call getting in touch with your ancestors... god damn."

"Right?"

There's the enormous thump! of an amplified needle

being dropped on vinyl, and a scratchy Moroccan go-go record begins to blast over the PA. "Is that an electric fish I hear?" The needle skips badly, tears across the record and goes silent, as if embarrassed by its own outburst.

Gil can't believe his luck. Sitting in the dirt in the sun, with a bunch of strangers. What could be better after a twelve hour flight and a four hour drive? And the best part is, it's only just begun. Five more days of this!

He never would have accepted the invitation in the first place if it wasn't for that new hippy shrink of his. She actually called it *portentous*. Christ almighty. Look at these people!

He pictures a slightly grimmer construction than the one before him. His consists of an attractor (he envisions a small white sun) and an immense teeming surge from a beginning/ground-state, composed of countless moving points, like a magnetic dust, with each point representing a human lifetime, and the aggregate forming a sort of wave (the outliers and exceptional cases serving as electrostatic blur, visually), bending upward toward the source (so much struggle! so nearly impossible even to rise at all!); up, up; cresting, exhausting, never reaching, but always, always falling away.... And if that's not happy enough of a story arc for you, the post—state is never at the same level as the pre—state. It's always lower, to compensate for the aberrant grasping salient. Infernal machine... forever ending lower. So even aesthetics are complicit...—but wait! What's this? Down here the sine is dissolving—no, it's interwoven into a bizarre vibrational fabric, in hypercomplex concert with helixes, figure-eights (and nines, tens, ...), spirals, circles, and countless other curves! Has he sifted his way to the string level? But these aren't strings at all. He perceives (patchily, like through a filter) a simmering, maddening to look at directly; all of the possibilities, after all, all... awh! It's... In all the churning static, he finds... balance? Peace? Return? It's teeming up; zooming out...—and here he is now, on a macro level he also can't pin down. He stands up, gathers a deep breath of air, rolls it at the top of his lungs... lets it fall, draws with it the sine wave of a roller coaster. He exhales until the echo-stain of his wave is absorbed by the sand. Who's he kidding? He feels just fine. Things could always be worse. See if he can't throw his back out on that boat over there. He wouldn't mind another glass of that lemonade, either. That stuff is delicious.

* * * *

Seventeen concrete stairs connect path to deep recess in wall of radar station. Mahogany door opens to hallway leading to skylit, mahogany-paneled room. Large Rococo swivel mirror stands alone in the middle of white wall-to-wall carpet. Skylit attendant in sky-blue skirt stands behind short counter near door. Another coat closet and another door, mahogany, behind her. She takes his helmet and jacket, disappears without expression into the closet, tight athletic ass swishswishing in synthetics, returns with a white cotton Gandoura and leather sandals, points him to shower and dressing room. He rinses off, visines, mouthwashes, does last-for-now minty fresh pop, stashes, splashes with fragrant water, strips, puts on robe and sandals and that's it. Walks back into room. Attendant's standing at the mirror, ready to swivel. That's it. Rotate me into the light...

At top of steps he bumps into who he'll call Captain Merica (every rich ex-brass faux-visionary pitchman CFO fuck) and the client (another very rich Constantine in latest East-West-hybrid monkeysuit) at the top of the steps—perf—"... and here he is now."

"Speak of the devil," The Man shouts, pointing at himself.

"I'd like you to meet our star pilot, Mr.—"

"Call me MecOne."

It goes all good. A bit of orchestrated serendipity; client's getting his tour and pitch, topic of extra-special hot-shit demonstrator comes up, bam! here's the demonstrator himself. Keep shit rolling. And what do you know? La di da and away we go! Along buzz-cut bluegrass putting greens either side of the gently curving path.

* * * *

"You're right," CAMEL says. "It shouldn't matter. The less predictable the better."

"It's reasonable to expect some... cooperation, though," Aisha says.

"No, it's cool," Ala assures CAMEL. "I think we'll be all right." A highly-processed Cheb Hasni dance mix swirls and pops through earthier noises. The scrap-quilt hull is coming together. Given that no two pieces match, and the walls were raised conterminously and with a minimum of cross-checking, it exhibits surprising symmetry. Makeshift buttresses are being removed one by one. Laughter rings out from the hold. More rugs are being dragged up to the quarterdeck floor, to keep fewer feet from busting all the way through the palette slats, while the three short masts and a bowsprit are being lashed together from freed buttress pieces and speaker wire. One of the QSCs sits on a crate in the center of the bilge like a treasure chest, blasting away, turning the hull into a giant speaker cabinet, and the T60's diamond needle into a plow, and the harvest an underworldly bottom-end.

"...transformed, through living channels. Relief to those for whom life is thirst," muses L. A. Vukosavljević to Peregrine as he paints 'Ayacucho' just behind the poop deck; "she describes for us the stories of our lives, lines forever traced and retraced, like a riverbed—"

"A most simple, graceful stroke."

"Complexity is often mistaken for simplicity, I think." He glances with concern at the growing, name-attacking... raptor, is it?

"Quite brings the Acjagchemem to my mind, all this," says the allegedly landed ornithopter.

L.A. holds his tiny brush upright in the air, sizes him up through it and its ghost-double both. "Please?"

"Annual ritual sacrifice of the divine vulture, represented by a more literal buzzard, of course... although to say represented does rather... misrepresent, doesn't it? Not only the very same bird but the very same woman, you see. That's all I'm on about. Don't remember much about the squaw I'm afraid, but every year she manages to get herself turned into a turkey vulture. Don't ask me how. A *Cathartes aura*. Marvelous creatures, those. One point of the ritual is to turn the vulture back into a woman. Don't ask me why. Used Jimsonweed as a sort of a... ticket in. According to old Sir Frazer, the savages couldn't tell the difference between species and individual—"

"Yes, I see. Perhaps we are all the same vulture then. Very good. But he was correct, in sensing this unity of difference there, in California, no? I think so..."

Aisha watches her dad's work buddy and his partner try to act like they're not looking for Avery. It's like a slapstick routine. The guy who just passed out standing up must be the writer Avery said he thought he saw earlier. He stood right next to her for a good ten minutes, muttering to himself. Here comes Avery now, with Karina, from the direction of the farmhouse. Karina's holding a film camera, and Avery's got a funny look on his face. What a day he's having. Good for him. Now he sees something she can't see from where she's sitting. He walks back around the hull out of sight, while Karina climbs aboard the vessel. CAMEL sees whatever it is too, but continues to work. His work outfit is a dirty feathered cap with a beak instead of a bill, and a leather crotch-wrap-thing. He's not wearing any shoes either, even with all the scrap and rusty metal going on. Pretty disturbing. Ala keeps coming up to him, staying just long enough to run one finger along one muscle-furrow, or whisper something in his ear, before flouncing away. Look; there she is now, a shimmering of semi-sheer fabrics, offering her eye for plumb, now giving someone a neck rub. She's very attractive for her age. She's given Aisha a couple of interesting looks. The word 'tropical' comes to her mind.

Aisha takes a picture of Ala chatting up Wieland. Zafer,

Uwe and that NZYME dude are letting Asulil and Rahiq film them with the Bolex, while Aghbalu and Usem take turns looking through the Eclair without touching it. Shula and the girl from Detroit alternate between filming Asulil and Rahiq's filming on a cell phone camera and popping into their shot from unlikely directions. Karina now stands over them all, framing the scene as a wide-screen landscape with her thumbs and forefingers. They were talking about filming a very-short later on tonight, starring a real soldier, and speed-narrated by a professional fast-talker. They've asked Aisha to write some dialogue.

"Think... Eisenstein in Laredo..."

"I can't do that—"

Here comes Ala.

"Pulque? Seitan? Ketamine?" Humid. "Kama Sutra?"

* * * *

"I understand your question," says Captain Merica. "And yes, the answer is no; the Ruptor AURAVOIDER is no more difficult to operate than your garden variety Ababil Sparrow," lying, natch, "though ours is of course a smaller and far stealthier machine. Is there a learning curve? Of course there is. I wouldn't think it something your pilots shouldn't be able to pick up fairly quickly. But will your intel analysts be astounded by its next-generation surveillance and data collection technology? You bet they will. I can assure you..." They enter the station through the main doors. Thirty-nine close-set donkey eyes pinned to twenty screens, all harvested by him personally. Haters. They resent him for showing them who they really are.. Because he's Lawrence of fucking Arabia; he's John the fucking Baptist; everybody please kneel. Now suck his dick. By the way, the Board would like to watch. They can't get enough of his ass. Looks real sexy on paper. When they want to really turn on the charm, they give it a jingle. So tough titty, little droney drones, who'd have Constantine staring at sand for an hour on some grid search. It's one thing to be a wizard with the wand — it's called "getting plenty of pussy and fame" — but what gets the Machine so fucking hot for The Man is his nose, raw for action. Speaking of which, today's contract stipulates no looking unless wearing clown nose, glasses/nose/'stache combo (no buckteeth), because 'any insistence upon mutual acknowledgement, or similar attempts at leveling corrupt his precisely honed, naturally rarefied talents...' Ca-ching. "... and the canard configuration and high aspect ratio wing allows the Ruptor to loiter above its target for longer than ever before...," blah blah blah.... They'd dismiss him as a dandy if they could, only he won't let them. "... less than deadly..." No Armed Force ever wrung his bad ass self onto no middling bell-curve (talk about tough titties), and they got to know it. "... peace business... Disruption not Prosecution is our m.o."

* * * *

"Avery." It's Al, the interviewer, wearing a wide-brimmed straw hat, cargo shorts and hiking sandals. Karina frames them, smiles, and heads toward the boat.

"Al? I wasn't expecting to see you here. But I can't say I'm surprised."

"It's a small world, yes?"

"I'll say." Avery has already recognized Endlicher and Guzman as the same two people from the station on that strange last night in Primera. He's been keeping an eye on them as best he can, considering. They're inching this way now. Now they're looking right at him. He sees Al look in their direction and nod, as if giving them a signal. He freezes. So *that's* what the interview was about! He knew something was odd about that whole thing. Al must be some sort of private investigator, working for Superior Life! "It was all my doing," he says to Al. "No one else's."

"Your partner in crime might disagree, no?" Al points at Aisha, who's busy attaching rigging to the mainsail, and smiles broadly beneath his straw hat. "Have you met my friends?"

"Those guys?" Avery waves at the investigators. "Not yet, but it looks like I'm about to."

After seeing Avery wave in their direction, Guzman and Endlicher abandon their cloak and dagger routine and start marching over. Endlicher raises his hands with reflexive relief, as if he's the one surrendering.

When Al sees who Avery is referring to, his sleepy eyes flare ever-so briefly, then narrow into happy crescents. "Not them!" he laughs, and points again, toward but not at the investigators. He nods again at Ljubomir Vukosavljević and Lila Vukosa, who seem to have placed themselves directly between Avery and his pursuers. "Them."

"We're commming to get themmm, Bahhbara," Endlicher moans under his breath, theremin-like. "Bahhbara…, we're—"

"Yeah Don. Good one. I get it." But she wiggles her fingers in the air and makes a brief theremin sound of her own. A deal's a deal. "Just flash them the paper, tell them who we are, and see what they have to say." They pass through a slowly rolling wheel of dancers, one of whose arms swings dangerously close to Guzman's head, causing her to duck and almost trip over the long wooden stick that's suddenly blocking her path. "Try to get them to ag—god—damn it—"

"Excuse me…"

"Watch your damn staff, hippy!" Guzman barks. "Jesus…" What is that thing, some sort of a flute? Oh it's just a cane. And it's not connected to a wizard, but to a little old man. "Oh! I'm sorry!"

"Not at all, investigator Guzman."

"I'm sorry?" Inv. Guzman shakes her head. She's clearly no longer sorry. "Have we met?"

Avery points. "You mean Mika Krizan?"

"And his daughter, Lila."

"I thought she was his lawyer."

"She is also that, yes."

"Oh!"

"So… you are disappointed now?"

"Why would I be disappointed?"

"You have not found your friend."

"No, but I wasn't—"

"He stays just ahead, no?"

"I—I was going to say I don't quite follow…"

"Yes. Come, let's walk. We are not so different, you and I. Like the bees, yes, who must gather pollen."

"I don't get it. You're saying we're drones?"

"Drones don't gather pollen, Avery. *L'ignorance artificielle est un affront à l'inexplicable.* And so little of what we really do is named, no?"

Avery nods. He feels a little bit guilty now for thinking Al was working for Superior Life. "Were you annoyed at the way we ended the interview?" he asks.

"I felt you were keeping your options too far open. Being less than entirely honest, perhaps. But I understood."

"I'm sorry." Avery looks uncertainly at Aisha, who has just walked up to them.

Al pats him on the shoulder. "No. I don't accept. I was also not being entirely honest. I do not write for a tourism magazine. But all good stories contain lies, no?" He nods at Aisha. "Hello again."

"Hello."

He smiles at the two of them. "Partners in crime."

"So if you're not… then what were you talking about last night with those two investigators?"

"I just told you. Gathering pollen. But you must tell me, you two; what are your plans now? Something tells me they do not include a residency at the Kasbah Kandisha."

"Remember those tickets I told you about, that the writer gave me in that carriage house in Primera?"

"Of course. You refused them, if I remember correctly."

"No, I took them." Avery undoes a shirt button and produces a small grouch bag he has tied around his neck. He takes the two Lisbon-to-Tokyo airfare vouchers from the leather pouch and hands them to Al.

"Ah."

"At the time it seemed so unlikely, but..."

"The latest plan is to visit Kyoto," Aisha says, "then go home to face the music."

"I see." Al hands the tickets back to Avery. "By the way, how much of that fifteen thousand dollars do you have left?"

"Most of it." Avery stashes the grouch bag beneath his shirt. "We had a little bit of our own money, and we've been... more than fortunate. We haven't really needed to spend much. Our plan is to make it back with most of the cash intact."

"And the bank account?"

"You're looking at it."

"Of course. So..." Al turns around clockwise, then counter clockwise. He puts his hand on their shoulders and whispers between them, "I think you two should go now, then."

Avery points at Guzman and Endlicher, who are on the other side of the clearing, busy talking with the artist and his lawyer. "We don't mind talking to them. We plan on coming clean when we get back anyway, so what's the big deal? As they say in the casino, right?"

"And the insurance company? You said they deserved what they got."

"Yeah, well… maybe it's not about them…"

"It's very interesting that you came here, no? You combined your crime and punishment into one act, and you will bring some stories home with you, no? You will share them, with those who ask the right questions?"

"I don't—"

"The secret society your friend Mara told you about?"

"Oh. Yeah. Sounds kind of silly when you put it that way."

"Oh, no; it is not silly at all. What I mean to say is, there is a way…" He points with his eyebrows toward a trio of shadowy figures tramping up the wadi toward the darkness. One of the figures turns around and waves. Al motions for them to stop. "You see those people up there?" Avery and Aisha both nod. "Follow them. They can take you to Oran now. From there you can get easily to Lisbon."

"Why now?"

"They prefer to travel by night."

* * * *

Hands one with joysticks, fingertips on nickel nippletips, hips ass thighs wrappedaround by sweet contoured leather seat. That's it…. Eyes one with screen. Tits cold launch and he's up… he's in…. Mmm mmm mm. There it is. Feels good. The Man kicks off his sandals, wraps his toes over the edge of the console, squeezes, adjusts the motorcycle mirror paperweight and… Mmmm… thrusts.

"We are great believers in disruption, as you will soon see," Captain Merica bullshits away behind him. "You have this concept?" In the mirror, Constantine dips his head demurely. The Man likes to let the voyeur know he's being watched. This one likes it. Freaky freakay. "Well, we like to think we've taken it to the next level." Captain waits for a bite, doesn't get it, reels in, recasts, "So, what do I mean by that? Well, the very first thing we did was approach prosecution in a brand new way, focusing on its inefficacy as a control mechanism, long-term... blah blah blah inherent risk of metastasizing proximate radical sentiment through traumatic experience etc. etc. That is, we came to see the conventional, explosive approach as being too... binary? That is to say, what results can you reasonably expect from an ordinary bomb? An explosion. Or nothing. One single, unrepeatable result. But what if a single device could produce a variety of effects, ranging from mild anxiety and discomfort to permanent incapacitation? And what if this full range could be focused on one individual, or broadened, much like a lens, to an area the size of a city block? And what if the results could be repeated at will?" In the mirror, Constantine leans in and focuses his eyes on the screen. "Ruptor is our next-generation AURAVOIDER—"

"What is this, AURA—"

"What's it stand for? Autonomous Unmanned Recon/Attack Vehicle/Onboard Intercept/Directed Energy Radiator. You'll see for yourself momentarily. Something to keep in mind as we proceed, is a wonderful benefit of a system of this type, which is the absence of payload—"

"Tell me what I am looking at, please?" Kinky Constantine's eyes on the mirror, on the man/machine; he wants it.

"Give me a reading on that, would you Carla?" Captain Merica waits. "She's new here," he apologizes. "Hey Zane, would you give Miss Conway a hand?"

Looks like the Captain will just have to do it himself, the old fashioned way. He'll bullshit. Leaning in, like that's going to help, "Let's see... we are..." That's it, Captain. Smooth. We wee whee, all the way home. "... looking at the undercarriage camera view, from approximately..." getting a quick, exaggerated horizon curve, so he can misjudge altitude out loud, "—five thousand feet?"

"One thousand feet, sir."

"Thank you, Zane. Ahem. Ruptor is equipped with modified Shahid Noroozi guidance and control system, and ultra-high-resolution CCD TV camera with internal image processing and stabilization softwares. As you saw, with a good pilot no runway is necessary. Launch can be facilitated by mobile pneumatic catapult that we can install on a Benz-Khawar L series truck, or by conventional RLS. The ACS is equipped with autopilot, base operable range of 35 km, increasable to 125, capable of launching, maneuvering, locking, tracking, loitering, disrupting, as well as chute deployment and recovery, datalink..."

"What about noise?"

"Engine noise? Nominal. At operational altitude the target might just sense a mild buzz, and that's only if there is little to no ambient noise. Of course—"

Constantine bows toward the screen. "Where are we now?" he asks, though he knows better. They all know better. They all ask.

"Yes, well... let me put it this way..." Put it, Captain... "we could have this same Ruptor, loaded on the Benz L2624 you just saw, waiting for you at in..."

"But we would not want that."

"No, of course not. We can also provide you with a list of storage facilitators, for a negotiable fee..."

"I see..."

"And we also provide safe launch coordinates, again negotiable."

"I see. Yes, good." Something fat, stinky and horny shifts its weight in the dark.

"These particular coordinates are not negotiable, I'm afraid."

"Of course." The dirty cliffs spread for him. The Man chose the coordinates. He's here to spread the word, and the seed. He'll be gentle. A—a—almost...

"Downside? Simple answer? There is no downside. Just watch."

* * * *

"You might even find yourselves implicated, if you're not careful."

"*Us?* I think you've got us confused—" Inv. Guzman shouldn't say more. Endlicher lifts himself onto the balls of his feet and peers over the head of the old guy. Avery Krizan and Aisha Sandoval are nowhere to be seen. What's with the olive-eyed chick in the cute business attire, is more what he'd like to know.

"Just who do you think we are?" he asks.

"May I ask you both a question?" The woman scans the eyes of both investigators, starting with Guzman's. She proceeds without waiting for permission. "Did Superior Life send you here?"

Guzman's eyes burn. She faces the woman like a brick wall. "And what possible business is it of—?" But the woman only arches her eyebrows as if to say, must I tell you everything? Guzman cinches her eyelids. Things begin to take shape in her mind. She lowers her eyes and stares blankly at the little old man.

"No; they did not," the woman answers her own question, reminding Guzman again that she and Endlicher are acting without Superior's imprimatur. "Strange," she pretends to ponder, with a pinch of cruelty; "I should think yours would be a priority case."

Endlicher curls his upper lip, bites his lower one, and masks his ignorance with feigned ignorance. "And whose acquaintance do we have the pleasure of making?" He looks at his partner. She's nodding, but not at him.

"This is the real Mika Krizan," Inv. Guzman says, "and his lawyer, I presume."

The woman extends her hand into the space between them. "Lila Vukosa. Pleased to meet you."

"Barbara Guzman." The women shake hands. Endlicher's eyes bug. His neck collapses forward while his head stays gyroscopically plumb. "So is it Bland?" Barbara asks. Lila nods.

"Huh?" Don asks.

"Rod Bland, Don. Vice president of the company. Our

boss."

"What about him?" There's so damn much delicacy going on around here; Endlicher wishes someone would just speak plainly. With a wide swivel toward the old man, "Did you say you're Mika Krizan? Were you also invited by the suspects...? I—"

"Not quite, Don." Barbara turns to Mika/Ljubomir. "Right?" She knows she's right. She's nodding, dancing almost, like she's got a song stuck in her head. "I thought you looked familiar. It's all quite decadent, isn't it? I even have a good guess as to why you're both here." She whispers to the old man, "you're not the only one who enjoys research."

"*Veličanstven!*" the artist replies with a mini-curtsy. "But is much more than decadent, *da*? He looks up at her with earnest curiosity, "If you already suspected—"

Barbara cuts him off. "Agent Sandoval and I come from a similar place. He needed to take responsibility for what he did."

"Yes… but he has taken all the responsibility, has he not?"

"He's… yes. Yes he has."

"But how—" Don's head swivels back and forth between his partner and the old man.

"So it's true, then, about Bland."

Lila nods again. "According to reliable sources."

"Hello?" Endlicher insists, hiking his voice up a key. "Anybody?"

Mika Krizan motions toward the paper Endlicher holds. "May I see that, please?"

Endlicher instinctively pulls the paper away. The tone of this conversation is... it's not unfriendly, but he sort of wishes it was. It's like he's acting in a play, and he's the only one without a script. And the old man's the director, and he knows it, and he likes it. There's something almost... brutal about the whole thing. He looks at Guzman. She got a script. She holds her hand out toward him. It's settled, then. He hands her the paper. She passes it to the lawyer lady, who gives it to the old Russian, or whatever he is.

"What's going on here, Barbara?"

She sighs, collapses her shoulder. "Do you happen to remember how the counterfeit Krizan sculpture was insured?"

"Market value, wasn't it?"

"Not counterfeit," Mika/Ljubomir says, with an impish grin.

Lila rolls her eyes at her silly father slash troublemaking client. After glancing over his shoulder at the paper, she gives the investigators her own tempered version of her father's grin. "Is this supposed to be some sort of subpoena?"

"It's... more of a summons, really..."

"A summons? Oh, that's very good! And of course you received for this an okay from the Hague?" The artist laughs heartily.

"Huh? Not... binding... exactly," Endlicher stammers on; "because it's more like... an enticement? A suggestion? We figured, since the tickets were free..."

"Yesss," Lila purrs at him, handing him back the paper

(and good luck with *that*, her eyebrows add). "So, tell me," leaning toward him conspiratorially, almost teasingly, "why did Superior Life not attach its stamp to this... enticement expedition of yours?"

"Don?" Barbara warns him.

"I would venture to guess," Lila says confidently, "that shortly after the arrest of Agent Sandoval, you both received emails from your superiors at Superior, encouraging you to consider the Krizan case to be safely in the hands of law enforcement. Or was it the courts? Not in yours, at any rate. Tell me, were you warned against creating a conflict of interest?"

"They didn't exactly put it that way—"

"But am I, as you say.., in the ballpark?"

"I give up." Endlicher turns to his partner for help.

"Better hold onto your seat, Don."

Meanwhile, with the setting sun in her eyes, Leona Bello leans over the forecastle like a figurehead, nods along to the guessing accompaniment of makeshift musical instruments arranged below her, and clears her throat. The flashy whites, pinks, and beiges of midday edge toward white, yellow and red golds. A flood of sound squeezes a shriek from the orchestra as she commences to bellow O Mio Babbino Caro. The sound is fine enough to find places Tripsy's system, for all its impressive strength, can't reach. Beneath the bowsprit, swaying like someone in religious thrall, a man in black rides her swells. Behind him, a Vulture is moved to silent tears, which are captured by Shula's cell-phone camera (this, and the immediately subsequent footage, will be streamed to Eden's agent's office, and from there to a major Belgian news aggregator...). While enjoying a quiet moment with Ala beneath the tower, CAMEL recalls his original idea to give this event away as a gift to the old tribe. Well not this, exactly. Apparently this wasn't his to give. Meanwhile, in a shadowy area of the trance floor, a new dance is developing. It forms with the patience of large things; it spirals inward but to a circumference whose distance from the yet unoccupied center is too obvious to be agreed upon; it is small but growing, gathering human force the way a storm gathers itself to itself, counterclockwise, and—if noon is north—following the path of the sun through the firmament, and under—. NZYME is struck dumb in the act of ingesting the mushrooms suppling in his palm. He sticks them in his pocket and joins the circle, not needing to have seen one before to recognize the birth of what could end up being a genuine naturitualistic phenomenon. Could it be the dance they've been waiting for? There's only one way to find out.... To those watching from the long tent, the sun seems to hesitate atop the opposite hill for an impossible period of time before finally letting go.

* * * *

The Man loiters the AURAVOIDER over a group of five, two females and three males, walking along a ridgeline. He's between them and the sun. One of them points up at the Ruptor. They all squint upward, then disappear into a ravine Uh oh. A squintet. Not cool, babies. He could... no, he can't. He will tag them.

Captain Merica grips the seatback behind him, covering his ass with reasonable bullshit, "What the pilot's doing now is what's called tagging. He's marked this group, enabling the AURAVOIDER to continue tracking it off-screen, leaving him free to proceed to the primary target, and return later if desired." Ya. He'll be Bach. And up, up, up... and crescendo.... and voila. "Ruptor can focus and transmit sound waves capable of shattering eardrums and even eyeballs, effectively incapacitating any individual or group target. Needless to say, while this operation is considered sublethal, it can be nearly as traumatic to witness as conventional prosecution, and just as liable to foment proximate radical sentiment, so we won't be demonstrating it today. I mention it only disclamana—as a disclaimer." Sure, Captain. Tickle him good.... "What we would like to present, rather, is a small range of alternative methodologies. We believe that by employing less... graphic measures, shall we say? particularly within a public, which these days is another word for publicized, you know, crowd control context, any governmental—or, as in your case, nongovernmental—entity might enjoy far higher rates of compliance." Captain puts his hand on his pilot's shoulder, leans forward again, points to the screen, "... zero in on those gentlemen there, with the leather jackets, if you would, MecOne... that's it... let's start off with some C-six..."

"Coming right up." The Man zooms in to an equivalent distance of fifty feet; not close enough to challenge his company's presumptions regarding target nationality, but close enough for him to know.

"While you may have noted similarities to the Kalandia Scream in this mode, its effects are much subtler. Watch closely as our target begins to experience some mild discomfort. Naturally, conventional prosecution is unconducive to counterintelligence potentialities. Keep an eye also on the individuals most proximate to the target...—Oh—Okay...."

Not quite the optics Captain was hoping for, just after tea.... "Did I mention that this particular mode, when coupled with a decent whisper campaign, has shown itself to be a highly effective deterrent against illicit food distribution?"

* * * *

You've done it now, professor. Congrats. Good luck playing it cool after puking in (euphemism for *on*) a crowd. That second bottle of contraband raki really packed a punch, huh? How blasted (that's explosively...) embarrassing; almost as bad as at the last panel you participated in, when you missed the chair after you jumped up to drive home a point. At least there are no colleagues around here to false-pity you (he saw right through their schadenfreudian slips that day, though, dintee...), unless you count the kid. Good thing she took off when she did. Boy, but that came on fast. It's true. Nothing quite that concentrated has ever hit him before. Weird beans. Not a good sign. Speaking of signs, what was that... premonitory... sound he heard just before, like an auditory migraine aura almost, made him think of flies on roadkill? Everyone sure scattered though, didn't they? Were they already starting to avoid him? Did they know already? Were they were expecting it? He wonders, what if it was a drone? What if he was just the target of a... projectile vomit projectile? Wouldn't that be something? That would explain—(Yeah. Then why's everyone ignoring you, Dave. You're beyond the bounds of plausible deniability, you know... you've graduated...) He pulls the bottle from his waistband, takes a desperate, congratulatory swig, rattles his head, wipes his chin with the back of his hand. "Someone want to bring me a shovel?"

****

"Well then. That was interesting. Let's broaden our focus, shall we?" When in doubt, pull out.

"Far out."

"Not too far out...." Back to the pitch, "Another effective counter-agitator is infrasound-induced visual distortion, or IIVD. In this mode, Ruptor effects vibrations in the eyes of the individual or group being targeted, resulting in disorientation and visual hallucinations. As you will soon see...—... that group there... there you go... disrupt that little Mecca dance...," leaning in, quietly but not softly," H-three...."

"Aye, aye, Kaaba."

****

At the center the darkness develops. The dancers dance in place around it, and let the earth spin effortlessly beneath their feet; they're coming and going, from dying-ember giants at the fingertips of an undiscovered galaxy, to minute traces of grit at the bottom of a dirty drain. In both ways the spiral continues beyond the visible. Light leads time in circles... growing, shrinking... the darkness rushes and recedes in equal measure, and they fall toward it, and away....

The dancers manifest an ululating drone that wobbles between C♭ and C♯. From the ship-speaker only a viscera of beat penetrates the respirating circle (dense quanta of sound, stripped to pulse, regions of higher density and stronger gravitational pull...), serving for each spinner as agent of oscillation, transmission for shifting between pitches. When the IIVD wave hits the choppy C surface, it shifts just enough for the expected, desired visual chaos to settle into (or discover) an unstable moiré pattern, and the spinners' vibrating optic lenses to slip or adjust into a peculiar 'false' focus, obscurely attuned to precisely this synthetic interference. They all "see" the apparition, but none quite possess the conceptual vocabulary to describe it. One thing they all will agree on later: the noise is definitely caused by the apparition, and not the other way around. The 'sense of euphoria' eludes expression as well, though a pile of words are spent trying to say that it exists.

* * * *

"It appears we may be witnessing an epiphany here, gentlemen." Captain Merica may have guessed right this time, but he doesn't like it one bit. His hand chokes the seat so hard the leather crackles. "Maybe they're looking at—," almost saying "Mohammed," not knowing if the ban on depiction extends to the imaginary, "—never mind."

"Maybe they're seeing Jesus," Constantine offers, smiling into the mirror, 'I'm hip, flyboy', in other words. "Now that would be a revelation."

"Could come in handy, though...." Captain sounds

worried, but Constantine is riveted.

"Yes," he whispers, "it could indeed."

Nothing exciting, as far as The Man is concerned. Not a smidgeon of panic. No thrilling thrashing around like ants, or engrossing balling-up like rolypolies. They're hallucinating, but so what? Who else can tell? Where the fuck's the terror? They're dancing just like before. Better, even. There's nothing to sink his teeth into. The Man feels a scoche fucked-with about now. Is someone having a fuck-with with him right about now? What will They think? What are They thinking now? Because this is the worst possible thing; it's boring. He could scream right now, with all this boringness. Sometimes the worst is your world gets liquidated by remote control; sometimes it's the fucking Program depends on you being The Man, and some stupid fucking... collaterals aren't giving you the love. Either way, the desperate man is justified in doing whatever it takes. God he wants to give it to them now!

But that's not the deal, bub. There's to be no deviation from standard procedures, the text said in no uncertain terms. He has to let Captain Merica call the shots, even though Captain Merica is an idiot nobody. It's other "people" he's concerned with. The Program. They hack his thoughts. They tell him secrets. They tell him they have use for one man and one man only. He is The Man. They are watching him right now, through their own very hidden camera, natchitty natch.... They take their deals real serious. Captain here thinks these people are just a bunch of camel jockeys; but The Program knows damn well what They're looking at (kinky research, fellow Americans and all that; real sexy.....). What will

They think of his ability to perform?

* * * *

"Have you never wondered, Mr. Endlicher," Lila maybe flirts a little bit, "as to why your executives at Superior Life exhibit so little enthusiasm for your investigation?" Don nods cautiously. "Or why they seem all too satisfied to have our Mr. Sandoval plead guilty to all charges, and leave it there? Superior Life has yet to recoup a dime of their so-called losses, isn't that correct?"

"So called—?"

"Have either of you asked yourselves why our fugitives have been allowed, one might even say encouraged, to remain at large, while you, their noble pursuers, are forced to resort to counterfeiting and public misrepresentation?" Lila flaps the summons back and forth to illustrate. "Or why the organizers of this event were allowed to keep and use the money to gather a random sampling of Americans to this relatively isolated place, when it would have been exceedingly easy for your agency to simply freeze and seize the funds? The real question to us is, who benefits when everyone else, including yourselves, is sneaking around?"

"I'm still not seeing what you're getting at."

"Here's the deal, Don," Barbara takes the reins, being more familiar with the territory they're entering. "The Krizan was covered under the building's umbrella policy, right?"

"Okay..."

"Which covered all losses at market value, right?"

"I'm with you so far."

"Do you remember who owns the umbrella policy, Don?"

"Yeah, it's that fraternal organization…"

"The Knights of Califa. You know who wasn't supposed to be living there?"

"Who? Krizan? You mean, uh, he was squatting…?"

"No, no," Lila butts in. "Avery Krizan was never made aware of this clause."

"What clause?"

"Don," Barbara explains sympathetically, "according to the terms of the umbrella policy, the policyholder was not permitted to have tenants. Now if—"

"How do you know that, Barbara? Isn't that Rod's policy?"

"He told me himself."

"He did? Why would he do that?"

She gives him a fed-up, but warm look. "I'm an investigator, Don. I swear, sometimes…." Mika Krizan just stands there beaming. Don stares at the artist, almost marveling at his flamboyant satisfaction that this scenario is playing out so goddamned interestingly for him. He's getting that feeling again, like he's playing a fool in a farce, for someone else's amusement.

"The Knights of Califa had been quietly using the building to store unused ceremonial objects and other valuables since the seventies," Barbara explains; "candle holders, scepters, chalices, stuff like that. But over the past two years or so, they've begun to store some pretty valuable objects in there, for certain individual members of the fraternity. These items were added to the manifest... though we'll never know if some of these items ever existed."

"And..." Don grasps. Slowly but surely, dawn breaks. "And they weren't supposed to have tenants in the building. And Rod... And Rod what?"

"Here's what we've learned," Lila says, to Don's obvious astonishment. "There were a total of three unauthorized units generating income at the time of the fire, okay; two studios and a one-bedroom. The fire originated in the one-bedroom. As you know, the fire was determined to be an accident. A very inconvenient accident, the case may well be. You see, we have very good reason to believe that an act of arson was already imminent for this building. Only a few loose ends were left to be tied..."

"But—"

"Like making sure that the drug addict who manages your property gets out of the unauthorized landlord business..." Barbara adds.

"Instead of seeing to its incineration as he was likely charged to do," Lila says, completing the thought. "Precisely. What is not in dispute is that even before the fire's cause was found, Mr. Sandoval, as a representative of your agency, was instructed to get rid of the unfortunate family in whose apartment it originated, by leveraging the wife's immigration status, which was problematic. She has since been deported, by the way."

"What about the third tenant? And the property manager you mentioned?"

"One and the same. Kyle Bland is his name. I believe

you know his father."

"You mean—"

"You might be surprised to learn that in addition to Senior VP at Superior Life, your Mr. Bland is also a Califan Knight Exalted."

"Rod Bland? Exalted? Get out of here."

"It's true, Don," Barbara says. "His son Kyle was in charge of the storage operation. And Rod certainly knew his son was also residing on Califan property. We don't know whether or not he was aware of the other tenants before the fire."

"Who is *we*, Barbara?"

"Okay, just me. I'm sorry I didn't tell you, but you see how delicate the situation is—"

Don gives Barbara a wounded look. "You could have at least—"

"As to the junior Bland," Lila jumps in charitably, "in addition to his landlording enterprise, he was most likely manufacturing methamphetamine in his apartment near the time of the fire. According to a recent interview given to an associate of ours by Avery Krizan, this was rather an open secret. Our other source strongly suspects that Kyle Bland was to be the arsonist, with instructions to make himself disappear after the act. Not that this person will ever publicly admit such a thing, at this point."

"Your *other source*? Who are you people?"

"We are what you'd call an interested party, Mr. Endlicher. A very interested party. And our other source is a very perceptive individual. And since you asked, Kyle Bland appears to have disappeared after all. Several speculations can be made regarding this fact, of course. He may have thought that his illegal laboratory was what caused the fire, or perhaps he simply decided that acquitting himself in public was not worth his effort. It's impossible to say at this time. Drug-induced paranoia may have played a role. One could of course also speculate that he did not vanish voluntarily, which would not be so outrageous, considering the reputation methamphetamine users have for loose tongues. At any rate he has yet to show his face, even to claim his belongings. This leaves only our Avery Krizan."

"What about Sandy?"

"Sandy was the sucker," Barbara says sadly, before a thought occurs to her, and she stares at the artist with something approaching admiration.

"Mr. Sandoval has placed a fine and noble bet," Mikal/Ljubomir says in response, "that his silence will translate to freedom and protection for his daughter. This is a very beautiful bet, I think."

"If you say so," says Don.

"In the same interview, Avery Krizan told our associate that Sandy Sandoval approached him for the first time while the building was still burning. Avery was told not to worry about a thing; Superior Life was there to take care of everything. And since Avery Krizan had no phone or computer at his disposal, Mr. Sandoval personally made arrangements for him to stay at a local residential hotel until better arrangements could be made."

"Or his claim was sorted out, whichever came first."

"Precisely. The building owner had a very good policy, Mr. Sandoval informed him. Avery was advised to make a list of his losses that night, and to contact him with it the next morning. The next day Avery was told that, as the commercial portion of the claim was being expedited, if he would be willing to attach his to that portion of the claim, not only could his claim be resolved in a matter of days or weeks rather than months but 'they'd be a lot less likely to nickel and dime him on every little thing.' Of course he would then be precluded from making a separate claim as a resident."

"So it had to be somebody who knew about Sandy's reputation."

"Somebody at Superior."

"Who was high up enough—"

"To have Sandy assigned the case in the first place, knowing his reputation..."

Endlicher, who has been shaking his head more and more resonantly, takes a step back and throws up his hands. "Okay. Wait a second..."

"What is it?"

"Are you telling me it's all a Masonic conspiracy? What is this, the *DaVinci Code*? Come on!"

"Don't be silly, Don."

"My old man was a Mason. So don't—"

"There is no Masonic conspiracy here, Don." Barbara grins. "It's The Knights of Califa—"

"Yeah yeah. Slippery slope."

Barbara gets serious. "Why aren't we prosecuting, Don? Huh?"

Don looks at Lila and Mika/Ljubomir. "So where the

hell do *you* come into all this?"

* * * *

Maintaining a clean signal was of the utmost importance. Prometheus said there was to be no interference. But Goddamn, They must be bored. He knows what They said, but he knows They want action. They always want action. Can't have bored boards. There are kids running around down there, for fuck's sake. They're playing! He blinks five times in rapid succession.

Captain leans in on him, getting all low. "What do you think?"

"The children—" He could use a pop right about now. They're getting on his nerves, the little –

"Bastards!" Captain Fucking Einstein thinks he's looking at a terrorist training camp. "How dare they have children down there."

"How dare they is right, Captain. What if someone got MAD?"

Quietly, "You read my mind." Even more quietly, "But why do you keep calling me Captain?" CFE turns around, smiles at Constantine that everything's peachy, leans in close again. "Not the children. But those four adolescents there? in the black hoods?"

"Good eye, Captain—"

"They look deserving enough, don't you think?"

"Indeed I do."

"Regrettably," loud again, back to his Toastmaster bit, "as we all know, all too often it is the young who are coerced to carry out the most heinous acts. As I'm sure you also know, they are typically recruited and manipulated by older men who take advantage of their youthful idealism and enthusiasm. What we'd like to demonstrate next is our AURAVOIDER's Magnetic Acoustic Device, or MAD, which emits a targeted blast of sound at a frequency that children, adolescents and very young adults find... maddening. I'd like you to direct your attention to these four—" he points at the center of the screen at the four figures in black. Four. "To use a colorful hypothetical, let's pretend we've targeted a terrorist recruitment center, and we wish to demobilize it, while minimizing radicalization of the local population. By first employing the MAD, any youths in the target area can be repulsed, self-removed to outside the target zone. This way it is possible for Ruptor to clear our recruitment center of new and would-be recruits, while sending them a clear signal, but leaving them with no other lasting effects... before stronger and more permanent means of incapacitation on the recruiters and facilities themselves can be deployed..."

* * * *

"So honesty is against the laws of nature?" Flyball tries to shake his palmed head, but he can only get it to pivot the one way.

Wyatt Timmon lies on his back, resting his head in a sling of braided fingers. "Squirrels run around all day, hiding nuts from each other," he bullshits. His gears are spinning. "And there's that mantis that looks like a stick."

"But isn't, I mean, if we're the only animal that strives

to be more than an animal, then if I'm to be a—ah, wait,—If I am an honest guy, then you say I'm nothing more than a... aww shit." Flyball tries to remember what he's just heard. "Spatio...? Spatio... temporary in... what scheme of things again?"

"Forget it, son. I'm just yanking your chain. But hey; honesty can go to your head. The truth'll set you askew. Ain't that right, Dave?"

"I call it ssspatiotemporally localized rebellion."

Tobi sits up, brightens. "Sign me up!"

"Just doing God's work."

"Thanks, brother," Flyball says, giving Wyatt a not-very-high-five. "I do believe I've seen the light." He giggles. "Or should I say the dark." Gil blows out a hookah hit and giggles too. The dark. Hu huh......

"Leasht out here they can't harvest our time," David Edwards rambles. He's feeling much better since he 'let it all out', so to speak. "-sswhat they do, you know.—sswhy time's going so mush faster, you know. Telling you, they're shtealing—" He stops talking but keeps waving his hand around, resetting his head on his shoulder again and again. "I write impenetrable books to return the favor." Gil giggles again. He rolls over, easy-breezy, remembering without pain, full of the grace of underlying complexity, and tries to passes the hookah to his right.

"Maybe later, amigo. Excuse me..." Wyatt ducks out of the tent and walks over to the rock band, who are busy standing in the sun in their leather jackets, ignoring everyone else. It takes him five nods before they acknowledge his presence. "Wasted Ute, huh. That's heavy...."

"Yuup."

"I got some Cherokee in me," he offers, his eyebrows hiking up hopefully, "but you probably can't tell by looking."

"Yeh?"

"Then you know."

"I know what?"

"Nothing."

"Say, where you boys from?"

"Shiprock."

"Shiprock, huh? So I hear you're going to rock this ship!"

"Yuup."

"Not now."

"After dark."

"Unplugged mufugginn uh..."

"Noise attack." Suddenly, as if someone just four-counted, the foursome all go silent, and stare into space like they've just fallen into the same deep trance. Facing Wyatt from the four directions, they close their eyes and start nodding in unison, then one of them starts humming a strange, hypnotic melody, and the others immediately join in pretty damn good harmony. Wyatt is mesmerized. The nodding grows in intensity until all four matching dutchboys swing like carnival rocking ship rides, forcing him to step out of their middle. As if enchanted, they chant louder, charming a small crowd from around the trance floor and tent area. There's an unmistakably improvisational edge to their impromptu performance, but also a peculiar *following* quality, like they're singing a raga beneath a silent drone note. They remain in a state of intense concentration for a couple of minutes or so, then they stop and look at each other. Through the applause, whistles and whoops, they engage in a wordless conversation:

"Where's this coming from?"

"It just like popped..."

"... like popped into my head."

"I know."

"Mine too."

"It's still in mine..."

"I know."

"Mine too."

"That mean we're mufuggin..."

"Trippin'?"

"Rock gods."

"Fuuuck..."

"We better practice..."

"Before it goes away..."

"So we don't forget." The first one starts singing again, on key like never before.

* * * *

"So this *is* rather unusual." Captain Merica's about to soil his Brionis. "What are your thoughts on what we're seeing here, pilot?"

"My thoughts? You sure you want to know my thoughts?"

Captain squeezes the seatback even harder. "Please."

The Man switches on the AutoLinger and turns around. "Well, Captain, since you asked, it would appear that your MAD is proving attractive to humanoids!" They're your fucking countrymen, Captain. They're not fleeing. See the applause? Do you like that? You ought to fucking salute. Now let's hear you spin it...

"Ahem... of course MAD can also be used to provide intelligence, as in this instance... it would appear that these four are not raw recruits after all. The MAD relies on the sensitivity of young ears; however, if the young person or persons being targeted have been exposed to high noise levels, perhaps caused by repeated exposure to explosions or even gunfire, they may become insusceptible, you understand..."

Not bad. But fuck those kids. He's going to get the mocking little shits. He swings the camera over...

* * * *

"They control what is as far as they control what is to be," David Edwards sputters, throwing himself into the tent shirtless, "Means and machines-s. The past gets shp—spun; our history's rerouted and we don't even... Our thoughts—Our thoughts! Channelled... into numbberless ditches. Show sheparate; show the shame! The shame. The same. Sepa—... all the shpectacles shpill into one shtultifying—"

"Uh huh." Huh? Tough chick; soldier? "You're a writer,

yeah? Don't that make you a professional spectacler?"

"I don't mean to be rude," suited man, laying flat on his back, searching his pockets asks, "but are your books like this?"

"You try killing the thing."

"Try killing for the thing."

"Am I a professional shpectacler if I don't cash their checks?"

Wyatt sits up. "That would make you an unprofessional spectacler."

"Touché." Outside, the Wasted Utes stop singing, open their eyes and look up at the sky in unison. If Wyatt wasn't convinced before, he sure is now. He's never managed a rock band before, but he knows 'it' when he sees it. Rock and Roll has just become his dream.

"You ever think about moving to L.A.?"

"Nope."

"That's where the money is. The beautiful people—" Wyatt's pitch is interrupted by bitter laughter. "—seriously; they'd eat you guys up, I'm telling you—" More laughter.

"No shit they would."

"Fuck Cali."

"All time fuckedest slaughter in American history..."

"The muhfugginn... Gold Rush."

"Yuup."

"The Golden muhfugginn... genocide."

"Yuup."

"Five bucks a head."

"Quarter a scalp."

"Took the money..."

"Yuup."

"The land..."

"The children..." Speaking of children, for the past minute or so Wyatt has been watching the kids play a strange game up on the hill. They keep taking turns collapsing, falling perilously, getting back up and doing it again. It's quite a convincing stunt, if that's what it is. Wyatt's not so sure it's fake.

"Buried what they did..."

"Hundred Wounded Knees..."

"Million dead..."

"Like it never muhfugginn..."

"Happened."

"So muhfugginn groovy..."

"They don't even talk about it."

"Fuck Cali."

Wyatt stops watching the children. "Ooh kayy...." He solves for how long he might could last in Shiprock. "Fair enough. Tell you boys h-what...."

The kids are huddled together now. One of them has a camera in her hand. It's pointed up at the sky.

* * * *

"Hear me?" Captain's face is so close he could bite it.

He could kiss it. He could lick it like a cat, or go stubble to stubble with it. Captain's voice is breathier, his breath hotter, "I don't care who the fuck you are. I said not the children!"

"I had no choice, Captain." The Man flicks on the AutoLinger. "I yam what I yam. If you'll excuse me, gentlemen...," he stands, picks up his rearview mirror, "your star pilot requires a visit to the men's room."

Captain looks at the mirror, does the canine head-cock thing again. Constantine watches.

"Helps me think."

* * * *

"So?" Don Endlicher repeats the question. "Where do you guys fit into all this?"

"Isn't it obvious?'

"Nope."

"Do you think we can simply sit back and watch the name of Mika Krizan to be used to perpetrate a fraud, when this fraud could have negative consequences for my own livelihood?"

"So you are also here to see Avery Krizan brought to justice."

The Brutalist laughs. "On the contrary, Mr. Endlicher. I am here to see justice brought to Avery Krizan, and so to my own good name."

"What do you mean by that?"

"I mean—excuse me, one moment please..." The artist pulls a small tape recorder from his coat pocket, holds it up to his face and presses Record. "I, Ljubomir A. Vukosavljević, acting as the legal entity "Mika Krizan", having presently arrived at the same conclusion, am now prepared to publicly declare that the performance presently unfolding before these investigators Guzman and Endlicher's fortunate eyes is the very manifestation of his solitary years of rarefied expense, his grand *remek-delo!*"

"In other words," Lila elaborates, "the legal entity 'Mika Krizan', as represented here by Mr. L.A. Vukosavljević, hereby represented by Ms. Dr. Lila Vukosa, J.D. would like to lay artful claim to the entire situation seen before you today. Naturally, as a necessary component of the Conceptual Brutalist masterwork projected here in scrap wood, sand and so forth, the ship destroyed in Avery Krizan's apartment fire will necessarily be included; grandfathered in, as it were."

The investigators are informed that they are of course welcome to peruse any of the literal reams of process materials Mr. Krizan/Vukosavljević has accumulated in his Alpine studio for further study. In the meantime, he will be publishing and marketing a magnificent coffee table book describing and illustrating the entire process and its execution, perhaps in collaboration with his new DarkArk friends. They are part of the creative team, after all. They may as well share the credit—"

"But this is absurd!"

"Isn't it?"

"And I suppose the money's part of the situation too?"

"Yes. Let us talk about the money." Mika/Ljubomir produces an umbrella from his cane. "And by 'the money', I assume you are referring to this... ninety thousand dollars American?"

"You say it like it's nothing."

"I do not think you understand," the artist says seriously, possibly even angrily, opening the umbrella. "You might think it is *something*, but I must not, nor will I ever, allow your agency to undervalue my work."

"Undervalue your work?"

"Are you not aware, sir, that even a minor Krizan can bring at auction several times your ninety thousand dollars American?" The artist nods confidently. "Very true. And I can assure you that this is no minor Krizan. I will see to that soon enough. As for how my attorney and I see it now, the Superior Life Insurance Company owes to Avery Krizan as much as one million dollars, American."

"I beg your pardon?"

"My pardon is inconsequential."

"You're full of shit." But Don's feeling somewhat vindicated. So he *is* in this guy's movie...

"Am I? So you've come all this way to remind me of the old Slavic saying, that for the liar there exists no honest man." Both men shake their heads—Mika in disbelief pretending to confusion, Endlicher the opposite.

"Your ninety thousand dollars American," Lila puts it clearly; "that is the fraud here."

Mika Krizan's grin is as impenetrably mystic as his daughter's is professionally inscrutable. "Do you have a card?" he asks Don.

"Why?"

"May I borrow it?"

Don grudgingly pulls out a business card and hands it over. The artist examines it briefly, then he produces a pen from the air, writes a list of names on its blank side, and hands the card back to Don.

While Don holds the card, Mika/Ljubomir taps the topmost name. "Very good, very knowledgeable," he says. "And incorruptible as gold, of course. She works with many of the finest auction houses in Europe...," "moving his finger down to the next name, "he helps to insure many major traveling exhibitions, including my own.... He may be of some help to you...; then again, he may not...."

"I'm not sure I—"

Guzman stops him with a squeeze of her hand.

"You would be doing us a great favor, in fact," Lila adds, "if you were to contact each of these people. Explain the entire situation to them if you wish, including your own involvement, et cetera, and see what they have to tell you. We will request that your conversations be recorded, and would like to thank you very much in advance for your continued participation."

"Huh?"

"Who knows what it may be in the end, no?" The artist winks at Don.

"I'm speechless. There's no way—"

"Very well, then. We will be in touch with your agency. By we, of course, I refer to very good American lawyers. Ahh..., but only after I consult with my publicity team. They are even better than my lawyers." He lowers his voice to a purr. "Really, I consider them to be artists. Media is their medium, you might say. A case like this one, with such potential for self-reflective amplification—" he claps once with delight, "—they will give special attention, let me assure you! It will be a collaboration, really. Think of the possibilities!"

"..."

"I can't tell you what publicity does to the market value of my client's work," Lila drives home the point. "This can only help *his* career..."

"Or...?"

"Yes...?"

Guzman looks around to make sure no one is eavesdropping. "Or, we could let bygones be bygones?"

"Indeed, that would be my recommendation..." the artist offers, "if I were not Mika Krizan."

"Mm Hmm."

"In either case," Lila adds, "might I ask, that in the event that you do decide to continue participating, don't hesitate to be creative in the writing of your recommendation."

The artist smiles once again. "Exhibit taste and discrimination," he directs them. "One never knows what one might become of this, after all."

* * * *

The night is moonless, and dark as a cave. Kwéte stops, gets low to the ground, becomes very quiet, and listens. He hears footsteps. Someone has been following him. But the humming sound he hears is not human. He jumps to his feet and starts running; he pitches himself into the black bar-

ranca below. The sound grows louder. He heaves the gold-veined stone at the light now upon him and turns toward the footsteps, into the darkness...

* * * *

Endlicher and Guzman stand in the dark. There's a break in the music. The fire has just been extinguished. They can hear the breeze. Endlicher points out a satellite in the sky. They watch it blink. Far off in the distance someone sings the Isha'a prayer. It must be coming from town. The sound swirls and darts in the night air like a thing caught in a stream.

"Looks like he'll get away with it."

"We'll see."

"I could get one of those rose hats that lady's selling."

"And something to eat."

"I could use a drink."

"There's nothing better than water sometimes."

"Nothing in the world."

A humming sound comes from the direction of the cliffs, followed by a low, distant boom.

"Did you hear that?" Guzman points up the wadi.

"Sounded like thunder."

They watch the sky, half waiting for lightning.

"Look at all those stars."

* * * *

ABOUT THE AUTHOR

David Scott Ewers was born in and raised in Pomona, California. He moved to San Francisco in 1989 and to Oakland in 2002, where he currently resides with his wife and daughter. He has been writing, making music and engaging in various marginal pursuits for decades. *Ultimate Resort* is his second novel.

CPSIA information can be obtained
at www.ICGtesting.com
Printed in the USA
FFOW02n1637140717
37683FF